RUNAWAY

ALSO BY PATTI DOTY

Finding Home

RUNAWAY

PATTI DOTY

For Quinn and Cecily,
who inspire my life.

CHAPTER 1

QUINN WILLED HER BREATHING TO SLOW and her heart to steady as the walls of the duplex she called home tightened around her. She recognized her own anxiety, escalating since her last client had dissolved into a puddle of tears and snot while she poured out her story of grief and loss. The usual remedies—housecleaning, hot bath, kitty snuggle, even *Romancing the Stone*, her second favorite movie—had failed. Now, backlit by intermittent flashes of fireworks from the Eldorado Casino's roof, Quinn slid tailor-fashion to the living room floor, readjusted her grip on the bottle in her hand and raised it high. "Through the lips and over the gums, look out stomach, here she comes." She brought the bottle to her mouth and drank deep—Jose Cuervo, a fit date for New Year's 2001.

Minnie the Mouser, 97 percent Siamese, nudged Quinn's hand. She scratched the cat's left ear, felt the golden tequila burn and waited for the relief Jose could bring. It didn't come. Instead her heart struggled to escape its confines. Her breath heaved. She scanned for danger. As Quinn watched, her old Hoover vacuum, abandoned on the threadbare orange and black carpet after the aborted cleaning frenzy, bucked and snorted and shuddered into life.

Damn, Quinn, she thought, *what have you gotten into now?*

Hallucination, her therapist mind reported, *panic attack—* pounding heart, shortness of breath, fear of dying—but that mind was no longer in control. She knew she was crazy; she knew the vacuum meant to kill her.

Terrified, Quinn scuttled backward, bumped against the kitchen wall and fumbled upward for the black plastic phone. Greasy with the remnants of long-forgotten meals, the coiled cord eluded her and her fingernail snagged the yellow daisies of the faded wallpaper.

"Damn." She sucked her bloody fingertip, grabbed again and caught the receiver. The numbers jumbled in unfamiliar combinations before they reconfigured into the seven-digit links to her sisters. Keeping a wary eye on the vacuum, she dialed DeMello sister number one.

"I can't come to the phone right now," Camille's mechanical voice responded. "At the tone please leave a brief message and I'll get right back to you. Have a nice day."

What message do I leave—hello, this is Quinn, your soon-to-be-dead sister?

Quinn clicked off, dialed 911.

"Emergency services. Do you want police, fire, ambulance?"

Where do you report a rogue vacuum cleaner? Quinn wondered, couldn't answer.

The dispatcher's voice repeated the question.

Quinn dropped the phone. With one last look at the monster in the living room, she fled the house. The street was dark, fireworks interrupted by the rain. In the window next door a disembodied face appeared and disappeared. Quinn DeMello did what she always did best—she ran.

TEN DAYS LATER QUINN DROVE EAST on I-80. She had gone this way before, years ago on a trip with her father to deliver a car, before she knew east was a destination. The Nugget Casino grew smaller in the rearview mirror and exits skimmed past, untaken. Tail lights flickered ahead like rubies flung from a careless hand, beckoning.

Quinn pressed her newly-acquired cell phone to her ear and strained to hear her sister's well-modulated voice as it cut in and out. "So what happened next?" asked Cecily, number five in the DeMello family hit parade. Their long-distance connection sputtered.

"The Reno police came," Quinn answered. She had already made light of the anxiety, the fear, the vacuum. "A woman cop who stuttered tried to cover me with a big umbrella."

She remembered: *Flashing lights illuminated the night, frosted the shadows with red and blue, and the police car rolled beside her as she ran. When she didn't stop, it pulled ahead and cut her off. The passenger door opened. A uniformed officer emerged. The umbrella in her hand fought back, mushroomed. Motionless in the headlights, Quinn ducked to protect her eyes. "S-s-sorry," the woman said.*

Quinn giggled at the memory. On location in Cabo San Lucas, her youngest sister giggled with her. "Just like Mary Poppins," Quinn said. "I expected her to rise up into the night."

Cecily's giggles stopped. "God, Quinn, is everything about a movie? Just tell me what happened."

Quinn felt the edge. If her movie-star sister couldn't appreciate the connections, who could? Her jaw clenched but she kept her voice light. "There were two, the stutterer—she said her name was Davidson—and a big guy, button-popping belly, eyebrows that needed a trim. His nametag said Smith and she called him Sarge. I told them I'd heard a noise and thought somebody was breaking in so I called 911 but then I got scared and ran. I don't think they believed me." Her story left out the details.

"*Did you call 911?*" *the grizzled sergeant asked while he scanned her rain-soaked nightgown and bare feet and the hair that straggled half-way down her back. His eyes said, "Now I've seen it all."*

"And?" Cecily prompted.

"And they stuffed me in the cop car, wrapped me in a moldy blanket and drove to the house. No handcuffs." She grinned, glad Cecily couldn't see.

They parked at the crumbling curb and looked at the single scraggly tree, the weedy yard, the strips of white paint hanging like icicles over the faded brick: home. Davidson and Smith exchanged a glance, got out and escorted Quinn inside. Nothing had changed: The old red Hoover sat clashing with the carpet; the bottle of tequila lay on its side, a few golden drops pooled beside it; the phone receiver dangled from its greasy cord. Sergeant Smith walked into the kitchen, his regulation oxfords stamping wet footprints across the linoleum, and hung it up. "Do you have any identification?" he asked as though expecting her to say no.

"I was afraid they'd haul me off to the Mental Health Institute. Wouldn't that be a hoot—locked up with all my clients?" A laugh covered the unease that vision produced. Cecily didn't laugh.

Their flashlight beams sent creatures scurrying as the officers scanned all four rooms. Then Davidson said, "C-can we call someone for you?" and Quinn sagged against the door jamb with relief. She didn't much resemble the spiky, bleached-blond image on her driver's license, and her story sounded feeble even to her own ears, but apparently they accepted enough of it that they could return to real police work.

"They wanted to call someone for me but I figured everybody would be out celebrating so I just asked them to take the damn vacuum out to the curb." Quinn laughed again.

"God, Quinn, this isn't funny. You could have lost your license, you . . ." The cell phone went dead. Quinn flushed with embarrassment as relief swept her.

The police car had finally pulled away. Quinn watched it blend into the night, then stared at the empty street until Minnie wound around her bare ankle. She scooped up her cat, shivered and closed the door and the red vacuum was just a vacuum sitting placidly at the curb.

On the roadside a plastic bag stuck in a leafless branch waved as Quinn passed.

Farther east the storm heightened. Quinn concentrated on the road, passed exits for Lockwood, Mustang, Patrick. Leafless cottonwood trees stood skeletal watch along the Truckee River, gray and dull thanks to the threatening sky. The Tracy power plant, a collage of structures veiled in steam and glowing in the dusky Nevada afternoon, reminded her of Frank Herbert's Arrakis, the spice planet *Dune*.

Her thoughts skittered. In the past ten days she had been granted a leave from Family Counseling Services, bought a new car and found a tenant named Ben—mentally renamed "Ben the Boarder"—who thought cats were "okay." *So many details when you don't just knee jerk and run.* Guilt and giddy relief mingled as Quinn released her home and Minnie to Ben's care. *The last runaway,* she promised herself with grim determination. She had "The Perfect Plan."

Beyond Fernley the landscape changed, bare hills in the distance while closer power lines marched across sagebrush flats like the robots in *War of the Worlds*. A Ford four-by passed, throwing a muddy spray over her only real possession, a yellow Volkswagen bug, circa 2000 and newly christened "Angelica the Auto." The pink slip dated January 5, 2001 was tucked safe in her wallet behind a faded picture. She clicked the wipers to high and patted the dash. "There, there, Angelica, we'll be fine," she said, but didn't really believe.

Her sisters, all but Cecily in Mexico, had visited her on New Year's Day, long after daylight had dispelled her fears.

"A man can't save you, you know," Caroline, newly out of a disastrous relationship herself, pronounced. "I know that's what you're looking for whether you admit it or not."

"Well, duh, of course I know that," Quinn responded like the little sister she was, "and I'm not." Inside however she wasn't so sure. *Maybe just once . . .*

"But Quinn," Claudia dismissed her younger sister's idea with a scornful glance, "you know it was just a panic attack. You've had them before. What you need is Prozac and a good therapist, not a road trip."

"But Claudia," Quinn defended, "I am a therapist and I do need this road trip. It'll clear my head and then I can start over." *Or not*, she added silently.

"Start over," groaned Camille, eldest sibling, sweet in her own do-what-I-tell-you way, who often spoke for them all. "Quinn, how many times have you started over?"

Good point, Quinn thought now as the wipers beat their asynchronous rhythm, competing with *Pagliacci* and the soggy darkness of her thoughts. A touch of her finger silenced Pavarotti. Her sisters were never so cooperative.

She tried to explain. "I just need to get out of Reno. It's a poisonous atmosphere for me." The truth, that she felt like a pretender and her clients' tragic stories left her retching on the bathroom floor, was too pathetic to tell. The even-more-secret truth, that she needed absolution more than they, was impossible.

As usual, they didn't understand. "Poisonous! My God, Quinn, everywhere you *go* is poisonous!"

In memory, she could hear the italics and the exclamation points as they continued. It was hard to be the DeMello black sheep. She supposed her sisters loved her but somehow it never felt that way.

Who could blame them, and they don't know the half of it.

The conversations coalesced. "You've got a cute house, a cat that hasn't run away (the *yet* was implied), a job that you're good at (*finally*, also implied), and—"

Coalesced; faded into imaginary voices which presented her self-doubt and criticism with sibling power; became the now familiar sister chorus, insistent and persistent—her personal Jiminy Cricket.

But now she had a plan. This road trip would be her driving meditation, a silent journey where she wrestled her anxiety into submission or—

She touched the brakes, felt her little car slide on the rain-slick road as she passed the Lovelock exits. *It has to work. No attachment, no connections, staying one night and then moving on until I kill the thing within or it kills me.* She was aware that the mysterious 'thing within' was also herself, wasn't quite sure what to do about it. *I'm a therapist, for God's sake. I should be able to fix myself.* She sang a few bars of "I have a plan" to the ABBA song on the radio, then sighed and switched it off. *Maybe I'll just see what happens.* A behemoth roared into the rearview mirror, blinked its halogen eyes and passed narrowly, throwing up a muddy spray. Its rear door queried, "How am I driving? Call 1-800" but the rest was lost in dirt and Quinn could not call to complain.

Rain fell like a stage curtain, limiting her vision, and she eased off the gas. The VW slowed to forty. *Pay attention, Quinn, no time to wonder what's next.*

CHAPTER 2

Headed east out of Reno on Interstate 80, Owen Johnson peered through the watery windshield, cursed himself for not replacing the wipers and listened to the cajoling voice cutting in and out of the cell phone held tight against his ear. His jaw worked. 2001 was not starting well.

"But Owen, honey, I only wanted you to stay here until the storm passed."

Owen almost smiled as he remembered a movie he'd seen, the woman on the floor, her arms wrapped around the man's legs, begging— His lips tightened. *This isn't funny,* he thought.

"If you hadn't kept arguing," he said, "I'd be home in Winnemucca by now. And I asked you not to call me 'honey.'"

Karle Moran didn't take no easily. "I know you're angry with me, honey, but can't a friend be concerned? We *are* still friends, aren't we?"

A CPA, he prided himself on his logical thinking and it had been easy in the beginning. *Too easy,* he thought now. They *were* friends then and when she'd offered the finished basement in her newly remodeled home for his use on days he worked in Reno, it seemed like a good deal. Low rent, nice place, a pleasant—well, okay, drop dead gorgeous—roommate. But somehow things had changed. And now—whoever said breaking up is hard to do certainly had Karle in mind.

"Karle—"

She overrode his interruption. "It's supposed to be just an awful storm. Not even predicted." Her words slipped into a southern drawl not obtained in the south as she absolved him of his obvious bad judgment.

He drew in a deep breath. This was another argument he wasn't going to win.

"You can't blame me," she continued. "I can't help worrying about you even if we—" The line went dead.

Owen blessed limited phone service and wiped the foggy windshield with his flannel sleeve. The exits skimmed by—Lockwood, Mustang, Patrick: unpromising names for unpromising places—barely noticed as he negotiated the familiar road and tried to blot his ex-lover from his thoughts.

MILES LATER THE OLD HEATER GRUMBLED as it waged a losing battle to warm the vintage Toyota Land Cruiser. Owen leaned forward and cleared the windshield again. *Should've just stayed in Reno.* But the idea of another night trying to convince Karle he was no longer romance material had him squirming for excuses. Now he was halfway home with a load of wood that could have waited weeks to transport and a timetable he'd have trouble keeping. *Never again*, he promised himself.

"Coward." He spoke the word aloud. "Coward."

Insistent rain challenged the wipers. Owen blinked as though this would clear his view. Cold air creeping up his pant legs made his left ankle ache at the old break. He wiggled the ankle in the heavy boot. *Worth it,* he thought now, *the price for catching a game-winning pass.* The old Toyota, heavy with its load, lumbered along.

Oughta call Vic and Viv and let them know I'm on my way.

He sighed. He loved his sisters but they worried about everything these days. Who could blame them? Their savings were dwindling. Their bed and breakfast operated in the red. I hated to say told you so but it was hard to get guests to a ghost town. He sighed again and felt like he'd let them down. He didn't want his sisters to worry about him, even though he knew they did, more since his cheating wife had divorced him. He was sorry they knew the whole story but small towns don't hold secrets tightly. Now they were unhappy that his romance with Karle had cooled. He knew they didn't much like her, but they liked the idea of someone taking care of their big brother. The notion that Karle Moran would take care of anyone but herself drew a laugh.

Then dusk and sleet outlined the SUV in his headlights—Explorer, maybe an Expedition—as it began its sideways slide and spun in the middle of the road.

"Son of a bitch." His laughter died.

"Fuck me." He groaned as he pumped the brake and struggled for control. His right hand sketched the sign of the cross—forehead, chest, shoulders—and returned to grip the wheel.

The SUV tipped, righted itself. Then, facing west, it slid into the eastbound lane. Blinded by its lights, Owen fought the wheel and cursed until the storm muffled the sounds of collision and his world went dark.

CHAPTER 3

ELPLESS, QUINN WATCHED THE SCENE PLAY out before her—the big black SUV plowing headfirst into the ancient Toyota, vehicles halting on the edge of the rain-slick road almost under Angelica's wheels. She swerved, braked and came to a halt just beyond the wreck. Stunned, she willed herself not to throw up. "Oh shit, Minnie," she moaned, forgetting the Siamese was safe in Reno with Ben the Boarder, "what have you gotten us into?" She fumbled for her cell phone, prayed for service and dialed 911.

It was easier to report an automobile accident than a rogue vacuum. In the eerie silence that followed her successful call, Quinn pawed through the detritus of her front seat—music stand, boom box, vibrator—found her yellow umbrella, touched her wallet for luck and scrambled into the weather. The biting wind snatched at her sweatshirt hood and whipped strings of hair across her face. The red and white sides of the Land Cruiser gleamed like blood in the glow of the Expedition's headlights as the two vehicles nuzzled.

Semi-protected by the yellow canopy, Quinn approached the Expedition. Angelica's emergency lights blinked on and off behind her. She peeked into the window, saw no movement.

"Everyone okay?" Her voice scratchy, whispery. She cleared her throat, shouted. "Is anybody hurt?

This time the wind whisked away the words. She pounded on the window, tried the door. When it didn't open, she assaulted it with a clenched fist. *Where are the damn cops when you need them?*

A window descended electronically.

"I think we're okay," a shaky female voice filtered through children's cries.

Heart racing, Quinn accepted the reassurance and moved along the side of the Toyota, scrabbling for handholds as the wet gravel moved beneath her feet, and wished for the boots left behind. To her left, darkness curtained the threatening unknown—*a ditch, a cliff, a hungry coyote?* She coughed to dislodge the fear, sharp in her throat, and the sound seemed too loud. She circled the conjoined vehicles, skirted the rear bumper and felt her way forward. Idling motors, children's cries, a sharp metallic clink as something settled—all muffled in the sleet. No cars passed. She reached out; a snick of sound stayed her hand.

The battered door opened. A man emerged. Quinn stepped forward just in time to catch him as he slumped. Umbrella abandoned, she took his weight and eased him to the pavement.

"Easy, easy, it's okay."

He mumbled.

"What? I can't understand you." Quinn leaned closer, saw a black substance oozing over his eye. Her heart fluttered, raced.

"Thanks," he said. "Dumb thing to do. I'm okay now."

He kept his head down though, and Quinn hoped he'd stay seated. *My height but heavier. I won't be able to hold him twice.*

The man gestured toward the Expedition, its interior lights now illuminating a youngish female and two small children. "Are they all right? Should you take care of them?"

"She said they're okay. They seem pretty lively at the moment. Just stay put." Forgetting universal precautions, Quinn reached toward his forehead, but he caught her hand so she waited.

"I was watching her in front of me but she must have hit a slick spot 'cause all of a sudden she was coming right at me and I couldn't get out of the way." He touched his forehead then, examined his fingers. "I think I hit my head. My sisters will kill me."

She made a small sound, a question.

"They've been nagging at me to get a new seatbelt installed in this old beast. I keep meaning to but—"

A shriek pierced the storm, and now *his* look questioned.

"Cell phone," she answered.

Flashing lights and emergency personnel surrounded them. A figure encased in yellow insinuated himself between them, shouldered Quinn aside and eased the man to the ground. "I'm an EMT," he said. "I've got him now."

In minutes Quinn sat in a dry patrol car and the man lay on a stretcher, a tarp almost protecting him from the wet. Her thoughts were distant, muffled, and the commotion around her seemed part of another world. *Shock*, she thought, and wondered about the man.

A little girl sat beside her as they waited. "My name is Naomi," she pronounced, her eyes tracking her mother as she paced in the rain, cell phone to her ear, a trooper in raingear at her side. "I'm six. My brother, Michael." Her forehead crinkled in a disapproving frown as she glared at the boy clinging like a limpet to the mother's neck. "He's almost four but he acts two."

Quinn ached to wrap the child in her arms.

Moments later, mother and children settled into an ambulance and she waited alone. A rap on the window startled her. She looked up. Outside, secure in his yellow rain suit, the EMT gestured toward the stretcher. "He wants to see you," he said.

Quinn pulled her frayed sweatshirt tighter and stepped into the weather. She stood where the man could see her.

A pressure dressing obscured most of his face and a cervical collar limited his motion, but he stuck his hand out in her direction and she took it. "Thanks for stopping," he said. "Most people wouldn't."

Quinn flushed. "It's okay."

His grip was firm, palm calloused. "I'm from Winnemucca," he said, "Owen—"

The rest was lost in the siren's howl as the first ambulance began its journey back to Reno.

Quinn gripped his hand, reluctant to disrupt the moment. "Hi," she said, "I'm Quinn." Then she added, "And I'm a runaway"—a joke.

Before the man could respond, the stretcher was borne away and Quinn, no longer necessary, squished back to her car.

ONCE IN THE AMBULANCE, OWEN LAY stiff and irritated and let the EMT fuss over him. "I'm Erica," she introduced herself. "Bob's driving. How are you doing?" She checked blood pressure and pulse, peeked under the dressing that covered his forehead and right eye.

The vehicle swayed as it gathered speed and Owen was glad he was secured to the bed. The collar around his neck rubbed when he tried to turn his head so he stared upward, waited. *Too much fuss for a bumped head.* "I'm fine, considering."

Erica laughed.

He laughed, too, and winced at the pain radiating from beneath the bandage.

"What's your name?" Erica's blond ponytail jiggled as she recorded his answer. "Well, Owen Johnson, do you know what day it is?"

My unlucky day, he thought, wondering how he was going to get back on schedule without calling his sisters, without calling Karle. He was in no mood for I-told-you-so's. "Friday," he answered, "not the thirteenth, the twelfth, January twelfth."

"And our president is…?"

"George Bush the younger—almost."

Erica considered the answer for a moment, apparently decided he was right before she patted his shoulder, checked his pulse again and turned her attention to her written report. He was dozing when she asked, "Who was that woman, the one with you, I mean?"

"I don't know. All I heard was 'runaway.' The guy talked to her; he'll know her name."

"Right. Lucky she came along."

He thought about the woman: *Cool enough to call 911; brave enough to stop and help; strong enough to take my weight; firm grip, eyes blue enough to drown in. A runaway, she said. Well, Owen Johnson, maybe it's your lucky day after all.*

CHAPTER 4

FRIGID AIR POURED OFF THE INN'S windows but Vivian and Victoria Johnson ignored it. Clad warmly in overalls and flannel shirts, they stood close together, Vivian wrapped shawl-fashion in an Indian blanket, Victoria unaffected by the cold. Two blond dogs lay at their feet, one to the left and one to the right: Patience and Prudence, Corgi bookends. Behind them a potbellied stove radiated heat. Snow swirled outside. The sisters could see nothing but the glow from a single bare street light which struggled to illuminate the dirt road meandering by their Wildflower Inn Bed and Breakfast.

"I wonder where she is," Vivian mused, "or even if . . ."

". . . she'll get here," finished Victoria. "Who knew this storm was coming? She's probably stuck in Lovelock or Fernley, or maybe on the road and . . ."

". . . that's why she hasn't called." A dog stirred at her feet. Vivian pulled the blanket tighter around her shoulders and bent down to scratch the Corgi's ear. "Easy, Patience, it'll be all right," she reassured, wanting to believe. The little dog settled and uttered a contented woof. Her mistress straightened and looked back into the storm. "We probably can't charge her for tonight, even if she doesn't cancel, can we? Won't that just add insult . . ."

". . . to injury?"

They both sighed. No charge meant yet another unpaid bill. Their ghost town, Unionville, had once been a thriving mining town with twenty new people moving in each day. But that was in the 1860's. Now on a good day there was a population of twenty and it seemed that no one wanted to visit a ghost town without roller coasters or ziplines.

"I am thirty-seven years old," Vivian said apropos of nothing, "and right now I feel old as . . ."

". . . dirt," finished her twin. "Me, too."

Once again they sighed in unison.

Changing the subject, Vivian said, "I hope Owen has sense enough to stay put tonight." Her frown suggested doubt about her brother's decision-making.

"Wennie," Victoria used their favorite nickname for their serious older brother "is a CPA. Too much common sense to come out in this weather."

The sisters leaned into one another and watched the snow fall.

SNOWFLAKES FELL, IMMOLATING THEMSELVES AGAINST THE windshield as Quinn left the accident site and drove into the night. Miles later the storm worsened and the adrenaline that had fueled her ran out. The wipers labored. Quinn, shoulders aching, hunched forward over the wheel and struggled to identify the edges of the narrow secondary road. Phantom lights flickered in the snowy wilderness outside Angelica's warmth. In the darkness, the life of Nevada's high desert proceeded but the only visible movement was the inexorable fall of snow. She wondered what it would be like to stop, just stop, and let the snow enfold her. What seemed like a good idea a week ago now seemed disastrous, Unionville and the Wildflower Inn Bed and Breakfast just faraway dreams.

The sister chorus clamored, sounding almost real in the darkness: *Unionville? For God's sake what's in Unionville? At least San Francisco has the symphony. If you don't want to be a psychotherapist any more, at least they always need flutists in the City.*

They're right, Quinn rebutted. *I've played my flute for rent money before—I just don't want to do it again.*

She forced herself to maintain a steady pressure on the gas. "Easy, Angelica, too slow and we're dead in the water; too fast and we're in a ditch." She spoke aloud but the sound of her voice was not reassuring and the VW bug crept on without comment. Exhaustion blanketed her as completely as the snow covered the road. *I'm even too tired to be anxious,* she thought, and wished she had toothpicks to prop her eyelids open.

The chorus again: Grow up, Quinn; just grow up.

Quinn tried to ignore the words as her eyes swept the roadside for a sign.

"Go seventeen miles on the paved road, then turn west," the woman at the bed and breakfast had reminded her. "Yes, right; there's a sign on the fencepost—turn right there."

Quinn had been to the B&B once before, two summer days a few years past when her romance with Harry the Hunk was new—before he left her in search of something, someone, more real. *But he liked my hair,* Quinn thought, remembering the way his hand ruffled the red spikes and then traveled down her neck in search of the rest of her. He thought it was funny that all of her hair wasn't red, until she did something about that, too. *He liked my hair.*

The Wildflower Inn, set in a ghost town at the foot of the mountains, deer coming down to sip from the stream, meals served under spreading cottonwood branches, no humans in sight, had seemed ideal for her purposes. No sad stories. No reminders. Maybe a cowboy on a white horse? She had found the inn's crinkled business card when she emptied her underwear drawer and called on impulse.

See where impulse leads me.

She almost missed the turn, the promised sign hidden in the storm, a right turn. Snow whirled, pushed by the wind, and the VW slid, caught and struggled uphill. *I think I can; I think I can.* No living thing marred the landscape.

The woman on the phone sounded young, young and anxious and apologetic, as though having Quinn there were important somehow. She said she and her sister now owned the place, that there were three guests already, but space for one more if she didn't mind paying extra for the room with the private bath. Quinn wasn't worried about money, not yet with her last paycheck uncashed in her wallet, so she made the reservation. *One day at a time*, she thought, *one day at a time*, and wished it were true.

Finally she could make out a fence, a gate. A light glowed.

A star in the east, she thought, forgetting she was facing west, and she wished Angelica were a camel she could flick with those little leather quirts that still smelled of their original owners—Quinn of Arabia.

The wheels of the little car slipped, caught, slipped again, and all Quinn could do was hold on as it slid. Nose pointed downward, the headlights giving life to a shallow indentation hardly big enough to be called a ditch, Angelica the Auto settled in. Then nothing moved but the snow.

Quinn revved the motor, felt the wheels whirr, nothing. Again—nothing. Finally she turned off the ignition. "I guess

I've got us in another mess," she said aloud.

Angelica didn't reply.

The car leaned into the snow. Quinn tried to open the door but it moved only inches.

How do I get out of here?

Her breath caught, her heart hammered and, for just a moment, a red vacuum filled her vision. She blinked it away—no time for panic now. *I can do this.* Twisting, bending, wishing her legs had extra joints like the camel, she clambered over the console and unfolded herself out the passenger door.

Flute case and duffel in hand, she stood in the snow and looked around. Just past the fence, lights brightened a window and shone weakly on the crooked step of a long and narrow porch. The house looked small and shabby, not at all as she remembered, and she hoped she'd come to the right place. The cottonwood, so protective in summer, stood menacing, a single branch striking the house.

The chorus raised its volume: Told you so, told you so, told you so.

SHOULDER TO SHOULDER, VIVIAN AND VICTORIA watched through the blizzard as headlights inched closer and a small car eased into view, struggled up the road.

"Is that her?"

"Must be. It's not Wen, and it's certainly not Scott." Victoria bit her lip, sorry that she'd mentioned Vivian's wayward son. She draped her arm around her sister's shoulders and Vivian Johnson, younger twin by seven minutes, snuggled closer. They watched the little car slide into the shallow ditch that fronted the inn.

Now they waited. The yellow car settled. The motor revved, revved again—then silence.

"Should we provide . . ."

". . . assistance? I think we'd—no, wait . . ."

Through the falling snow, they could discern a flurry of movement inside the car.

Neither was sure when they had begun to pin their hopes on this unknown woman, this last guest. Both were aware of the absurdity of their belief, but there it was, nonetheless, an intuitive sense that this woman could somehow help them rescue the Inn, maintain the life they loved, perhaps even help with Scott. A slender figure emerged through the passenger door, rummaged inside, then turned and plodded toward the house. Long strands of hair dripped over her face, and her shoulders hunched as though she carried a great weight.

"It must be Quinn," Vivian stated the obvious.

"A pretty slender reed, sister." Victoria shook her head as they stepped away from the window and prepared to greet their guest.

CHAPTER 5

N THE PORCH, QUINN SKIRTED A stack of firewood poised as though waiting to pounce, lifted the tarnished doorknocker and let it fall. Its *thunk* startled the night. In the distance an animal yipped, fell silent. *Alfred Hitchcock, here we come.* Exhausted, Quinn waited.

The door opened.

"Come in. Welcome." Two women were outlined in the doorway; two low, round voices spoke almost in unison.

Quinn gasped. *Tweedledee and Tweedledum.*

"I know, it's quite a shock at first but you'll soon get used to us." The speaker laughed, held out her hand and pulled Quinn through the door. "I'm Vivian Johnson, and this," a wave of her free hand at the identically short and stocky person beside her, "is my twin sister, Victoria. Please come in and get warm."

Miniatures. They're like miniatures, Quinn assessed from the elevation of her 5'10" height. Identical rows of tiny pearly teeth gleamed from identical smiles.

A dimpled hand grasped her elbow. "Come in, you're letting out the heat. Victoria, get her . . ."

". . . things. I know, I know. And what's this?" She plucked the slender case from Quinn's limp grasp. "Oh, I know, it's a flute. Do you play?"

Quinn threw a desperate look over her shoulder at Angelica, disappearing under a frosting of snow, and stepped into the house. Overheated air wrapped around her. An orange cat of sumo wrestler proportions gazed from its perch on a crowded shelf and then closed its yellow eyes as if she were of no importance. *Through the Looking Glass.* Quinn closed her eyes. The door slammed shut behind her.

"Of course she plays, you ninny." The twin identified as Vivian snapped. "Why else would she carry a flute case around in the middle of nowhere?" She turned her attention to Quinn, shivering and silent, her back to the door. "Victoria, this poor girl is soaked to the bone." She pulled Quinn toward a potbellied stove glowing dusky red in the small room. "Vicky, don't just stand there, get . . ."

". . . some towels. I'm going, I'm going." Victoria stomped from the room.

Whoa. Really down the rabbit hole. Not Hitchcock at all. A protest rose to Quinn's lips. "I..."

The twin returned with an armload of white towels. "Sit and dry off," she interrupted as she pushed her unresisting guest down on a sofa near the stove and dropped the towels beside her. "What in the world happened to you anyway?"

Stranger and stranger. Quinn tried again. "I . . ."

Vivian silenced her. "Patience, Victoria, she'll tell us in her own good time."

Younger than me but they're pushy like Gran. I should.... Fatigue and a sudden yearning for her grandmother's touch rippled through Quinn, and with a sigh she surrendered to this very odd situation.

Cooing softly as though to a child, Vivian peeled Quinn's soggy gray sweatshirt up and over, then wrapped Quinn's hair in a towel transparent as tissue which bore the scent of the winter air that had dried it. She started to pat moisture from Quinn's bare arm, then stopped and stepped back. Hands her hips, she looked down at her guest. "You must be Quinn DeMello," she said as though just recognizing that her actions were not ordinary, "and we must seem quite much. Our parents were anglophiles, you see, and we were a bit much for them, too, but you'll soon get used to us and tell us apart ..."

"... right as rain," finished her sister.

Quinn wasn't sure how 'anglophilia' explained *this* situation. She was formulating her question when the women looked at her feet, exclaimed and went to work removing her sodden Keds and wrapping each foot in yet another thin dry towel.

Instant relief. Gratitude escaped Quinn's lips, a low moan. *Just waiting for my lines,* she thought and let the women fuss.

Efficient hands propped the wet shoes by the stove. One twin said, "Now you just sit here and finish drying and we'll ..."

"... be back quick as a wink," the other finished. They bustled from the room.

Heat and damp and the smell of wet hair quivered. Images doubled and then separated. *Not more hallucinations,* Quinn hoped. Her heart was too tired to race. The furniture-laden room challenged her sense of place and time: High ceilings collecting heat; armchairs flanking the sofa on which she sat, doilies that her grandmother called antimacassars protecting their overstuffed extremities; stacks of magazines vying for space with multicolored figurines and spindly-legged tables bowed with their weight. *Just like a movie set,* she thought but didn't recognize the scene. Her eyelids drooped.

Wherever I am, it's warmer than snow. She dozed.

IGNORING THE COLD AIR THAT CREPT across the scarred kitchen floor, Vivian set the water to boil and fiddled with a box of tea leaves. Faded light from an old ceiling fixture illuminated a room busy with pots and pans, cuttings rooting in faded cups, dishes that overflowed the cupboards. A braid of garlic, partially stripped, hung on one wall next to a collection of trays secured in a creation of cheerful ribbons, a gift from a long-ago guest.

"Well, what do you think?"

She addressed the query to the ancient enamel range—better to see its chipped surface than the disappointment on her sister's face. "We knew it was stupid to . . ."

". . . have such expectations just because she sounded so good on the phone." And because of your damn intuitions, Victoria thought but didn't say. She moved to the side of the stove, stepping over a bushel basket in her way and forcing Vivian to meet her gaze. "Of course it was stupid." Troubled brown eyes held as they considered the bedraggled woman they'd left in their parlor, her oval face with its tentative look, her eyebrows straggling toward each other. It was hard to assess the character of a wet cat.

Victoria continued. "But I'm not so sure we were wrong. There's something about her—"

"Of course, Victoria Marie, whatever was I thinking? Carrying a flute through the storm must mean something." But the wry glance Vivian afforded her usually pessimistic sister was tinged with hope.

A CACOPHONY OF YIPS AND YAPS filled the air as the parlor door swung open. Quinn jerked awake. She peeked under half-opened lids expecting hovering figures in ruffles and bustles and crinoline petticoats. Instead, one twin shushed two small dogs and the other laid an overflowing tea tray on a low table, adjusted her shawl, and sat beside Quinn on the settee.

"Eat. You'll be fit as a fiddle in no time." She situated a steaming cup into Quinn's flaccid hands.

Quinn grasped it like a lifeline. Without hesitation, she guzzled the hot milky tea, and the sudden rumble of her stomach and the urgent complaint of her bladder restored her to the room which no longer shimmered like movie land. She blinked and held out her cup for a refill. After she slurped the last of the tea and released the cup gently to its saucer, a twin passed a flowered china plate piled high with sandwiches quartered, crusts removed. Resisting the urge to grab the whole pile, Quinn took one and bit in—bread and butter, the comfort food of childhood.

"Ahh." She shoved the soft bread into her mouth, added more, then more. Conversation seemed unnecessary.

Sipping from mismatched cups, the sisters perched on an elderly ottoman and watched Quinn gobble.

"I knew she'd be hungry," said one.

"Well, she had to get dry first," retorted the other.

They nattered as their guest ate: Details of the inn, the other guests, the heroic brother. Finally the plate was bare. When Quinn swallowed hard, wiped her mouth with the edge of her hand and looked around, one directed, "Bathroom's that way," and nodded toward a door on the far side of the stove.

Tucked in a stairwell, the bathroom was modern enough to finish off the Victorian vision. Quinn washed her hands and face, drew fingers through her hair. The mirror reflected no improvement. With a grimace, she returned to the parlor.

"Feeling better now, are we?"

Quinn nodded.

"You *are* Quinn DeMello, aren't you?"

She nodded again.

"And now you're here?" The statement held questions.

Finally my scene. "Well," Quinn coughed, cleared her throat and began again, "well, I was heading east and . . ." The abbreviated version of her recent adventures flowed over tight lips. *Just the facts.* Quinn didn't want these two to join her critical sister chorus. Color and texture crept in as she described the crash, the children, the fear. The sense of connection she'd felt with the injured man, her desire to sink into the snow—these she held close inside.

The twins remained silent.

"And the stupid snow kept falling," she said, dismissing the two hour struggle to find her way. "Then Angelica just couldn't hold on any more and we landed in ..."

"... the ditch," Vivian finished her sentence. "Your poor little car, all alone out there in our ditch. Vicky, I told you . . ."

Head tipped to one side, Victoria ignored her sister and addressed Quinn. "My dear, you said 'Angelica.' Is someone still in the car?" Her voice rose. "Should we ...why didn't you—?"

"Oh, no." Quinn laughed, a contagious sound, and she didn't understand the hopeful expressions that crossed twin faces. "Angelica's my car—'Angelica the Auto,' she is."

Without warning, the sister chorus mocked: Angelica the Auto, really, Quinn. What will these women think of you now?

Her laughter faded.

The grandmother clock in the hall chimed into the silence—one, two—

Three faces turned toward the sound.

Vivian jumped to her feet. "Oh, my, Vicky, it's eleven o'clock. This poor girl must be exhausted."

Her words mobilized them. The speaker—Vivian, Quinn concluded—gathered the tea things and scurried from the room.

The other twin now clearly identified as Victoria checked the sweatshirt steaming beside the stove. Quinn reached for her shoes and Victoria waved her back.

"Just a minute. Those just won't do tonight," she said, and left the room. Minutes later she returned with a pair of leather work boots, worn but sturdy-looking. She handed them to Quinn. "Here, try these. They're our brother's but I think they'll fit you."

"Thank you." Quinn slid her narrow feet into the boots—warm, dry. She pulled the laces and the boots snuggled tight against her bare ankles. "These are great. Thank you."

Victoria produced an 'I've-got-a-secret' smile.

What? Quinn thought. *Ruby slippers in disguise?*

Before Quinn could consider further, Victoria left and Vivian returned with a blanket which she tossed around the taller woman's shoulders. "Here." She pulled her own shawl up over her head. "Ready, sister?"

"When you are." Victoria had reappeared, stuffed into a dark blue parka and struggling with the zip. She gave up, pulled the hood over her curls and opened the door. Fat snowflakes dashed in as the dogs dashed out. The snow rode the wind up from the ground to mingle with the flakes still falling. The guesthouse stood stark in the distance.

"You remember, Quinn, your room is …"

Quinn wanted to finish the sentence "… in the guesthouse across the way," but a twin beat her to it.

"… in the guesthouse across the way. Of course she remembers." She smiled at Quinn and stepped into the snow. Quinn readjusted her blanket and followed.

Women and dogs plodded across the yard toward the wood frame structure. The staccato rhythm of wind-whipped branches accompanied their approach up snowy steps onto a porch which extended the width of the building.

"Careful, it squeaks," Vivian whispered as she opened the door. Her sister shushed the dogs and Quinn remembered there were other guests. She hadn't finished knocking snow off her loaner boots when she was pushed inside. "Here you are, dear, you know where your room is. We'll see you …"

"… in the morning." Victoria handed her the flute case, set the duffel at her feet. Bemused, Quinn watched sisters and dogs disappear into the snow.

In the house, the kitchen, usually alive with the scents of baking bread and simmering spices, now held the stale odor of defeat.

"So what do you think now?" Victoria Johnson inhaled against the tight knot in her chest. She stared over her sister's shoulder at the black window as though answers might lurk in the dark.

Vivian kept her hands busy with the teacups, applying the threadbare dishrag as though the bone china suffered from baked-on grease, gaining comfort from the warm soapy water and the familiar task. She let the question hover.

"Well?"

She sighed. "Vic, you saw her. She's just a child. How can she help us?"

"I know, like a drowned rat she was, that wet, stringy hair and all. And so thin—" Victoria shook head. "She looks like she needs more help than we do. But—" Her voice trailed off as she recalled the promise in Quinn's laugh.

Vivian placed the last cup to drain on the faded tea towel. "So you still believe…?" She stepped away from the sink, faced her sister, and for once a sentence hung, unfinished.

Victoria averted her eyes and didn't reply so Vivian voiced what she knew her sister was thinking. "You think we need help with Scottie, that he's in some kind of trouble and we can't help him. You think that this girl, this therapist from the big city, can somehow do what we can't." She turned away then, willed the tears not to fall. "All that and save the Inn, too?"

The dark windows mirrored her skepticism.

Thoughts flowed between them, a twin communion as old as they but uncomfortable for all that, the worry about Vivian's son, the boy they'd raised together—suddenly distant, seldom home or closed up in his room—combined with the fear that they would lose the Inn.

Vivian spoke again. "I know you don't want to talk about Scott, but I know you're worried, too. Like father, like son, you've been thinking, and you're hoping I won't notice."

Thoughts of the boy's father, a misshapen joint pinched between stained fingertips, a mocking smile on his perfect mouth, twisted Victoria's lips and brought her eyes to her sister's. "You know?"

"Of course I know. I haven't smelled it in a long time but who could forget …"

"… the sweet, sweet smell of burning hemp," Victoria finished with grim humor. "And speaking of smells," she grabbed an onion from the basket at her feet, tossed it to her sister and changed the subject, "let's prep for breakfast."

CHAPTER 6

QUINN WOKE FROM A DREAMLESS SLEEP to the darkness of the Wildflower Inn Bed and Breakfast's premier room. *Early*, she thought, *just a few more minutes.* She burrowed into the covers and was almost asleep again when the memories flooded her. Pain with remembering—never again would her baby's cry be her alarm—death to forget. Happiness vanished. Heart racing, she whispered, "I'm sorry, baby, sorry, sorry, sorry." She pressed her hands against her chest and forced her thoughts to the now, the only way to survive.

THE TWINS HAD LEFT HER STANDING in a darkened room with only a flute case clutched to her chest as a ward against the panic that darkness spawned. When her eyes had adjusted, she picked up her duffel and made her way to her room. Exhaustion claimed her. She flopped onto the bed, her last movement a wiggle to keep the wet boots off the spread. Now she rested in a soft nest of smooth warm sheets and heavy blankets wearing only her tank top and red thong and wondered how it had happened.

The brother?

Vivid imagination portrayed the unknown man's hands peeling away her clothes and tucking her into bed. Her skin tingled. Her cheeks flamed. Unwanted arousal spurred her up into the frigid morning air. A quick rummage in her duffel scattered its contents across the room. Her fingers located her pink wallet and she held it to her cheek for a beat before sliding it between mattress and springs. A quick trip to the frigid bathroom and then, clad in threadbare sweats, purple yoga mat in hand, she went in search of space for her morning routine.

Bare feet silent on the cold wood planks, she followed the hall into a large room replete with horsehair sofas, stiff chairs, and a hodge-podge of tables circa long ago. A mullioned bay window filled the far wall, its watery glass panes exposing a white landscape punctuated by cottonwood exclamation points. Nothing moved. A sense of time dislocated once again engulfed her. She released the mat and its vinyl *plop* dispelled the notion.

Freed, Quinn turned her attention to the porcelain stove in the corner, its surface cool enough to touch. She fed it kindling and laid on four pieces of split wood. When a satisfying flame licked the pine, she spread her mat on the thin Oriental rug and turned her attention inward.

I breathe in; I breathe out. No room in the mind for anything else—no babies, no guilt, no rough hands on her body. Toes spread like roots, arms motionless at her sides, every muscle activated, ready: Mountain Pose. She reached skyward, inhaled deeply and swooped like a bird of prey, folding fully until her chest lay flush with her thighs—her first Sun Salute.

Five perfect fingers curled around her pinky—an instant ache as memory filled her. *If I could just go back,* she thought, and forced her attention to her breath.

THE WHITE ILLUMINATION OF DAY ON fresh snow filled the room and a rooster crowed as Quinn finished her final Sun Salute and realized she had an audience. On a faded green sofa, three women sat side by side in silent observation. With her hands at Namaste, prayer-like, Quinn returned their gaze.

The redhead spoke. "Sorry to intrude. We've never seen anyone do that before."

Quinn frowned. Sadness edged out social skills. This was supposed to be a journey into solitude, not society. She said nothing.

"It looks like we're stuck here for a while," the same woman continued, gesturing at the scene outdoors. She held out her hand. "I'm Michelle Morgan. And you are?"

No one moved.

Just as time stretched forever, Quinn stepped off her mat and reached for the woman's hand. "Quinn." *More voices to the chorus,* she feared and wished she could use Greta Garbo's line, "I vant to be alone."

The woman didn't seem to notice. The hand clasping Quinn's was soft and the nails were long and pink. Diamond rings almost buried in flesh adorned the left hand she laid atop Quinn's right, deepening the handshake and preventing escape. "Would you show us how to do that," she asked, "since we're stranded here together and all?"

She made it sound like a picnic. Quinn shuddered.

"Please," chimed the second woman, petite, with blond hair tastefully assisted. "I'd like to learn, and it would while away the time—there's no TV, you know." She giggled. "Oh, yes, I'm Barbara ... Barbara Lathrop." She shook the hand that Michelle released.

They looked at the woman still seated. Noncommittal, she looked back.

"That's Allison Brown," explained Michelle. "She's shy. We're here for a girls' weekend. Escape from reality, you know." Both women laughed. "We're supposed to leave today, but the radio says the roads are closed. Besides, there's a yellow car in the way and we can't get out anyway." She didn't sound like she cared one way or the other. "What's your name again?"

Quinn's frown deepened as they spoke. *I don't want to be stranded. I don't want to while away the time. I don't want any more stories.*

"Quinn," she repeated, mind racing for a graceful exit. Finding none she muttered, "Uh, I could show you some basic poses and we could do some meditation, I guess."

Two expectant faces turned toward her. Allison gazed out the window, unreadable.

"But," Quinn continued, her words just behind her self-protective thoughts, "good learning conditions require concentration and silence. So if we're going to do this we can have no verbal communications in the common areas." *God, I sound like a prick.* Shame mixed with the sadness.

The fire crackled and the scent of pine filled the room. A snow-laden branch snapped and everyone jumped. Quinn longed to escape.

"No talking?" Michelle looked stunned.

"Oh, let's try, Michelle, it'll be fun."

Quinn imagined Barbara's story at her next bridge game. A little humor glimmered.

"But … no talking?"

"She gave you her conditions. Take it or leave it." Allison's high voice came as a surprise. "I think I'll take it." She rose gracefully a full six feet and extended her hand. "Quinn, Allison Brown. When do we begin?"

Before Quinn could reply the Johnson twins and the dogs arrived in a flurry of snow and good cheer, effectively interrupting the discussion. "We stamped out a path for you, so come on. It's …"

"… time for breakfast, you see. Bundle up. You'll be warm as toast if you keep moving."

Their guests stood in the great room, motionless, as though caught in some underhanded deal. Quinn pulled away from Allison's handshake.

The twin who spoke didn't seem to notice the awkward silence. "Good, you've all introduced yourselves," she said.

The other twin, Victoria if the blue parka was a reliable clue, checked the stove, nodded approval. "Somebody fired her up." She quirked an eyebrow at Quinn when the other women just stared. "Thanks. Now let's get moving."

Getting bundled up took several minutes as the women struggled with boots and coats. Quinn stood to the side and watched. Victoria muttered, "Three-ring circus," and hustled back into the cold morning.

Her sister, a pink parka replacing the previous day's shawl, handed Quinn a heavy jacket. "Here. This will work better than the blanket."

Quinn slipped her arms into the coat and froze as its bittersweet scent rendered her breathless and aroused, her imagination flaring. *The brother's, too?*

Vivian's voice shattered the moment. "Come on now, time to eat," she said and shepherded her charges toward the main house.

IN DAYLIGHT, ITS DISREPAIR WAS OBVIOUS. Ribbons of paint hung from the fascia. A cardboard square stood in for a window pane. Straggly bushes and old rose canes proclaimed their neglect. What years ago had been charming was, in this cold light, bleak.

Vivian seemed to notice Quinn's glance at the window. "Oh, it's covered up tight as a drum," she explained. "You won't get cold. Just too many things and not enough money." She didn't seem to realize such financial candor was unusual. "Our brother helps with repairs when he can. We're not too good at that, you see, but he's been busy. Beginning tax season and all."

The brother again, some kind of money-man—the "Wennie this" and "Wennie that" of last night's conversation. *He should be helping his sisters more*, Quinn decided as she followed the women into a living-color version of the movies that sustained her.

THIS MORNING THE BARN-LIKE KITCHEN SHIMMERED with heat and the smells of sweet bread and fried onions—welcoming. A chipped enamel stove, an economy-sized refrigerator and a deep porcelain sink with a scarred Formica counter clustered near the back door. Opposite, under a chandelier that should boast candles instead of light bulbs, a trestle table set with mismatched china presided.

"Hurry up, get it while it's hot." Victoria, her white chef's apron dragging on the floor, urged them out of their coats and into chairs around the table.

Quinn looked for the maid in black smoothing her starched and ruffled apron, the gentleman in riding clothes idly flicking his crop against highly polished boots, the woman with smooth white skin and a seductive smile—Sir Lawrence Olivier, Joan Fontaine. She was disappointed at their absence.

"Dig in," invited Vivian as she donned her matching apron.

They did—scones with Devon cream and strawberry jam, fried eggs, rashers of bacon, piles of crusty toast, bowls of applesauce and cooked prunes, a chipped milk glass pitcher filled to its brim with fresh-squeezed orange juice. The women ate.

Michelle and Barbara chattered through the meal, pausing only long enough to swallow, and Quinn was reminded of a Harvard study she'd read somewhere about women speaking 30,000 words a day. *They're well into their allotment*, she noted as she mopped up her egg yolk with the last bit of her toast. She considered just one more scone and was surprised at her appetite. Allison's egg congealed on the faded flowers of her plate.

Sated, Quinn pushed back from the table and sipped coffee laced with thick cream. *Incongruent—fancy food and peeling paint, drafty floors and dress-up dishes, cheery good will and a funny undercurrent of something, worry maybe. What does this have to do with me?* The twins had stopped fussing over her but they still bustled around more like grandmothers than the 30-somethings she knew them to be. Uneasiness and curiosity battled for supremacy.

Coffee cups filled, the twins joined their guests. Victoria rapped her cup and conversation stilled. "Saved the bad news until you were all full as ticks," she began. "I know you were planning to leave this morning but there's no way out of here today. Although together we could move Quinn's lovely yellow vehicle, the …"

"… snowplow won't be by until late today or tomorrow morning," finished her sister. "We plow our own lane, you see, but the main road isn't a very important one so it doesn't get very prompt service."

"Not to worry, Vivvy. We'll just bite the bullet and manage, like we always do." Victoria turned to her guests. "Won't we, ladies?"

Drama? Comedy? It felt like a movie Quinn had seen but couldn't quite remember. *What's my role?*

Allison's high voice commanded attention. "We suspected as much and have recruited Quinn to instruct us in yoga."

Oh, yes, that role. Quinn flushed, hated that she flushed.

The clock ticked and radio voices conversed in the background.

"Tell us, Quinn," Victoria invited.

They expected something like this. How weird.

The women waited.

"Well, uh," *what the hell,* "yeah, this is what we'll do. First, some mild after-breakfast exercise. Can't do yoga on a full stomach. Maybe—" creating a plan as the words emerged, "after helping with the dishes, about ten laps back and forth between here and the guesthouse." *There, that should keep them quiet.*

Michelle groaned and Allison glared her silent. Vivian and Victoria exchanged a look that Quinn again couldn't interpret. She continued, "Then we'll have thirty minutes of quiet time before we meet in the great room for the lesson. And don't forget—silence."

"Silence?"

"Quinn said we can't talk in the greatroom. It's bad for concentration or meditation or something," Michelle explained.

The twins looked at Quinn but she didn't elaborate, just stood and began clearing the table. The others, their enthusiasm varied, joined her.

DISHES WASHED AND DRIED, THE WOMEN donned their gear and followed Quinn back and forth in the snowy expanse between the buildings. Four brown and black goats pranced along a wire fence pacing them, a supportive audience. The Johnson twins and their dogs closed themselves into the house.

A woodpecker worked in the distance but the sister chorus almost drowned him out: What in Heaven's name are you doing,

Quinn? Forty-three years old and leading a bunch of spoiled women through the snow? You should just say no, Quinn, when will you ever learn to just say no? This is the dumbest thing you've ever done, Quinn. Why don't you just grow up?

Well, at least these women are quiet. Quinn forced her attention to the woodpecker.

"I TOLD YOU SO," VICTORIA SAID as she held her hands to the stove as much for comfort as for warmth.

"We'll see." Vivian wasn't so sure. Coffee mug in hand she stood at the window—back and forth, back and forth like watching a tennis match—and suddenly a snowy volcano erupted. "Vic, Vicky, come look. Hurry!"

"Oh my God."

Snowballs flew as Quinn pelted the others with deadly aim until they joined forces and pelted her back. Moments later Victoria, boots flapping, arrived to find the women collapsed upon each other, laughing. "Ladies, ladies, are you all right?"

Allison's voice rose from the pile. "Of course. We're fine." A hard-packed snowball caught Victoria's shoulder. Cold snow spattered her cheek as Vivian hurried up just in the time see her sister plunge, snowball in hand, into the melee.

LATER, BACK INSIDE, VIVIAN PATTED THE damp from Prudence's blond fur and watched her sister towel-dry her own short dark curls. "Well, that was fun. I haven't had a snowball fight in years. In fact, I never ever …"

"… liked them. I know, Viv, neither did I, but that was fun, wasn't it? And the ladies, especially that prickly Allison woman, acted like she was having …"

"... the time of her life. She did, didn't she? They were all still laughing like hyenas when they went off to get dry. But Vic," Vivian draped the wet towel over the drying rack and looked at her sister, "maybe we shouldn't tell Owen?"

CHAPTER 7

Miles away, preparation for landing American Airlines flight 4401 to Denver slowly drew Owen Johnson's attention from the letter he'd been reading. He'd memorized its contents but still didn't believe them.

"Dear Owen Johnson," the letter began, pencil scratching on cheap white paper, "This will probably come as a surprise . . ."

What an understatement.

His head ached.

He'd meant to deliver his load, check on the twins and be back in Reno in plenty of time for his flight. The accident changed all that. It was a full eight hours in the emergency room before he'd satisfied everyone that his head was too hard for serious damage. The Physician Assistant who stitched up his forehead had urged Vicodin on him, and once he'd arrived back at Karle's he'd been happy to have it. He'd hoped to get in and out without her notice, pick up his overnighter and run. His plane left early.

Karle's basement, his home-away-from-home, had an outdoor entrance. Eight concrete stairs, dark and familiar—he brushed against a rosemary hedge and its fragrance surrounded him. For the first time in that very long night he smiled. The sky was growing lighter. The cab waited at the curb. He turned his key in the lock, waited until its click disappeared into the crisp air. Nothing. He eased the door open, stepped inside. The overnighter sat where he'd left it, packed save the toiletries kit which he pitched in now. Maybe—

His fingers were still on the zipper when his bedroom light blazed on.

"Owen, what are you doing? Oh . . ." Karle gasped as he turned and she saw the bandage. "Baby, what happened?"

His lips twitched. At least she wasn't calling him honey. He caught her hand as she reached to touch his forehead, thought of the other woman. "It's nothing. Bumped my head in a little fender-bender." He grasped her wrists and put her away from him. "Go back to bed, Karle. I just needed clothes and then I'm out of here." She didn't know about the letter, about this trip he dreaded. What he did was no longer her business.

She pouted. Clearly, *she* didn't see it that way. The full lower lip which he'd convinced himself was delicious now just irritated him.

"Honey, you're hurt. You can't go haring off somewhere. What if you've got a concussion? What if—"

"I'm fine."

The lip trembled. Tears threatened.

"Karle, stop it. I can't stand it when you cry."

She slipped her arms around him, laid her head on his chest and he held her, not knowing what else to do. It wasn't her fault he couldn't love. It seemed he didn't have any love left in him, not any more.

I've made a mess of everything.

Now the floor trembled beneath his feet as the landing gear slid into place. He braced for landing. Life had been simple, predictable—*just what I wanted*—until his wife fell in love with her boss, until his father died and left a mysterious trust, until this letter.

"Dear Owen Johnson." He folded the pages and tucked them into the pocket of his leather jacket, removed his glasses and shoved them in, too, and wished for the Vicodin he knew he couldn't afford to take. He didn't care much for flying and this trip was worse than most. Now the plane was about to set down in Denver and he would drive a rented car into hills he'd never seen to meet a brother he hadn't known existed.

IN THE GUESTHOUSE OF THE WILDFLOWER Inn Bed and Breakfast, on the threadbare Persian rug, three women struggled into assorted sitting poses.

Ungainly children. On her purple mat Quinn sat in a lotus position, facing her new students and nodding encouragement while trying not to laugh out loud. If the snowball fight hadn't restored her good humor, the sight of these three certainly would. And they *were* quiet. Rain forest music—frogs, birds, dripping water—rose from the CD player at her side.

Michelle, Barbara and Allison finagled themselves to attention. She could tell this would be a short meditation. Quietly, she began. "Ladies, let yourselves be comfortable where you sit."

Barbara squirmed. Quinn offered her a lacy white pillow from the nearest chair and waited while the woman settled with a lusty sigh. The other two laughed.

Quinn squinted to disguise an involuntary eye roll. She could almost hear her mother's voice warning, "Don't do that. Your eyes will get stuck in the back of your head."

She grimaced at the stab of pain that always accompanied mother-thoughts and continued, "Now place your left hand palm up in your lap and bring your right hand to join it, palm up, on top." She demonstrated. "And when you are ready, please let your eyes gently close."

They wiggled, followed her instructions.

"Just for now," Quinn spoke softly, "there is nowhere you have to be, nothing you have to do—" and wished she believed it.

Her yoga instructor phase was an early one, about twenty years ago during a brief sojourn in Marin County. She couldn't remember the man she'd been with but her hair had been waist-length, white-blond and frizzy from a perm gone bad.

Surprised that it came back so easily, she went on, "Now sit tall ... imagine a line of energy entering the top of your head moving straight down your spine, anchoring you to the earth and the sky."

She paused after each command and memories skittered in and out. She was twenty-four, fresh out of someplace, and she'd followed the man's promise of peace—veggies and grains, no booze, just a little pot now and then. Somehow peace hadn't shown up but it wasn't until he wanted to share her with just a few of his best friends that she'd roused herself to move on. No peace—but not many thoughts of her daughter either.

"Take a deep breath." She took her own and pushed the memories—intrusive thoughts, really—away, buried them like . . . She drew a ragged breath and hoped no one noticed.

She coached them softly. Barbara's eyes peeked open, darted and when she caught Quinn's eye, squeezed shut again. Allison seemed intent on her breaths. Michelle's fingers twitched and Quinn was sure she wanted to say something. The tinkling sounds of the rain forest seemed tiny in the large, cool room.

Six meditation minutes later Quinn relented and began a yoga warm-up, demonstrating and then waiting as they copied her movements—bending, stretching, holding.

That accomplished, she coaxed them into Down Dog. Barbara collapsed in giggles as she tried to push her bottom toward the sky. Allison hissed her silent, but Quinn saw a smile. Finally, they all stood in Mountain Pose—feet together, back straight, head high—and finished with a series of ratty Half Sun Salutes. *This is what got me into this mess in the first place*, Quinn remembered as she at last released them into Shavasana, the corpse pose. "Lie on your back, legs apart, arms away from your body, close your eyes and collapse into total relaxation."

Ten happy minutes later they sat facing Quinn. Hands at her heart, she bowed to them. "Namaste."

Eyes everywhere but on each other, they murmured, "Namaste," and returned her bow.

THE BEDROOM WAS DARK WHEN QUINN woke from her unexpected nap. She rubbed sleep from her eyes and squinted at the clock—4:30. Light flickered at the Inn's kitchen windows as she rose from her bed and, carrying her flute case like a purse, went in search of a practice room. Meditation, yoga, music—the rigidity of her practices held her together.

She walked across the silent great room and tried a door. It opened into a space walled in glass and permeated with the pink remnants of sunset. She entered. Lining the perimeter, a ragtaggle family of chairs waited. She set up her music stand and opened the case.

The gleaming flute invited her touch—silver cylinders on a blue velvet bed. Her hand tingled as it closed around the first piece, a cool metal body, and she brushed away imaginary lint before she picked up the second, the foot-joint, and slid it into the tenon-and-socket joint at the body's right end. The corners of her mouth turned upward. *I could do this in my sleep.* Her left hand lifted the head-joint and aligned it onto the body, adjusting its depth of penetration.

Face relaxed, eyes half closed, Quinn lifted the flute, pursed her lips and began a warm-up as familiar as her own breathing. She blew a gentle stream of air across the embouchure, adjusting the angle and velocity until a perfect tone issued forth. As her lips assumed their proper shape and her fingers danced, the notes segued from disciplined scales and arpeggios to gypsy abandon, and she was lost.

As the sweet sounds of Mozart's *Flute Concerto Number 1* faded, Quinn turned away from the windows, their view now hidden in the dark, and applause greeted her. Allison, Michelle and Barbara clapped. Behind them, Vivian and Victoria Johnson stood beaming as though something wonderful had just happened. At their feet, Patience and Prudence panted in appreciation.

Christ, Quinn thought, *I feel like January, February and March of the entertainment-of-the-month club.*

Vivian announced, "Dinner time, ladies."

CREED, COLORADO—*TOWN'S A MISNOMER,* OWEN THOUGHT— MORE a cluster of low buildings surrounding a larger, barn-like structure, certainly smaller than Alamosa where he'd spent a few hours tossing and turning on a mattress that had known a hard life. Tires crunched in leftover snow as he pulled his rented Explorer to the side of the narrow gravel road and turned off the engine. He was beginning to understand yesterday's strange conversation at the airport Hertz counter.

He'd asked for directions while his driver's license was being photocopied.

"Are you sure that's where you're going?" The agent, a freck-led engineering student on night duty, looked up from the copy machine, no longer bored. "That's not where tourists usually go this time of year."

"I'm visiting." *What's it to you?*

The freckles stood out on the pale skin giving the boy a shocked look. "Sorry, Mister Johnson, it's none of my business, but the car you're renting isn't likely to get you there."

"What do you mean?" Ashamed at his own irritation, Owen made an effort to keep his voice neutral.

"Well, uh, it's kind of not really a town, you know. And it's up in the mountains a ways on an old mining road that ... well, just say it's not well-maintained in the winter."

"Oh?"

"And the folks who live there, well, my folks say—" A pink glow suffused the boy's face and the freckles almost popped off his cheeks. "Sorry, my folks tell me I talk too much. I suggest a truck or at least an SUV—bad road and possible snow and all that."

The boy provided a map, the destination circled in black, but no further information. He prepared documents for the new rental, a white Ford Explorer, and sent his customer on his way with what seemed like relief.

Now Owen observed Creed, his newly-discovered brother's hometown. Pickup trucks lined the street. A flash caught his eye, and his head swiveled. Nothing. The early sun didn't pen-etrate this unsuspected valley; the air was dark and crisp as he stepped down from the vehicle. He sensed watching eyes. *Shake it off, Johnson, it's just a town.*

He started up the gravel walk.

CHAPTER 8

N CENTRAL NEVADA, THE BUENA VISTA Valley's roads remained unplowed as the sun cast its rays and snow turned to slush. Day Two, sans snowball fight, mirrored Day One at the Wildflower Inn Bed and Breakfast. By dinnertime, the slush had become ice. Michelle and Barbara held hands, steadying each other as the women trudged between the buildings. Quinn's loaner boot slipped on the frozen path and she went to one knee. Allison caught her and pulled her up, then tucked Quinn's hand into the crook of her arm.

Quinn started to pull away, stopped. "Thanks."

Arm in arm, they followed the others into the overheated, magical kitchen.

In minutes, they clustered around the old table, its mismatched china and shining glasses greeting them like old friends. Allison uncorked a bottle of white wine with professional aplomb. "Rombauer, my new favorite."

"And … bonus … the winery's only an hour from her front door," Michelle announced and the others laughed as she handed distributed wine glasses. No one refused. A second bottle waited chilling in an ice bucket.

"Mud in your eye," Allison toasted.

Crystal clinked. "Hear, hear."

Quinn tipped her glass, emptied half, then forced herself to sip as the women found their places at the table and the tight fist inside her loosened its hold.

Spinach salad with a raspberry vinaigrette dressing sat on individual plates but the rest of the meal was served family style and tonight the twins ate with their guests. Victoria's blue turtleneck and Vivian's frayed pink cashmere made their identities easier to discern. Barbara's compliment on the puffy corn soufflé elicited an organic gardening discourse from Victoria that lasted through the meal. "But of course the best food in the world is only as good as its cook." She tipped her glass toward her sister. They already knew that Victoria only cooked breakfast.

"Hear, hear." Glasses clinked again.

Vivian blushed and twisted a loose thread at her wrist.

Relieved to be offstage, Quinn ate and listened, and she attributed her unfamiliar well-being to the wine.

Finally, Vivian topped off the coffee. Mouths full of poached pear and crème fraiche, the women listened to Victoria's weather report. "Everyone was surprised that it snowed again last night, but it's supposed to be clear tonight. No more snow ..."

"... so the road should be cleared tomorrow," Vivian chimed in, "and we'll plow the lane—"

"So we can head out?"

"Right, Michelle. We'll push Quinn's vehicle out of the ditch—"

"Pull, you mean pull, Vivian."

Vivian flashed her sister a look but corrected herself without rancor. "Push, pull ... whatever. We can use the tractor and it'll be out in a jiffy. Then once up and down the lane and you ladies will be good to go."

Quinn finished her dessert in silence, savoring the last of the cream. *Where will I go?* It was hard to look to the future, but right now it was slapping her in the face.

"Let's get packed, ladies, so we can get an early start in the morning." Allison stood and donned her coat. Michelle and Barbara followed.

As Vivian reached past Quinn's shoulder to remove the dessert bowl, she whispered, "Quinn, could you stay back a minute, please?" Apparently taking assent for granted, she went on clearing the table.

Curiouser and curiouser.

THE OTHERS GONE, QUINN FOLLOWED VICTORIA and the tea tray into the parlor and settled onto the settee. The potbellied stove glowed red and warm. The coffee laced with cream and something stronger burned a welcome path down her throat. Her eyelids drooped.

Vivian joined them and the twins again perched on the ottoman, hands clutched in their laps. Except for the sweaters, Quinn still couldn't tell them apart. She waited, willed herself to stay awake.

Victoria of the blue turtleneck cleared her throat and straightened her shoulders. "Quinn, you're probably all a-twitter wondering what we wanted to talk to you about.'

No answer seemed necessary.

"As you've probably noticed," Vivian took up the explanation, "we're not exactly in good shape around here right now. Not enough guests to make ends meet and—" Tears trembled in short black lashes.

"Oh, sister," Victoria patted her hand, "never you mind. Wen says Daddy's estate is almost settled and things will be better soon. Besides we have our plans. Remember that's what we want to talk to Quinn about."

Another scene without a script, Quinn thought as Vivian's tears retreated.

All three jumped as a wood knot exploded in the stove. A piney fragrance filled the room and memories of campfires with her father flooded her. *Silly*, she thought, *and it was usually sage anyway*. Quinn shook memory away and brought her attention back to Victoria's words.

"You know, Quinn, this bed and breakfast was Vivvy's idea. She loves it here and wanted to be out of the city. We'd been living in Las Vegas and …"

"… we'd been living in Las Vegas where we could be anonymous," Vivian interrupted her sister, "but we both wanted to come home." She took a swallow of her coffee, and the sisters exchanged a glance.

That sister look again. Quinn wondered and waited.

The story was simple: They'd been college-prepared in hotel management and home ec. Thanks to a homemaking mother they had mastered canning and baking and gardening. They thought they knew it all.

"We inherited a little bit of money from Aunt Sarah—she was really Daddy's cousin but we called her 'Aunt' anyway. She didn't have any kids of her own so …"

"… so we thought running a bed and breakfast would be as easy as falling off a log and we decided to invest her money in this place. Our brother wasn't sure it was a good idea. In fact, he really tried to discourage us and suggested a bunch of other ways to invest, but we were adamant." Lips tight, chin set, a nod for emphasis, Vivian looked like a petulant toddler. Quinn raised her cup to hide a sudden smile.

Victoria nodded. "Yes, we were determined. One of our school friends used to live here, you know, and we already knew it and loved it, so when her parents decided to retire we made them an offer."

An offer they couldn't refuse? Woops, wrong script. Quinn's mouth twitched. She wasn't sure where this conversation was heading, where she fit in, but even she could see the humor of the moment.

Vivian assumed the narrative. "As you can see, we get a few guests and the place is serene and the rooms are comfortable and beautiful and we don't have television, and—" She took a deep breath, sipped her coffee, and mopped her eyes with a pink cashmere sleeve. "And we serve wonderful food and people enjoy being here. But we don't get enough guests to cover expenses. Our father died a little while ago and left some money and Wennie keeps saying we'll get it soon, but in the meantime we keep digging into our savings."

Quinn frowned. *Down a rabbit hole for sure.*

Victoria seemed to notice the frown. "Sorry, let's start over." Vivian bobbed encouragement. Side by side, they were now clutching each other's hands. "Quinn, we need something to make people sit up and take notice or we'll lose Wildflower Inn. We think you're it, Quinn. We'd like you to stay and work here with us."

Shocked, Quinn said nothing. Whatever she'd expected, it wasn't this. This was not according to plan.

Vivian persisted. "What Victoria means is, we watched you with the guests and saw how they responded and we ..."

"... talked into the night and came up with a plan."

"A plan to entice guests to the Inn."

"We'll offer special retreats for women …"

"… and we want you to run them."

IN CREED, COLORADO, GRAVEL CRUNCHED UNDER Owen Johnson's feet as he walked toward the building. "Please come," the letter ended, "and we'll talk."

Well, I'm here. What's next?

A man in faded overalls stepped from the building and stood on the step. In the porch light, Owen could see him clearly. *Short and spare, black curls shot with silver, a beak of a nose taking up most of his face . . . not much question who his father was.* Owen's doubts disappeared. Disbelief remained.

Michael Johnson stepped forward and offered his hand.

Over coffee in the hulking structure that seemed to be Creed's church, community center and storeroom, Michael Johnson told his story, referring to the man Owen called "Dad" as "our father" with no apparent ill-will.

How would I feel if my father just didn't come home? Owen wondered. *If I woke one morning and my mother told me that from now on it would just be the four of us?* A groan rumbled deep in his chest.

Michael heard, and his eyes held sympathy. "He had to make a choice, Owen, and he no longer loved my mother. He loved yours, so his choice was easier." He held up a hand as Owen started to speak. "I know, he should have thought of that sooner, but he didn't. He always sent us money, my mother said. And we were so little when he left and he wasn't here that much anyway, so after a while we didn't really remember him. Mother told me just before she died that he'd set up a trust for us."

Owen shivered, chilled by the familiar voice and his father's lies. He wrapped his hands around the hot mug and cleared his throat. "I don't know what to say. Obviously, what you're telling me is true."

"You've consulted an attorney, I'm sure." Michael's right eyebrow raised and his lips turned upward.

God, do I look like that when I talk to the girls? Owen nodded.

"And he found us to be what we say?"

Owen nodded again. He had known about the insurance policy. He didn't need it but his sisters did, desperately. It was odd that a trust held it and nothing else, and his father had often done odd things. *But this?*

"I knew that our father had died, but he was just a memory, and we, my sister Martha and I, decided it would be best to just let things be. That was fine until Martha's granddaughter Emily got sick. "

"And you needed money?"

Michael nodded, expression unchanged. "We remembered our mother's words but we were reluctant to pursue the matter. What grief it might stir we had no idea. Then a treatment became available, an expensive treatment that our community could not afford. We couldn't deny Emily the chance to live so I contacted the bank. You know the rest."

"I do." As executor of his father's will, Owen had uncovered his father's secret life. And then Michael's letter arrived.

"I thought I should contact you, that you at least deserved to hear the story from me."

"Thank you." Owen gulped his lukewarm coffee. History as he knew it had changed. He had never felt so unsure of his course. *It will take some time to make sense of it all,* he thought. *If I ever can.* "So what happens next?"

"Well..." Michael Johnson grimaced at his own coffee, made an imperceptible movement and waited. Nothing happened. He shook his head as if reminding himself they were alone, rose from the table and retrieved the blue enamel pot from the wood stove that warmed their corner.

He's used to being waited on, Owen thought, uneasiness filling him.

Michael replenished their coffee, replaced the pot and resumed his seat at the table. "Well, you can always contest our right to the trust." He brought his mug to his mouth but didn't drink, gazed at his brother through the steam. "You might even win. The next step is yours."

Their offer to Quinn having been made, the sisters stood alone in the Wildflower Inn's kitchen. Vivian's hands paused deep in the soapy water. Victoria waited for a dish to dry.

"I think she liked the idea. I think she'll do it."

"Honestly, Vivvy, you are the most optimistic …"

"… person you know. I know, I know, you've already told me that a hundred times. Sure it's a long shot, but she didn't say no."

They stared across the dark expanse to the guest house. Nothing moved. What was Quinn doing now—sleeping, worrying, calling friends or relatives to tell them about this strange turn of events? That's what they would be doing, but neither could imagine her on the phone. She seemed too alone, and besides—she didn't seem the type to take advice kindly.

"Maybe we should have asked her questions, you know, like …"

"… like interview her?" Vivian shot her sister an impatient glance and busied her hands with the flowered plates. "Honestly, Vicky, it's not like it was a job interview. If anything, she should have asked us questions."

"Yeah, yeah, but did we …"

"… make a mistake? I don't think so. If she's the right person, then she's the right person, whether we know her particulars or not." A saucer waited, dripping, in her hands. "But did we do the right thing, not talking about …"

"… about Scottie? Who knows, Vivvy? I don't, but like you said, if she's the right person, and if it just comes up . . ."

The look Vivian gave her sister was filled with hope and anguish. She rinsed the saucer and set it carefully in the draining rack, and Victoria could do nothing but hug her and silence her own doubts.

They finished the clean-up in silence.

WHILE THE SISTERS SPECULATED IN THEIR kitchen, Quinn, alone in her room, reviewed the evening. *Bizarre.* The twins had gleaned her wandering state and made an offer she couldn't refuse.

But she *had* refused. "I don't have any qualifications," she'd told them, "and I don't know anything about business." Everything inside her was crying—*run.*

When they persisted she blurted, "And I really don't like people." *The truth would never do.* The sisters had just exchanged that look again and ignored her protests. The property might look slovenly, but the proposal they put forward was not. In spite of her misgivings, she listened.

Victoria summed it up. "Quinn, we need a hook, a way to bring in paying guests. You need a place to be, for whatever reason."

Quinn flushed, surprised and embarrassed at her own transparency.

Victoria's raised hand forestalled explanation. "You don't have to tell us anything. We've been watching you, and we think together we can make something exciting happen here."

Vivian took up the offer. "We can't pay much right now, nothing really, but we can give you room and board and a free hand in setting up your program."

"And a share in the profits?" The smart aleck question just slipped out.

Run, her inner voice urged.

The twins exchanged glances, turned identical brown eyes back to her. The fire whimpered and Quinn shivered as Vivian said, "Yes, and a share of the profits," and held out her hand.

What else can I do? Quinn shook the proffered hand.

Audacious.

At the memory her lips twitched into an almost smile before the sister chorus took over: Good God, Quinn, what are you thinking? Working in Unionville? In a bed and breakfast? In a ghost town? For room and board? Honestly, Quinn, you are a professional woman, you know.

Ah, yes, she told herself above the clamor in her head, *but I just can't bear to hear another sad story.* She squinted as though she could see her sisters, convince them. *Maybe it will be different this time.*

The reassurance didn't stem the voices: And what will all this do for you? Make you happy? Just grow up, Quinn.

Then they hummed in unison: What if it doesn't work?

She lay back against the metal headboard, wished for another glass of Allison's Rombauer. *What if it doesn't work—that's the question, isn't it, Quinn? What if it's just like everything else?*

She switched out the light as her memory obligingly ticked off a long list of failures. *They didn't even ask me questions. What would I have told them? That I run away from everything, that I like old movies and Tequila shooters and—* The rest seemed too risqué for Victorian ears. *But there's something with them, too. In* the darkness, under her mountain of covers, Quinn remained awake and pondered the words unsaid.

In Colorado, Owen guided the Explorer down the icy road. He hadn't met the others, the sister and her family, the cancer-stricken two-year-old who had started this process. *No,* he corrected himself, *not the child. My father . . . damn it, my father started this process. Dear God, Dad, what were you thinking?*

He braked at a sharp turn, checked the rearview mirror. The cluster of buildings that was Creed had disappeared into the valley as though it didn't exist.

What am I going to tell the girls?

CHAPTER 9

ARLY MORNING LIGHT PENETRATED THE BEDROOM. From under her covers, Quinn watched the sun rise through the shining diamonds of ice that decorated the window. In the background women's voices murmured and doors closed. *I wonder what happened to that man,* she thought, remembering the sense of something special she'd felt as he grasped her hand. *Maybe the Highway Patrol will give me his name, and I can call . . . I saved him, maybe it's his turn.* Wishful thinking faded as she dozed, and when she woke again she knew she was alone.

Yoga mat under her arm, Quinn padded through the heavy silence to the great room. An envelope lay on the threadbare carpet where she spread her mat. Brow furrowed, she picked it up—thick parchment bearing a hint of vanilla, perfect black calligraphic letters, *Quinn*—and ran her finger under the flap. The paper inside matched the envelope, creamy and thick, the message brief:

> *Dear Quinn, I was ready to spice up my life with an affair, but your two days of silence provided opportunity to reconsider. I am returning home to discuss my feelings with my*

husband in the hopes that our marriage of thirty-two years can be preserved.

Thank you, Allison.

Quinn sat back on her heels and tried to sort her jumbled thoughts. *Maybe the twins are right? Maybe I can do something good even if I don't know what I'm doing? Maybe—* Her heart raced. The possibility that things could be different brought excitement and fear in equal measure. Yoga and her plan for non-attachment abandoned, Quinn found pen and paper and settled into deep thinking.

Outside Baggage Claim at the Reno-Tahoe Airport, Owen climbed into the back seat of a Yellow Cab. "Jafbros Auto . . . on Glendale."

The cab pulled away from the curb and Owen leaned back against the sticky head rest. Except for the thinking loop that prevented work he'd intended to complete, the flight back to Reno was uneventful. He closed his eyes.

"We're here, sir."

Owen roused himself, climbed out and handed the cabbie a twenty.

His old Land Cruiser sat in the lot ready to go. "Just some scratches, Owen. I rubbed 'em out. Sorry they had to tow 'er in." The Jafbros owner nodded at the vehicle. "They don't make 'em sturdy like that anymore. I bet the other guy don't look so good." Both men laughed.

Good news for a change.

Owen tossed his overnighter into the Land Cruiser and headed east. The old truck rumbled along as though the collision had never happened. *Sturdy.* He patted the steering wheel. It had been love at first sight, the skinny boy and the shiny red and white vehicle, John J. Johnson's newest toy. Thoughts of his father tightened Owen's chest. *Wish I felt sturdy.* His fingers explored his tender forehead. He wanted a hot shower; he wanted his own bed; but most of all he wanted to erase the past three days.

The hundred miles to Winnemucca sped by unnoticed.

At 8:35 in the morning Quinn pushed open the wooden gate, lifting it upward to assist its tired hinges. Even with help the gate barely cleared the tufts of listless grass. She thought about the day this move would be automatic, then laughed at the notion and added *repair the gate* to her mental To Do list. The snow had disappeared leaving the ground so spongy she wondered if she'd sink.

I've only been here three days, seems like more.

Beyond the fence, gray geese swished their bottoms like the bustles of little old ladies as they honked and hissed, and the precise little goats, Nubians, she'd been told, meandered among them unperturbed. From an adjacent enclosure, the melody of bells worn by dirty-white sheep accompanied her walk toward the narrow porch with the crooked step.

She locked away her doubts, avoided the woodpile, and rapped on the front door. Without waiting, she stepped into the parlor. The stove glowed red, and the aroma of coffee drew her toward the kitchen.

Vivian and Victoria Johnson sat side by side, curly heads bent over papers strewn across the trestle table. A red account book served as paperweight. Both women looked up as Quinn strode into the room.

"Good morning, ladies."

"Good morning, Quinn. We didn't want to bother you too early." Victoria's hand crept protectively onto the red book. "We were just going over the accounts."

Quinn noted the motion. *Last chance to back out.*

"Morning, Quinn." Vivian flashed a half-smile and wiggled from her chair. "Coffee?"

"Absolutely. But sit, I'm not a guest any more. I'll get it myself." She tossed a legal pad, the yellow of its first page almost hidden by the letters, black and mysterious as Egyptian hieroglyphics, which marched across its lines. "Here . . . I jotted down some ideas for our adventure."

Vivian crumpled back into her chair as though the bones had disappeared from her legs. Victoria's whispered "yes" held relief.

When Quinn folded into the chair opposite and sipped from a Welcome to the Bahamas mug, Vivian swiped at the tear trickling down her left cheek. "We thought you'd probably change your mind," she said, "in the cold light of day and all . . ."

Quinn hunched forward, elbows on the table, and her blue eyes went dim; then she straightened and, like a horse shaking its mane, flipped her hair back from her face, and the corners of her mouth turned upward. "I admit I had second thoughts, and then third and fourth thoughts." She raised the mug to her lips, and the twins waited. "And then I thought . . ." *Stop,* she ordered herself, *stick with the script—no fear stuff, no past history, and certainly nothing about the letter from that Allison woman. Life starts right now.* She cleared her throat and finished, "And then I thought, what the hell, this sounds like fun. I'm yours 'til fall."

Heedless of the paper they disrupted, dimpled hands reached toward her, and so did the words they'd held back— "You won't be sorry; we'll have a great time; this will work

63

out, just wait and see." Quinn set her mug carefully aside and joined her new partners in the three-way handshake that sealed their deal.

Much later, Vivian scrubbed at her tears with a pink flannel shirtsleeve as she passed out bowls of oatmeal and refilled coffee cups. Victoria popped up and down like a marmot at a golf course, powered, it seemed, by equal amounts enthusiasm and relief.

Too much relief, Quinn's inner wisdom counseled. *Just wait for the next act.*

Breakfast over and dishes cleared, the women settled around the table. No television, the twins reminded Quinn, just radio. And no money, at least for a while. "But we can get started right away, can't we?" Vivian asked, her eyes on Quinn. "Make plans, start work, get ready . . . a routine?"

This is crazy, Quinn thought. *I've just agreed to work my butt off for people I don't even know here in the middle of fricking nowhere for nothing. And as soon as the brother finds out, I'll probably get the boot anyway. My family's right . . . I am nuts.*

Without warning, bubbles like champagne filled her. Her heart beat faster and before she could squelch it or even understand it a chuckle emerged and then another and another, like hiccups, each rounder and fuller than the last. The twins stared, and the sight of their open mouths, identical O's in round faces, incited her, and the laughter outgrew its restraints. Infected themselves, the twins giggled and then, like children admonished to be quiet in church, they too couldn't keep it in and all three were holding their sides. Their laughter filled the kitchen. Tears rolled down their cheeks.

Winnemucca—home. In the evening darkness Owen maneuvered the old Toyota into his narrow driveway, parked and let himself into the white frame house he'd just refurbished. In the darkness he sniffed and smiled: Lemon Pledge—Vivvy had cleaned again. He liked that she cleaned up after him, even though he urged her not to. He wandered through the dining room, ran his fingers over the keys of his mother's baby grand, then into the living room where his mail sat neatly stacked on the table beside his leather chair. His hand reached for it, detoured to the remote and one click freed the opening strains of *Aida*. Humming, he left the mail untouched and carried his bag to his bedroom.

What am I going to tell my sisters?

He ignored the answering machine blinking on his nightstand and tossed the bag beside his bed. In the adjoining bathroom, he started the shower, and, still in darkness, began to undress. He knew who'd called—Karle, Vivian, Vicky maybe, if she needed something. If he heard their voices, he'd have to call back. *Can't call yet*, he thought as he pulled off his shirt, tossed it into the laundry bin, folded his trousers and laid them on the dry cleaning pile, *not 'til I know how to tell them.*

The only person he wanted to talk to was Mike, the friend who'd need nothing more than a fast game of pickup basketball or a couple of beers at the Winnemucca Hotel. He stepped into the steaming shower.

His thoughts raged as he soaped away the travel fatigue: *It was Dad's decision, and Dad's money. Well, Mother's, too, but not mine. He took care of her, of us. Who am I to say he shouldn't take care of his other children, too?* His eyes stung. Would he ever get used to this new reality?

"There'll be no fight, Michael," he'd told the man whose resemblance to his father tore at his heart, "at least none from me."

"And your sisters?"

"Up to them," he shrugged, "but I think not." He couldn't imagine his sisters fighting anyone for money. More likely they'd want to donate some of their own, once they heard the story.

Did they need to know?

"Honesty is the best policy, son." His father's words. "Don't ever forget that."

He snorted. His chest ached.

Can't I cook up some story about the money? Do they need to know that our father was a liar, a cheat, a bigamist, and worse, that he'd abandoned one family to play house with another. It was bad enough that they wouldn't get the money. Did he have to spoil their memories, too?

The phone rang just as the hot water turned icy. He stepped into the frigid air and reached for a towel as he let the machine pick up. "Wen," Vicky's voice, "Wen, if you're there, answer me. I don't know where you've got to but we've got really good news. Call as soon as you can. Love you." A pause, then Vivian spoke. "I mean it, Owen, call us. Good things are happening here but we need your blessing."

Letting the message light blink, Owen dropped the towel, slid between his sheets and let exhaustion silence his confusion.

CHAPTER 10

HE NEXT DAY THE SUN SHONE and Quinn knew it was time settle into her temporary home. Unwilling to forego privacy, she had refused a room in the main house. Now she explored the guest rooms—one bed too soft and one too hard, one room too dark and one too light, a *Goldilocks and the Three Bears* kind of dilemma—and then, finally, tucked into the front corner, the fifth bedroom with its thick adobe walls and adjacent library was just right.

A hidey hole more than a bedroom, it reminded her of the cubicle under the eaves in her grandparents' home, before they had abandoned her for retirement in Florida. That room had been hers by default, her sisters afraid of the scratchy noises emanating from the walls. Now she wondered if anyone had found her box of treasures hidden and forgotten in the rafters above her cot.

The twins joined her and surveyed the room. "The bathroom is way too small," the practical Vivian pointed out.

Yep, I could poop and shower and brush my teeth all at the same time.

"Janet's parents, the previous owners, remember, thought the room needed its own bathroom, but the only space left . . ."

". . . was the closet," finished Victoria, "so they carved this mini thing out of closet space and you only have that for your clothes." She gestured at the pine wardrobe which commandeered an entire wall.

Mine, thought Quinn, *and who has anything to hang up, anyway?*

Victoria enumerated more of the room's faults. "And the windows face west so you'll never see the morning sun. And the fireplace smokes."

They all studied the ancient fireplace painted with the soot of many fires, its fender dented from the weight of booted feet. Then Vivian told her about the movie star who had slept there, stretched out on the floor in front of the smoking fire until she finally healed her broken heart and danced on the kitchen table.

Mine, thought Quinn.

"This will do nicely, thank you," she said. The twins shrugged their shoulders and shook their heads and acquiesced.

IN HIS OWN BED, OWEN woke to the click of a door opening. In his dream he had waited in a dark room, a barn . . . he could almost smell the hay. Michael had promised to bring his sister Martha, and together they would explain. Another click. *Am I awake or asleep?* His alarm hadn't rung so it couldn't be six yet. He wanted to stay asleep, to meet his new sister or maybe the woman with the turquoise eyes. His chest filled with anticipation. The mattress moved . . . *she's coming.* Heart thudding, he turned and familiar arms slid around him.

"Karle?"

He scrambled out of the bed and switched on the light just

as his alarm blared. Karle Moran, thin strap of a black teddy slipping off her bare shoulder, raised herself on one elbow. Her eyes moved from his face downward and she smiled.

"Dreaming about me, lover?"

He looked down at himself, grabbed for the sheet. "God, Karle, what are you doing here?"

She stroked the rumpled bed.

He ignored the invitation and stalked into the bathroom, the sheet dragging behind him.

When he returned, wrapped in a damp towel, he saw she hadn't moved, but a pout marred her pixie features.

"This is not the desired response, Owen Johnson."

"What are you doing here?"

She exaggerated the pout. He wanted to slap her, the way he'd slapped his sister Vivian when she'd stuck her tongue out at him, before his father's hand taught him that hitting women wasn't okay. *Dad . . .* Heaviness settled in his chest, and he felt like he'd just finished the championship game—and lost. He rested his rump on the edge of the bed. "Karle . . ."

"Oh, all right. I have a client in Elko so I thought I'd stop off here and start my day with a smile."

He frowned.

"But I guess you're not in the mood?" Karle's voice held the sneer that would never mar her beautiful features.

He ran his hands through his hair. "Karle, we decided."

"No, Owen, you decided that we needed a break. Well, I've had all the break I want, thank you very much." She scooted toward him, ran a delicate finger down his side and loosened the towel.

His body responded.

Her lips brushed his shoulder, followed her fingers downward. "Looks like somebody else is done with breaks, too."

Cursing his body for its betrayal, he caught her hand, and, not knowing what else to do, brought it to his lips. "Karle, I thought you understood. I can't—"

She smiled, shifted her breasts, let her nipples press hard against him. "Looks to me like you can, like you want to."

Christ. He wanted her, just in this moment he wanted her so much he ached, and that was the problem—the feeling lasted only as long as the ache. *How do I tell her I can't love her? It would be so much easier to—*

He stood.

She sat back and shook out her long red curls. Her tiny body arched toward him.

He ran his hands through his hair again and the towel slipped. He grabbed for it.

"Karle, you know how much I want you. You are beautiful and sexy and—"

She chopped her hand downward in the air, cutting him off. "Cut the crap, Owen. If I'm so beautiful and sexy and blah blah-blah blah-blah, then why are you standing there clutching a towel like a high school virgin?"

Damn, she's not making this easy. He sat back on the bed beside her, took both her hands and, ignoring the ache in his groin, tried once more to explain.

CHAPTER 11

HREE DAYS AFTER THE SCENE WITH Karle, a scene he would rather purge from memory, guilt and responsibility overtook him and Owen called his sisters.

Victoria answered. Neither mentioned the string of messages ignored. When Victoria cleared her throat and then went silent, Owen grimaced. He knew he didn't want to hear whatever was coming next, but he asked quietly, "So what's up, Vicky?"

She told him. In the background he could hear an occasional prompt from Vivian. He didn't say a word as she told him about a new partnership with a stranger named Quinn DeMello and pie-in-the-sky plans that he tuned out. Then Vivian came on the line. "Wennie, you've been gone so long. We miss you and we want you to come right out and meet Quinn."

A poke in the eye sounded more fun but Owen knew his sister's wheedling tone. Some days it irritated him. Today, ensconced in his favorite chair in front of a roaring fire, a stubby glass of Maker's Mark in his hand, he missed his family almost enough to meet the mystery woman. *Almost.*

Then she added, "Besides, I think you've been avoiding us."

Ouch. He'd conferred with his attorney and with the trust manager and withdrew his objections. The money had been dispersed. There had been no further word from his new half-brother and that surprised him. He was both relieved and disappointed at the silence. He still didn't know what to tell his sisters.

He gulped the scotch warming in his hand, felt it burn, and lied. "I've just been busy, Viv, and I've got a seminar coming up next week, and it is tax season, you know."

"Sorry, Wen, I didn't mean to nag. We know how busy you are, and you know we're pleased as punch that you take such good care of us."

Sucker-punched. When he'd finally convinced Karle that he had neither time nor energy for a relationship, she had chastised him. "You spend way too much time with those sisters of yours and their little problems. You're not getting any younger, Owen Johnson. You need to think about a life of your own."

Right now he didn't feel like a benevolent older brother.

As though used to her brother's silences, Vivian chattered on. "But we are so excited about the Inn. We've worked out a schedule so we'll be ready for Valentine's Day. It is so romantic here." She drew out the *so*, and a fragile smile hovered on her brother's pursed lips. The fist that gripped his chest loosened. He settled into his chair and propped his feet on the ottoman. *At least I can listen.*

"Tell me about this schedule."

"Well, Quinn's working outside assessing the property and its potential—"

I'll just bet she is.

As Vivian outlined their plans, Owen's thoughts turned to deceit. *A cheating wife and a bigamous father—it would be a while before he believed much of anything. As for trust—* He grimaced. *That ship had sailed.*

"Wen, are you still there? I'm trying to tell you how much fun we're having. We have planning sessions every day and we're all working really hard and we laugh. You just won't believe it here, Wen. And I get to plan all the food. Wait 'til you see . . . You are coming, aren't you?"

He sighed.

"What, I can't hear you."

"I said I'll try, Vivvy." He struggled to inject interest into his voice, his thoughts clouded and distant. *God, how will they keep going without Dad's money? How can I tell them they'll lose the Inn? What could this woman possibly want from them?*

"You don't sound very enthusiastic, brother. I'm sorry to fuss at you when you've got so much on your plate, but we've got so much to tell you, show you, and we need your approval. You're our accountant, after all."

"I'll try . . ."

"It's okay, sweetheart. Just come when you can. But you won't believe how much fun we're having and how much good stuff is happening. It's like a miracle. Quinn's like a miracle. Come really soon. We miss you."

"I promise, Vivvy, I miss you, too, and I'll come as soon as I can."

"OK. Love you."

She hung up before he could respond the traditional "Love you, too," and he sat staring into the ashes of his fire. *You'd better go soon, Johnson, before that woman takes them for everything that's left.*

QUINN'S NEW LIFE FIT HER LIKE oft-washed Levi's, but still the sister chorus invaded her thoughts: 5:00 a.m., Quinn? Chores? For Heaven's sake, you don't even know what morning looks like.

True, but there's so much to do.

A share in the profits, Quinn? Get real. This will never fly, and you'll be left with nothing.

Maybe . . . but what else would I do?

And what about the brother, Quinn? What will he think about this crazy scheme?

Ah, now that's the question.

QUINN CLUNG TO HER MORNING ROUTINE, ignored her doubts, and thought about repairs, improvements and advertising, and the pile of yellow legal pads on the kitchen table grew taller. She walked the property, her feet marking her territory, sometimes accompanied by one twin or the other, most often alone. She missed Minnie the Mouser, invited the dogs Patience and Prudence, but they preferred to keep their feet clean.

"Watch out for wild things," Vivian warned.

"Did we tell you about the mountain lion?" Victoria detailed mayhem in the chicken coop. "A professional hunter and his dogs finally got her."

"I was afraid she'd get into the infirmary," Vivian added, the infirmary a wire-roofed pen presently home to a hawk with a broken wing and a raccoon healing from The Attack of the Fierce Unknown, a common local malady, Quinn was informed.

Victoria passed a photo across the table. Quinn looked into the eyes of a magnificent beige cat tucked into the arms of a leafless tree.

She shivered.

Victoria turned to her sister. "It's too early still for snakes, Viv, don't you think?"

S UNSHINE WARMED HER BACK AS SHE tromped the low hills carrying her cell phone and a big stick. Like her hero, Indiana Jones of *Lost Ark* fame, Quinn hated snakes. Occasionally she scuffed up an arrowhead, but she let it lie. The brother's boots rubbed blisters and she knew she needed to get her own things soon. Angelica the Auto, out of the ditch for weeks, stood ready, but each morning Quinn just applied new moleskin and promised, "Soon, girl, maybe we'll go tomorrow."

Surrounded by sagebrush and dispirited Donkey Ears, Quinn shaded her eyes and surveyed her temporary domain. *Sacagawea,* she imagined herself, *or maybe Meryl Streep in* Out of Africa*? Maybe* . . . She redirected her attention to the Wildflower Inn: a stream, a sticky dirt road, rickety fences and pens and sheds, and three buildings, four if you counted the partial ruin farthest up the canyon. Ghostly or no, the air tingled with promise.

Under the cloudless sky, Quinn wondered about the people who had lived here before her. She had read the pamphlets in the guesthouse that told of a mining town that expanded to become the county seat, produced some three million dollars worth of silver and boasted both a courthouse and a school.

The sister chorus wasn't so generous: An old mining town, for Heaven's sake, dead for years. What in the world are you doing there?

What am I doing here, in a ramshackle bed and breakfast, and no Starbucks for miles? Absurd. Tickled, she ignored the chorus and considered the structures below.

Except for the small corner that housed her bedroom, the guesthouse was a young fifty, but the main house, one hundred yards closer to civilization, was two stories of poor insulation, peeling paint and drafty windows surrounded by century-old trees.

Charming?

At breakfast, while Quinn still shuddered from the cougar story and worried about the snakes, Vivian had produced pictures of the mining camp and the house in its youth— fresh white paint, immaculate lawns, women and children in church-going finery—and she could imagine them now: Parties on the lawn; stories told around a crackling fire before the children were tucked under thick down comforters; kisses stolen in the shadows.

Get real, Quinn, the sister chorus intruded.

Gallons of white paint, she answered, imagining the house restored to its original glory presiding over summer suppers, Easter egg hunts, ice cream socials, maybe even an old-fashioned Fourth of July. She visualized the dress she would wear, that is, if she had one.

Quinn assessed the third structure. Weathered to a blue-brown hue attainable only from Mother Nature, the building stood aloof across the road and halfway between the two houses. Its green aluminum roof flashed in the morning sun.

"The former owners—my friend's family, remember— put a new roof on the barn just before they decided to move," Vivian explained. "They thought they were going to live here forever."

"Lucky for us," added her sister.

The barn was watertight and clean, home to pigeons, mice, four barn cats, and the horse, George, a compact sorrel with three white socks and a bald face who should have been christened Georgina.

"She came with the property and we just thought she was old and fat until Wen pointed out she was ready to foal."

"What an introduction to country life." The twins laughed, continued, "But that little foal kept us in spare change for quite a while and still makes her new owner happy."

Chuckles rose from the brush behind her. Quinn jumped backward. Her boots scuffed sand and pebbles, and she lost her balance. Whump, flat on her bottom. Two small bodies, bullets with wings, shot across her path, and then . . . dead still.

Her own heartbeat thudded in her ears. *Quail,* she panted, *I think,* and felt silly for interrupting their conversation. *You need a bird book, Quinn.* When her heart resumed its original rhythm and her breathing returned to normal, she stood and dusted off the leaves and dirt. *I'll get one when I go to town,* she decided as she headed down the hill to her newest and most welcome chore, the care and feeding of Girl George.

QUINN FELT A KINSHIP WITH THE little mare the moment they met, but since Joseph Gastanega—like the horse, a leftover from the previous owners—was the self-appointed mainstay of the barn, she had been reluctant to intrude. She contented herself with hanging over the corral rail, scratching and petting whichever part Girl George presented.

She didn't notice the old man until he waved and motioned her toward the barn.

"Hello, Mrs.," he greeted her, the word sounding like *miss us* as it emerged from lips clamped around the stub of a crooked cigar. "I am Old Joseph." He handed her an enamel mug so hot she almost dropped it, filled from a blackened pot that boiled on a camp stove in the doorway.

Quinn held the battered blue mug in the potholders of her pulled-down sleeves and ventured a swallow. The viscous black liquid burned her mouth, her throat and her stomach, but if sipping the vicious brew earned her rights to the horse, she would sip.

"He's Basque," Vivian told her later, "and the sheepherders just live where they live. There's a cot for him in the barn, but I don't think he ever sleeps there."

Al DeMello, Quinn's jack-of-all-trades father, had entertained his fascinated daughter with stories of the Basque sheepherders: how they wandered the hills alone but for their flocks; how they carved their marks in the white bark of the aspen trees he called "quakies;" how they whittled away the dark nights and left an art gallery of small carved figures in their wake. Now she watched Old Joseph, twisted and wizened like the black cigars he favored, as he struggled with the hay. His gnarled hands, trembling like the aspen leaves under which he slept, left tangles and straw when he tugged the comb through George's mane. She had appointed herself his apprentice.

"The horse she likes you," the old man said as George announced her early-morning arrival. Apparently that was the only recommendation Quinn needed. Joseph Gastanega taught her how to cut the bale and distribute the one or two flakes of alfalfa hay the mare needed each day, its musty smell a reminder of summers past.

"Always the fresh water, Missus, fresh not frozen." He wheezed at his own humor as he broke up the ice in the tin trough. Another morning he mixed oats and molasses, stirring them in a rusted Folgers can before he offered them to the mare. "She doesn't need this much," he instructed, "only after exercise and," his hand hovered over George's soft nose, "for special treat."

Now he was gone.

"I go to the city to live with my daughter, Mrs., just for a little while until," he spread his hands for her to see, and the tortured fingers hurt her heart, "until these get better, or," his eyes lit up with the secret he held from his daughter, "or until the warm weather comes."

Quinn had shaken hands with the daughter, Anne, a heavy-set and pleasant woman, but couldn't watch as they drove away. She knew he had willed the daily care of George to her.

SHE CALLED CECILY TO TELL HER about Old Joseph, about Girl George, whispering her conversation into the black plastic receiver in the parlor.

"A horse? Quinn, what are you doing schlepping around after a horse? You have a Master's degree in psychology, for God's sake. You're not a stable boy. Come stay with me. I admit I was too hasty."

Quinn was surprised at the offer, after the incident with the pills and all on her last visit to Cecily's lovely yellow bungalow in La Jolla. Because it warmed her toward her sister, she tried to explain. "I like it, Cec, the smell of the barn and . . . and, and Cec, she nickers like she's glad to see me." At her sister's silence, Quinn gave up explaining the comfort she felt when she stroked the soft neck and buried her face in the warm curve of the mare's shoulder. She emphasized the practical. "Besides, the brother usually does the heavy work, and he's not here."

"And what's that about? I've been meaning to ask that. What is it with the brother?"

Quinn felt a familiar tightening in her stomach. Her heart thumped. She didn't want to think about the brother.

"I don't know, Cec. He's an accountant. He does the books for them and for their mother's business." *And he has life and death power over this little adventure I'm having,* she thought but didn't say. "The twins say he's up to his ears during tax season." She added, grinning at her use of their cliché.

Cecily's voice held no answering smile. "Sounds like he should be helping his sisters. Woops, gotta run . . . it's my scene."

Cecily gone, Quinn remembered Vivian's words. "Don't fret; he'll be here as soon as he can. We told him about you, and about our plans, and he says he wants to hear more. And," she added, "he's eager to make your acquaintance, you know."

Check me out, more likely.

CHAPTER 12

QUINN WASN'T SURE HOW IT TRANSPIRED—"MEET our suppliers in town" and "help Vicky shop" had been bandied around. Now, she rode shotgun as Victoria wheeled the banged-up Ford truck over seventeen miles of country road toward *town*—Winnemucca, Nevada—and unwanted civilization. She squirmed on the hard bench seat of the inn's only means of transportation as it rumbled along. Sunlight streamed through the windshield, and the temperature in the truck cab rose.

She felt scalded, *scoured*, she thought, an imaginary Brillo pad scrubbing away her skin, her defenses. She had succumbed to the peace of the ghost town where only the wind whispered questions and demanded no answers. Rational or not, *town* threatened exposure. *On display—and found wanting.*

Sagebrush dotted the sere landscape. Fear nibbled at her as the twenty-five miles of Highway 80 East went by too fast.

They gassed up first. She pumped and Victoria went inside to pay, staying awhile, Quinn assumed, to visit. Winnemucca seemed the kind of place where everybody knew everybody else, like her hometown used to be. She grimaced, vowed to keep her distance and wished that her original plan for solitude and nonattachment hadn't slipped away. The Wal-Mart on the hill was no problem, bright lights and clerks who wouldn't remember your name if they waited on you every day. Quinn bought a bar of lavender soap and hefted grocery bags into the truck bed.

Hannigan's Feed was personal.

Victoria parked the truck, and they entered through the rear of the store.

A plain man with an overhanging gut greeted them. "Well, saints preserve if it ain't a twin. How're ya doing, Victoria Johnson? And who's this pretty little thing you've got with you?" Thing sounded like *thang* as he shifted his chew to the opposite cheek.

Quinn felt her bitchiness level heighten. His roaming eyes marked him another taker.

"Hi, Larry." Victoria greeted the man, didn't seem to notice his avid gaze. "Quinn, meet Larry Martin. Larry, this is Quinn. She's working with us these days."

Karl Malden on a bad day. Quinn offered her hand, mentally detached it from her body as he held on a shade too long. She tugged at her green sweater but it refused to meet the waistband of her faded 501's so she wrapped her arms around herself and leaned against the 6x6 that supported the counter. *Larry the Looker,* she christened him and tried not to feel undressed. She concentrated on the display of boots that marched along the wall and searched for her sense of humor.

Larry's glances flickered back and forth as he did business with Victoria, interrupted by an army of men in boots and Levi's who greeted Victoria like a long-lost relative and directed inane questions at Larry while they ogled Quinn.

Jerks.

Larry's eyes swept her, the wrinkles at their corners deepening, as though he knew her thoughts and was amused.

Yuck. I hate men, Quinn thought, *Nah, not hate . . . they're just trouble.* She sighed and yearned for red cowboy boots and cowboys on white horses.

"Ready, Quinn?"

Finally. She shouldered a bag of organic chicken feed and followed Victoria out the back.

Truck loaded, Victoria drove further into town. "I need to stop at my brother's and drop off some stuff. Maybe he'll be home so you can meet him."

Run, Quinn, run. Her feet itched to hit the pavement, but she just shrugged. What choice did she have but to ride along? What excuse to sit in the car when Vic said, "Come on in"?

The white frame structure, surrounded by an old wire fence and a winter brown lawn, occupied a small lot on a busy street. "He wanted to live downtown, Quinn, so he could walk to the movies and the store, and he eats out a lot so he wanted to walk to dinner, too."

Everything the brother did seemed worthy of notice.

They let themselves through the metal gate and Victoria latched it behind them. "He's always working on it, fixing it up, but now he says it's done. He's got these two really good friends, John and Mike—the three of them started kindergarten together—and they helped a lot. They should have. Wennie's done their taxes for years for nothing, and he worked just as hard on Mike's house as he did on his own."

And where's the little helpmate wife? Quinn wondered but didn't ask. An uncomfortable feeling lodged in her throat. *Green with envy—really, Quinn?*

As though reading Quinn's mind, Victoria finished, "He says it's perfect for one person." She retrieved a key from under the mat and opened the door. "Anyone home?"

No answer. She replaced the key and stepped inside. Quinn followed.

The 12x12 room had burgundy walls and high tin ceilings and pristine white crown molding. No ceramic figurines, no doilies, no sense of time dislocated. A tidy stack of mail and two remotes on the table beside a deep leather chair; horn-rimmed glasses resting on *To Kill a Mockingbird*; Hemingway's *The Sun Also Rises* and Norman McLean's *A River Runs Through It* on the matching ottoman. Quinn noted the worn covers and dog-eared pages.

Victoria led her through a second room. "Here's the dining room, but there's only space for Mama's piano."

Quinn's fingers skimmed the keys. *Perfectly tuned.*

"Wen keeps it for her. She's in assisted living, you know. Mama could have been a concert pianist; that is, if she hadn't fallen in love with Dad and had us." As though she sensed Quinn's curiosity, Victoria gestured toward the rest of the house. "Go ahead and look around. I'll just put these things away."

Quinn thought about the piano and the mother and her children as she wandered down the hall, stopped at an open door. *What the heck.* She took one step into what was obviously the man's bedroom and looked around. King-sized bed, blue plaid quilt that looked homemade smoothed over white sheets, another pair of horn-rimmed glasses beside a clock radio on the night stand. The door to his closet stood open. She edged closer.

Dark leather cowboy boots, scuffed tan work boots, blue and white athletic shoes and black dress shoes lined up on the closet floor, above them a row of pants—Levi's, khaki's with military creases, dark dress slacks, each encased in its personal plastic. On the higher rod, obediently facing right, hung eleven shirts—two plaid, two blue denim, six crisply white and one Hawaiian flowered print. Quinn counted them as she reached out toward the flowers. The silk was soft, and her touch loosed a fragrance so sharp and sweet that she gasped, dropped her hand and, feeling as though she'd rummaged his underwear drawer, fled the room.

In the kitchen, Victoria leaned into the refrigerator putting away the containers of food she'd brought. She closed the door and looked up when Quinn entered, fanning her cheeks.

The kitchen boasted granite countertops, shiny appliances with no sign of wear, and cherry wood cabinets. Quinn slid one finger down the smooth surface surprised when it didn't release the man smell, too.

Victoria watched her. "Wen made the cabinets. When he moved in the original metal ones were still here. Nice, huh?"

"Very nice, beautiful."

Beautiful and lonely. She crossed the room, its only sign of life the Christmas card photographs decorating the refrigerator door.

Victoria pointed at the likeness of a middle-aged couple and three children, two teens and a toddler, all blond and all sporting red velvet Santa hats. "This is John Perry and his family." Quinn moved beside her for a closer look. "They're such nice people."

The dark and handsome couple with the Great Dane was "Mike and Patti Sakelaris, Wen's other best friends."

Two preteen boys with round faces and teeth too large for their mouths stared from school pictures. "Basketball players— Wen's coached at the Boys and Girls Club for as long as I can remember. He likes kids and they like him. But who wouldn't?"

Yeah, right. The man seemed too good to be true.

Quinn ran a finger over the largest picture on the door, not a card but a snapshot—a man and a woman, both wearing hardhats and each wielding a hammer, perched on a roof. The man's face was turned away from the camera, attention focused on the laughing woman whose hair cascaded over her shoulders like a red waterfall.

Victoria laughed. "The duel of hammers. That's Karle, Wen's landlady in Reno. They worked on her house together. I swear she is the cheerfullest person I've ever known."

Quinn jerked her hand away as though the picture were hot.

Victoria didn't seem to notice. "Come see the workshop and then we've got to go. I thought he might show up, but I guess not."

They descended into the basement. Power tools in boxes, paint cans with readable labels, wood pieces sorted and stacked lined the perimeter shelves. Over the workbench, screwdrivers, pliers, and hammers clustered in homogenous groups on a pegboard. No dust. No cobwebs.

Neat freak. She turned and gasped. An unfinished armoire occupied most of the underground space; its beauty took the thought away. She stared.

"Really something, isn't it?

On the way home, they were quiet, each occupied with her own thoughts.

It was the house of a man set in his ways, a man in love with his life—just the way it was. Quinn twisted a strand of hair around her finger and tried not to think about the laughing woman. *I really should go home and get some other clothes.*

"You said we didn't need much," Vivian groused as Victoria deposited the eighth grocery bag on the counter. She pounced on an escaping onion and tossed it into a bushel basket in the corner.

"Now or later." Victoria nodded at the hearts that adorned the brown paper bags. "I thought we should get a head start on Valentine's Day. It'll be a full house, remember."

"Finally, thank goodness." Vivian folded the last of the bags, smoothing out the wrinkles over the hearts. "How was the trip to town anyway?"

All the way home, Victoria couldn't wait to tell her sister, but now she wasn't quite sure what to say.

"Well?"

Victoria put away the last milk carton, found a cold Corona and joined Vivian at the table. "You wouldn't believe it, Viv, but they were all over her like white on rice."

"Quinn?"

"Yeah, our Quinn. I didn't think much about how she looks, but you should have seen them. We went into Hannigan's to pick up feed and by the time we left half the guys in town were there, drooling like they'd never seen a woman before. Larry ogled her like you wouldn't believe."

"Feed store Larry?"

Victoria heard the real question. She had dated the store owner a few times before giving it up. He liked the store more than he liked her. She knew her sister feared a broken heart.

"No skin off my nose," she reassured Vivian and then described the scene: Quinn leaning against the check-out counter, her green wool sweater a little short at the waist and wrists from too many washings, her faded 501's sitting loosely on her slender frame. "She looked about twelve, well, maybe sixteen, just standing there twisting her hair like she does, and Larry looked like he wanted to lick her clothes right off her. Moths to a . . ."

". . . flame," Viv completed. She seemed to accept her sister's nonchalance. "Who would have thought it? Did you see Scottie?"

Victoria frowned—her sister's troublesome son worked part-time at the feed store since he finished high school in June. Uneasiness curled in her middle. "Uh, Viv, there's something that's . . ."

"You saw him? Is he okay?"

Oh well, I guess we'll just talk about Quinn later. Like a cat on a blanket, the uneasiness kneaded. "No, I didn't see him, Viv. Yes, he's okay."

Victoria watched the worry fade from her sister's face and regretted her own crabbiness. "Larry did manage to get his tongue back in his mouth long enough to tell me that Scott's been on time every day since Christmas. That's a good sign. Larry also said something about Scott's not being there much longer. I didn't get the whole of it, but it sounded like he thinks Scottie's planning a trip."

As the wrinkles reappeared across her sister's forehead, Victoria soothed, "It's probably nothing, just another Scott escapade." Scott slept on friends' couches, had no phone. He was hard to track down. "Maybe Owen can find out."

They brooded at each other across the table. A querulous owl called.

Mood shaken, Victoria jumped to her feet. "I'm taking a shower. Call him, and then we'll eat."

Vivian picked up the phone to call her brother.

"Bye, Vivvy, love you, too." Owen set down the phone and wandered back toward his cold and tidy kitchen. His sister had called to ask about Scott, tell him Vicky and Quinn "stopped by" and issue a dinner invitation. He wasn't sure which part to worry about first: Scott's escapade, lying to his sisters or that woman in his home.

The moment he'd stepped in his front door he'd known someone had been there. The air itself felt rearranged and here, in the kitchen, a faint odor of lavender lingered. He opened the refrigerator, removed a Tupperware container: Lasagna. Spoon in hand, he went from room to room, sniffing the air for the scent that seemed to have taken up residence. He knew he was over-reacting. It was natural for Vicky to drop by, bring food. *But she should have asked. Just because they think that woman's a miracle doesn't mean I do.*

He forced his thoughts to Scott. *What's the damn kid up to now?* He would check out a few of Scott's friends. No one in Winnemucca kept a secret very long.

But dinner?

Now I'm in for it—couldn't think up an excuse fast enough, could you? Dinner Sunday at 5. No reason to refuse. *Well,* he decided, *unless they ask about the money, I just won't bring it up.* His conscience kicked in. *What about the brother and sister they don't know about yet? When are you going to tell them about Michael and Martha? About their father's two lives?* He wanted to groan and pull his hair the way frustrated movie characters did. Instead, he ate the last bite of noodle, set spoon and container in the sink, and sniffed the air again.

The phone rang. Reprieved, Owen picked it up and almost groaned with pleasure when he heard his old friend's voice. "Mike, how's it goin', man?"

Mike Sakelaris and Owen Johnson exchanged the small talk of men who didn't need to converse to be understood, so Owen was surprised when Mike asked, "What's the deal out at the Inn? I heard your sisters have a new employee. Since we haven't seen you in a while, I guess you must be out there puttin' on the moves? Quite a looker, unless Larry's blowing smoke." His tone was light, but Owen recognized the underlying concern.

"Is she?"

"You don't know?"

"Haven't met her yet." Owen's grip tightened on the phone and he told his first lie. "Too busy in Reno."

"Karle again?"

Damn the man, this is what happens when your friends know everything. Well, almost everything. He tried to keep the irritation out of his voice. "No, Karle and I are finished and now even she knows it. I don't know what I was thinking."

There was a pause indicating that Mike might know something he didn't, but the man returned to his earlier subject, "So what's up at the Inn? And why haven't we seen you lately?"

Owen swallowed hard and opened his mouth but words wouldn't come. It would be treasonous to talk about his father's perfidy, about his fears for his sisters, about his distrust of this new woman, even if she was 'quite a looker', even though he knew he could trust Mike with his life. "Taxes. Busy earlier this year. And I'm going out early tomorrow to find out what's going on. You know my little sisters, always adopting strays."

Mike laughed and let the awkward moment pass. "John's at the gym, want a game?"

"When?"

"An hour? I'll pick you up."

More relieved than it warranted, Owen agreed. His relief would have evaporated if he'd seen his friend's frown.

DINNER OVER, THE SISTERS SAT IN the upstairs sitting room, a miniscule space between their separate bedrooms. The meal was simple, conversation sparse, and Quinn said good-night before the dishes were off the table. Flames flickered in the miniature cast iron stove that heated the upstairs, but cold air encroached. Vivian propped her feet on the fender and let her mug of steaming decaf warm her hands.

"Owen's coming for dinner this weekend, and he'll try to bring Scott."

"I know. Heard you on the phone. Maybe we'll find out what's going on." Victoria sipped from a squat crystal glass, her expression bland. "Karle coming, too?" She shifted in her chair. Disturbed, Patience wuffled and rearranged herself.

"Back hurt? I told you not to lift those feed sacks."

"I know, but I couldn't leave it all for Quinn. It'll be fine in the morning. What about Karle?"

"He didn't say and I didn't ask." Vivian kept her gaze down.

Victoria's eyes narrowed. "You didn't ask?" Vivian was never afraid to interrogate their brother.

"I didn't want to bring it up, but I don't think there's anything there, at least not since they got back from Hawaii."

"Maybe you're right," Victoria agreed, "but it won't be for Karle's lack of trying."

Vivian sipped her coffee, returned to their earlier conversation. "How was Quinn? I mean, how did she act in the store? She sure didn't have anything to say at dinner."

"It was amazing to watch, Vivvy. She didn't even notice them."

CHAPTER 13

Q UINN GLIMPSED A FLICKER OF LIGHT as she approached the barn. Air like shaved ice stung her cheeks. She paused, switched on her Mag Lite, and listened. Nothing. The owl and the rooster both slept. Absolute predawn stillness.

Overactive imagination.

Satisfied, she moved forward, concentrating on her footing, avoiding the patches of dirty snow and the thoughts of yesterday's trip to town.

Larry Martin had caught her elbow as she followed Victoria out of the store. "Can I call you this weekend?" he said as though she was just dying to be asked. Then the young guy loading the feed sacks, she didn't even know his name, offered her a ride home if she wanted to stay in town a little longer. She evaded both invitations, but thinking about it later she remembered a funny look from Victoria as they climbed into the truck.

Uneasiness swept her like a blast of arctic air. *I knew I should have stayed home.* Now she contemplated ways to escape Sunday dinner with the brother. *Malaria, Dengue fever, an urgent summons from the White House?* Amused by her own wishful thinking, she picked her way toward the barn, then paused at the corral and listened again. When she heard nothing but early morning crackling around her, she slipped under the rail.

Girl George stood silent. Reassured, Quinn felt her way into the darkened interior. A silhouette materialized, backlit by the rising eastern sky, and she froze.

The silhouette spoke, "Sorry. Didn't mean to scare you," and pulled the cord of the overhead light.

"Indy," Quinn gasped. Fedora, leather jacket, face still in shadow—her movie hero come to life.

The man stepped toward her, hands away from his sides in a non-threatening stance. "Sorry, ma'am, left my whip at home."

Omigod, he got it.

"I never expected anyone here so early." He wiped his hand on a pant leg, stepped further under the light and reached out to Quinn. "I'm Owen Johnson."

Now she could see his face and the pinkish-purple slash that traversed his forehead and dimpled his right eyebrow. Her breath caught and her world tilted as she remembered—the wreck, the blood, the tingle as his hand clasped hers. " Wow. Wennie?"

He laughed. "Yep. The curse of baby sisters. And you must be Quinn."

Quinn stepped into the puddle of light where they could see each other clearly. The man's eyebrows rose as he recognized her and the handshake froze, midair.

"Well shit, it's the runaway. What are the odds?" Owen pulled his hand back, hooked his thumb on his Levi pocket and stared. "Huh." The air changed between them. "I wondered where fate had taken you. It never occurred to me that my sisters' magical 'Quinn' could be my own illusive rescuer." Quinn discerned surprise and irritation in his voice.

"What a coincidence. It looks like you're recovered." Quinn put nasty in her own voice, defense against his less-than-welcoming tone and her own embarrassment—she'd cast him as hero, not nemesis. "I wondered if I'd ever meet the brother-who-does-all but not much lately. I thought you'd arrive on your white horse sooner—to protect your sisters, I mean."

The welcome surprise in his eyes hardened to something dark. "Not my intention, I assure you," he said. "I come to help as often as I can."

"Yeah, right." She wanted to rewind the scene, but she had already relegated the brother to enemy status so she changed the subject. "Have you fed the girl yet?"

The man adjusted his hat, fingered the brim. "Yes, she's fed and watered. As I said, I didn't expect anyone so early." Thrust and parry. "Viv says *you're* a city girl."

OWEN PUSHED HIS HAT BACK AND watched Quinn stalk up the muddy road and disappear into the guesthouse. "Isn't she the feisty one?" George's lips worked into his jacket pocket looking for the treat she always expected and always found. "I wonder what the girls see in her." Owen polished the apple against his plaid flannel shirt. The little mare nudged him in sympathy before she accepted his gift. He rubbed her neck and tried to unclench his jaw. "Well, old girl, at least you haven't fallen under her spell."

George munched as the man mucked out her stall and gave no notice to the ferocity with which he attacked the task.

That his sisters' *savior* should turn out to be his own rescuer was an unexpected turn, amazing really, and her gasped "Indy" amused him. "What do you suppose she wants here?" he asked as he shoveled. George masticated and didn't answer. "Right, you're right," he murmured as though she had, "but did I really sound that bad?" The memory of turquoise eyes and a firm grip which surely hinted at more than roadside rescue stayed with him.

Just my rotten luck, stupid rotten luck, never happen to anyone else. Quinn had surrendered the barn to the man, escaped before she said something else she'd regret. Now she sat on her yoga mat and dithered: *I blew it. Bad first impression. I should have just been nice and surprised to see him, not all 'in your face' about his sisters. God...* She moaned in frustration but her yoga mat refused comfort. *I don't even have George to talk to,* she fussed, separated from concentration by the width of a brown fedora. Finally she gave up, pulled on the man's boots and charged up the hill.

What if he makes me leave?

"What do you mean, she's a nice person?"

Owen stood in the kitchen and fumed at his siblings. They hadn't complained that he'd come a day early, just hugged him and started his favorite coq au vin. He'd worked until dusk repairing winter ravages and worrying about lying fathers and empty trust funds and cheeky women who raised his blood pressure. Now, showered and changed, he pulled the cork on the pinot noir he'd brought because neither sister liked the darker, heavier reds that he preferred. Feeling ill-used, unable to pinpoint the reason, he glowered. "She's like a cat with her claws out just waiting for someone to scratch."

The twins exchanged glances.

Owen's thick black brows drew together over the bridge of his nose and stretched the tender new scar. "I don't know what you two have planned but I can tell you I'm not happy about it." He poured wine into three glasses, emptied his in one swallow. "What do you know about her anyway?"

Victoria looked at her sister, raised a shoulder in question. Vivian returned the shrug. Owen recognized the maneuver— they'd decide who could twist him best and that one would answer. Tonight it was Vivian.

"Wen, I don't know what happened but please just give this a chance. It's hard to explain, but there's something about her that we think is special." Vivian paused and the only sound in the room was the click of her spoon as she stirred the savory dish simmering on the stove. Its sweet fragrance filled the room.

Victoria took her turn. "Vivvy's right, Wen, there's something about her that makes us hopeful, and this time I think we're right. You just need to . . ."

"Keep an open mind," they ordered in unison, "and help us see this through."

Ha, I was right. Owen refilled his glass and sipped, this time letting the swallow linger as he internally bolstered the case against Quinn. *They don't know anything about her beyond the babble of "magical laugh, caught on quickly, enthusiastic" and their own wishful thinking.* He squelched the memory of turquoise eyes and forced himself to relax. He had his work cut out for him.

Quinn entered and was properly reintroduced. The perfunctory handshake elicited no tingle. Relieved, Quinn sat across the table from "big brother" whom she dubbed Owen the Omnipotent and refused to meet his gaze. The twins twittered as they served the organic greens dressed with Balsamic vinegar, home-baked bread still warm from the oven, fragrant coq au vin.

"Coq au Viv." Owen earned a pleased smile. "Wonderful as usual, Vivvy."

Ugh. Quinn picked at her chicken and listened as he relayed news from town and then, in answer to a question from Victoria, an update on their mother. "She had a good day yesterday," he said, "and we played rummy before breakfast." Meeting Quinn's eye, he offered a polite explanation. "She's been in an assisted care facility for eight months. It was her decision, rather than to live with me or the girls, when she knew her memory just . . ."

". . . wasn't up to snuff," completed Victoria. "Wen visits her every morning he's in town, and Viv and I get in to see her as often as we can. Vivvy wanted her to come here, thought we could convert the back room and . . ."

". . . take care of her, but she'd have none of that. 'I won't be a burden to my children,' she said, and she meant it. Thank God, Dad planned well financially—thanks to Wennie, that is."

Quinn was surprised when the man flushed and changed the subject. Sitting at the head of the table, blue denim shirt hard-pressed and buttoned to the top, hair slicked down, dark-rimmed glasses in place, he didn't look at all like her Indiana Jones, and she wondered how she could have made such a mistake.

"Enough of that," he interrupted her thoughts. "I'm ready for coffee, and ready to talk about the big plans, but let's take care of the other business first, get that out of the way."

Over coffee and deep dish apple pie, the three of them went over the books. Quinn added extra sugar to her coffee and resisted the urge to keep stirring. *What am I doing here, anyway?*

Item by item, Owen went through the papers Victoria set before him. Only his occasional hums and uh huhs interrupted the otherwise silent room.

"What's this—window pane?" He pulled off his glasses and glanced over his shoulder as though looking for the cardboard. "It's fixed?"

"Quinn did it. We found the glass in the shed and she just put it in."

He turned back to Quinn. "You know how to do windows?"

She shrugged, didn't explain that when you're raised as the only boy in a family of girls you learn to do odd and unfeminine things. "Misspent youth," she muttered.

A quizzical look, then he dropped his eyes and examined the rest of the papers without comment. Finished, he scooped up the remnants of pie and ice cream and pushed his dish away. "Okay, girls, now the new venture."

He didn't look at Quinn.

Pain settled like a sliver in Quinn's left eye. She twisted a strand of hair and mumbled, "All we need is a drum roll." The man glanced at her, lips twitching, as though he could hear.

Victoria handed him the red folder, smiled reassurance at Quinn. "And Wen, we've got a full house already for Valentine's Day and we're going to serve breakfast in bed. That was Quinn's idea, too."

Selling me, Quinn thought, tucking in her mental insulation. *I hope it works.* She couldn't remember when this project had become *her project*, not just something to while away the hours until it was time to leave, and she knew the brother's approval was crucial. They'd made it clear that his word was law.

How can you be that powerful when your name is Wennie?

OWEN JOHNSON RE-SETTLED HIS GLASSES AND shifted in his chair seeking a comfortable position in yet another uncomfortable situation of his sisters' design. *Pay attention, Johnson, you've got to be fair about this.* He knew how much his opinion mattered, wished it didn't. *How can I be fair when I know this won't work?*

The woman wandered away, returned with fresh coffee, and he nodded a thank-you as she refilled his cup. Bare hands, no tell-tale pale band branding her fourth finger. In her faded Levi's and green sweater she didn't seem much of a threat. He felt an odd sensation in his stomach, blamed the second helping of pie.

The accounts were as he expected, not close to breaking even, but was surprised at the repairs. Victoria's "We've got a full house for Valentine's Day" put him on full alert for sister manipulation.

"Okay, Victoria Marie, now the new venture."

He accepted the red folder. Vivian clenched her hands and closed her eyes and he wondered for a minute if she were praying. He discerned a muttered "drum roll" from across the table and looked up just in time to see the woman playing with her hair. With difficulty he staunched a smile, and it took willpower to focus on the papers in front of him.

Words printed in a bold hand he didn't recognize captured his imagination and, as he read, he could almost believe. *Too good to be true*, he chided himself. *Can't expect manna from heaven these days.*

Struggling for a neutral tone, he prepared to defend his sisters. "Your work, Ms. DeMello?"

As if in slow motion, the man perused the pages she'd written out so carefully, the only sign he'd moved from one word to the next a faint change in the deep crevice between his eyebrows. Quinn pushed her chair back, twisted her hair, and observed this trio that had become part of her life—the brother rangy, not quite handsome, his hair falling over the scar on his forehead; the sisters identical in manner and form, as full-figured as the brother was spare; three hawk noses proclaiming their relationship. Like a good accountant, he focused on the details; rapt, they focused on him.

Too much influence, Quinn thought, her own sister chorus blessedly silent.

Owen Johnson raised his eyes from the page and pinned Quinn with his gaze. "Your work, Ms. DeMello?"

She took a deep breath. "Theirs. I just added the details."

"Why only two- and three-day stays?"

Though she'd been warned, she was unprepared for the abruptness of his manner, the challenge in his tone. She bristled, took another deep breath and prayed that her voice wouldn't betray her.

"One day doesn't provide the flavor we want. This is an experience to savor, to soak up, to remember. Everybody does spa-day kinds of things." She dismissed spa-days with a flick of her fingers. "They're not special any more. But more than three days can overdo a new experience. We want them to leave begging for more."

"How do you know?"

"Drop out rates in therapy, other classes."

"Therapy?"

He has a right to ask. Her fingers tortured another lock of hair and she tried to shrug off his staccato questions, his dark eyes pinning her in her seat. *I feel like I'm on trial*, she thought, and knew it to be true. "Drug and alcohol, marriage and family. I'm a therapist." She didn't mention that she was also an EMT, a Red Cross mental health volunteer, a part-time flutist, a . . . but then she'd already told him she was a runaway so what could he think?

"Okay." He shifted in his chair, rearranged his glasses. "Why organic food?"

Happy to direct attention away from herself, Quinn gestured toward the kitchen and the remnants of their gourmet meal. "Ambience, stage setting . . . the unusual, and it's already here." Vivian's face flushed. "Give them health in an unexpected, total environment, but pleasure as well. Delicious food . . . almost exotic. Palatable wines . . . but just a tease."

His prominent Adam's apple rose and fell as he swallowed. She wondered what he was thinking.

"Good selling points, I suppose." He looked at the paper in his hand as though refreshing his memory. "I don't get the kitchen and garden work part. Explain."

Quinn grinned and straightened. *He can't find anything wrong with it. He's just picking because he thinks he has to.* Flooded with unexpected confidence, she was ready to spar with this man. Her face lit up, and the twins exchanged their nothing-to-worry-about-now look.

OWEN STRAIGHTENED, HIS EYES FIXED ON the woman across from him, the corners of her mouth turning up and her eyes flashing as she spat out answers to his inane questions. *She's toying with me.* Incredulous, he listened to her explanation and didn't remember the question that had prompted it. He couldn't quite put his finger on it but something had changed and this room, more familiar to him than his own kitchen, crackled.

"Simple," she explained, her voice so soft he had to lean forward to hear, "we're building a community here, a connection that's different from the others in their lives. We want our guests to leave feeling they've been part of something bigger than themselves. Timing and environment help create this feeling. So does shared work—it's like glue that binds people. We're letting them be participants in this creation."

She paused. He leaned in further, afraid he'd miss her words, and she turned her turquoise eyes to his. For just a moment it seemed she would say more. *This is what she wants, this connection*, he realized, but then she shrugged and her voice returned to normal, and he was sure he'd been mistaken.

Leaning back in her chair, Quinn cleared her throat, shook her hair back, and continued. "Anyway, we've got hours of the day to fill—why not something useful rather than just entertaining?" She shrugged again. "Make them work for their fun."

He nodded, appreciating the amount of persuasion it must have taken to get his traditional sisters on board with this idea. He glanced at them now, side-by-side on the edge of Vivian's chair. Vivian beamed at Quinn. Victoria nodded. Neither looked at him.

Not yet ready to concede, he announced, "Needs work, good concept. And the silence part?"

The woman stiffened and glanced at her hands, and he prepared for the lie. She twisted her hair. *Deciding what not to say?*

Her eyes met his and held, and doubt niggled him as she answered, "To provide a novel experience and enhance the spiritual atmosphere without promoting any formal doctrine or dogma."

Huh? Not what I expected. He eyed her curiously, ignorant of the expectant silence that had taken possession of the room.

Silence. Quinn sensed the twins barely breathing. *Too much? Not enough? And why did I say that about spiritual atmosphere? He'll think I'm a loony.* A giant hand squeezed her stomach and she wanted another glass of wine.

The man tidied the pages into the folder, placed it on the table, squared it, and positioned his glasses beside it. "What about the other days, the non-retreat days?"

The twins exchanged glances, looked at Quinn.

"Non-retreat days will be like a regular B & B except . . . music and tea in the afternoons, elegant organic meals, no TV, and silence in the common areas except at dinner time. All this spiced by the retreat presence—" Her voice trailed off. *Shut up, Quinn, let well enough alone.*

He repeated the straightening ritual, put his glasses on and off. "It looks possible, ladies."

What a pain. A quick glance in the man's direction caught him running his fingers over the fresh scar on his forehead, his eyes on her and, again, his lips twitching. For a second she thought she'd said the words aloud.

Then pudgy hands clapped, reached out to her. "See, we knew he'd like it. Now we can get started. Wennie, it will be great, just you wait and see."

Owen Johnson didn't seem quite so sure. Lips no longer twitching, the look he cast Quinn was full of challenge.

FEET PROPPED ON THE FENDER IN their sitting room, the sisters discussed the evening. Quinn had gone to settle George. Reneging on his promise for Sunday dinner, Owen was on his way back to Winnemucca.

"I thought it went well, didn't you?"

That butterflies-in-the-stomach feeling again. Victoria Johnson scrunched up her face and looked at her sister for a long moment. "Yeah, that's why Wen ran out the door like the house was afire, but—"

"But what? The way he looked at her when she wasn't looking? That *what?*"

"Yes. It was exactly like I told you, like Larry Martin looked at her. And he was so . . ."

"... so unpleasant—lawyerly. Yeah, not his usual mellow self at all. And he forgot to take his leftovers. Oh, Vic, what are we doing?"

"Oh well, what's done ..."

"... is done. And Scottie's coming tomorrow."

CHAPTER 14

Armed with brother Wennie's tepid blessing, the women began. Vivian seemed preoccupied the day after her brother's visit and then sad. Quinn wondered but didn't ask. The to-do list was formidable and there was little time for anything else.

The invitations looked presidential—special ordered in fine linen stock, ecru with black letters, thin gold cord—and they were sent west to prominent women who might be searching for something new and who, the trio admitted to themselves, could afford to pay. *Next time Boise, Portland, Seattle.* Quinn chuckled at her own inflated thinking.

Quinn's miniscule budget included sticky mats, and she decided a trip back to Reno was in order . . . soon. She ordered real yoga pants—stretchy blue fabric folded low at the waist, tight at the hips—and a tiny top to match, and after her morning moments with George she worked on yoga routines suited for their expected guests.

Each room in the guesthouse was stripped, cleaned, and redressed. Victoria's friend, Cassie, proprietor of Timeless

Treasures, Winnemucca's most interesting antique store, provided an endless supply of old linens. The Inn's down comforters, refreshed from an afternoon draped over the clothesline in the sun, wore duvets of Battenberg lace and gingham checks and toile prints. Plump pillows donned lace cases and leaned like aging coquettes against the old brass headboards.

"Polished to an inch . . ."

". . . of its life," pronounced the sisters as they surveyed the great room and its gleaming piano. Faded landscapes hung on white walls, antimacassars protected the old velvet chairs, and an arrangement of dried hydrangeas filled the corner behind the piano. The murmur of the heater and the ticking of the grandmother clock vied in the background.

"I think we're ready," Vivian whispered as though afraid to tempt fate.

"I think we are, too," Quinn whispered back, closing her eyes to the peeling paint and weedy yard and the tiny holes in the carpet beneath her feet. "Valentine's Day, here we come."

VALENTINE'S DAY: THE FIRST GUESTS SINCE Quinn's arrival— three couples already in residence, the other two expected at midday with the promise of a candlelight supper at eight. In the pitch black of early morning, Victoria grumbled sleepily, "Breakfast in bed, whatever were we thinking?" and stumbled down the stairs to put the coffee on. She flipped the light switch and gasped.

"Viv, Vivian Elizabeth, hurry up. You're got to see this."

Running her fingers through still damp curls and stumbling over the loose edge of her slipper, Vivian Johnson scrambled down the stairs.

Hearts lay everywhere: Hearts of every shape and size, pink hearts, red hearts, white hearts, and hearts sparkling with silver and gold glitter. Hearts hung from the walls and the ceiling and they created a pattern on the shiny wood floor. What might have appeared childish and tacky instead looked fun and romantic.

"Wow. What happened here?"

The fragrance of newly perked coffee filled the room, and on the long table the breakfast trays stood ready, adorned, like the room, with hearts. The twins looked at each other. "Quinn."

When they found her in the barn, Quinn just shrugged. "I couldn't sleep so I got an early start."

"Listen to this, Wen."

Two days later, Owen held the receiver against his shoulder as Victoria read from the guest book. "'Best Valentine's Day we've ever had;' 'the Ms. Johnsons have outdone themselves this year;' 'Breakfast in bed was such a treat. We're ready to sign up for next year;' 'February 14 is our anniversary and this was the best gift ever.' They're all like that, Wennie. You should have been here. It was great, and Quinn's decorations made everybody smile, and Viv made the loveliest Chicken Marsala and the Crème Brule turned out perfectly, and—"

"I get the picture," he interrupted from his office in Reno. "Keep up the good work." He was glad she couldn't see his frown.

Victoria's back pain persisted. After much nagging from her sister, she consulted their family physician who prescribed a new anti-inflammatory called Vioxx and forbade heavy work, so Quinn assigned herself the repairs and tackled them with vigor.

With the advent of warmer days, Old Joseph returned. "Only for the Saturday and Sunday, missus," the old Basque sheepherder told Quinn as they watched his daughter drive away. "She comes again for me on Monday." He laid out his bedroll, set up the camp stove, and began work on the saggy front gate.

First light, earlier each morning as the sun slowly began its journey north, found Quinn replacing cracked window panes, reattaching wayward pickets, cutting away the brambles that engulfed the house. For several days she worked alone, but on a sunny Sunday after news of the Valentine's Day success had had time to circulate, a crowd from St. Paul's Catholic Church showed up to sate its curiosity and offer assistance. The Johnson family had attended St. Paul's Catholic Church on Malarky Street—"How can you take it seriously if it's on a street named Malarkey?" they joked—for their entire lifetime, albeit sometimes more regularly than others.

Quinn, hair tied back with a pink bandana rescued from the hall closet and sweat pouring down her cheeks, had abandoned her jacket and shirt, another orphan from the brother's wardrobe, and was working in tank top and jeans when the crowd descended. Apparently unfazed by the audience, Quinn had produced black Hefty bags and assigned tasks, and pretty soon the gawkers were working as hard as she and laughing at the incongruity of it all.

Vivian and Victoria watched as Ian, one of the altar boys from church, danced from foot to foot at the bottom of Quinn's ladder waiting for a chance to serve. Their conversation was inaudible, but his flushed cheeks and Quinn's grin suggested a meeting of the minds.

"She's quite a worker, that girl," John Perry commented to his best friend's baby sisters as he came to stand beside them.

Alerted by something in his voice, Victoria afforded him a sideways glance. John was without a doubt the oldest and dearest of her brother's many friends. At 5'4", he had been the unlikely fifth of the Lowry High's basketball team starters—John and Mike and Owen and two other boys whose names she couldn't remember. Unlike her brother, John had remained in Winnemucca after their graduation, working his father's ranch and marrying his high school sweetheart, Mary, now inside making sandwiches for the working crowd.

As he spoke, his wistful gaze rested on Quinn, stretched out long and lean against the rickety wooden ladder scraping peeling pink paint from the fascia. The movement accentuated the muscles in her arms and the generous curve of her breasts. When Victoria didn't respond, John laughed, "Everyone's curious, you know. Mysterious strangers don't show up here every day." A long pink curl descended, intact, and the workers below cheered. "Where's Owen anyway? What does he think about all this?" He grinned at Victoria's scowl and wandered in the direction of the kitchen.

Victoria turned to her sister. "She attracts them like flies, doesn't she?"

"Bears to honey. Pretty amazing, isn't it?"

"Even John Perry—looking at her with those eyes. He called her the mysterious stranger and wondered what Owen thinks about all this." Victoria sighed. "Maybe we should . . ."

". . . ask her some questions? I'm not sure that's a good idea, Vic, 'cause then she can ask us questions, too."

Chapter 15

HE FOLLOWING DAY, PAINT CHIPS IN hand, Quinn went in search of the twins. The fascia was primed and ready for color, and she wasn't going to make that decision alone. She found them upstairs in the blue room, largest of the guest rooms and restful with its cerulean walls, bright white woodwork and blue plaid bedding. One at each side of the bed, they prepared to turn the mattress, an old trick Quinn remembered from days with her grandmother. *I wonder who turned our mattresses*, she thought. She flinched—the mother who had never turned a mattress in her life could still instill pain.

She watched them for a moment, *two peas in a pod*, as they worked in perfect harmony, and she realized the sister chorus had been quiet all week. Startled, she wondered if they'd abandoned her, then remembered they existed only in her head. *Maybe I don't need them anymore. Maybe I'm just a lost cause and finally even I realize it.*

She forced her attention back to the twins. Expertly, they flipped the mattress, panting with exertion. Quinn realized they didn't know she was watching and longed for the intimacy they shared.

Stop. Don't go there.

She sighed. There were so many places in her mind that were forbidden. She imagined boxes full of thoughts and memories, tied up tight and labeled *Danger! Do not open!* Some even wore the skull and crossbones of the iodine bottle hidden high in the medicine cabinet at home.

Shaking off her black thoughts, Quinn slipped into the room, plucked a feather pillow from the pile by the door and launched herself onto the bed, flailing wildly. "Pillow fight, pillow fight."

Viv shrieked and stepped back, tumbled over more pillows and landed on her bottom. Forgetting her sore back, Vic snatched up a pillow and attacked and in minutes all three were pummeling away. Soon the air rained feathers and down and they collapsed, panting, on the disarrayed bed. Through tears of laughter, they surveyed the wreckage.

"Quinn?"

Out of breath and panting, she explained, "I just thought we needed another snowball fight."

DESPITE PAINTING AND PRUNING AND CLEANING, Quinn continued her hikes. Guided by a wavery map sketched on the back on an old envelope, she explored Old Joseph's hills, ostensibly in search of the *guided walks* promised in their invitations, really in search of the old man's peace, and the hills unfolded themselves to her. She carried her stick but no snakes invaded her path. Music sang in the creek, birds rustled in the trees and the brother's boots grew accustomed to her feet. The sister chorus provided only a ripple of background noise, and sleep claimed her instantly when she fell into bed.

On Sunday, still sweaty from an early hike, her own body odors mingling with the scent of the man whose shirt she still wore, Quinn sat in the barn doorway in Old Joseph's spot cleaning tack as he had taught her. The daughter had fetched her father, promising to return him "but not until it's really spring." Quinn hoped the old hands were keeping warm.

We've gotten a lot done in just a few days, she congratulated herself as she picked at bits of ochre enamel around her thumbnail. *Great color.* The earthy hue perfect for the fascia that had almost defeated her—four coats of paint after a week of scraping and sanding. Relieved that the job was done and warmed in the circle of sunlight, she gave audience to hopeful thoughts. *Full house for the first retreat. Yoga routine finally comfortable. House paint good enough until a real painter can tackle it. Maybe that will satisfy Mr. Owen the Omnipotent.* Her hands worked the leather and smoothed away the butterflies that thoughts of the brother awakened. Alone in the barn, the smell of horse and dirt and spring surrounding her—*what could be better than this?*

She sensed a presence and froze. In the corral to her left, George flicked her tail, unperturbed, but Quinn's hackles rose. She lifted her eyes from the bridle in her hands.

He lounged against the rail, illuminated by the rising sun, the most beautiful human being she had ever seen. Shiny black curls, a wisp longer than the fashion, clear olive skin, fathomless black eyes, lips even and full. His aquiline nose seemed vaguely familiar. Against the pale green blur of the valley, he posed for Quinn's admiration.

After an adequate time he straightened away from the fence as though pulling himself to a taller stance, paused while his garments realigned themselves, and moved toward her. The rays of the sun seemed to follow him.

Closer, he was younger than Quinn had first thought, nineteen or twenty at most.

"You must be Quinn." Each word emerged round, as though formed deep in his throat, carefully considered and then blown out like soap bubbles through a little plastic hoop.

The bridle slid off her lap as Quinn jumped to her feet, and the boy reached to retrieve it, brushing against her sleeve on the way. She stepped back. "Who are you?"

He picked up the bridle and placed it in Quinn's hand, his cool fingers sliding along the exposed flesh of her wrist. Blindingly white teeth distracted her and she almost missed his reply. "I'm Scott, Viv and Vic's son. Didn't they tell you?"

"Will you tell her, Vivian, or shall I?"

Palms up, Quinn fended them off. "Hey, nobody needs to tell me anything. I just wanted to make sure he was who he said."

The young man named Scott was gone, tarrying with her just long enough to arouse disturbing emotions. He told her he was from Winnemucca and was off to join his father in New York City. He shook her hand, his own politely ungloved, and held it just a fraction too long—smooth fingers pressing hers. What should have been amusing—the blatant attention of a younger man to an older woman—was not. Quinn shivered. His teeth flashed and she knew he'd felt her response. His gaze lingered as her tongue sneaked out to moisten her lips, and then he turned abruptly and was gone.

Vivian interrupted her thoughts. "I'll tell her, Vicky." She turned her tear-stained face to Quinn. "Scott is my son." She sniffed, rubbed at her nose with an overused tissue. "He was supposed to stay for dinner. He was going to come last week and he didn't, but today he promised. I'm making his favorite . . ."

A hiccup interrupted her and Victoria, as usual, finished the sentence, ". . . Sloppy Joe's. Ungrateful twit." She grimaced and handed her sister a fresh tissue.

Vivian folded it and wiped her eyes, then blew her nose, unfolded the tissue to check its contents, refolded it and wiped her eyes . . . again and again until there was only a soggy ball in her hand. Nauseous, Quinn plucked new tissues from the box, put them in the woman's hand, and watched as the performance was repeated.

I can't stand this. Quinn waited for the story to unfold. She didn't know much about these women, she realized, recognizing the irony as she settled back into the chair, hands loosely in her lap, body aligned toward the tearful woman, and waited for the tissue ritual to end. Victoria, eyes averted, sat quietly beside her sister. Quinn wondered if her tissue ritual would be the same. The bouquet of sweet simmering hamburger filled the kitchen.

"We never dated much during high school." Vivian rubbed her nose hard and began her story. "Mostly a group of us just hung out together."

"And even when the others started pairing off we didn't. I expect it's formidable, the idea of choosing just one twin."

"But we really didn't mind." Victoria's voice held no conviction.

Vivian nodded. "Then, just before graduation, a young man came to town. He was the grandson of a prominent rancher here in the valley. We know now he was sent to the country to get straightened out, but we didn't know that at the time. Not that it would have mattered. Oh, Quinn, he was the handsomest boy I'd ever seen."

Flashing teeth and cool white fingers—again, Quinn shivered.

"Even our mother was smitten. She called him 'young Mr. Darcy' and invited him to tea." The laugh was practiced, humorless. Vivian continued, "Not to make a short story long, he liked both of us, and silly girls that we were, we both liked him, too."

Victoria's voice was like sandpaper. "Not surprising, really. He was the first person who could tell us apart."

Unhappiness flooded her sister's face. "We'd never had secrets before."

The scenes rolled through Quinn's imagination—a tall man, boy really, indifferent in his flowing black greatcoat and opaque shades; two girls, their identical faces soft with youth and innocence, looking over their shoulders as they followed him into the fields, leaned against him in doorways, convinced themselves that they enjoyed the smell of his tobacco in their car, all the while disappearing from each other—no happy ending in sight. The stuff movies were made of—but this was real life.

"And no one realized what was happening until I turned up pregnant."

Quinn assumed a professional silence and hoped her feelings didn't show.

"Vicky was hurt and angry so she went off to college without me. I got packed off to have the baby—we had an aunt in California, you see—but Vicky didn't stay mad, and when Scottie was born we couldn't let him go, so Wen helped us and we set up housekeeping together."

"They almost died." Victoria looked at her feet as she added this piece of the story. "Both of them. Mother even made me come to say goodbye." A tear slipped down her cheek, and with the tissue Vivian handed her, Victoria repeated her sister's ritual.

"But we didn't die, and we're fine, but it's been hard on Scottie. Too many mothers . . ."

And no father. Quinn waited.

The kitchen clock ticked off the minutes. A round gray bird perched on the sill behind Vivian's shoulder. Quinn watched its little black head bob as though keeping time. The clock ticked and the head bobbed until, therapist or no, she couldn't endure the silence. "And the father?"

Victoria shrugged. "Don't know. Viv never heard from him again."

"His grandfather talked with our father. A check came, comes every month."

"A large check."

"So Scott doesn't know his father?" Quinn recalled the boy's words.

The twins looked at each other. Quinn wasn't sure what she read there—shame, blame, secrets—

"We thought it best," they answered in unison.

CHAPTER 16

"I DON'T NEED HELP TO GET THE stuff on your list, and I certainly don't need that woman telling me what to do."

Alone in his own kitchen, Owen scowled, glad Vivian couldn't see him. The phone had rung just as he poured his first cup of coffee. Like most early morning phone calls, it was full of bad news that just kept getting worse.

Because his sisters didn't like Reno, he'd already agreed to do the big shopping for their fast-approaching and probably disastrous first retreat. He had not planned on the annoyance just dumped on him. "I told you I'd do it. I was just going to do it when I was working in town."

"Well . . . you haven't been around so much, and we've got to get cracking."

She could really turn the guilt screws. Owen squirmed. *Avoiding my sisters, avoiding Karle. Avoiding this new woman and the odd feelings she aroused.* All this avoiding bred irritability. "I do work, you know."

"We know you work hard, Wennie, and we appreciate that you're doing this for us." Vivian's soothing voice fed his guilt.

"I'll do it, Vivvy. I just don't know why she has to come with—"

"We just thought it would be a chance for Quinn to pick up her stuff. Your truck is much better for hauling than her little car and—"

And you want me to get to know her and like her. I get it, I just don't like it.

His left thumb massaged the crevice between his brows, hard, and he shook his head. Even over the phone, he couldn't say no to his sisters. "Well, all right, but just this one time. I'll do it tomorrow and she'd better be ready when I get there."

LATER THE SAME MORNING IN THE Wildflower Inn's sunny kitchen, Vivian flipped three pancakes onto the empty platter and Quinn snaked her fork in to get a fresh one. Vivian shook the spatula in her direction and they both laughed.

Victoria lifted her gaze from the pile of papers on the table. "Hey, keep it down."

Fork poised halfway to her mouth, Quinn looked askance. Vivian bopped her sister with the spatula.

"Sorry, but it's almost here." Victoria waved her hand over the yellow pages.

"One more week."

"Only one week, and look how much we've still got to do."

Quinn filled her mouth with pancake and syrup. *Opening night jitters?*

From behind, Vivian wrapped her arms around Victoria, rested her chin on her sister's curls. "We'll get it all done, sister mine. We always do. And I just talked with Wen this morning. He says he and Quinn can do the Costco run tomorrow and—"

Quinn went on alert. "Me? Owen?" She coughed and choked as maple syrup slid down the wrong way.

Vivian abandoned her sister to pound on Quinn's back. Spluttering and coughing, Quinn cleared her throat. "Me? Owen? Costco? No way."

Victoria waved away the protest. "Wen said he'd do the shopping but he never gets it right so we thought you could go along to help and pick up your stuff at the same time."

"That's right, Quinn," Vivian chimed in. "You need stuff from home. And yoga mats—you did say we need yoga mats, didn't you? And that thing to fix George's bridle."

"And you wanted to check on . . ."

"Minnie."

"Yeah, yeah, I know what I said, but this just sounds like a plot to throw us together."

Quinn meant it as a joke, but the look the twins exchanged had her wondering. "What?"

THEY COAXED.

Quinn searched for reasonable alternatives, finally acquiesced.

It was arranged.

Friday morning, 6:15, Quinn sat high on the seat of the old Toyota Land Cruiser, none the worse for its earlier misadventure, as Vivian leaned in and gave Owen final instructions. "Quinn's house to pick up her stuff and check on Minnie. Yoga Shack, Quinn will direct you, for those mat things. Sierra Feed, you know that place. And Costco. Here's the list." She thrust a folded yellow sheet at him.

"I've got it, I've got it." His jaw worked. Irritation or amusement, Quinn couldn't tell. His voice stayed level. "I've got to stop by Karle's, too, before we start home so we'll probably be kind of late."

Vivian kissed his cheek and stepped off the running board. He gunned the motor and the truck lurched down the road. "Sorry. Didn't want her to think of anything else."

Thirty minutes later, Owen Johnson turned onto I-80 heading west. Only the skull that decorated the sign for the Star Point Trading Post and General Store noted their departure.

A familiar fist strangled Quinn's insides. Errant thoughts struggled to escape their duct-taped boxes and she wished she were driving Angelica, that she hadn't agreed to this trip. The man aroused feelings she couldn't afford. *Get a grip, Quinn.* She counted her breaths and kept her eyes fixed on the road.

The landmarks passed by too slowly for comfort.

The man exuded stories, seemed intent on being pleasant as he told her about the antelope ground squirrel who, in the heat of the playa summer, creates its own shade by curving its bushy tale forward, umbrella-like, over its own back and head; describing the habits of hawk and eagle and the antics of the little birds who harass them in the sky; spinning the tale of a rancher friend, mending his irrigation system, who found himself the object of target practice when his neighbor's son started shooting across the alfalfa field, ". . . and the kid's father didn't seem to get what Tom was upset about. 'It's just a twenty-two,' he whined when the sheriff went out to talk to them."

His driving reflected what she had come to know about him, competent, stolid, and, in part due to the age of the vehicle, slow.

As though he read her thoughts, Owen apologized. "Sorry this is so slow. The old truck just doesn't move as fast as it used to."

She glanced at him, then back at the road. He didn't look any happier than she felt. "It's okay," she said and decided to make an effort.

The sister chorus crooned: Watch out.

"What year is it, the truck, I mean?" *Odd vehicle for an accountant.*

"Sixty-six, not the usual transportation for a stuffy CPA."

She made a noise that could be mistaken for a laugh. Sometimes it seemed that he really could read her thoughts. The tight fingers inside her loosened just a little and her eyes strayed to his hands, light on the wheel, then to his face. He was smiling.

"It was the first 4-wheel drive vehicle that Toyota imported. Trying to get into the American market, I think, cheaper than jeeps. My dad bought it new from Dan Flammer Pontiac in Carson City, paid $1400 cash for it."

She murmured *hmmm* but he didn't need encouragement. She leaned her head back against the hard leather seat and listened as he outlined the merits of the vehicle.

"Four door . . . straight six . . . steel springs . . . The paint is red over white and it's all soldered not welded." He glanced right, noted her closed eyes. "Sorry, didn't mean to bore you."

"You're not." In her self-imposed darkness, she could speak freely. "This reminds me of my father. I'd ride along when he delivered a vehicle and he'd talk car talk the whole way." Her face softened but her eyes were closed so she didn't see Owen's eyes widen in surprise. "How did it get to be yours?"

"I learned to drive in it—across fields and stuff. It'll go just about everywhere. And I fell in love with it." His voice deepened and he went silent. She opened her eyes, turned to look at him. He frowned as though he saw something unpleasant.

She looked at the road, saw nothing amiss. She waited.

He cleared his throat hard. When he continued, his tone was light and good-humored and she decided she had been mistaken. "Anyway," he said, "when I was a senior Dad let me buy it. He would probably have given it to me, but I didn't know that at the time. He was ready for a town car by then. I guess the novelty of having a 4-wheeler gave way to the need for comfort—he bought a Buick sedan with all the bells and whistles."

He cleared his throat again.

Watching him, Quinn saw a furrowed brow which belied the lightness of his words. *I'm not the only one with secrets*, she thought. She said nothing.

"It wasn't very practical for a college boy, but I didn't care, and now I can't bring myself to part with it. There are only twelve still registered, you know, but I found a parts place in Texas and a Toyota club in the LA area so I can keep it running. I've got another car, an Audi, for the commute, but I still really love this old girl."

He clicked on the turn signal and she looked around, startled—Fernley, only twenty-nine miles from their destination. "Gas?"

"Nope. This is the reason we had to start early. You haven't lived out here until you've had breakfast at the Wigwam. Hope you're hungry."

He did seem intent on being pleasant, so Quinn nodded *yes*, sure she couldn't push anything over the lump in her throat.

They shared Main Street with a Volkswagen bus and two trucks. On either side shops were closed, some boarded up, Closed or For Sale signs in their windows. The town felt deserted but Mary and Moe's Wigwam Restaurant, Casino and Indian Museum occupied half a block and its parking lot overflowed.

"Looks like the whole town's here for breakfast," she said as he held the door for her.

Before he could reply, a short woman, one hand smoothing a Welcome to the Wigwam apron, the other darting up to check the status of her beauty-parlor-red hair, hurried up to them. "Owen Johnson, well, aren't you a sight for sore eyes."

"Good to see you, Millie. How's Harry?"

"Well, you know Harry. Harry's my Maine coon cat," she added in an aside to Quinn as she grabbed menus. "Two for breakfast?"

Half-listening, Quinn looked around as they followed the voluble woman. Indian artifacts—arrowheads, beaded leather gloves, baskets, porcupine quills and yellowing black and white photos—filled every inch of space, covering the walls and crowding the museum-style glass cabinets that served as room dividers. Harry's saga was interrupted several times as men stood up and shook Owen's hand or slapped him on the back in greeting.

The outcome of Harry's latest adventure remained unclear as Millie seated them in the Lahontan Room. "Holler when you're ready," she ordered and hurried off. A scowling girl, dyed black hair falling over her pale countenance, sauntered to their booth, slopped hot coffee into two mugs and left without a word.

"Prom queen?"

Quinn laughed. "Elvira. Good we survived."

Owen chuckled.

Quinn hid her surprise behind the menu. *A sense of humor lurking?*

All the breakfast choices were identified by name—Sleeping Moon, Great Beginnings, Walking Hungry—and Quinn settled on Little Bird: two eggs any style, hash brown potatoes and toast, English muffin or homemade biscuit. Without consulting his menu, Owen ordered the Heap Big Breakfast. A peek told Quinn he'd be having chicken fried steak with country gravy, two eggs—"scrambled," he ordered—hash browns and a similar selection of breads. When he said, "Wheat toast, hold the butter," she raised her eyebrows and he laughed. "Gotta watch those fat grams."

They'd just started on a second cup of coffee when the food arrived. Quinn eyed his breakfast with respect as she wolfed down every fat gram on her own plate. They didn't talk much as they ate. Sated, she waddled off to find a restroom.

OWEN JOHNSON KEPT HIS EYES ON his plate, resisting the urge to turn and watch Quinn walk away. *That went well,* he told himself as he chewed his meat into something that might slide over the lump in his throat. *She seemed to get a kick out of the stories. Too much car talk probably, but I'm glad we stopped here. Good food always goes over well.* He wasn't sure why it mattered.

He jumped. At his elbow, Millie reached into his space. "How's Karle?" she asked as she topped off his almost-full mug. "Haven't seen her around in a 'coon's age."

Interpreting the question to mean *who is this woman and why is she here?* he ignored it. "Karle's fine, Millie, just real busy. I'll tell her you asked for her."

Millie wiped imaginary catsup scum from an already clean bottle and refilled Quinn's cup, but Owen had nothing to add, and he heard her "humpf" as she finally turned away.

Should have just introduced her. She's just my sisters' business partner. With unnecessary vigor, he slathered strawberry jam on his last piece of toast, but the corners of his mouth turned up as he remembered Quinn's unrestrained laughter as he described the squirrel mincing its way across the playa, its bushy tail poised just so above its little head. *She's been a good partner, so far. Good ideas, good work ethic.* On his visits to the Inn he'd seen her mending fence, mowing grass, shoveling manure. He was surprised at how much she could do and how much she did.

He conjured Quinn's image: Long skinny legs stretched out on the rickety ladder as she applied a dirt-colored paint to the house trim, her breasts straining against the stretchy top she wore like a uniform. Then he remembered how her incredible turquoise eyes had gone flat as she'd caught him watching her, how he had felt himself a voyeur. That feeling returned, and he coughed as the toast stuck in his throat and coughed again as the big gulp of ice water went down the wrong way. *No wonder she didn't want to come with me today.* He didn't like the muddiness she evoked.

When Quinn returned to the table, Owen was mopping up the last of his gravy. He didn't meet her gaze as she slid into the booth.

"Where's the museum?"

"You're in it, city girl." He grinned and shoved his thoughts aside. "This is it." He was still grinning as they climbed back into the Toyota.

The remaining miles sped by as a surprisingly voluble Quinn told her personal food service stories. Owen started laughing when she described chatting with a customer and then forgetting to turn in his order, "...and he still left me a tip." As the mishaps tripped off her tongue, he laughed harder and harder. By the time she finished, "...and chocolate was everywhere, the damn milkshake flinging itself around and around and around and the customers, the ones that hadn't already escaped, hiding under their tables like it was a war zone, and me with my head under the counter trying to pull the plug when my boss got back from lunch," tears ran down his cheeks and he could hardly see to drive. She shrugged. "That was the end of that career."

A BRIEF SKIRMISH AT HER HOUSE almost disrupted their new-found amity. He opened the truck door, started to get out. "I'll help. Tell me what to do."

"Stay. I don't need help." Her smooth forehead furrowed. "Stay," she repeated as he stepped to the ground, jerking her hand in the motion used to command dogs. "I really can do it myself."

Tapping the steering wheel with aggravated fingers, he waited until she reappeared, arms overflowing with clothes. Something long and plaid dragged behind, threatening to trip her, and a pair of scuffed boots topped the pile. He thought about letting her struggle with the door, decided that was juvenile, so, feeling pouty, he jumped out, opened the rear door and smirked behind her back when she didn't protest.

"Thanks." She dumped her things in, circled the vehicle and hoisted herself into the front seat. Blood trickled from the edge of her lower lip.

"You're bleeding."

"No, I'm not."

She dabbed at her lip with the edge of her sleeve. He handed her a clean handkerchief. "Minnie wasn't happy to see me."

He thought her eyes were wet but she kept them averted and he couldn't be sure. When she launched into Minnie vignettes, each funnier than the last, he couldn't help laughing, and by the time they reached the warehouse store the moment was forgotten.

In the midst of Costco consumer abundance, they haggled over who got to negotiate the cart, then giggled and pushed and shoved like teens in a mall as they competed to embellish Vivian's shopping list.

"You win, you win." Almost knocking over their wine bottles, Quinn threw up her arms in surrender when Owen balanced seven pounds of dark chocolate cake on the counter.

After a quick stop for the yoga mats and an explanation of their necessity that had him picturing Quinn in a variety of poses, Owen was smiling and licking chocolate frosting off his lips as he left her at Sierra Feed and went to gas up the truck.

QUINN WAS LAUGHING AT SOMETHING HER old friend, Pete, had just said when she heard Owen enter the store. The latch clicked, the bell announcing customers tinkled and the air in the room electrified. Then she heard it: the audible woof of air as desire and jealousy hit his solar plexus. She stiffened. She'd heard it too many times before. The laugh dwindled.

Owen paused at the door and then stepped inside, eyes only for Quinn, and she was abruptly aware of herself leaning over the counter, jeans stretched tight, skin visible where her sweater no longer met the waistband. She straightened and turned toward him, her hands tugging down the sweater, pulling herself inside.

His hands reached out as though to touch her, and he brushed against a display of bridles. The metal pieces clanged together. He looked at the hand as though it belonged to someone else and then dropped it to his side.

Behind the counter, Pete, a rangy fellow in his forties with thinning blond hair pulled into a pony tail, looked up and nodded at the new customer. Two cowboys who had sidled up to enjoy the view took one look at Owen's face and found business elsewhere.

"Owen, you ready? This is Pete Murphy." Quinn indicated the man behind the counter. "Pete and I went through grade school together and he knows everything there is to know about horse tack. See," she waved George's bridle, newly repaired. She knew she babbled, couldn't seem to stop, anything to avoid the naked look she would see on his face.

"Murphy, Owen Johnson." The two men shook hands. Owen turned toward Quinn and without meeting her eyes muttered, "Truck's ready. I'll wait outside." Gaze still on the floor he turned, nodded in Pete's direction and strode from the store.

Pete watched the interchange with a knowing expression. "Another one for your collection, Quinnie?"

She glared at him, tossed money toward the register and followed Owen outside.

He was already in the truck, book in hand, pages still. She watched him, waiting for her breathing to quiet, feeling like she should apologize, like she'd done something wrong that she didn't mean to do. Nausea rose as she remembered the open longing on his face, the expression men get when the wanting hits too fast to hide. The jumble of thought and emotion churned up anger, and she marched up to the truck, climbed inside and slammed the door. *Damned if I'll apologize for something I didn't even do.*

"Good book?" she asked, knowing he hadn't read a word.

HE WINCED. *Now I've done it*, he thought, not quite sure what *it* was, and laid aside *A River Runs Through It* which had never failed him before. When he walked into the feed store he'd been thinking that his sisters were right. Quinn was fun and funny and did, indeed, have some special quality. Her laughter reached him as the door clicked shut. His body betrayed him and he wanted her all for himself. Appalled as he felt need rise in him, he could only mutter and then escape.

Now he chastised himself. *How stupid am I?* He felt her simmering beside him, ignored her quip about the book and started the engine. *Smart ass. She shouldn't wear clothes like that.*

He drove into the heart of old Reno, pulled to the curb in front of an old brick house with a look of success about it and

Pella labels still stuck on the windows. He turned off the engine and looked at the woman beside him, her face turned toward the window. An invisible wall had replaced their laughter. Neither had spoken a word since Quinn had climbed into the truck at Sierra Feed. "Home away from home," he murmured, thinking *Hope Karle's home; it'll even the score.*

Before he could exit the truck, a redheaded woman burst from the house. Laughing, she leapt onto the running board and threw her arms around him. He suffered the hug a moment, then extracted himself from the truck and the hug.

The woman noted Quinn. "Who's this, Owen honey? Aren't you going to introduce us?"

Jaw working, he muttered, "Karle, Quinn. Quinn, my landlady, Karle Moran."

Karle's bare feet grasped the running board as she reached across to shake Quinn's hand. "Hello, I'm sure I'll be hearing about you." Her smile didn't contradict whatever sting might be intended. "Want to come in?" she asked, but before Quinn could reply, Karle's attention returned to Owen and she was dragging him toward the house, her hands as voluble as her lips. His laughter trailed behind.

LEAFLESS TREES BORDERED THE STREET. A calico cat scooted across the brown grass, disappeared over the neighboring fence. Karle's front door slammed shut, and Quinn picked up Owen's book. Her thoughts roiled. *I don't want to be desired, just ignored—or maybe just friends. God knows I wasn't trying to attract him. I almost forgot he was a man. Now there's a problem.* She chewed on a fingernail and contemplated the ruins of The Plan.

When Owen returned, Quinn had read no more of *A River Runs Through It* than he had. Discomfort reared inside and she touched her wounded lip, wishful, as she watched the hearty kiss and enthusiastic hug that sent him on his way.

"Sorry about that." Owen settled an overflowing cardboard box on the backseat. "I didn't mean to take so long. I needed this stuff before the weekend and Karle needed a strong back." He laughed, no doubt at the pleasant thought of the tiny, titian-haired woman so clearly enamored of him, and nodded at the house they were leaving. "The outside is done and she's renovating the inside herself. 'No more bossy contractors,' she says, but sometimes she needs brute strength, and that's me. She says it's good when a man knows his place." He laughed again.

Ha ha.

"I rent her basement," he explained as they wended their way through the old streets toward the freeway. "Gives her a little extra income, not that she really needs it, and a male presence, and I have a home away from home for the days I work in Reno. I've been here almost five years now, but these last few months, with her tearing down walls and pulling out plumbing and all, have been almost too big a challenge."

His voice was light but the muscles on the side of his jaw worked. As she tucked herself into the dusk, glad no response was required, Quinn wondered what he wasn't saying. Questions swirled in her head faster than she could box and label them. *What just happened? Did I imagine the lust? What difference does it make anyway?*

The sister chorus was louder than usual: God, Quinn, what did you expect?

He talked around the danger that lurked in their silence, his eyes glued to the road as though it was new territory, and cataloged a history of construction misadventures. All she heard was the amusement in his voice.

As they drove toward a sky finger-painted in reds and pinks, Quinn's silence finally prevailed. She set her shoulder away from him and stared out the passenger window, *pouting*, her sisters would call it, and she wasn't sure why.

Minutes passed and the Tracy power plant came into view. He broke the silence. "Looks just like Dune, doesn't it?"

Interested, she kept her jaw tight and didn't let him know it. Then movement in the sage caught her eye and her grievance disappeared. She pointed. "Owen, look."

He saw it, too, and slowed the truck to the shoulder of the road. A coyote, sleek and silver, stood captured in the headlights, one foot raised, interrupted in mid-stride, head up, nose foreword: alert. Owen slid across the bench seat toward Quinn, arm draped along the seat behind her. She shifted her body to accommodate his, felt his weight against her back as they watched a second animal, darker and smaller, emerge from the brush. The two stood together for what seemed an eternity as the humans watched and then, in wordless communication, turned together and melted back into the landscape. Their memory hovered like smoke, and then like smoke was gone. The man and the woman sat unmoving until the pink faded from the sky.

"WHAT HAPPENED TO THEM?" VIVIAN ASKED. Victoria shrugged. They stared at the rattling kitchen door.

Owen and Quinn returned from Reno after dark and unloaded the truck in silence. Then Owen left "to get things done." Quinn disappeared into the guest house without a word, then returned and unceremoniously dumped Owen's worn boots on the kitchen floor. They made more clatter than they needed to.

The screen slammed shut behind her.

"Who knows. At least they didn't come to blows, but I agree, something . . ."

". . . happened." Wrinkles in Vivian's forehead deepened. "Do you suppose they—"

"No." Victoria's voice brooked no argument. "No romance there. The divorce hit him too hard, and all those lost babies and then the, you know. If he'd been interested in anyone, it would be Karle. Remember, I told you he was done after . . ."

". . . Mimi. I know you did, but what if you're wrong?"

CHAPTER 17

"In like a lion, out like a lamb."

A gentle breeze stirred the remnants of a shamrock wreath, as Victoria described March's progress. Wrapped in blankets against the chill, the women took their coffee on the porch. On the uneven steps, flakes of green leprechaun feet gave evidence that St. Patrick's holiday had been honored. The few B&B guests seemed appreciative.

"Yes, sister, and April showers bring May flowers, too, but so far we've not had showers and," Vivian gestured toward the fence, outlined in daffodils and crocuses, "we already have flowers." Worry crept into her voice. "But it still might freeze."

Cold nights, warm days, threats and promises—everything changes. Quinn sipped her hot coffee and considered the past few weeks. The bush alongside the house, so bare and straggly on her arrival, now glistened purple with the promise of lilacs. The old apple trees hinted at life, and the peach tree was dusted pale green. Along the stream that meandered behind the guest-house, yellow-green willows stretched. Even the dirt smelled like spring. The odd day with Owen Johnson seemed far away, dreamlike, its confusion lost in the well-being of the moment. *I wonder why I'm still here* collided with *I could stay here forever.*

She watched a robin stalk its prey through the grass.

"Two more days," Victoria was saying when Quinn's attention returned to their conversation, "and they'll be here. I'm pretty—"

"Nervous?" ventured her sister. "Me, too. No, scared spitless is more like it."

Quinn looked up. "Viv, you nervous? Why? You've been doing this forever." It had not occurred to her that these women could be afraid.

"I know, but this is different. What about you, Quinn?"

"A little edgy, I guess." Her stomach clenched.

In two days, on Friday, the seventh of April, the first retreat group would arrive.

Vivian fluttered her hands. "I'm a-twitter for sure. I just wish Wennie was going to be here. I'd feel ever so much calmer if I knew he was standing by."

"Me, too, but he won't be." Victoria's face scrunched up in irritation. "April 15 is coming up and all those tax problems need him more than we do. We're just lucky he can transport them." Early Friday morning, their brother would pick up four Berkeley women at the Reno-Tahoe International Airport and deliver them to the wilds of Nevada.

Vivian patted her sister's arm. "We've all worked hard and it'll be fine and dandy, Vicky—food's ready, house is clean, program's planned. The weather is beautiful. And we have Quinn. Whatever can go wrong?"

THE SKY WAS STILL BLACK THURSDAY morning when Quinn woke, sweaty and disoriented, arms and knees folded in to ease the ache in her belly, the familiar nightmare clinging. Her head filled with images: pudgy arms, tiny fingers, the sharp outline of a woman's back, and when she sniffed she could just catch a whiff of Johnson's Baby Powder.

Why now?

Desperate to dispel the dream webs, Quinn stretched, and the bed seemed too small, her legs imprisoned by stiff cold sheets. She pulled her knees back into her chest, curled onto her side and slept again.

LATER, THE MORNING SUN STRUGGLED TO penetrate her gloom. As the ache in her heart and the fragrance of baby powder lingered through meditation, yoga, and George like the clouds of an impending storm, Quinn could appreciate its frustration. Still seeking refuge, she dug her hands into the cold earth of the garden plot.

The stream behind her, freed from its icy restraints, tinkled a merry and incongruent accompaniment to the sister chorus: It's your fault. They can't save you. Why not run?

A fierce thrust deep into the earth ripped Quinn's fingernail, and the pain blotted the words. She tasted blood and dirt as she sucked on the finger. *This isn't working. I can't do this anymore.*

The sun rose higher but didn't warm her; the creek sounds and bird song withdrew as though filtered through cotton batting; and the boxes in her mind, set loose by the dream, tumbled out their contents. Breathing ragged, heart keeping time, she rocked back and forth in the dirt, and a Lincoln town car eased its shiny white way up the lane. *Mother.*

Horrified, Quinn hunkered down behind the blackberry brambles and watched the vehicle come to a halt at the gate. She heard the cough of the engine dying, the screech of the brake being set, and then, like dust settling—silence.

Into this new scene, set like an old Western in sepia tones, three women emerged, conferred in strident whispers and then started along the path to the house. The tallest led the way, head high, shoulders up, back straight, her gait lopsided as her high heels sank into the soft earth. The Nubians clustered at the fence to watch. Side by side, the other two followed, and the three passed from Quinn's view. On her knees, not really surprised, her only coherent thoughts: *How did they find me? I don't want to go.*

ALERTED BY PATIENCE AND PRUDENCE WHO'D been sunning themselves on the porch, Vivian stepped to the front door, open to let in the crisp spring air. "Vicky, that you? How'd it go?"

Victoria had gone into town early for an appointment with her chiropractor, leaving Vivian to "put the finishing touches" on the retreat preparations. Really, Vivian knew, her sister had wanted private time with their brother to talk about Scott, missing since his encounter with Quinn in the barn. Her breath came out in a rush. She hated it when they tried to protect her. "Did you find out anything about—?"

The question died. Vivian stared at the three formidable women on her doorstep. With an effort, she closed her mouth, opened the screen and stepped out. The door snapped shut, yapping dogs inside, and she surreptitiously wiped doggie slobber on the seat of her overalls and extended her hand. "Ladies, good morning. I'm Vivian Johnson. What can I do for you?"

"Good morning. I'm Camille Strickland." The taller woman grasped Vivian's hand with just the right amount of pressure for just the right amount of time, then released her and gestured toward the two women now balanced on the second step. "And these are my sisters, Caroline and Claudia. We're Quinn's family, and we'd like to see her."

VIVIAN SETTLED THE TRIO IN THE parlor and went in search of Quinn. She found her, frozen, behind the blackberry bush. "Quinn, your sisters are . . . Quinn, for Heaven's sake, what's the matter?"

She dropped to her knees, put her hand on Quinn's trembling shoulder and then reached up and pulled her against her own ample form. Quinn stiffened but didn't pull away. A moment later she shuddered and relaxed her head to rest on Vivian's curls.

Vivian crooned nonsense and rocked the sobbing woman.

Finally Quinn grew quiet, muttered, "Sorry," and wiped her runny nose on her sleeve.

Vivian released her. "I didn't know you had sisters."

"Is anyone else with them?"

"Anyone else?" Then it occurred to her that Quinn was asking about a man, and she wished for Victoria with all her might. They dealt with things much better as a twosome. She wondered what the right answer might be, said, "No, just three women." When Quinn said nothing more, she added, "They seem quite nice."

"Oh, yes, they are. They're really very nice. They've come to rescue me."

"Rescue? From what?"

A mirthless laugh. "From myself. It's their job."

THE MORNING FIRE HAD BEEN ALLOWED to die down and only spring sunlight warmed the room when Quinn entered the parlor. On the sofa, flanked by Claudia and Caroline, Camille spoke without preamble, "It's Mother, Quinn; she is ill." She waited as Quinn slid boneless onto the twins' ottoman perch and covered her dirty knees with dirty hands. As though they could sense her discomfort, Prudence draped her heavy little head over Quinn's left foot and, with a cool, wet nose, Patience gently prodded her hand.

Camille continued, "As I was saying, Mother came back from her African trip pale and shaky, but she said she was just tired."

Caroline interrupted. "We told her it was too big a trip but does she ever listen?"

Claudia ignored her sister's comment. "After resting for two weeks, doing virtually nothing . . ."

Camille took back the telling. ". . .she still was weak and pale and, according to Caroline and Claudia, looked even worse. They called me, and I went home and we convinced her to see her doctor.

Quinn heard the reproach: *Where were you when we needed you?*

Caroline answered the unspoken question. "We knew you were busy, Quinn, so we didn't call you. She even fooled Dr. Mason at first."

Claudia nodded and irritation sharpened her words. "Yes, she got all dolled up like Mother can and didn't take one of us with her." Claudia didn't like to be fooled. "So it wasn't until he got the blood test results that the doctor suspected something really wrong."

"After that, he admitted her to the hospital for more tests."

Quinn watched their mouths but could barely hear their words. It couldn't be *her* mother, weak and pale, lying in a hospital bed, ill with who knew what. "So what is wrong with her, anyway?"

At that moment, balancing an overflowing tray, Vivian re-entered the room. "Refreshments anyone?"

Amidst the flurry of food distribution, Quinn watched her sisters—Camille familiar and solid in a voluminous dress and matching jacket designed to cover a much heavier woman; Claudia and Caroline, brunette and blond, alike nonetheless in casual sweaters and carefully pressed jeans—as they positioned themselves around the tray. A lonely fly circled, and Vivian shooed it away. Quinn picked at the dried mud on the knee of her own Levi's and welcomed the interruption.

Vivian had arranged tiny cakes and the banana bread that was her specialty, and Quinn knew she was trying to make a good impression. The bread was for tomorrow's tea. She wanted to tell her it wasn't necessary.

"Is everything okay, Quinn?

"No, Viv, they just told me my mother is ill."

"Nothing serious, I hope?" Her expression said I didn't know you had a mother, either.

Quinn winced as her secrets were revealed.

Another glance at the sisters, a quick pat on Quinn's shoulder, and Vivian fled back into the kitchen and the radio's soothing tones.

Claudia and Caroline helped themselves to the sweets. Camille wiped her fingers on the hanky she kept in her purse, sipped her black coffee before she answered the question that should have been Quinn's. "It is serious, Quinn. Ovarian cancer."

Cradling her cup in both hands as though it were a baby bird, Quinn placed it down, adjusting and readjusting until the tiny circle of its bone china bottom fit perfectly into the tiny circle of its bone china saucer. In the movies there would be music now, she thought, as the world changes. The hot tea in her mouth didn't want to be swallowed. Quinn wanted to be somewhere else.

Camille scattered words into the room. "Carson Tahoe Hospital . . . tests, CT scan or MRI, I'm not sure which . . . pelvic mass . . . anemia—"

Quinn couldn't take in the details. Camille's voice seemed far away, cutting in and out like a bad phone connection. "She had surgery, "de-bulking," they called it, and she's started on chemotherapy."

She finished and the sisters sat in silence. The fly settled unmolested on a cinnamon cake. Quinn struggled to assimilate what the others already knew.

"She already had surgery?"

"We knew you were busy, Quinn."

They all looked at Quinn expectantly.

"I can't come home right now."

"No need." *No one expected you to* hung unspoken. Camille cleared her throat. "Claudia has taken a leave of absence and is staying home with Mother. We just didn't want to tell you over the phone."

And it took a little doing to track me down. Quinn frowned. "What about John Paul?"

At the mention of their baby brother even Camille fussed with her cup and didn't make eye contact. Quinn knew he must be on another runner.

"He's managing the store now, you know," she said, and that was all.

HOURS LATER VIVIAN FOUND QUINN IN the sun room fingering "Flight of the Bumblebee" as though, if she just played hard enough, she could join the bees. Her hair had slipped out of the pink bandana she'd taken to wearing when she worked outside and lay damp on her forehead. Vivian lifted the flute from Quinn's trembling hands. "Enough, Quinnie," her tone perfected on a very young son. "Sit." She pushed Quinn onto the love seat. "Now talk to me."

Quinn sat. Dust motes danced in the afternoon sun. She wiped her sweaty face on her sleeve and raised empty turquoise eyes to the woman at her side. "Are they gone?"

"Yes. After you left I served them more tea and some lunch. We chatted a little and they left."

Quinn's jaw clenched. "Sorry."

"It's okay. They wanted to drive home before the sun was in their eyes. Camille liked my cucumber sandwiches."

Quinn ignored Camille's eating preferences. "What did they tell you?"

Vivian sighed and wished her sister would get home. "That your father died several years ago and your mother had had a hard time since. That you have another sister, Cecily, I think they said, who lives in California and is in the movie business. That your brother is managing your father's business, has a gift for cars but no head for finances, that he is something of a . . . 'mama's boy,' I think Caroline called him."

"Yeah. He still lives at home." Quinn's face was toward the window, her eyes opaque. "But then so does Claudia." She stopped, and the silence between them stretched into the corners of the room, now darker as the shafts of sunlight migrated west.

There's something she doesn't want me to know. Vivian shifted in her seat. *Damn you, Vicky, where are you when I need you?*

Quinn cleared reluctance from her throat. "What else did they tell you?"

"About you?"

She nodded.

Vivian squirmed, waited until Quinn raised her gaze from the floor, and tried to read her immobile face. She stared. Quinn stared back. Vivian had never seen a living face so still, and her resolve to outwait her new friend collapsed. "They said you were very smart and very talented but that you don't stay in one place very long."

"And?"

"That you and your mother don't get along very well, that you have a . . . Claudia called it a 'love-hate relationship.'"

Quinn's eyes brightened, and, in her lap, her hands loosened their grip.

Well, Vic, Vivian thought, *I guess her secret's still safe.*

Quinn spoke. "I guess that says it all."

AFTER A HASTY SPIT BATH, QUINN settled herself at the kitchen table where Vivian had laid out a cold supper. Ravenous, she reached for a piece of the warm bread. Vivian and Victoria were already in their usual seats, and their presence together was comforting. It had seemed odd, Vivian completing her own sentences.

The sisters exchanged glances. They had obviously been discussing the morning's surprises. Quinn could imagine Vivian's description: *The tension was so thick you could cut it with a knife.*

Victoria shook her head.

"What?"

Vivian cleared her throat. Patience and Prudence stirred restlessly at her feet. "Quinn, do you need to go home?"

LATER, ALONE IN THEIR SITTING ROOM, the twins re-hashed the evening.

"I still think she should go home."

"So do I, but Vicky, we can't make her go." Vivian sipped her sherry. "Besides, the retreat starts tomorrow and we need her here." She bounced out of her chair to pace the little room. "God, I can't believe I said that. I am so selfish."

"No, honey, you just said what we've both been thinking. And I'm so sorry you had to go through this all by yourself." She poured another two fingers of Scotch. "Did you tell Wennie?"

"Left a message. And he hasn't called back. He doesn't seem to want to talk to us much these days, does he?" Her eyes moistened. "And I didn't even ask about your back." She collapsed into her chair.

"My back's fine. Or it will be if I do nothing but put heat and ice on it and stretch every minute of the day." Her face wore irritated wrinkles. "And I didn't see Wen either. I thought I'd catch him at home but he was nowhere to be found. But about Quinn—the way I see it is this . . . Quinn and her family have some problems, else why would she be here in the first place? Maybe the problem is with the mother and that's why she doesn't want to go home. So she'll stay here and, thank God, we'll have the retreat as planned." She set her glass on the tray and held up two sets of crossed fingers. "I hope."

1:00 A.M. QUINN TRIED TO PULL the room around her but it refused to budge, and she lay wrapped in the vestiges of her dream. They had come again—the arms, the baby powder, the cold and unyielding back— to wrest her from sleep and sit like a stone in her belly. She'd heard Joan Didion talk once about the "dark in the middle of my soul." *This must be it*, she decided, surprised that dark was so heavy.

Memories bubble-wrapped and distant, she considered her mother and their last conversation, twin to others of their past, when Mary DeMello had looked at her fourth daughter without expression, uttered "Do whatever you think is right, Quinn, I'm sure it's nothing to me," in a flat, cold voice, and turned away. Quinn shivered.

The discussion with the twins had persisted past exhaustion. Neither understood why she needed to stay. After all, they *wanted* their mother to live with them. Patience and Prudence had prowled, circled, and sniffed, and finally settled against Quinn's feet.

"We can do it without you," Vivian had urged without conviction.

Beside her Victoria nodded. "Wennie will help." There was no conviction in her voice either.

The mental picture of Owen Johnson cross-legged in Lotus position before their sophisticated guests drew a wobbly smile and the tension lifted. In the end, guilt warring with relief, they accepted her decision.

CHAPTER 18

SHOWERED AND SHAMPOOED, CHORES BEHIND HER, Quinn lingered on the guesthouse porch reading lips as the Johnson sisters greeted their first retreat guests. Four women ascended the steps to the house. No longer piled high with unsplit logs, the porch was inviting in a rustic sort of way—wood planks, old lawn furniture, new floral cushions—at least that's how she hoped these women would see it. By the twins' reckoning, the fate of the Wildflower Inn rested on this retreat, and Quinn felt guilty that yesterday's personal drama had distracted from their last-minute preparations.

"I'm Vivian Johnson and this is my sister, Victoria." The twins had chosen completely different outfits and their identical nature seemed less prominent. "You must be—"

"Thalia Monroe." The thin woman grasped Vivian's hand, the smooth blond curtain of her hair swinging over one eye only to be encouraged back behind her ear by a slender, well-manicured finger. A diamond stud sparkled in the lobe. "These are my friends, Carol Carlisle, Nancy Martinez, and Angie Edwards." Handshakes all around.

Showtime.

The red and white Land Cruiser stood side-by-side with an antique yellow cab—transportation fitting an adventure back in time. Owen and the taxi's owner, Martin Edwards, a young Winnemucca man whose plan to renovate the vintage car was taking a back seat to earning money for the next Winter Olympics, carried luggage into the guesthouse. Tags color-coded bags to owners in the manner of European tour groups—orange for Thalia, red for Nancy, pink for Carol and baby blue for Angie—and Quinn wondered if the colors matched their personalities. She ignored Owen as he brushed past her through the door and hoped he noticed the new western shirt with flat mother-of-pearl snaps that covered her black tank top.

"Hi, my name is Quinn." She shook hands with the women and waited while they looked her over, then, striving for enthusiasm rather than tour guide ennui, she escorted them through the guesthouse. "This is the great room. Down the hall are your rooms." Anxiety fluttered and she pushed it away.

Both Thalia and Nancy eyed Owen as he brushed past them with the bags.

Ignoring their wistful looks and her own tightening gut, Quinn pointed out the kitchen and the porch and then ushered them to their rooms, Thalia and Nancy to the two identical loft rooms—Ying and Yang—and Carol and Angie below—Romeo and Juliet—and invited them to explore house and grounds. "Lunch will be at twelve-thirty in the main house," she told them.

Enthusiastic voices floated after her as she left them to settle in.

THE KITCHEN SIMMERED WITH HEAT FROM the range and four anticipatory females. Outside the window a horde of black and gray birds chattered and picked at lunch.

Around the trestle table dressed in white linen with spring-colored napkins, the guests sipped ice tea, finished their spinach and sun-dried tomato quiche and listened attentively as Victoria outlined the retreat schedule. Prince Charles, the cat who so assiduously ignored Quinn's arrival, staked his claim to Nancy's lap and purred like a rusty engine as she scratched his yellow ears.

"We will begin each day," Victoria told them, "with coffee or tea in the great room, then a sitting meditation followed by your yoga session and then . . ."

". . . breakfast," finished Vivian, breakfast her favorite meal.

From the far end of the table, Quinn picked up the instructions, and four perfectly coiffed heads swiveled in her direction. "After breakfast we will have a brief stroll, then quiet time followed by another meditation and lunch under the tree," she indicated the big willow, pale green with its new leaves still tightly furled, "weather permitting."

Outside, the sun smiled its blessing and no one doubted that weather would permit.

"After lunch," promised Victoria and again the heads turned, "and food preparation for dinner, you will enjoy a walk into the hills." A slight murmur followed this announcement.

Quinn ignored it and went on. "After our walk, there will be time for reading or for a nap, and at five o'clock tea will be served in the great room. Dinner will be here at seven. If you have any questions, please ask. And remember, conversation at mealtimes and in your rooms only."

There were no protests as Vivian handed out aprons from Grandmother's Johnson's stash and directed the guests to their tasks. With a sigh, Nancy reluctantly dislodged the sleeping cat, brushed yellow hair from her new jeans, and joined her friends.

The twins exchanged satisfied glances and Quinn considered the half-moons that her fingernails had dug in her palms. Angie's pink nails flashed over onions on the cutting board. Soapsuds went unnoticed on Nancy's cheek as the friends mimed conversation.

Day One bumped along, a little stiff but without mishap except for the slice out of Angie's finger—Carol's "Oh, for Heaven's sake, Angie, it's just a scratch," taking care of that emergency—and the blister that Vivian's boot rubbed on Thalia's heel. Quinn made a mental note to add moleskin to her equipment and a reminder about hiking shoes to the instruction packet. The guests were not complaining.

Day Two followed suit. The weather cooperated.

In the waning light of the third and last retreat day, the bell rang for tea and the women, bringing with them an air of suppressed excitement, gathered in the great room. Quinn was playing her flute and Thalia had just finished pouring when Owen Johnson entered, nodded to the guests and sat down at the Baby Grand that dominated the room. His fingers found Quinn's notes, and Ave Maria soared as the resonance of the baby grand merged with the high sweet tones of the flute.

Whoa, I thought it was the mother who played.

Only years of discipline kept Quinn's breath flowing evenly, her fingers moving on their predetermined journey. Her quick glance discovered his shock of damp brown hair, his attention directed downward as his fingers moved over the keys. She wondered what she would see if he raised his eyes to meet hers, and all the electricity in the room coalesced within her. Summoning her willpower, she directed her attention to the music.

FOR AN HOUR THEY CHASED EACH other, the piano leading into Haydn's "Serenade," then the flute calling them to the "William Tell Overture." Owen's shoulders shook, his hair bumped wildly over the purple scar, and the air shimmered with regal Egypt as his hands pounded out the "Triumphal March" from Verdi's *Aida*. Quinn breathed liquid honey, crisp snowflakes, sounds of ruby red and emerald green as she gave him the Kasbah of Rimsky-Korsakov's *Scheherazade*. Her fingers danced, moved the music as they never had before—playful, exhilarating, demanding—and she reached into herself to find the notes.

Owen laughed out loud as she presented the Beatles' "I Want to Hold Your Hand." A wicked smile turning up the corner of his mouth, he countered with "Don't Be Cruel" and Quinn lost her concentration for a moment before she could suppress her own chortle. The song ended and the music disappeared into silence.

Owen lifted his eyes. Quinn's skin tingled and the fine hairs on her forearms stood up as he looked straight into her soul. Then his fingers rippled over the yellowed ivory keys, pulling her with him into the haunting melody of "Annie's Song."

As John Denver's love song to his wife faded into the last rays of the sun, Quinn, exhausted, dropped her arms to her sides and bowed her head, and her hair, like a curtain, covered her face. A maelstrom of applause roused her, and when she raised her eyes Owen was gone and she was left to accept the accolade alone.

DEAR GOD, JOHNSON, WHAT WERE YOU thinking?

Not quite sure how he'd made it to the car, Owen clutched the wheel of his silver Audi and headed toward Winnemucca, the sound of applause still ringing in his ears. His heart pounded and his groin ached. He knew he'd made a huge tactical error.

It seemed innocuous enough when Vivian pleaded for his company at dinner. "They'll love to visit with you, Wen, and they are such nice women, you know, you met them already."

He knew she meant him for entertainment and once again he couldn't say no. He'd given them so little lately, and, besides, the odd day with Quinn had faded into its proper proportions. Any red-blooded American male would respond as he had. It was nothing more than a normal physical response to an attractive, albeit unusual, woman.

It was that damn flute, he thought, *and the way she slid the pieces together.* Even now he could imagine those hands, knowing and gentle, touching him, but then in the darkness as he watched, he hadn't been able to resist. His brain clearly hadn't been working as he strode across the room and seated himself at the piano opposite her. *So this is what taking leave of your senses feels like.* He groaned and ran his fingers though his hair.

He didn't know what he'd expected when his hands touched the keys; maybe even, God forbid, he had wanted to steal a little of her thunder, take her down a peg. He certainly hadn't anticipated the way she blended her notes with his, the teasing choices she offered him, certainly not the electric shock he'd experienced when he looked into those unguarded turquoise eyes. Lost, "Annie's Song" had come from his heart.

"You are fucked big time, Johnson," he moaned, banishing love from his thoughts.

IN THE MAIN HOUSE, DINNER CONVERSATION swirled around the musical entertainment.

"You should have been there, Victoria. It was beautiful, the way the music flowed, the feelings, and how cleverly they played together." Nancy's praise was effusive. "Have they played together long?"

Vivian and Victoria exchanged a glance. *Where was Wennie? What was up with Wennie?* By the sound of it, this night's performance was totally out-of-character for their self-effacing brother. *It did go well,* they telegraphed in their twin way. *A brilliant finale.*

"What a surprise ending," commented Carol, "to a most wonderful experience."

"Will he be back?" Thalia got right to the point. "I'd like to tell him how much I enjoyed the performance." Next to her Nancy nodded with enthusiasm.

Vivian peeked at Quinn. At the end of the table the woman made soup of her Bananas Foster and didn't seem to notice the curious glances directed her way. As soon as she could, Quinn made her excuses and ran.

AFTER DINNER, TOO RAW FOR CONVERSATION, Quinn said her polite goodbyes, accepted thank-you's and ducked her head at the praise. She even endured a quick hug from Angie without flinching. The screen door squeaked behind Thalia's "Good night, Quinn" and after a while quiet settled over the guest house as the women completed their packing and fell into sleep.

Now she curled up on the guest house porch, her down comforter the only defense against the whirlwind of her thoughts. There was no doubt that the retreat had been successful, highly successful if tonight's enthusiasm was any measure. Owen's addition had been brilliant. These women would certainly spread the word.

The twins must be relieved, she thought. *There will be another retreat. I should go celebrate with them.* Instead, feeling too heavy to move, she tipped her head backwards to consider the starry darkness and the concomitant head rush muffled her own wistful *I can stay.*

The lights of the main house were as far away as the stars.

Silence enveloped her and Pachelbel's Canon whispered in her head. *Owen. What was that all about, his music, the look in his eyes, his escape?* The swing moved restlessly beneath her as she replayed the afternoon—his music, his hands, his eyes. *Into my soul . . . how stupid is that? This is not going according to plan.* She flushed and pushed the comforter away, longing for arms to hold her.

As though called up by that longing, her daughter filled her thoughts. *Samantha.* She rocked on the swing, remembering the round baby cheeks, the dimpled baby hands and the sweet, sweet smell of almond and spice and Johnson's Baby Powder found only with her nose tucked deep into the crevice of Samantha's neck.

She didn't notice when the tears began to fall.

EARLY THE NEXT MORNING VIVIAN AND Victoria Johnson stood in the middle of the lane, still waving as the rented van, Martin Edwards at the wheel, carried their first retreat guests out of sight. Quinn, the sick feeling that exhaustion and too many tears produce unrelieved by her sleepless night, watched from the porch, knowing that just one more word would plunge her into the darkness. "It was a success; it was a success," she repeated under her breath, but the fog crept in anyway. She thought about the barn and George's nurturing bulk, but her bed beckoned, and she slipped away before the twins turned back toward the porch.

On her pillow, still balled up from her sleepless night, lay a feather, a round black rock, a sprig of sage tied with a pink ribbon and the arrowhead fragment that Thalia had discovered on yesterday's hike. Quinn crawled into the unmade bed, careful not to dislodge the offerings. *Maybe it's time to go.*

THE TWINS WATCHED QUINN DISAPPEAR INTO the guesthouse.

"I think this was hard on her." Vivian's voice was tinged with worry. "Will she . . ."

". . . stay? I hope so, but you know what her sisters said—she doesn't stay in one place very long." Jittery with excitement and exhaustion, Victoria didn't want to focus on troubles right now. "It went really well, though, don't you think?"

Vivian's face lit up as she thought about the thanks rained on them, each guest separately commending the retreat. "Oh, yes, Vicky, yes, yes, yes. It went brilliantly. It was wonderful." Pausing in search of superlatives, she grabbed her sister's hand and pulled her into a whirl of movement that conjured road dust to dance with them. "It couldn't have been better."

"Contain yourself, sister dear, there's still work to be done." Victoria brought them to a halt, a hand to her back but her own smile still in place. "One retreat does not a success make."

"I know, I know, but Vicky, it was so good, and I just know the next one will be even better. Thalia said she really, really liked the silence part. Quinn was right about that for sure."

"And Angie, even with that big bandage around her finger, said it was the best three days she'd had in a very long time."

"Carol wanted all my recipes. You know, Vic, I argued with Quinn about it but I think the most fun for me was sharing the kitchen with those women."

They turned and looked at the silent guest house. "She seems so young, our Quinn, more like a daughter than someone even older than we are. It's like she got stalled somehow, her development I mean. And she's so . . . quiet, so . . ."

"Distant?"

"Yes, distant is a good description. She is distant, but she really gets people, doesn't she? I wonder why she doesn't understand . . ."

". . . herself? Yeah, I wonder, too." Victoria eyed her sister. "And speaking of wonder—I wonder what's up with Wennie. Playing the piano like that and then not even staying for supper? That is not like him at all. And this morning sending Martin in that van? Did he say anything?"

"Not really, but we only talked a minute before he went off to the great room for tea. He didn't mention the trust fund. I thought that would be settled by now. Just said he hadn't located Scottie, but he's still trying." Vivian sighed. "Wanted to know if we'd heard from him. Vic, maybe we should have told Quinn. Maybe she could have talked some sense into him. Maybe we should make a clean breast of it."

Her sister shrugged. "What's done is done, Vivvy. We just have to trust Wen now."

"And hope Quinn doesn't run away, too."

The lane was quiet, only the drone of the eight o'clock news and the song of a single bird heard in the distance. They started back toward the house. "By the way, did you hear anything about a squirt gun battle? Nancy told me . . ."

CHAPTER 19

DAYS LATER OWEN ARRIVED, UNANNOUNCED, AT supper-time. He'd stayed away long enough. Time and daylight and a few brief but safe encounters with Quinn had convinced him that one night of music meant nothing. Now he parked the truck and its loaded trailer by the barn, set the squeaky brake and strode across the lane. "I've got a plan," he announced as he entered the kitchen. His sisters surged forward and, after hugs all around, Vivian handed him a plate and waved him toward the table. Quinn nodded and passed the potatoes.

"This retreat was even better than the first one, Wen," Vivian brought him into the recap he'd interrupted. "Allison Brown's mother . . . Allison was one of the women who got snowed in here in January, and I guess she really liked us because her mother didn't even wait for an invitation, and she brought her sister and two of her friends. Such nice ladies . . . but you know, you brought them from the airport."

Their voices became background for his thoughts. Of course he remembered Mrs. Calhoun, tall and brusque, and her old lady friends. Mostly, though, he remembered his encounter with Quinn.

He'd finished distributing their luggage and found Quinn staring out the kitchen window. She jumped as he touched her elbow.

"Sorry, I didn't mean to startle you." They had reached an uneasy truce, their few conversations brisk and businesslike. Still she acted like she didn't know what to expect.

She turned, eyes shuttered. "It's okay. I thought you'd left already." Her raised eyebrows screamed suspicion.

"Soon." He handed her a book, faded and thick. Her fingers brushed his as she automatically accepted his offering and the tiny contact raised the hairs on his forearms. Hating his response and praying for a steady voice, he said, "Here. Vivian said you wanted a bird book, and Sibley's is the best I know. Sorry it's so ratty. It's had a hard life, but it's my favorite and I thought you might use it until you can get your own." He turned and left before she could refuse.

Now he watched as she sawed her chicken into tinier and tinier pieces. *She doesn't like it when I'm here.* He couldn't stay away. He shook his head and tried to focus on Vivian's description of the Easter Egg Hunt.

"These ladies are as old as Mother, and they huddled around the table laughing and laughing and laughing. Quinn mixed up Easter egg dye and offered a prize for the fanciest egg. We all voted. Then Sunday morning there they were, scurrying around the field picking up colored eggs like giant children. Vic and I, well, I thought they'd think it was babyish, but they loved it."

Envisioning Tom Hanks in *Big*, Owen wondered whether everything with this woman was a party. "Sounds like a total success." He said, and his tone made the words churlish but he didn't know how to retract them so he just shrugged and went on. "So I've got news, too."

The twins leaned in. "All ears," they said in unison, then, "Jinx, you owe me a coke," and giggled. Quinn twirled a lock of hair, and for a minute his whole world centered on the golden curl and the languid finger.

"Sorry, Wen," Vivian said as their giggles subsided.

"Earth to Wen," said Victoria. "Hey, earth to Owen."

"Huh." Startled, he grabbed his coffee mug, swigged, and his scalded tongue refocused him. "Sorry. Okay. Remember you wanted some ideas about trail rides? Well, they tell me the eagles are back in the canyon, working on their nest."

He glanced up. Even Quinn was paying attention now. He said, "I think eagle viewing would be a great trail ride event, don't you?"

Quinn's lip curled. She opened her mouth as if to protest, and he watched irritation chase across her face. *Shit, she thinks I'm telling them what to do, taking over. For God's sake, I'm just trying to help. Quit while you're ahead, Johnson, you'll never get it right with this woman.*

Ignoring her look and the warnings exploding like fireworks in his head, he addressed his next words to Quinn. "So, would you like to explore?"

Quinn's antagonism evaporated and anticipation prickled up and down her spine even as her lips parted in surprise at the invitation. Trail rides were planned. They were worrying about what to do with their next guests, two teens and their best-friend mothers. Just because it was The Omnipotent's idea didn't automatically make it a bad one. Did it?

Before she could respond, he added, "I brought Trigger, John's horse, in case you wanted to. You can ride George."

Making me an offer I can't refuse, she thought with glee, but obviously he wasn't reading her mind this time because before she could accept, he went on, "Otherwise I can scout it out my—"

She raised her hand to silence him. "Sure. That'd be great. When?" He looked so startled she clapped her hand over her mouth to keep from laughing out loud.

Vivian and Victoria exchanged glances.

"Tomorrow early," he replied, his voice an emotional kaleidoscope. "Trigger and George ride well together. We'll take lunch."

The twins exchanged glances again, said nothing.

MID-MORNING, PICKING THEIR CAREFUL WAY ALONG the trail, the two horses and their riders rode deeper into the canyon. George dawdled and then hustled to catch up and nip at Trigger. The big blond horse simply sidestepped and moved forward, swishing his tail, unmoved by George's attempts to gain his attention. Quinn patted the mare's neck in commiseration. Around them the high granite walls cast shadows, and she was glad for the protection of her jacket.

A wisp of sunlight bounced off the reddish cliff face, and a cluster or rocks dropped like a waterfall into the canyon ahead. Quinn's startled "huh" sent Girl George dancing and her hooves scrabbled against the loose gravel.

"Spring thaw," Owen Johnson said without looking back, "loosens the rocks and some of them come down."

Her hand soothing George's neck and her own jumpiness, Quinn concentrated on her companion. She hadn't seen much of him since the ill-fated trip to Reno, even less since the impromptu duet, and she felt his absence as acutely as she now felt his presence. Their duet had been a tease, a promise unfulfilled, and as she played each evening she tried not to long for more. He no longer watched her in silence, but his comments, via his sisters, seemed instructive, and Quinn rankled at his high-handed approach. Today in his brown fedora and dark leather jacket, easy astride the big gelding, he again resembled her hero.

Trigger maintained a two or three length lead, picking his way over the still muddy trail and finding his footing among the slippery pebbles. Swollen with melting snow, the stream tumbled loudly in its narrow bed. Except for the occasional nip at her companion's rump and an attempt or two to graze from the clumps of grass growing out of the rock, George seemed content to follow and, for the moment, so was Quinn.

The trail widened, Trigger paused, and George snuggled up beside him. As she bumped him coquettishly, the big horse snorted and danced away. Owen shifted to maintain his seat. Under his firm hand, Trigger settled, and Quinn stifled a grin. Without comment, Owen raised binoculars to his eyes.

After a few moments, he handed them to her. "Up there."

Quinn's eyes followed his gesture, and in the pale morning sky she caught the motion. Training the binoculars skyward, she saw the wide wings of a raptor high above, its markings indeterminate to a novice. "The eagle?"

"I think."

He moved Trigger along the stream to a grassy clearing and dismounted. "We'll go on foot from here."

Quinn imitated his actions, set George to graze, and followed the man along the narrow path that appeared like a miracle at his feet. It wound up out of the creek bed and Quinn hugged the rocky wall on her left. Carrying saddlebags full of picnic lunch, Owen set a brisk pace, unmindful of the increasingly steep drop to their right.

At a sharp turn, Quinn hesitated, and, without breaking stride, Owen ordered, "Don't look down. You'll be fine."

Hating her fears but even more their discovery, she lengthened her own stride, kept her eyes on the path and almost forgot the plunge to the canyon below.

For forty minutes they moved steadily upward. Without warning, he threw his arm across Quinn's chest like a mother protecting her front-seat child and pressed her back against the rock wall. "Shhh."

She followed his gaze up and across the ravine.

There they were—close enough that Quinn could see both with unaided eyes. One bird thrust at the raggedy nest, easily big enough for a human baby, that perched on the rocky ledge. A larger bird swooped in and settled beside his mate. Suspended motionless, the humans waited until, tired of providing entertainment, the eagles abandoned their nest repair and let the wind currents carry them away. Mesmerized, Quinn stared until they remained only in her imagination.

"One always stays after the eggs are laid, you know," Owen's voice broke her reverie. "They make their nests out of leafy sticks and twigs so they're thin the first years, but they get bigger as they repair and reuse them. The old ones get to be five or six feet across."

As he spoke, he moved away, and Quinn realized she'd been clutching his hand. He hadn't protested. "Come on, let's find a sunny spot and eat before we start down."

Eyes still on the empty sky, willing the birds to return, Quinn hesitated, then scrambled up the trail and found Owen already sitting on the edge, feet dangling. After one careful look she found a patch of sunshine as far back as she could get.

"Don't like heights?" He rummaged in his saddlebag, handed her a sandwich neatly wrapped in waxed paper.

She shrugged. "Not much," she said and accepted the food. After sharing the eagles there was nothing he could do to make her angry.

He bit into his sandwich and made no further comment. She took a bite of her own sandwich.

"Water?" He twisted the top off and handed her a bottle of Crystal Geyser.

Stifling the I-can-do-it-myself impulse, she accepted the water and ignored his knowing smirk. A big swig washed down salami and cheese.

"Tell me how this trail ride will work."

"Adam Singer's the trail boss. He'll arrive in the early morning—he usually brings a helper or two—and they'll match up the women with suitable mounts. Then we'll come up the way we just did."

"We?"

"Sure. I wouldn't miss this for the world."

She couldn't misunderstand the challenge in his eyes. What could she say? It was his idea, after all. And his horses. And his sisters. She chewed on her lip.

He just grinned. "Adam will leave us at the creek where we started up the hill and take the horses back, and we'll continue on foot to the eagles' watch. Then up here," he indicated the open space dotted with scrubby pines directly behind them, "where Martin will meet us with lunch and a vehicle."

"Just like an English country picnic." Hugh Grant in *Sense and Sensibility* popped into her thoughts.

"Just like."

"And no hiking home?"

"None."

Quinn grinned. "Brilliant."

He replied, "Glad you approve," in such a wry tone that she knew he'd appreciated her earlier scorn.

She flushed, ducked her head. "Sorry."

"I suspect I've been somewhat high-handed."

At that they both laughed, and when he held out his hand Quinn wiped sandwich crumbs off her own and reached out to him.

She wasn't sure what happened next—did his movement loosen something or was it just that ledge's cosmic turn to crumble?—but without warning Owen slid out of view. The roar deafened. Flattened, Quinn cringed, clinging as the earth reverberated, then sucked itself in and left a vacuum. A few stones tinkled on the boulders far below. Silence.

OWEN, SADDLE BAG STILL DRAPED OVER his left arm, balanced rigid as the dust and noise settled. A single rock bounced off his shoulder on its journey downward; then all was still.

"Shit."

Balanced on a narrow outcropping built up around the single tortured pine that had broken his fall, he looked down at the boulders and scrub brush waiting their turn. He shivered. Above was silence.

"Quinn. Quinn, are you okay?" Guilt and apprehension rose in the seconds he waited. *What if she's hurt? I should never have brought her here.*

She sounded far away. "I'm okay. What happened? Are *you* okay?"

"Ledge slipped. I'm down about six feet. I need your help."

"I'll call." He heard her fumbling for her phone.

"No reception."

He waited while she checked, heard her sound of angry disbelief, "Damn."

"Quinn, slide to the edge. I'll hand you a rope and—"

She made an undecipherable noise, and a shower of pebbles clattered around him. She was backing away. *Christ, she's afraid of heights. What now?* He noted the sudden change in the air that promised rain, glanced at the ominous sky. Even as he watched, the sun disappeared into the clouds, and he knew if she didn't help him they were both in trouble.

"Quinn . . . pay attention." He winced at the sharp tone his helplessness produced, took a deep breath and softened his voice. "I'm on a ledge about six feet from you. If you can secure my rope I can climb up."

"Can't I go for help?"

Whining, she's whining. Peril or no, the corners of his mouth turned upward. "No, it'll be dark too soon and you don't know your way."

He gave her time to consider this, didn't hear any movement, and in the voice he'd used on very young sisters, coaxed, "Quinn, honey, just lie flat on your belly and inch forward. You don't even have to get to the edge. You don't have to look down. I'll just hand up the rope and you can grab it. We'll be fine."

Nothing moved. Guilt and tension shaped his next words. "Quinn, you can do this. It'll be easier if we get out of here before it rains. Just scoot on over."

"All right, all right. Just give me a minute, will you?"

He knew she hated him then and he didn't blame her, asking her to do what was clearly impossible. *I shouldn't have been showing off, sitting on the edge like I own the world. I should have been more careful.* All the same, he was relieved by her normal snappiness. He heard her muttering and hoped her anger would translate into action before the heavy sky opened. He crossed his fingers and waited.

PATRONIZING SHIT. QUINN TOOK A DEEP breath and glared toward the sound of a voice used only on idiots and children.

Her heart thudded against her ribs and frustrated tears turned dirt to mud beneath her cheeks as she huddled on the path. Aloud, she ordered herself to action.

"Step one, gloves on." *I'll show The Omnipotent I can do this.* She located the worn leather gloves he had handed her just that morning and pulled them on.

"Step two, lie flat." *Do this right, Quinn. Don't let him see you fail.* It was easier to think about failing than about spending the night huddled on the mountain, knowing any moment his perch could release and send him to his—

"No," she said aloud and didn't care if he heard.

She willed her muscles one at a time to release their hold on the tiny patch of dirt she inhabited, to relax into the stretch she needed to approach the edge. Sharp rocks bit through her shirt and she rolled to her side, the shift sending another cascade of pebbles downward. She heard him suck in his breath. *Serves him right.* Anger felt better than fear. She fastened the metal buttons on the Levi jacket, resumed her prone position and, ignoring the panicky noises in her head, she wiggled forward.

"Good girl," he encouraged as plinking stones marked her progress. Unwillingly warmed by his approval, Quinn paused as he continued, "Just move slowly, Quinn. I'm holding up the rope. You can see it."

She hated him then, hated that cool, calm, unemotional man who was tempting her to her doom. *When we get out of this I'm gonna kill him.* Resolve strengthened, she scooted another millimeter. It didn't help that she knew he was right.

"Good girl. Just a little further."

She imagined her fingers squeezing his throat and lifted her gaze from the gravel under her nose. Visible above the edge was the stiff old lariat she'd seen hooked on Trigger's saddle.

"Step three, grab the—" She inched forward just as lightning split the sky. "Oh, shit." She froze.

"Just lightning, Quinn. Thunder in a minute." The boom reached them. "Here, grab the rope."

She grabbed it, slithered away from the edge, heart racing. "Now what?"

She heard another ragged breath as a jagged streak of lightning illuminated the heavy sky and random raindrops splattered the rocks—maybe not so unemotional after all—but his voice was calm as he directed the rescue. Slip knot already in place, rope secured to a sturdy pine and fed back to his waiting hands. In minutes he stood on the trail beside her.

"Good job, Quinn." He grabbed her in a bear hug as rain began to fall in earnest.

THEIR SILENCE ON THE WAY DOWN was a friendly one, tension gone as though something had been decided. Unperturbed by the rain, Trigger and George whinnied when the bedraggled pair arrived and then slogged off down the hill without complaint. Water coursed off Quinn's hat and down her neck. Owen rode ahead, slouched forward in the saddle, impervious to the weather.

Cold, wet, exhilarated. *I went to the edge and it didn't beat me back. I showed him.* She was glad no one could see her grinning.

As the lights of the main house came into view, Trigger paused and George moved up beside him. Owen turned toward Quinn and the sudden movement sent his horse dancing away. A firm pull on the reins brought him back, and Owen reached out, traced Quinn's jaw as he pushed the wet hair away from her face.

"Thanks again." His murmur was barely audible in the wind. "Saving my life is becoming a habit, it seems." She saw the flash of his teeth. "You do rise to the occasion."

He let her hair fall and kicked Trigger forward. The memory of his touch lingered on her cheek.

The Wildflower Inn shone like a lighthouse and Quinn almost expected the low moan of a foghorn to herald their approach. Weary, they dismounted and led the horses into the barn. Her wet jeans clung like shriveled skin and she shivered, excitement, cold and the aroma of wet horse contributing to the jitters in her stomach. She unsaddled George and threw a blanket over her steaming back. "Extra oats for you, my girl," she promised as she reached for the Folgers can and stumbled over Bessie the Barn Cat.

At her side, Owen wiped Trigger down with spare, efficient motions, then reached over and plucked the tin of oats from her shaking fingers. "I'll finish the horses, Quinn. I'm not as wet as you. Why don't you go in and let the girls know we're okay. We've been gone a long time."

"Thanks." She wanted to touch him, stay by his side. She relinquished the can and walked toward the blazing lights. *Later*, she thought, *but not too much later.*

She squished across the wooden floor. No one greeted her. She wanted to sneak off to her own room and savor the day. Instead she struggled out of her wet boots and wandered through the kitchen. "What's going on?" Her voice echoed. "Where is everybody?"

She heard voices, and as she approached her excitement faded into a sense of impending . . . something. She looked into a room she'd never entered. From the tin ceiling a bare light bulb dangled on a frayed cord and sent more shadow than light over apple crates, cardboard boxes and a hodgepodge of unidentifiable implements that covered every inch of the wide-planked floor. An old cider press stood proud in one corner. Vivian and Victoria Johnson, backs to the door and mirrored in the bank of windows that comprised the south and west walls, stood hip to hip in twin communication.

"Hey, guys, what's up?" Quinn stepped gingerly into the dank room.

As though on the same string, they started and turned towards her. "Quinn," Vivian said. "We didn't hear you. Where's Owen?"

Victoria turned. "Hey, sweetie," she said, "you look like a wet hen. What happened?" She threaded her way across the room.

Vivian skirted the jumble and hurried after her sister. "We wondered where you'd got to." She shooed them toward the parlor. "This is quite a storm. The weather man didn't even predict it, and here it is. Did you hear the thunder? Dumb question, of course you did. We knew you'd be wet. Your coat's soaked. Take it off right now or you'll catch your death." She pushed Quinn closer to the stove which was just starting to take off the chill. "Victoria, get some towels. Quinn, where did you say Wen's got to?"

Déjà vu, but now she knew who Wen was. "Owen's in the barn. He'll be here in a minute." Teeth chattering, Quinn peeled off her jacket and stretched her hands toward the heat. "What are you guys doing, anyway?"

No answer.

Victoria returned with the towels. Vivian produced tea, and after a worried look toward the barn, settled beside her sister on the footstool. "Tell us what happened, Quinn."

Steaming by the fire, Quinn recounted the less momentous parts of the day until it became clear that neither woman was attending. She looked down at the identical faces. "Okay, ladies, what's going on?"

A conspiratorial look passed between them.

Vivian put on a matter-of-fact tone. "Your sister Camille called. She wants you to call her tomorrow. She says your mother is ready for hospice and refuses to go. And Claudia can't take care of her at home anymore."

Hospice. Quinn doubled over, the word a sucker-punch to her mid-section, and the memory of Owen's touch disappeared. Vivian reached out a steadying hand. Quinn waved her away, remembered to breathe. "I'm okay," she lied.

She'd had a client in hospice once, a nice sixty-something lady who hovered four days in a morphine stupor and then died. Hospice—a death sentence. *No, I'm not done with her yet.*

She stepped back from the hot little stove, the need to do something, anything, strong upon her. She retrieved her wet boots and propped them against the fender; she hung the Levi jacket on the drying rack; she picked up a mug from Vivian's tray, looked at it as though it were a foreign object and put it down, the tea untasted. She didn't look at the women watching her.

They don't understand. They can't understand. Her head seemed full of clouds that separated her from the room and from herself, leaving only black and white thought without sensation. She looked around, eyes blind.

Patience and Prudence whined and wiggled.

Then her legs refused to support her and she sagged against the wall. Victoria jumped up and steadied her unto the couch. Vivian patted her knee. *I can tell them apart,* Quinn realized. *I can really tell them apart.* For a moment this seemed more important than Camille's phone call. "So what do they want from me?" The words rubbed like sandpaper in the hot air.

Again the shared look.

"Camille didn't say, Quinn." Victoria pulled a chair close to the stove and sat, her knee brushing Quinn's. "She didn't say, but Viv and I have an idea."

As though she'd stepped out of the wardrobe and into another world, Quinn waited, docile. The scene would play and she would watch and—no matter what she did—it would end. *She can't die; she still hates me.* A moan escaped her lips as she rocked back and forth and tears trembled.

Vivian wiped her own eyes. "We think you should bring your mother here."

The world blazed into full color.

"Here? Bring Mary here? Why would I do that?" Quinn stared at their earnest faces, then slumped, face in her hands. She knew they didn't understand the thing she had with her mother, so different from their own. *It's my fault but I can't tell them. They'd hate me, too.*

Victoria blinked at the given name. "Yes, here. Vivvy is an EMT, you know. She took the classes because of Scottie, in case something happened. We live so far away from help and all." Her explanation faded, didn't include the times her sister had plied her trade on the injured animals that came their way, the way she'd cried when she couldn't help their father. "No matter, we could do pain meds easy enough, and there's always at least two of us here. And the hospice nurse could come out from town."

Vivian shaded in the details. "We could fix up that back room, the one with . . ."

". . . all the windows, the one we wanted our mother to use."

"And you could spend time with your mother."

Her first thought was that the room was too full to fit a dying mother. Then it all crashed over her. *It won't help. Nothing will.* Her protests died unuttered as a blast of cold air swept the room and Owen entered, spraying water like a dog shaking himself after a swim. He pulled off his sodden gloves and jacket and tossed his hat toward the drying rack.

His sisters jumped up to greet him.

"Owen, you're getting water all over . . ."

". . . everything."

They nagged at him as they spread out his wet garments and handed him a warm towel and a mug of tea. "And guess what, Quinn's mother is coming to stay with us."

Quiet settled like the closing curtain of a play. Owen turned his gaze toward her. "Quinn?"

She sat without words, no longer the star, as the twins filled her silence with their enthusiasm. They explained about Camille's phone call, the mother's need for hospice, their own availability. As they talked something tiny and hopeful fluttered in her chest.

"So, Wennie, we can fix up the sunroom for her, and we can all take care of her."

Almost to herself, Quinn murmured, "I'd be doing something useful for her." A little half-smile turned her lips upward.

Owen's face closed. He said nothing.

"WHAT IN THE WORLD WERE YOU two thinking?"

Owen stalked back and forth in his sister's sitting room, interrupting the flow of heat from their tiny fire, running his hands through still damp hair and, in the sisters' estimation, acting like a madman. Quinn, cup of soup in hand, had gone off to bed, and the siblings gathered upstairs.

"Don't be upset, Owen, it's a perfect solution," Vivian stated.

Outside the storm continued, and thunder punctuated his words. The restraint he'd shown downstairs had disappeared. "Perfect for who?"

"Whom, Wen, whom. It's a perfect solution for all of us. Quinn's mother has a comfortable place to stay until she dies, a place with her daughter. We'll make a little extra money. Quinn gets to spend time with her mother and not have to leave us. It's perfect for everybody."

"It really could work. Wen," she chided as her brother made a huffing noise, "don't be rude. I know you think it's because of Mother, that she wouldn't let us take care of her, but it's really not."

"No, it's not about Mother. We just love Quinn and this will give her a chance to mend her fences with her mother . . ."

". . . and keep working here at the same time. A win-win situation."

Owen threw himself into the only chair left, leaned his head in his hands. "Girls, girls, girls . . . you don't know anything about this woman or her family." With resolve, he put aside the memory of Quinn's face, frightened and determined, as she reached down to rescue him, the feeling of her body full against his own. "I think you're getting in over your heads on this one."

His sisters exchanged their look; he gritted his teeth. "I hate it when you do that."

They grinned. They always won arguments with their brother.

"She's not one of your wounded birds, you know."

Her voice gentle, Vivian responded, "I think she might be."

CHAPTER 20

HE BEDRAGGLED RIBBONS OF THE MAYPOLE fluttered in the drizzle as Mary DeMello arrived. Flanked by geese, goats and dogs, Vivian, Victoria and Quinn crowded out through the gate and watched the ambulance slither up the hill and come to a halt in the center of the gravel lane. Owen, looking as though he wanted to be somewhere else, leaned against the corral fence. The rear door swung open, Quinn hurried forward and Owen strode across to her side as two garrulous attendants wearing EMT badges flirted with their patient and lifted the gurney to the ground.

Quinn hovered, the battle between eagerness and dread shielded from her face. She leaned down to greet her mother as she emerged from the vehicle. At just the right moment, Mary turned her face away and Quinn kissed the air beside her ear.

"Quinn, you didn't cut your hair. You're way too old to wear it like that."

Quinn pushed the offending strands back from her face and darted a glance around to see if anyone had heard. Only Owen, arms crossed over his chest, was close enough, and she couldn't read his face. Relieved, she stepped aside. One of the EMTs winked at her as they passed. The twins retreated to the porch to welcome their guest. Voice wooden, Quinn performed the introductions.

"Vivian and Victoria, what lovely names, but I shall have to call you V and V because I'm quite sure I'll never tell you apart." Mary DeMello's tiny smile was so sweet no one could take offense at her words, delivered in such a breathy whisper they had to lean in to hear.

Quinn was reminded of an old perfume ad, something about whispering and they will listen, as she observed her mother's performance. Mary's emaciated hand with its Cherry Blossom Pink nails fluttered like a semaphore toward the Lincoln Town car, Claudia's Pathfinder and Caroline's old Ford truck, previously unnoticed and now, packed full, parked along the ditch behind the ambulance. "My things. Just a few. You know, things I couldn't do without."

No one said anything for a moment. Mary DeMello smiled. *She doesn't need a supporting cast*, thought Quinn and tried to think of something to say that would ease the moment. Vivian broke the silence.

"Well, just you come in," she said, "and let's get you settled." Victoria held the screen open and Vivian lead Mary's entourage through the parlor and into the newly refurbished sunroom. Claudia and Caroline fluttered as the EMTs transferred Mary to the hospital bed that hospice had provided. Vivian smoothed a soft pink coverlet over her new charge and patted her gently. "There you are, almost home."

Mary didn't respond. Expressionless, she watched her belongings take over the room—wheelchair in the corner, recliner beside the bed, pictures in silver frames on the antique rosewood dresser that Victoria had polished until it gleamed.

Camille lifted pastel garments from the suitcases. With an imperious nod, Mary directed their distribution, and Quinn wondered where she thought she'd be wearing those things, or when. She said nothing.

Claudia held up a small polished box and placed it into her mother's outstretched hands.

"Oh, Mitzi, we're here." The dying woman wrapped her arms around the casket. She cut a glance at Owen, but directed her explanation toward the twins who watched openmouthed. "I just loved Mitzi so much—the sweetest dog I've ever had—and I can't stand to be without her. You do understand, don't you?"

Owen stood beside Quinn in the doorway. "Who's Mitzi?"

"Mother's toy poodle. A present from my father. Mary adored her almost as much as she adored Daddy."

"So she just died?"

"Well, no, she died about ten years ago." Quinn didn't understand the odd look Owen gave her.

"Quinn, come in here." Mrs. DeMello's contralto voice, full and soft as a ripe plum and made richer by her weakness, demanded obedience.

Quinn shuffled to the bedside, her eyes on the floor. "Yes, Mother?"

Mary fixed her daughter with a stern gaze. "Go thank those nice boys who moved me in. I know they won't take tips but be sure to offer them refreshment before they start back. It's such a long trip, you know. These nice ladies," her smile encompassed the twins like sunshine, "will get me tucked in."

Two stars twinkled in the night sky as Owen found Quinn, wrapped in a bulky white comforter and curled in the porch swing like a small child. Down leaked from a hole near

174

her shoulder and he tucked a bit back in, tried to ignore his body's unbidden stirring. "This isn't working out the way you hoped, is it?"

She shook her head but said nothing. He felt her gaze on him as he balanced two juice glasses on the porch rail and filled them with purple liquid from an unlabeled bottle. He placed one glass in Quinn's hand, jerked back from the fleeting touch of her fingers, and leaned against the porch rail swinging the bottle by its neck, his own drink forgotten. *I'm just visiting my sister's partner. It doesn't hurt to be nice.*

"She seems a little . . . cold, your mom," he said and looked away from the torment in Quinn's turquoise eyes.

SURPRISE DENTED THE ARMOR SHE'D DONNED at her mother's arrival as Quinn accepted the glass Owen handed her, wished for a tequila shooter. Things *weren't* working out the way she'd hoped; worse, she wasn't even sure what she had hoped for. Her shoulder tingled where his finger had messed with the down.

"Ahh." She sipped the liquid he'd given her, relieved to find wine not juice.

"Vicky's famous blackberry wine. I hope she doesn't miss the bottle."

He leaned against the rail, pensive, and she wondered why he was there. The full moon cast enough light to read by, but, not wanting to see pity in his eyes, she kept her attention on the glass in her hand. His words seemed to come from a great distance—"She seems a little cold, your mom"—and were offered so gently that Quinn couldn't reject them. Instead, she looked up at him, and their gaze held for a long moment before he turned away. Tears welled. *It hurts, my heart hurts.*

He stared at the darkness, raised his glass to his lips.

Quinn thought about her mother, and when she spoke her words disturbed the silence, but she kept her voice light as though what she had to say didn't matter. "She and Daddy were so tight it's like there wasn't room for anyone else. What a pair to have six kids. I think he liked her best when she was pregnant—at least, that's my psychobabble theory—so she kept herself that way as long as she could. Presented him with babies, and then we just grew up willy-nilly."

Tongue loosened by the tart fruity wine that slid over the lump in her throat, its purple coolness soothing the sore spot in her chest, she continued, knowing full well that she would suffer for this, that guilt would take over when her body's flashing message *quiet, TMI* reached her brain.

"It's not that we were abused really, just . . . unnecessary."

In the background, the sister chorus thundered, and she realized how quiet they'd been. The real sisters had deposited their mother and departed; the chorus remained in her head: what did you expect, Quinn? Mother is just mother—and Daddy *did* love you best.

She realized she'd been quiet a long time, but the man didn't seem to mind. He leaned toward her to refill her glass. Empty—Quinn didn't remember drinking it.

"Penny for your thoughts," he said.

"Not worth it." She gulped the cool purple liquid. "No, I was thinking about my father." *Daddy loved you best?*

"Tell me."

"He wanted a son. Or at least that's what everyone said. After three girls, when I arrived they'd given up on ever getting a boy and gave me the special name—the boy's name. I was Quinn Michelle, the next best thing to Quinn Michael."

He opened his mouth as though to protest, closed it again. When he replied it was just, "I wondered why no C name."

What didn't he say?

"Yeah, I guess they thought this was their last chance. When John Paul was born I was afraid they'd want it back."

"Want it back?"

"My name."

"Huh," he said. Then, as an afterthought, "Who's John Paul?"

"Oh, of course you wouldn't know . . . he's my brother, the only DeMello boy. He's the youngest of us all. I was lucky to be a tomboy 'cause he was never much interested in sports, working with Daddy, stuff like that, and I was. About the only girlie thing I ever did was . . . play the flute." If Owen noticed her momentary hesitation, he didn't show it.

Quinn pondered her struggle to emulate Al DeMello—a little girl in faded blue and white striped overalls with a greasy rag hanging from her hip pocket peering under the hood of whatever vehicle he was fixing; clinging to a horse ten times her size desperate not to be left behind as her handsome Portuguese father cantered out of the corral with the confidence that had captivated his wife and antagonized his in-laws.

"I wanted to be like him." She drank, rocked the swing harder. "I wanted to be just like him and know something about everything, like he did, but I was just . . . a girl."

She wanted to be like him, compact and dark and mysterious. Instead she was a gangly girl, not very good at anything except playing the flute and . . . fucking, as it turned out.

Shut up Quinn, just shut up. She jerked her glass up to her mouth. Wine sloshed out and painted a purple blossom across the white blanket.

BUTT AGAINST THE RAIL, INCENSED AND aching for the little girl, Owen noted Quinn's pause. *Secrets, too many secrets—like lead in the pit of my stomach.* He gulped his own wine. *No, make that lava,* he thought as the tart liquid burned its way down. An open book, his sisters described him. *Ha.* He could only see the pale oval of her face. He gulped again. *What didn't she say?*

The moon slipped behind a cloud and her eyes were hidden by the night.

As though keeping time with her thoughts, the swing rocked faster, and when the wine sloshed onto her comforter, she looked up at him, defiance and apology and helplessness in her eyes. Like sirens of old, she drew him nearer. His weight slowed the rocking as he eased himself down beside her and, lifting her feet into his lap, tucked the blanket around them. She held her glass with exaggerated care and accepted his attentions.

"Tell me about you." A faint slur marked the effects of the alcohol, and he understood she felt she'd talked too much. He wanted to kiss the purple from her lips.

Instead, he focused on the father he thought he'd had. "My dad owned the local shoe store. He'd been a traveling man until the twins were born and my mother insisted that she couldn't raise three kids alone." *Michael. Martha.* He swallowed bitterness. "Dad had no interest at all in sports or outdoor activities. He and my mother sat and read every evening—they each had a special chair and good light—my mother worried about poor light ruining her eyesight—and listened to opera on the phonograph. I used to lie under the table and make up stories for the music." He chuckled. "It was a huge disappointment to find out what the stories really were."

Quinn received his story with a flickery smile; he felt like he'd won the Nobel Prize.

FUNNY, HE'S FUNNY AND SWEET. SHE managed a smile before she emptied her glass. *And sexy,* she acknowledged as his hands caressed her feet and she began the inner tingle. *But something's not right.* His story created distance from her angst, safer than desire, so she swept her empty hand around to include the barn, George, the mountains. "So how did you learn all this?"

"Uncle Charles, Dad's baby brother. He thought it was his duty to rescue me from *Aida* and piano practice and Henry James. Thankfully, Mother never suspected 'that sweet boy, Charlie' had a rowdy streak a mile wide."

A movement caught her eye and Quinn scrambled from the swing, nearly falling as her feet tangled in the comforter. She grabbed the rail for balance and pointed. "Look. There."

His eyes followed her finger upward.

An owl glided through the night—two strong wing strokes, then swooping down, spectral in the moonlight, gliding . . . then suddenly down again, out of sight.

"Poor mouse."

Disentangling himself from swing and blanket, Owen Johnson stood beside her at the rail and his shoulder steadied her. "Fulfilling its destiny."

"Or karma." She shivered.

He laughed and wrapped his arms around her. She nestled back against him and found she fit, her head against his shoulder, and she relished the hardness of his body. His arms tightened as a second owl swooped across the sky.

"An owl picnic."

He laughed again and hummed a few bars of "The Teddy Bears' Picnic." His breath ruffled her hair. She turned her face toward his, shivered, and he stepped back. His eyes glittered hot but his voice was mild as he said, "Sorry. It's late and you're cold." He retrieved the comforter, forgotten at their feet, and draped it around her, keeping it between his hands and her body, and pushed her toward the door. "Good night."

As she crawled under her covers, the sister chorus started: Quinn, what do you— She tuned it out. She fell on her bed and, for the first time in days, slept well.

CHAPTER 21

I N HIS BASEMENT, OWEN MAINTAINED A steady pressure as he rubbed wax over the fine wood of the armoire. *Stop. I've got to stop before I wear this away to nothing.* Tax season over, he spent hours in his basement and the piece was now complete but the peace of mind he sought eluded him.

Every day he conferred with the private detective who was searching for Scott. Every day he checked the mail for word from his brother in Colorado. Every day he longed to stand behind Quinn and feel her warmth against his body. Yesterday, in Reno, Karle had called him on his distraction, said he was acting like a menopausal women.

Get a grip, Johnson. Disgusted with himself, he cleaned up and went to visit his mother.

HE FROWNED AS HE ENTERED HAPPY Acres, the assisted living facility which had become his mother's home. The high school aide who monitored the door skittered out of his way. He frowned. He hadn't meant to be wearing his black look.

"Good morning, Owen," Thuy Woods, the nurse-administrator greeted him. "We don't usually see you this time of day. Your mother's in the sunroom." Her voice dropped as though telling a secret. "She'll be happy to see you. She's having a really good morning."

Making an effort, he smiled back, inquired about her children, both students at Lowry High School, and then headed toward the sunroom. The cheerful colors and sunny landscapes on the walls only darkened his mood.

Gertrude Johnson sat alone, head bowed as though she slept. Binoculars too large for her frail hands lay in her lap. The pale green cardigan looped around her neck complemented her darker green skirt, and sensible shoes completed her ensemble—a proper English matriarch. Just a hint of silver highlighted her soft dark hair. For a moment she was the mother of Owen's childhood and his stride quickened. Outside, visible through the bank of windows, the bird feeders trembled with activity, and budding trees gave the illusion of countryside.

"Mother."

At the sound of his voice, she raised her head for his kiss, captured his hand and held it against her cheek. Today she knew him. "Owen, look at the birds."

The softness of her wrinkled cheek almost undid him. He yearned to bury his face in her lap and let her tell him everything would be all right. *Absurd.* He forced his attention to the bird lecture he was receiving. From day to day, his mother's brain fascinated and saddened him, but she never seemed to lose the knowledge she'd gained from long nights with her good reading light and a book in her lap. His interest in birds came directly from her, but today his thoughts wandered.

Does she know? About them? Should I ask? What if she doesn't know? Do I have the right to pollute her memories?

"Owen, I don't think you're paying attention to the birds at all." Gertrude Johnson looked up at her eldest child. "And you're scowling. My dearest boy, what's wrong?"

"Nothing, Mother, nothing's wrong." He looked out the window and didn't meet her eyes.

Her voice was firm. "Owen Johnson, I may not be with it much of the time, but I'm with it today, and I can tell something is troubling you. You've been a grown-up for a long time, but sometimes even grown-ups need their mothers."

He dropped onto the small sofa, his hand still clasped in hers. He couldn't meet her eyes. "Mother," he asked, "were you or Dad ever married to anyone else?"

QUINN SAT IN THE COCOON OF her mother's sickroom. Each day she came, each visit the same: Mary propped on her fine linens, attention riveted on her teacup; Quinn perched beside the bed, silent after her clipped recitation of the day's activity. Each day Quinn remembered the teas of her childhood—Mary DeMello, Madonna-like, pouring a sweet Jasmine brew from a Limoges teapot: each child with a special cup, Quinn's Belleek china with tiny shamrocks, and the pressure to keep it intact was intense. The memories filled the room but only Quinn seemed to feel them.

Talk to me, Mommy. Talk to me.

Mary DeMello's purring snores often filled the room.

Quinn looked up from the cuticle she'd shredded, stared at her mother's hands. Her chest tightened. Those tiny hands, translucent but still perfectly manicured thanks to Victoria's unexpected patience, filled Quinn's most vivid memories—hands holding aloft a pure white sugar cube in silver tongs, waiting for an answer to "one cube or two?" while Quinn pondered

her choices and savored the moment of her mother's full attention; hands soothing wrinkles from the white folds of a First
Communion dress; hands flashing like lightning across a child's
face leaving a bright red slash and confusion in their wake.

Quinn's fingernails dug into her palms. *I'm a grown-up now.
That was then.* She felt ten.

The purring stopped. Quinn watched her mother wince as
she scanned her daughter's ragged cuticles, the chewed wisp
of hair, the longing. Mary said nothing and Quinn knew her
mother just wanted her to leave so she could ring her silver bell
for the magic potion only a twin could offer.

She reached for the teacup. "Can I get you something else,
Mother?"

The room waited, cold despite the summer sun.

"Quinn." Mary's voice was so thin Quinn had to reach for
the words. "Quinn, what do you want from me?"

How could she say, Mommy, I want you to love me? She'd
said that once, a long time ago, and Mary had replied, "Why,
Quinn Michelle, of course I love you," and that was that.

Now she said, "Nothing, Mother. Just rest."

Mary's gaze fixed on her daughter for just a moment, then
her eyes drifted shut. So that was that.

Tears streamed down Quinn's cheeks as she yearned. After
a minute she scrubbed them away with the heel of her hand,
pulled the pink afghan up over her mother's emaciated form
and tiptoed out to find a twin.

"She seems content, doesn't she?"

The twins stood on the back porch, the old Kenmore washer
agitating in the background, and watched Quinn assemble
yet another contraption. Thus far, frames for climbing beans

and teepees for peas leaned along the fence, waiting for work. Something for tomatoes would be next. As spring moved into summer and Victoria's back pain persisted, Quinn took on the gardening tasks. Victoria had tried to ignore her chiropractor's prescription "No lifting and no digging" written in bold and legible letters, but her sister pestered and Mary DeMello's "Oh, it's outdoors, let Quinn do it," had decided the matter.

Quinn had just smiled and, after a few days' work, suggested the retreats might offer gardening also. Their most recent guests, four women from Georgia with impeccable manners and syrupy voices who had discovered the Wildflower Inn on its new website and now couldn't wait to tell their friends about the organic garden they'd helped to prepare, had just departed in Martin Edwards' yellow cab.

Quinn hummed as she worked.

"She does," agreed Vivian in a cautious voice. "She works so hard, and the guests love her, but . . ."

"I know, Vivvy, the mother—"

They sighed in unison at the memory of Quinn's words—"Be careful, she'll enslave you"—and how foreign they'd sounded.

The truth was, and they both acknowledged it, that while Quinn worked outdoors, Mary DeMello *had* enslaved them. A tinkle of the silver bell that sat on her bedside table summoned Vivian or Victoria Johnson to her side. A request in her papery voice was instantly granted, the reward an exquisite Estee Lauder *Cotton Candy* smile. She refused the Hospice suggestion that she self-administer her pain cocktail, preferring instead to ring the bell and wait for "her girls."

"I really don't mind, Vicky, really I don't. We knew she'd time-consuming."

"That's not it, Viv, and you know it. She sleeps most of the time, and she's so little that taking care of her isn't much more of an effort than taking care of Scottie was. It's just the other . . . the attitude part. I watch Quinn while she sits with her in the afternoons, and it breaks my heart."

Vivian looked at her sister in surprise. It had always been her job to notice other people and here was Vicky worrying about Quinn's feelings. Things were happening around her, she thought, changing—Scottie, Owen, now her own twin. She wasn't sure how she felt about all this, but kept it to herself.

The bell tinkled and they both sighed again.

CHAPTER 22

ARLY-MORNING, JUNE, ALMOST SIX MONTHS SINCE the fateful snowstorm. *Surprise, still here.* Quinn discarded her gloves and worked her bare fingers into the cool, moist earth. In this moment she held the power of life and death—weeds, off with their heads; seedlings, live long and prosper. An earthworm, round and fat, slid into her hand as she crumbled a dark clod, and she waited while he—or she—returned to the underworld.

Four women had just departed, each to her home in Seattle, each with memories whch, if you could believe their words, they would treasure. Quinn thought of her own treasure trove, an antique basket that should probably be in the Nevada State Museum filling rapidly with tokens—a heart-shaped rock, a piece of polished glass, a snippet of barbed wire and more—that had joined Allison Brown's parchment thank-you. Quinn's fingers dug into the dirt. *A unique gift from each guest: why?*

As she knelt in the damp, hands busy, voices murmured themselves into her awareness—Mary DeMello's low but still musical this early in the day, Vivian's soft and soothing,

Victoria's heard seldom but brisk and bracing—and if she looked over her shoulder she could see movement in the sun-room. Once in a while she could decipher a word or two, mostly the murmur just teased her, and her hands paused as she listened.

OWEN JOHNSON SLOUCHED AGAINST THE FENCE and watched her, appreciating the decisive movements of her hands. He noted the pauses when her breathing seemed to stop, and he wondered what she was thinking—men, career, mother—probably about the mother, he decided, and wished she would think of him.

It was cool where he stood, the sun still low. The aroma of dirt and animal and stream moved around him, easing the discomfort that had become his most recent garb. He hadn't been around much lately. He claimed a new client and the continuing search for Scott as his excuse. In truth, he felt uneasy, a walking-on-eggshells sensation both foreign and unpleasant. He'd arrived late last night, settled John's horse Trigger into a stall beside George, and slept in his room in the barn, but he couldn't avoid his sisters forever. The news he carried weighed heavy. Even with recent practice, dissembling didn't come easy so he had been glad when Mary DeMello's bell summoned them from the breakfast table.

He escaped out the back door and there was Quinn, kneeling in the dirt, her back to the house. Feeling like a voyeur, he paused, taking in the liquid honey of her hair in the flickering new light, imagining it trickling through his fingers as he lifted it to reveal— He shook off the vision and, wishing he carried a cup of coffee for her, he strode across the newly mown grass toward the garden plot.

"They do talk a lot, don't they?"

The man's voice startled her. Quinn looked up, shading her eyes with her dirty hands and welcoming the familiar wriggling, the achy presentiment that began deep in her belly. In her imagination the Chinese symbol that meant both opportunity and danger unfurled.

"Owen, hullo. I didn't know you were here."

She hadn't seen him in days, knew he'd been looking for Scott, wasn't sure how she felt about his absence, or his presence, for that matter. "Any luck with your search?"

He hunkered down beside her, pushed back his hat. The scar, barely pink now, still startled her. The ache intensified.

"Actually, yes, and I'm thinking it won't be good news."

"Oh?" Part and not part of this drama, she let the question rise in her voice. No one had seemed concerned about Scott Johnson's absence until she happened to relate his words to his uncle.

"He said he was going to work with his father?" Owen had looked like he wanted to shake her. "Are you sure?"

She had taken three steps back, nodded. "I didn't know the story then, but it seemed a little strange after the twins told me."

"But you didn't say anything?"

She shook her head. She'd been embarrassed by her own feelings and, after all, they hadn't confided in her either. She'd recognized the problem instantly— Scott had drug issues and was heading for trouble.

"Well, don't," he said. "I'll take care of it."

Owen had been searching for his nephew since that day. As far as Quinn knew, his sisters didn't know that Scott was looking for his father.

Now Owen's fingers worried his scar. "Yeah," he said, "they are not going to like this one bit."

She waited. He had obviously decided to confide in her but still he struggled to get the words out.

"I finally talked with the CEO of the firm that manages Scott's trust, convinced her to contact his father and explain the situation—appeal to his better nature, if he has one. The long and short of it is . . . Scott's with his father. He's fine and has promised to write to his mother and his aunt."

"What a relief. Where's the father?"

"New York." Owen didn't look relieved.

"So what's the problem?"

"I don't know what to do. I got the information only with the promise that I let Scott tell them. Stupid promise. What do you think I should do?" His brow wrinkled, distorting the scar into a sideways question mark.

Why ask me?

He waited for her answer.

"Well, it's none of my business, but I think they need to know he's safe." She swallowed hard. "I'm not a mom, but if I were I'm sure the worst torture in the world would be not knowing."

Like an eraser attacking undesirable words, his index finger scrubbed at the scar, and Quinn stifled her impulse to capture his hand and hold it still. He stopped rubbing and nodded. "You're right. His letter should get here in three or four days, if it comes as promised. I'll wait that long, 'til Saturday, and then I'll just tell them. You're right," he repeated. "They need to know. Damn kid. This isn't the first time he's brought them grief."

He stood, and Quinn did, too. The leather of his jacket brushed her arm and she wanted to bury her face in his sweet smell.

"But that's not why I'm here. If I help with your chores will you go back up the canyon with me?"

As though anticipating her response, he backed away a little, his hands up in a fending-off motion. The crooked grin of a mischievous ten-year-old transformed his face. "No more cliffs. I promise. Besides . . . the eggs have hatched."

The day's chore list spiraled through her head—the Romeo Room, stripped and ready for paint, new guests due on the twelfth, the twins' birthday and . . . hatchlings. She felt like a kid playing hooky. She was already wiping down her tools. "Horses?"

"Horses. I planned ahead."

"Saddle 'em up. I'll meet you in the barn."

Tools stashed, tennies exchanged for boots, Quinn stepped into her mother's room. "Bye, Mary," she whispered, reluctant to startle the fragile figure almost lost among the pillows that secured her, like a doll or a baby, into her recliner.

Mary DeMello stared at the doorway and didn't respond.

"Are you really sure you want to go?" Vivian asked from behind her. "We're supposed to break heat records today."

"Go, Quinn, you need a change of pace." Victoria, herself leaving for her weekly physical therapy, pushed her out the door.

Always alert, the sister chorus turned up its volume: Quinn, Quinn, when will you ever learn? The answer is not a man.

Geez, she defended, it's just birds. But she didn't believe it for a minute.

In less than an hour they were on the trail, Vivian and Victoria, Patience and Prudence, even Mary DeMello disappearing behind them. Trigger picked his way along the creek, water tumbling with snow melt, and George assumed her place a few lengths behind. The sun's warmth already penetrated the canyon, allowing the shade only an illusion of cool. Perspiration soaked Quinn's shirt and her hair lay heavy against her neck. Uncomfortable, she pulled the long strands through the opening in the back of her baseball cap and welcomed the air that whispered like a lover against her skin.

Apparently wrapped in his thoughts and unmindful of the damp that stained his own shirt, Owen rode ahead, and to Quinn's eyes the man blended seamlessly into the saddle and the movement of the big blond horse. Once more, like George, she followed.

A haunting emptiness settled over them—birds and bees stunned silent by the heat—and images from old movies filled her mind: Indians waiting in ambush; mountain lions poised to leap; tumbling floodwaters just around the next bend—Roy Rogers country. Uneasy, she kicked George's sides, urging her forward, but the scrub brush and willow hung dense over the trail, grabbed at her pants, snapped at her cheeks, and narrowed the passage until nowhere could they ride abreast. Trigger's tail swished. Quinn's legs tightened around George. She leaned forward to lay her cheek against the coarse black mane, anything to stem the rising tumult. Patches of wild rose, purple and yellow, gave up their sweet aroma. Deep in the canyon, when they finally stopped for water, she could hear the bees working the blossoms.

They left the horses tethered in the grassy clearing and began the climb. As before, Owen strode out ahead, saddlebags flapping over one arm. Ignoring the drop, Quinn moved easily behind him. As they climbed up the canyon, the sun, high and hot, baked away her foreboding.

"There."

Her gaze followed his gesture and she saw them—a parent and two babes, the eaglets, small and white—on the nest.

"They look like ducklings."

He laughed. "They're downy at first. They feather out in a month or two. These have already started. Pretty soon they'll look just like their parents, only smaller."

They watched in silence.

"There were three. One died." His voice changed, and she wondered what he knew about dead babies, but he only added, "That's pretty common."

"They're magnificent." Through the binoculars he handed her, Quinn could see the babies and their gaping black beaks. As she watched, the second eagle carrying something in his talons glided into the nest.

"Lunch." Owen stood beside her, hat pushed back and eyes shaded by his hands, as they observed the feeding. "Dad brings the food and mom feeds the kids."

"When do they fly?"

"A month or so after they feather. These'll fledge in July probably; they're early. Mom and dad encourage them to get out of the nest. It takes a while before they're ready to leave home, but they get stronger and smarter pretty darn fast."

"And then what?"

"The babes leave and don't come back, but the parents nest here each year. Unlike humans, they mate for life."

"A little cynical, aren't we?"

A cold breath from the canyon brushed her as he stepped away from her side. His laugh struggled. "A little."

The sky was empty. The big eagle had disappeared, not even a contrail to mark his passage. Babies sated, the nest was quiet. Quinn thought about babies and eagles and taciturn men.

"Let's eat and then start back," he said, and she reluctantly returned his binoculars. He wiped the lenses carefully, capped them and stowed them in the leather saddlebag slung over his shoulder.

A hollow carved into the cliff by water and wind offered shade and distance from the edge. While Quinn relieved herself behind a bush, Owen set out the lunch Vivian had provided.

"Fancier than last time." He handed Quinn a bottle of iced tea and then a deviled egg as she settled down near him.

Mouth full of tea, she nodded. An approving lunch, she decided—deviled eggs, fried chicken, potato salad—but approving of what? They chewed for a while in silence.

"How's it going with your mother?"

Chicken leg cleaned to the bone, Owen licked his lips, leaned back against the rock wall, and appeared ready to listen forever. As the sun invaded their shady hollow, he moved away from its heat, closer to Quinn, and his shoulder settled against hers. She leaned forward, gathering up the remnants of their lunch, hoping he didn't feel her shiver.

"Okay, I guess." She stared at the chicken bone in her hand. "Okay's a relative term, of course."

He nodded, and she remembered how often he sat with his own mother.

"She gets weaker each day, dozes most of the time I'm with her. She seems livelier in the morning, chats with your sisters. I hear them when I'm in the garden. You know."

He nodded again. "Vic says the morphine's working pretty well."

"Uh huh. Makes her sleepy. She doesn't seem to be in pain though. That's a blessing. They warned us the pain can be pretty bad. And pretty hard to control."

"Hold still."

She froze.

He leaned across her, flicked something out of her hair. "Bee."

Desire set off by his touch rippled through her body, and the sounds of the day dropped away. Only the susurrus of the quakies and a subtle change in breathing remained. Guilt rose in the color of her cheeks. *Wrong, wrong, wrong . . . we're talking about my dying mother . . . I should not feel like this.*

His eyes swept her face, narrowed. "What?" His fingers touched her chin, urged her face toward his. "You know I want you, don't you?"

She could see every detail, the creases fanning out from the corners of his eyes, the scar on his forehead, the stubble that proclaimed his need for a midday shave, the hunger that muddied his dark brown eyes. She inclined her head, chin still caught in his grip, silent so her voice could not betray her.

He leaned toward her and placed his lips firmly over hers, and of its own volition her mouth softened under his, allowed his tongue entry. She held the rest of herself firm, resisting the urge to melt into the length of the body heavy against her own.

Finally, with a rueful laugh, he released her. "Let me know when you're ready." Without another word, he began packing up the saddlebags.

Like a lit firecracker, hating that he seemed so cool and controlled, Quinn waited for steady legs before she stood, her thoughts as rambunctious as her emotions. Owen's wasn't her first proposition. Usually she just shrugged *Why not?* and let them fill her. Sometimes they stayed, sometimes not, but eventually, as if they noticed that was all they got, they left, or she left first, disgusted with herself for thinking the emptiness could ever be banished.

Without a word, she stood and strode off down the trail.

WHAT WAS I THINKING? WE WERE *talking about her dying mother, for God's sake. Talk about rotten timing. Stupid!.* Cursing his own clumsiness and bewildered at Quinn's response, Owen gathered up the remnants of their lunch and followed the woman stalking down the trail. Ready to explode, his desire bigger than its container, anger provided the only restraint. *You know I want you . . . what a stupid thing to say. Even "What's your sign" would have been better.*

Like an inexperienced school boy, he replayed the previous few minutes as he hurried to catch up, Quinn's fear of heights apparently cured in her rush to escape him. *Was I wrong? Maybe she's just not interested. But I thought . . .* He felt again the heat that had risen between them, her withdrawal as his shoulder settled against her, the softness of her mouth as it melted under his own. *At least I'm not imagining that.*

The blue of her shirt disappeared around a curve. They were almost to the horses. "Quinn, wait."

George nickered and hooves click against pebbles as the horse moved off the grass. Quinn didn't answer. And she didn't wait.

PROPELLED BY HER OWN DISQUIET, QUINN ignored Owen's call, threw herself up on George's back and urged her down the trail. She pounded her thigh with a clenched fist. *What's wrong with you? He's not the first guy who's come on to you. You usually can't wait to get your clothes off. And look at you . . . you know you want him.* No stranger to lust—her motto: you don't have to love 'em to fuck 'em—she was bewildered by her reticence.

The trip down blurred, providing no answers to the questions circling like flies. *So what are you waiting for? Why? He's just another guy with the hots for you. Just do it or get over it—who cares?* Lost in her thoughts, Quinn didn't notice when George left the trail and trotted gingerly onto the hard-packed road. *Who cares?*

Without warning, the mare side-stepped, a little up and down hop, and left her inattentive rider in a surprised heap on the road. In the settling dust, Quinn heard the rattle.

She froze.

Behind her, Owen whispered, "Quinn, don't move."

Fat chance. Motionless, winner in the game of Statues, Quinn stared into the eyes of the rattler.

Coiled, head extended, the diamondback flicked its tongue and stared back. In and out, in and out, Quinn mesmerized, her world motionless but for the tiny forked tongue, the rattle like dried peas in parchment, the conversation of bees in the nearby sage.

Owen's boots scraped the sere earth. "Don't move, Quinn. Just don't move."

Thwack . . . sudden sound, involuntary jump . . . and the snake jumped, too, and then collapsed in a lifeless heap near her knee. She scrabbled backward, bumped Owen's leg and looked up.

He stared at the snake, gun dangling at his side.

Even as her heart careened against her ribs, Quinn chuckled. *No cool blowing of smoke from the gun barrel for this hero.*

"It's okay, Quinn. He's dead." Transfixed, his gaze on the motionless body in the middle of the road, Owen whispered again, "It's okay."

"You have a gun?"

Hooded brown eyes moved to the object in his right hand, and his eyebrows crinkled as though he was surprised to find it there. "In the saddlebag. Never needed it before." He looked from the snake to the woman and back again. "Omigod, I could have killed you."

Dismay took possession of his features, and he looked worse than she felt, so Quinn hoisted herself out of the dirt, brushed gravel off her backside and took the pistol from his unresisting hand. It was a .38, its four inch barrel still warm. Thanks to her father—"If you're going to shoot with me, Quinn, you have to know your weapon"—she could assemble and disassemble, clean and load this gun with her eyes closed. Holding the muzzle down and away, she flipped the revolving cylinder open and cleared it, the empty shell still warm, the five unspent bullets heavy in her palm.

She unhooked the Victorinox tool from her belt, sliced the rattles from the sad, limp body and tossed them to Owen. "Here, my hero. Your coup. Thanks."

They stood in the road and looked at the snake for a long time before they remounted, George again her placid and biddable self, and left the snake carcass to the turkey vultures circling overhead. Owen stayed at Quinn's side until they rounded the bend and the inn came into view.

CHAPTER 23

HEAT WAVES RADIATED FROM THE PACKED dirt, distorting the two figures on the Inn's porch. Sweat dripped from under Quinn's cap and blurred her vision. The horses, anxious to be home, now fidgeted at the corral gate as their riders sat motionless under a spell neither wanted to break. Trigger snorted. George flicked her tail. Finally, Owen swung his leg over the saddle horn and slid to the ground. Without a word, he tossed Quinn his reins and strode toward his sisters.

The twins sat on the porch, sipping tea, waiting for a breeze to lower the temperature, and hoping tomorrow's guests loved unseasonable heat when Quinn and Owen came into view. The pair stopped at the fence as though talking, then Owen tossed his reins to Quinn and started across the hard-packed dirt toward the house.

"Man with a mission." Vivian fanned herself with her hand and watched her brother approach.

"Wonder what happened."

Their brother mounted the steps in two strides.

"We'll be finding out soon, it seems."

Hat pushed back on his head, sweat staining his shirt, jaw tight, Owen Johnson confronted his sisters. "Girls, we've got to talk."

"Inside or outside?"

He took off his hat, mopped his brow with his denim sleeve, and darted a quick glance toward the barn. "Let's go in."

QUINN WATCHED THROUGH HAZE AND SWEAT as the man, like a figment of her imagination, grew less and less distinct and then vanished from her sight. She couldn't imagine their conversation—*Scott's safe? I'm in lust for your employee? I just rescued a damsel in distress?*—so she let the horses drink their fill and then they followed her into the barn.

She undid the cinch and lifted George's saddle from her back, and the mare rumbled in gratitude. She struggled with Trigger's saddle. The blond horse, taller by four hands than George, shied away from the unaccustomed touch. When she finally coaxed her way to his side and loosened the cinch, Owen's saddle was so heavy and high that taking its weight in her arms pushed her backwards into the wall. The saddlebags slid unnoticed to the floor.

Familiar noises created harmony in the dark barn—the deliberate grinding of horse's teeth, the scurry of mouse feet in the musty hay above her head, the gurgle of pigeons in the rafters—as Quinn considered the events of the day.

Bessie the Barn Cat observed with unblinking eyes.

It was real, the danger, not a stupid vacuum cleaner. She remembered how her heart raced, how still she held herself as she peered into the flat black eyes, how afterwards she'd laughed. She moved the stiff brush in short strokes over George's flanks, removing caked-on sweat and dirt, and thought about it. *Maybe I don't need to run. Maybe I can just look it in the eye.*

George's ears moved back in protest as the woman, heart rate accelerating, brushed faster and harder. Looking it in the eye seemed too frightening to consider, and she thought about her rescuer. *Whoa, an accountant with a gun.*

HANDS AND FACE WASHED, OWEN ACCEPTED the sweating glass of iced herbal tea that Vivian handed him. The women had communed in their silent way and now sat waiting for whatever their brother had to say.

"I have to tell you something that I promised I wouldn't tell," he began, restless in his chair, "but Quinn said something that got me thinking, and I've decided this is important enough to tell you anyway."

Again the twin glance. An old-fashioned man at heart, their brother's word was his bond. Vivian straightened in her own chair. Whatever was coming probably wouldn't be good.

"Quinn?" Victoria focused on the second anomaly. "What did Quinn say?"

A light came on in his face. "Quinn." The name rolled off his tongue wrapped in velvet. "You know, that woman has quite a good head on her shoulders. I asked her opinion about this, and she reminded me that secrets aren't always good to keep."

The sisters exchanged another look, incredulous this time.

"What? Oh, I know I've been kind of hard on her but really we didn't know much about her and . . . well, ah, I think you were right. She is an incredible person, even if she doesn't talk much. Her ideas have certainly turned the inn around and . . ."

Part of her wanted to explore this conversation, but Vivian's inner voice prodded. "What secret, Owen?"

"Oh, sorry."

He turned toward Vivian, perched on the edge of her chair, and covered her hands with his own. "I promised I'd let him tell you himself, but Quinn reminded me that mothers need to know their children are safe. Vivvy, I located Scott and—"

Their joyful voices drowned his words.

IN THE HOURS QUINN HAD SPENT with the horses, the sun had finished its run and was only a red rim in the western sky. The siblings were nowhere to be seen. Disappointed and relieved, Quinn entered the guest house. In the narrow kitchen, she warmed leftover tomato soup and sipped it, her thoughts miles away.

A gun!

She saw herself at his feet as he coolly eyed the body— Michael Douglas and Kathleen Turner in *Jewel of the Nile*—and that seemed more real than these suddenly unfamiliar rooms.

A scrawny bit of parsley stuck itself in her teeth and she worked it out with her tongue. *He kissed me. I wanted to climb inside his skin. What am I going to do?* She imagined the man's tongue in her mouth and forced the thought away. A new retreat would begin tomorrow. *Think about that.*

As twilight sparkled and *Das Ring* thundered from the CD player, Quinn paced, dusted, scrubbed. Her muscles quivered, her heart raced and her mouth filled with saliva as she thought about the bottle of Jose Cuervo buried deep in her cupboard. She swallowed hard and resumed the scrubbing until every surface sparkled and the aromas of Lemon Pledge and Mr. Clean filled the rooms.

The lights blinked on in the kitchen across the field. Squinting, she could discern movement. Like the little match girl, she watched, loneliness heavy upon her, then turned away.

In the book-lined room adjacent to her own, she flopped into the green velvet armchair that had reluctantly assumed her form, picked up her book—Carson McCullers' *The Heart is a Lonely Hunter*—and thought about the mute, Singer, so full of secret woe that he'd ended his own life. The cracks in the right-hand corner of the room arranged and rearranged themselves. The window reflected a flickering candle, and the shadows deepened around her. Finally she laid the book aside, beautiful lines unread, and stared into the gathering night.

The stink of her own body roused her.

WELL, THAT DIDN'T HURT TOO MUCH.

Under the weak spray of the old shower in the barn, Owen scrubbed trail dirt from his sweaty body. He'd answered their questions as best he could, at least able to reassure his sisters that their boy was safe. Vivian spoke for them both. "Well, you sure don't know much, Wen, but at least we know he's okay. I guess we'll just have to wait until we hear from him."

He rinsed the lather from his hair, ran his fingers through the curls, and turned off the taps as the water ran cold. *Maybe tomorrow I'll tell them about Dad.* He splashed cologne on his smooth cheeks and padded naked through the barn, his hands touching the leather, imagining Quinn's hands on each piece, on him. He was ready by the time he reached his barn cubicle and slipped into clean Levi's and a short-sleeved blue shirt. Impatient, he leaned against the barn door and waited for the light to come on in his sisters' sitting room.

VIVIAN PEERED AT HER SISTER IN the dusky light and flipped on the switch of the Tiffany lamp that lighted their little sitting room. The radio on the kitchen counter downstairs murmured on, unattended, and the ceiling fan stirred the hot air. Vivian sipped her usual sherry but Victoria held a more substantial Scotch and let its bite wake the pleasure in her mouth.

"What happened to him, Viv?"

They'd been talking about Scott's father but now Vivian knew her sister referred to Owen. She wasn't surprised when the conversation swerved toward their brother. You can only hate somebody so long before you run out of things to say. Scott's father was wicked; Scott was with him—end of story. At least she knew her son was safe, and the sick feeling inside had dissipated. For now that was enough. Wennie was another story.

"He's a good brother, Vic."

"I know, but . . ."

"I don't know what happened, but I sure as shootin' know what's going to happen."

"Quinn?"

"You were right, Vicky, he is ready to fall in love." Vivian shook the rattles, dry and without menace, left on the table during his tale of adventure—Owen the hero, Owen the rescuer of damsels in distress—while he praised Quinn's bravery, her cool-headedness, her . . . "Did he really say *sangfroid*, Vic?"

"Yep." They both chuckled at his florid description of Quinn laughing in the face of danger.

Vivian couldn't explain why she felt such apprehension. After all, they had trusted Quinn with the Inn and were ready to trust her with their son. In fact, they'd banked on her help when they invited her to stay. They had come to love and respect the woman who seemed young enough to be their daughter. Vivian tossed the rattles back on the table. "I'm afraid he's going to get hurt."

Victoria didn't argue. She accepted that her identical twin had a knack for understanding people, sometimes even predicting the future. Sometimes wondered what had happened to her half of this, but didn't spend much time worrying about it. "So what should we do?"

She covered her mouth with her hand to keep back the laughter growing inside. Vivian's worries were not to be taken lightly but she couldn't hold it back. She giggled. Vivian cast a dark look. "Sorry, can't help it. I keep seeing Wen with that damn gun in his hand and Quinn laughing."

Vivian chuckled with her sister. It was a pretty remarkable response, and the picture it inspired was right out of the movies, but the fine squiggles marking her forehead persisted, and she held out her glass for a refill.

Surprised—her sister rarely had more than one drink a week, never more than one in a day—Victoria lifted the crystal decanter from the tray between them and poured the amber liquid into the glass that had been their father's. "There."

"Thanks." Vivian sipped, laughter abated. "So what should we do? The right answer would be 'Nothing.' They're adults and have to manage their lives on their own."

"And your answer?"

"I don't know, Vicky. Maybe we've been wrong, not asking questions, not getting to know about Quinn's past. Fancy her advising *him* not to keep secrets." Vivian's laugh held a tinge of bitterness. "It won't do any good to talk to Wen, but maybe we can talk to the Queen of Secrets herself."

"And her mother?"

"Good thought, maybe the mother, too." Vertical lines shot upwards between her brown eyes. "Yes, the mother. I don't want Wennie to get hurt again and it's our fault that Quinn's here."

IN HER TINY BATHROOM, QUINN SQUIRMED out of Levi's redolent of horse and fear and lust, pulled her sweaty green tank top over her head. She peered into a mirror so small only her chest reflected back—nipples at attention, breasts overflowing as she cupped them in her hands—and felt the ache. She bent to observe her face, an oval streaked with sweat and dirt and hopelessness, framed by strands of dishwater blond hair streaked by the sun. The dent which her father had always called "my dimple" marked one cheek. She remembered another dimple in another cheek. *I can't stand this anymore. It's too much.* Blue eyes stared back.

Darkly amused at her own self-absorption, Quinn stuck out her tongue at her mirror image and climbed into the miniature shower stall. The scalding water startled her but there was nowhere to escape so she held firm in its cascade and grew accustomed to its heat—*Lamb of God, you wash away the sins of the world . . . wash away . . . sins . . . wash away*—and her soapy hands washed away the day's sweat and dirt, not lingering even for a moment in spots where they might normally linger. The scent of lavender filled the room.

Stars twinkled now. Temperatures in the desert plummet with the sun's descent and, chilled, she pulled gray sweats over her damp body. The worn fabric comforted her bare skin. She left her wet hair hanging down her back, no mother to admonish "Quinn, you'll catch your death," and went in search of earthly comfort.

IN THE DARK KITCHEN, EYES BLINDED by the refrigerator light, Quinn fumbled for the wine bottle, quickly closed the door, and the room plunged back into darkness. The Lamb of God had failed—why deny the release that alcohol could bring? Nursing a water glass filled to the brim, she stepped onto the porch. The screen clicked loudly behind her.

"Shhh."

She jumped. The cold liquid sloshed over her hand.

Butt on the porch's top rail, booted foot on its second, Owen Johnson, outline barely visible against the dark sky, pointed toward the garden.

Quinn stepped closer, knees suddenly liquid as his scent—*Jaipur* and man familiar from the clothes she'd borrowed—enveloped her. She resisted the urge to nuzzle his shirt and stood beside him at the rail while her eyes adjusted to the moonlight. Three deer nosed greedily against the garden fence.

"I didn't know you were here."

"I wasn't sure if you'd ever come out."

"You could have knocked."

"I know."

The deer, a young buck with budding antlers, a medium-sized doe and a large fawn, pushed against Quinn's fence. Tempted by green carrot tops, the fawn insinuated its nose under the wire. Someone, Victoria probably, flicked on the outside light and they froze, deer statues carved in time, and then faded into the brush, leaving not a whisper of themselves behind.

"Our day for wildlife," the man commented.

"Owen." Quinn took a gulp from her glass, choked a little, swallowed. "Owen, about today . . ."

"Hey, I'm sorry about that. I shouldn't have shot so close to . . ."

"No, I didn't mean that. That's fine." The wine she drank intensified the internal fireworks. "That's really great. You saved me. I meant about . . . earlier. You know."

"Oh." He turned to face her. "Well, I've changed my mind about that."

Heat mounted her neck as she assumed his meaning. "Oh." A stone settled in her belly and she stepped back. Cool night air encircled her.

"No, wait, I didn't mean—" He grasped her arms and pulled her against him. The wine sloshed over them both and, without releasing her, he removed the glass from her paralyzed grip and placed it on the rail. She stood still in his embrace, hardly breathing, as his newly shaven chin brushed her cheek.

His words were as warm and minty as his breath. "What I mean is . . . I don't want to wait until you tell me you're ready. I want you to be ready now."

Empty clothes, like breadcrumbs, marked the trail to her bedroom.

CHAPTER 24

ORNING LIGHT FOUND QUINN ON HER knees in the garden. Remnants of the night's electricity persisted, and her whole body quivered like a foot newly awakened from sleep. Energy abounded, and it seemed a small price that beet and carrot seedlings joined their weedy cousins on the compost pile. She resonated with music—Ravel's Bolero, Pachelbel's Canon, Tchaikovsky's Serenade for Strings—and she knew she'd never be empty again.

They had come together in frantic heat, Quinn's condom and Owen's laughter as he tossed his own pack beside them on her bed blending seamlessly into the grappling of new lovers. He'd been fast, but she never expected more, was accustomed to furtively fanning her own tiny flame after the man had rolled off in sleep or drunkenness, so she hadn't been surprised when he left her throbbing in the rumpled sheets. She was surprised when he returned, wrapped in her damp bath towel, bearing wine and glasses, her CD player, and renewed evidence of his desire.

In the candlelight, she watched.

"Do you mind?"

She shook her head no.

Under her flat gaze, he pulled the cork, poured the wine and replaced Handel with Andrea Boccelli. Trembling with an eagerness she could no longer hide, she welcomed him back into the bed, and she didn't try to still the moan that escaped as she touched him and his hands claimed her breasts. His heat cooled to deliberate, careful passion, but it was not until his mouth found her that she gave herself up completely.

After, frosted with the sheen of sex, she lay drowsy beside him and sipped the warmer wine as he continued to peruse her geography.

"You have a tattoo." His fingers outlined the miniature rose on the point of her left hip.

"Uh-huh." There was no need to tell him about the drunken night in Boca, how surprised she'd been to wake in the morning and find a bright red rose on her body, how relieved she'd been that it wasn't big letters spelling Montello.

The tantalizing fingers explored further, found the tiny vertical lines, exclamation points on a taut belly. In the flickering light she recognized the question in his eyes, and she squirmed down to silence it with her mouth.

Much later, he slid from the bed, returned with a hot wet washcloth and gently wiped her clean. He was gone when she woke.

The thoughtfulness of that simple act kept the smile on her lips as she sentenced vegetables to death. She didn't need a sister chorus to question what she'd done—*Of course this is risky. I just slept with my employers' big brother*—but the chorus's *Time to run?* slipped in unbidden, and Quinn shivered in its dissonance.

The new guests arrived today at noon.

OWEN STOOD DRIPPING ON HIS BATHROOM floor, the towel forgotten in his hands. *What am I doing?* Thoughts of the woman
hovered like hummingbirds, shimmering, darting, diverting
his attention. The steam seemed to carry her scent—lavender,
sweat, lust—and he sucked it in. *What on God's green earth am
I doing?*

Last night had been unplanned. In fact, all of yesterday
seemed to have been lived by another Owen—an Owen who
could calmly shoot a rattlesnake, seduce a beautiful woman, rise
to previously only imagined heights of passion. The memory of
her damp, lavender-scented towel around his middle aroused
him, and he looked down at himself in surprise.

She'd noticed when it happened, when the damp cotton and
her scent refreshed his desire. He'd seen her eyes widen before
she tugged the towel away and exposed him to her touch.

I could have lasted forever.

His lips twisted upwards as he recalled smutty locker room
jokes and imagined what his friends would say if they knew. *She
knows more about sex than I do,* he realized, *and I don't even care.*

Still smiling, he tossed the towel on the tile floor and ran a
comb through still wet hair. *Time's a-wasting.*

The sun dipping into the west cast long shadows across his
open closet door. As puzzled as a teen dressing for his first
date, the almost forty-four-year-old Owen Johnson examined
his wardrobe.

What should I wear?

Blue shirts and white shirts stared back. Hibiscus flowers—
red and yellow and purple—glared from the Hawaiian shirt
Karle gave him their first night in Honolulu. "Everybody wears
matching shirts," she'd said, laughing at his discomfort. In a
spirit of conciliation he wore his shirt whenever she wore hers.
He touched it and seven months of dust sifted over his shoes.

I wanted to be in love with her. I just wasn't. It had been a relief when they returned to their previous easy camaraderie. He lifted the silk shirt from its hanger, folded it neatly and laid it on the rummage sale pile near his boots. Finally choosing a blue chambray, he slid his arms into the sharply pressed shirt, turned up the sleeves and left the collar unbuttoned. *I wish I'd bought that red shirt I saw at Macy's.* He headed out the door.

THE FIRST EVENING'S FESTIVITIES COMPLETE, QUINN bid good night to their guests and, guided only by moonlight, hastened toward her bedroom sanctuary. After the long and difficult day, layers upon layers that stretched forever, all she wanted was the simplicity of her bed and the memory of last night.

Their new guests, five writers, had their own agenda. Members of a Reno-based critique group, they had intended this time to promenade their work and had been aghast at the starkness of the Inn and its environment.

Don't people read what they sign up for?

Quinn fumed as, step by step, she reiterated the agenda and answered their questions: "No, we don't have a hot tub; yes, all of us work in the garden and prepare the evening meal; yes, silence is expected." By the time they reached a compromise and dinner was endured she had long since exhausted her irritability quotient and was on her way to angry.

"Don't fuss, Quinn," urged Victoria as she and Vivian washed up the remaining dishes and Quinn set out the breakfast things. "It's not your fault they didn't get what our retreat is all about. Actually we should have anticipated trouble when . . ."

"When they had to have this date and we booked the retreats so close together," Vivian finished with a sigh. "Just don't worry about it, sweetie. They can't all be perfect guests." She held her breath as Quinn slammed another cup onto its saucer. "They'll probably come around. And I thought the compromises you worked out—that they would take their silent time for writing and have a critique time in the evenings after dinner—seemed to pacify even that bitchy one. What's her name, Vicky?"

"Peaches," grumbled Quinn, "Peaches Smith. That must be her pen name. What parent in her right mind would name a kid 'Peaches'?"

Vivian decided to change the subject. "Wen found Scott, Quinn. Did he tell you?"

"Finally."

"Oh, I know you've heard us complaining, but he had good reason. It's not a piece of cake growing up with two women."

"Okay, I'll ignore the fact that he left the two of you not knowing whether he was dead or alive." They gaped at her, startled by the harsh words, and she relented just a little. "Okay, tell. Where is he?"

Vivian slumped. "He's in New York, New York *City*, with his *father*. He says . . ."

"He says," Victoria picked up the tale, "we've been wrong about his father. He *says* that he's a great guy and we shouldn't have kept them separated all this time. At least that's what Wennie heard."

"I don't think he really understands the whole story." Vivian dabbed her wet eyes with the wet dish towel.

Quinn patted her shoulder. "When's he coming home?"

"He's not. *That man* . . . that man is going to teach him the stock business."

Sensing the despair beneath the sarcasm, Quinn's inner defenses wobbled. *No more. Please, no more.*

She changed the subject. "Have we decided yet about the Fourth? It's almost the middle of June and—"

The sisters exchanged the glance that signaled enough and allowed the change. "Let's just do it. I think a big party sounds fun, and we have the retreat booked already so we can just add the party into the entertainment."

"And maybe Scotty will be home by then." Vivian's wistful look stabbed at Quinn's heart. "No matter. We'll just look on . . ."

". . . the bright side. You're right, Vivvy, keep our chins up." Victoria turned to Quinn. "We'll invite all our friends, and you should invite your family, Quinn, if you want to. Your sisters might like to come, and your mom can sit out on the lawn for a bit if she feels up to it."

"And we'll get the new organist from church to do the music."

Quinn raised her eyebrows.

"It's okay, Quinn. You remember Harold, the tall skinny guy Martha Jones brought to your famous ice cream social last month?" Victoria paused, her mouth remembering the homemade peach ice cream and how much fun the gathering had been. "Anyway, Harold's a disk jockey, too, and has a great selection. Vivvy was talking with him after choir practice and he showed her the menu or list or whatever. It'll be good."

Quinn folded the last napkin, smoothed it into place beside the flowery china plate. "It's settled then, a Fourth of July celebration. Let's figure it out later. I'm beat and we have two more days of Peaches to endure."

She let the screen close gently behind her.

HE WAITED ON THE STAIRS.

At first she didn't notice, drained as she was from the conflict and the hopefulness. She wondered if he'd come. All day he had filled thoughts she couldn't brush away. Didn't want to brush away. *Tonight, tonight, will he come tonight?* Twice she caught herself humming tunes from *West Side Story*.

Her long strides carried her quickly across the lawn that separated the buildings. She approached the porch and paused. His stillness alerted her.

"Owen? Owen, you're here."

"Of course. You knew I would be."

"I thought you might have come earlier."

"I just wanted to see you," he said softly as he unfolded himself from the step and held open his arms. She hadn't quite dared sing it but she did feel pretty. Her fatigue dropped away as he gathered her close.

Holding hands, they slipped into the night.

Owen led her into the barn and up into the loft. She turned a surprised face to him when she saw the nest he had created, blankets spread on fresh hay.

"Didn't want to alarm your guests." He pulled her down beside him.

Shadows thrown by an electric lantern played across his face, his dark eyes held hers and it seemed, as it had the day of their duet, that he could see to her soul. She trembled. The wanting rose in her and she felt wetness between her legs. As though he could feel it, too, Owen stilled and his eyes darkened, then he pulled her hard against his chest. Released, mouths and hands ravenous, they fell back into the hay.

Later, in the quiet, they heard the owl's voice.

"Another owl picnic," he whispered, and, taking his role, Quinn hummed "The Teddy Bears' Picnic."

Shared memories.

When he smiled and held her tighter, she knew their thoughts were the same.

His free hand roamed her body as though he couldn't get enough.

CHAPTER 25

HE HOURS BLURRED AS QUINN WAITED for darkness and the length of Owen's body against hers in their hayloft getaway. He arrived late and left early, leaving no sign of his presence but the primal energy that fueled her.

"I feel like I'm on speed," she told him, laughing as they watched dawn creep in through the cracks in the walls, "and I don't even need to sleep."

His eyebrow quirked and she realized he'd probably never used anything much stronger than the wine he drank at dinner. She changed the subject but the disconnected feeling that thought produced stayed with her

Will he come back? Her heart beat too hard when she saw his truck behind the barn.

In her outer life, *my unreal life*, she called it, her enthusiasm even coaxed the writer-guests into cooperation. She invited three instructors from Great Basin Community College for dinner and a reading and Peaches Smith left in smiles, clutching an introductory note to Amy Culbertson, owner of the Coral Hills Literary Agency. On the foot of her bed Quinn found a poem titled *High Desert Love by Peaches Smith* on a dog-eared magazine page and she added it to the ever-growing collection in her basket.

When she was with Owen they didn't talk much, mostly anecdotes about town and childhood and an innocuous detail or two. No military, he told her, between wars. He didn't travel much, liked being at home watching movies, listening to music. What he didn't tell her, his sisters already had—Rotary president more than once, mentor at the Boys and Girls Club, school board treasurer, a man with a full life and a large group of friends. "Always ready for pick-up basketball," he admitted. No one mentioned a wife, children. And she already knew about Karle.

How respectable, how stolid, she would think, and then he would tickle her until she cried "Uncle," just before his tongue found her secret places and she decided he wasn't all that stolid after all.

"Happy Birthday, dear O-wen," caroled both sisters from their separate telephones as they finally connected with their brother. "Thank you, thank you, thank you for the discer." He'd had the attachment for their tractor delivered that morning. "Now we can really plow a garden. Did you have a good day?"

"I did." Owen sat in his office in Reno, impatient to be off the phone and on the road. "Did you?"

Their voices tumbled through the air as they answered his question. He heard something about Quinn and breakfast. Laughing, he shouted, "Girls, girls, one at a time. I can't understand a word you're saying."

"It's Quinn, Wen, she did it again. It started with breakfast."

"Breakfast in bed, Wen, us . . . breakfast in bed. Can you just . . ."

". . . imagine that? And then every time we started to do something we found it was already done."

"She did *all* our work for the whole day. It was the *most amazing* thing." Emphasis on the superlatives had Victoria sounding like an excited child. "We've *never* had a more special birthday."

He grinned, wondered when his half-brother Michael's birthday was, pushed the thought away but not before a scowl transformed the grin.

Vivian jumped into the conversation. "And she fixed an early dinner, just for us, Wen. We don't have any guests today, and just for us there was Salad Nicoise and a pasta dish with eggplant and tomato. I don't even like pasta and it was wonderful and—"

He interrupted. "Does she know it's my birthday, too?"

Assured that she did not, Owen wished his sisters one more Happy Birthday and left the office. A quick shower, a quick change and he'd be on the road.

Karle was waiting when he pulled up to her house. Her riotous red curls fell loose over her shoulders and the pale green silk of her dress slithered around her as she walked to the car to meet him.

"Happy Birthday, Owen honey." She placed a chaste kiss on his cheek and laid a coaxing hand on his arm as he stepped from the Audi. "Dinner's ready. Ribs on the barbeque, and that sauce you like."

He knew the sauce she meant, the one she had invented just for him, and his mouth watered. "Can't stay, Karle. I need to get back to Winnemucca." He didn't say *home*. Even now she pitched a quiet fit when he referred to anything but Nixon Avenue as home. He tried to avoid fits at all costs.

Her hand stayed on his arm as she brushed against him. "Just dinner, honey, just dinner. We need to celebrate your birthday. After all, that's what friends are for. And besides, there's a birthday cake from Josef's. You know how you love chocolate cake." Her pout warned *Eating mandatory* in neon letters. He followed her onto the patio.

The ribs fell off the bone. The coleslaw was cold and nippy. The chocolate cake from Josef's Austrian Bakery lived up to its reputation. Each bite kept him from home.

Kaile chatted about her newest renovation mishaps and didn't seem to notice his impatience. Flickering candlelight and the dancing flames from the fire pit produced a celebratory ambiance, and he shouldn't have been surprised when she handed him a small wrapped box.

I should have just said no. He accepted the box. "What's this?"

"It's a birthday present, silly. Open it."

He picked at the bow.

She dug a pointed red fingernail into the Happy Birthday paper and ripped it down the side. "Open it, Owen. It won't bite."

He peeled off the paper and lifted the lid. A flat leather heart lay ensconced in white tissue. He raised his eyes to hers. Hers glittered. She leaned toward him. He stepped back.

She looked at him for a moment with an expression he could not interpret. With a harsh laugh she grabbed the box. "Oh for God's sake, Owen—I got it before we . . . you know . . . and it was too good to return." She thrust it back into his hand. "It's a paperweight. Use it. Happy birthday."

She was in the house as he gunned the Audi away from the curb leaving his after-work shower and the new red polo shirt from Macy's behind.

Now he glanced at his watch. He wasn't sure why he didn't want Quinn to know about his birthday, was glad his sisters hadn't told her, but his present to himself would be Quinn in his arms. 9:14. He could just make it if he hustled.

11:38, THE FASTEST HE'D EVER NEGOTIATED the trip. *Thank God the Highway Patrol was busy somewhere else.* No lights showed as he pulled up behind the barn, and only the owl greeted him as he strode across the lane to her door. He tapped lightly, then louder, but received no response, and, his disappointment as acute as heartburn, he almost missed it, the puffy red heart hanging on the door. He ran his fingers over its smooth shape and felt a little better. *Where?* On the step was the outline of another heart.

He followed the heart trail to the barn. George, a heart with an arrow pointing upward decorating her forehead, nickered softly as he entered. He mounted the ladder. Only cloud-filtered moonlight illuminated the loft, but he could discern a shape on the blanket. He threw off his suit jacket and loosened his tie. As he knelt, the clouds drifted and he could see her clearly, naked on the blanket, wrapped in red ribbon and tied with a poufy red bow.

As he stared in disbelief, Quinn opened her eyes, murmured sleepily, "Happy birthday, lover," and opened her arms.

"LISTEN TO THIS," VIVIAN ORDERED HER brother when she finally got him on the phone. "'Best B&B I've ever stayed at;' 'My husband and I felt like royalty and plan to return next year;' 'Loved it! Already booked our next visit;' 'Most B&B's aren't kid-friendly but yours is wonderful. Our children loved milking the goats and Tommy—our four year old—said Please, Mommy, can we live here?' They're all like that, Wen. We can't believe how well things are going."

"When are you coming out again?" Victoria interrupted from the phone upstairs. "We haven't celebrated your birthday yet and we want to tell you about the Fourth of July party

Quinn's organizing. I think that girl's found some new vita-min—she's got so much energy we're just trying to keep out of her way."

Owen was glad she couldn't see his face. "Fourth of July party?" Dissembling had become a way of life. If his sisters knew how many nights he'd slept in their barn they didn't let on.

"Uh huh. We're inviting all our friends, and yours too, of course—Mike and John and anybody else you want. What about Karle? Will you bring her? We'll keep a room for her if you want."

Guilt hit him hard. *Too many secrets.*

"No, no, Karle's busy over the 4th. Oh, yeah, did I tell you I'm out of town for a few days? San Diego, for a seminar, but I'll be back in plenty of time for the party." He hung up before they could ask any more questions.

I'll be back on the third, and then I'll tell you everything, he promised the silent phone.

Two TRIANGLES OF CHEESE TOAST, GORGONZOLA on Vivian's homemade sourdough, curled on the otherwise empty platter. Only a scatter of broccoli florets remained on the vegetable plate. Quinn stirred sugar into her iced tea as she outlined the retreat's agenda to the four women seated at the trestle table. The big fan in the corner moved the hot air around as Victoria cleared the dishes and Vivian ladled whipped cream onto the raspberry tarts.

This group seemed different, softer, more present—Quinn couldn't quite put her finger on it.

"So every day we have yoga, meditation, quiet time, garden and kitchen chores?" Annabelle Pierce, Shirley Temple-curls bouncing in time to the words, seemed the spokesperson. The others—Karol Williams, Kristin Amundson and Shirley Brown—watched and listened in silence. Karol's eyes kept darting toward the tarts.

Quinn nodded.

"And tomorrow we hike to the Arizona mine?"

"Uh huh."

"Then next day is the Fourth of July party?"

Quinn nodded again. No prompting needed.

"We help with that?"

Two curly heads bobbed assent. The twins had been adamant that the guests assist in the party preparations, especially decorations—"They always like the meal prep and the gardening; they'll *love* this"—and every red, white and blue item Victoria could find at Wal-Mart now waited in the hall closet.

"And our last day we ride horses to see the eagles?"

Quinn nodded a third time. Usually this irritated her. They knew all the details before they arrived, but these women and their questions made her smile.

"I like the silence part," offered Kristen, a thin blond who looked like she needed a week in the sun. "It sounds . . . challenging." She flashed an impish grin at the others.

Karol, a plumper blond with similar features, put her hand on Annabelle's arm, and they allowed the subject to change. As soon as the tarts were consumed, the women went off to unpack.

"THERE'S SOMETHING DIFFERENT ABOUT THIS GROUP. I can feel it. But I don't know what."

"I thought so, too, Quinn," Vivian agreed.

Vic, hands deep in the soapy dishwater, disagreed. "They just seem like regular folks to me. Except that one woman, Kristin I think, she does seem a little . . . peaked."

A discreet cough from behind startled them. Karol Williams stood in the hallway. "I am so sorry to interrupt. Quinn, may I talk with you for just a moment? I can wait until you're done here."

"Dishes can wait." Quinn tossed her damp dishtowel on the counter, never unhappy to escape dish duty. "Come on."

The screen slapped shut behind them.

"Here?" Quinn indicated the porch swing.

"No. If you don't mind, can we walk down the road?"

Intrigued, Quinn assented. The chickens set up a clamor as Karol led the way through the gate and away from the Inn.

"I shouldn't be talking to—I promised I wouldn't say anything but—"

Secrets again. "This is about your sister?"

"My sister? How did you know?"

Quinn shrugged, kept silent. A good guess—she didn't really know anything yet.

Karol laughed. "Of course, we do look alike."

Again Quinn nodded and waited for the woman to continue.

"It's this way . . . and please don't say that I talked to you. She'd kill me."

Silence was better than a promise Quinn might not keep.

"Kristen has been ill. You may have noticed how thin and pale she is."

Having no other role in this conversation but to nod, Quinn nodded.

Karol continued, "She had a blood clot. It was in her leg, or maybe an infection in her foot that made a clot. I'm still not sure. I don't understand all the medical jargon." Her face clouded. "Anyway, they kept taking off bits and pieces, toes, part of her foot—amputating—and she kept getting sicker. We didn't think they could help her. The doctors didn't love her like I do. I thought she was going to die."

It was hard to keep nodding when she felt like crying herself. *Run, Quinn*, her inner voice screamed.

Karol rummaged in her Sierra Club backpack, pulled out a Kleenex and honked into it twice, looked at the tissue as though someone else had used it, then folded it and tucked it back into the pack.

Quinn waited.

"Sorry. Sometimes I think Kris is handling this better than I, and she's the one who lost her leg."

Quinn stopped, stared.

"She has a prosthesis. She's been doing rehab, and our trip here is her maiden voyage, so to speak. She just wants to be normal."

But she's not normal. Quinn wondered why the sister was telling her this. Then she got it. "Can she do the hike, the ride?"

"That's why I wanted to talk to you. She thinks she can. Rehab thinks so, too, but I'm afraid she can't. We're twins, you know, just not identical, and I'm the elder. I'm supposed to take care of her." Unspoken was the failure of that trust.

"Why are you telling me?" The words struggled over the lump in Quinn's throat. The story was sad but it was the trust thing that clenched her stomach. Quinn knew all about failure of trust.

"I don't know. Maybe, maybe you can help her."

"Maybe she doesn't need help." Quinn was surprised at her response but didn't retract it.

"Really?" Half question, half hope.

"Let's just see how it goes." Quinn turned back toward the house. "Let's just see how it goes."

LET'S JUST SEE HOW IT GOES. Quinn's disciplined fingers found their places on the silver flute, but fluttering thoughts distracted her practice. *What should I do? What is it like—to lose a leg, to wear a fake one?* She already knew what it was like to betray a trust. *Who am I to take this chance?* As the last notes faded she decided to do nothing and say nothing—as she told Karol, just see how it goes. She cleaned her flute, tucked it into its case and rejoined her guests for dinner.

Around the table, the women relaxed into their wine and their desire to be pleased, then tensed as conversation veered down one of many apparently forbidden streets. A cleared throat, a look darted at Kris and the voices swerved and the pretense that nothing had occurred lingered ghost-like in the summer heat. Quinn winced as Karol orchestrated the evening in protection of her sister's secret.

NEXT MORNING, QUINN GAVE EXTRA ATTENTION to the sitting directions, willed herself to stillness as the women settled themselves into the early morning meditation. *Let's just see how it goes.*

"*Om Mani Padme Hum, Om Mani Padme Hum,*" they chanted, and she thought the day might turn out all right. After all, *every* day of her life hadn't turned out badly. During yoga, Karol, Annabelle and Shirley spent more time watching Kristin than stretching, but Kris, red tee and black stretch pants concealing whatever needed concealing, seemed oblivious and moved through the exercises without breaking a sweat.

After breakfast and chores, while the sun still hung low in the east, they began their trek to the Arizona Mine, once the center of Unionville's existence. A ghostly silence settled as the group moved further into the heart of the town, and Quinn experienced once again a sense of time disjointed. She set a moderate pace. The women assumed her rhythm and her silence and she wondered if they felt the ghosts as well.

Carrying extra water and the promise of strength should the need arise, Martin Edwards strutted behind them with the importance of his solo male presence.

As they hiked the narrow path through pungent sage, Quinn stepped aside to observe her charges. They passed—Shirley and Annabelle in hiking shorts, plaid long-sleeved shirts and broad-brimmed hats all fresh from REI; Karol and Kris in faded jeans, sprung at the knees. Kris's baseball cap celebrated San Francisco Giants and Quinn couldn't see her face as the four moved along at a brisk pace, Kris still in the protective circle of her friends.

If she can't make it we'll just stop. Maybe I should have told the twins. No, they'd just worry and they've got enough to worry about. We could even carry her if we had to. This is what she wanted, after all. Sometimes people should get what they want. Protected by reassuring thoughts, Quinn hurried to catch up. *We'll just see how it goes.*

As the elevation increased and the path became rockier, they strung out and rested often. Near the top a small round-bodied lizard scurried over Annabelle's boot and the silence was shattered.

"What is it? What is it?" Jumping up and down and shrieking, Annabelle brought the party to a halt.

"It's just a horned toad, Annabelle." Quinn tried not to laugh as the women clustered around her and Martin rustled in the brush hunting the tiny culprit. "He won't hurt you."

They giggled about the tiny creature the rest of the way to the mine.

FRESH FROM THE SHOWER, HAIR TWISTED on top of her head, Quinn entered the kitchen to pick up the tea things. "Any word from Scott?"

An Audrey Hepburn neck! Victoria noted with surprise. "Not yet, tomorrow probably. No," she corrected herself, "tomorrow's the Fourth. Thursday, then." She'd made a special trip to town to pick up Scott's promised letter and hurt her big toe kicking the wall when it wasn't there. "Mail's probably slow because of the holiday." She was determined to maintain a positive attitude for her sister's sake, but inside she cussed her nephew and his worthless father. "Besides the toad, how did the hike go?"

Quinn grinned. She'd left their guests napping, exhausted from the hike and Annabelle's animated retelling of her adventure with the "horny toad." When Quinn had corrected the name, Annabelle spluttered, "But, Quinn, I thought it was trying to hump my foot." She looked baffled when the others convulsed into laughter.

"They did well, especially Kristin, and she's getting some color in her cheeks." Quinn paused and Victoria tried to catch her sister's eye, but Vivian's back was to them as she mixed the dressing into the macaroni salad with dill that she was serving for supper, along with grilled trout and blackberry sorbet. *What's the secret this time?*

Quinn blotted her damp forehead with a tissue, tossed it into the trash. "Martin was kind of a nuisance, but I'm glad he went along. We used up all the extra water he was carrying before we got back, and he's making enough money to go to the Olympics in Olympian-style. Shirley found two arrowheads, and I didn't say a word when she pocketed them. We did say we aren't the antiquities police, didn't we?"

They both laughed, and Quinn had to repeat herself for Vivian who never wanted to be left out of a joke. Victoria handed Quinn the tea tray, ready except for hot water, and Quinn bumped the screen open with her rear end and left the kitchen.

Victoria watched her saunter across the lawn. "What's up with her, do you think?"

"Just a good day?" At the counter, Vivian hadn't been paying much attention.

"More than that, I think. She's kind of . . ."

"Kind of what?" Vivian asked when her sister's voice trailed off.

"Well, kind of . . . glowing, I guess. Yes, that's it, glowing. And she's wearing a dress."

STILL IN HIS SUIT, SHIRT RUMPLED from hours of travel, Owen was waiting when Quinn entered the barn, and relief coursed through him. Three days without her had seemed like three years. In the Hotel Del Coronado, a basket of wine and fruit and an arrangement of flowers bigger than his suitcase welcomed him back, but the spacious room, the spa and the majestic ocean view seemed duller, somehow, and he'd tossed and turned alone on the California Queen.

What am I doing? She'll be gone, and then what?

He tried to find a comfortable spot in the damp sheets, found his body responding instead to an errant scent of lavender released by his sweat. *What if she's already moved on?*

The thought was intolerable, and he rose to look out on the ocean. The crash of the waves, usually so soothing, only emphasized his longing, his fears, and he turned away. *I'll just keep it casual, a summer fling, and then I won't mind when she leaves.*

Now she stood before him, just out of reach. The folds of her dress caught between her thighs, the burnished gold of the fabric so much the shade of her sun-bronzed skin that she seemed to be wearing nothing.

"Nice." His eyes caressed her as his hands wanted to. *Thank God, she's still here.* "You look good in that dress."

She pirouetted, teasing him with her distance. Her skin glowed. He stepped toward her, the summer fling idea dissolving. *No. She can't ever leave me.* He followed her up the ladder.

LATER THEY LAY QUIET IN THEIR hayloft, the dress he'd admired crumpled at their feet, and only a hint of bronzed shoulder peeked from the wrinkled white shirt that now covered Quinn's naked body. Her head nestled in the crook of his arm, and he wasn't sure if she was still awake. He was ready again and flushed in embarrassment. *Randy. She'll think I'm some randy old goat.* His lips curled upward.

As though she could hear his thoughts, Quinn shifted in his arms and her breasts tantalized his chest. Her body assessed his situation and she drew back. In the moonlight he could see the twinkle in her eyes. "Ready again, my randy old goat?" she teased, her voice husky as she raised herself to straddle him, and he wasn't embarrassed anymore.

After, Owen reclined against a hay bale, blanket across his middle for disguise. Wearing his shirt and looking well-used, Quinn sat opposite, arms wrapped around her knees, voice rising as she described the day's events. He watched, not caring much what she said, savoring her excitement and the delicious look of her.

She imitated Martin, "Just let me carry that little ole water bottle, Ms Kris" and "Come on this way, Ms Shirley, that ole rock is just too big to step over," getting his youthful pomposity just right.

Owen smiled, savored the flush of her cheeks, the huskiness of her voice, ached to touch her again.

She mimed Karol's furtive glances whenever food was present. *The hell with Karol. I want you.* He could hardly breathe.

Then she rendered Annabelle, "But Quinn, I thought it wanted to hump my shoe," and his sense of humor prevailed. He laughed until tears ran down his face and a pleased smile stayed on Quinn's face. *Almost as good as sex*, he thought as he reached for her. *Almost.*

In the lull that laughter brings, she snuggled against him. *Comfort, she fills me with comfort I didn't even know I needed.* He wasn't surprised to hear his own small voice say, "My father had another family before us."

She tightened under his arm, but said nothing, and, emboldened, he continued, exposing the secret. "Two children, before I was born. We never knew. He left insurance in a trust for them. I'm the executor, you know. It came out when he died and they needed the money."

Terse sentences, long silences—as though the sin were his own—as he told her of the letter and of his visit to Colorado.

"I asked my mother the other day, but her memory . . . I don't know if she ever knew." He shook his head, bewildered by his father's secret, by himself for revealing it now. "The boy, man, is only seven months my senior, so . . ." His voice trailed off. He still couldn't talk about the brother he'd just met, about the war inside himself for his father's memory.

She stirred. "Do your sisters—"

"No, they don't, and I don't know how to tell them, but I'll have to because the money they were expecting to help with the inn won't be coming."

"Good then that they're doing so well."

"Good then," he agreed.

She lay still, muscles tensed, afraid that any movement would dam the flow, and listened as the man revealed himself to her. He shook his head again, and she understood how hard it was when the parent you loved was really someone different. *He trusts me with his secrets*, she thought, and wondered why this felt so heavy.

"I was married once, you know," he spoke again as though, once allowed, everything must be disclosed, but then he paused, old habits still strong.

"And—" she prompted, secure at his side. She blew over the hairs on his chest and he shuddered.

"We divorced."

The story unfolded in fits and starts like an old car jolting along a bumpy road. *Remembering? Deciding what to tell me?*

"Her name was, is, Mimi, and we got married while we were still in college. She came here to Winnemucca with me after we graduated even though she didn't want to. She was from Southern California and the desert didn't make her happy, but I guess she knew before I did that I couldn't leave, so she tried to make this her home, too. I thought she was doing a pretty good job of it. My mother loved her."

Quinn pictured the young couple having Sunday suppers with the in-laws—*Your pie crust is so flaky, Mother Johnson, please teach me your secret; Yes, Mother Johnson, I'd love to see his baby pictures again*—couldn't quite feel the reality of it. Her hand played up the inside of his leg—*this is real!*—pleased at the reaction it drew. She didn't want to hear any more about Mimi, loved by his mother, making a home with him. She did want to know about Karle, but didn't ask. He watched her hand. His own played with her hair and a small smile hovered on his lips.

"So what happened?" she asked when it seemed he would say no more. Her voice emerged coarser than she intended.

She flushed, dropped her gaze and sat up to get the wine bottle. He didn't reach out to bring her back. The space between them chilled.

"We wanted to have children. I wanted children, and I thought it would help us be more of a family, give her a reason to belong here with me, I guess."

She took a big swallow of the merlot, handed the glass to him. He drank and wiped his mouth with the back of his hand. "She got pregnant right away, but the baby was born early, stillborn. And then there were others. We kept trying, and she kept miscarrying, and finally it all just got too hard."

Over the lump in her throat, Quinn whispered, "I can't give you children."

He thought about the stretch marks on her abdomen as he pulled her toward him then, roughly. He hadn't told her about Mimi's affair that had finally ended the marriage. He didn't tell her how he felt about lying women. The wine glass fell to the side: merlot like blood stains on the hay. Hurt and confused he snarled, "That's not what I want from you." His cruel weight forced her down.

Chapter 26

HAPPY BIRTHDAY AMERICA.

The red, white and blue banner hung catawampus between the old willow and the older apple tree as Quinn secured the last tie. *Deep breath, another, one more.* Quinn squeezed her eyes shut and willed the nausea to pass. *Jitters, just jitters.* She blamed them on the height.

Vivian steadied the old wooden ladder with one hand, shaded her eyes with the other and looked up. "You okay up there?"

"Fine." *Get a grip.*

Perched on the top rung, Quinn opened her eyes and surveyed the cheerful sign. "It's crooked."

"It's fine."

"No, it's not perfect."

"Perfect enough. Come down."

Quinn heard the impatience in Vivian's voice, tweaked the banner one more time and started down just as Victoria shouted, "Music's here," and Vivian abandoned her without a backward glance.

The ladder wobbled. Quinn's stomach lurched. She made her careful way down. Halfway she paused and looked around. Tables and chairs dotted the lawn. Annabelle and Shirley spread red and blue tablecloths and secured their edges with clothespins. Karol set out candles rooted in sand inside pint-sized Mason jars. Victoria stood on the porch, hands on her hips, and watched her sister flutter around tall, skinny Harold Anderson as he set up his sound system. Kristin was nowhere to be seen. Neither was Owen.

The nausea rose. She stepped onto solid ground, didn't feel solid inside. *He's not coming. He doesn't want people to see us together.*

Victoria clapped her hands. "It's noon—time to get cleaned up." She moved across the grass shooing guests toward their rooms.

One more hopeless glance. *Not here.* Quinn trailed the others into the guesthouse.

"It's never looked better." Satisfied, Vivian looked over the grounds of the Wildflower Inn Bed and Breakfast. Even the old American flag, gift from Vicky's Timeless Treasures friend, Cassie, looked lively and cheery as it fluttered in the breeze. Lights sparkled from every tree and bush.

At exactly three o'clock, as the first guests motored up the lane, the opening bars of the "The Star-Spangled Banner" filled the valley and for the rest of the day people arrived and departed to the rousing sounds of "God Bless America" and "Born in the U.S.A." and "This Land is Your Land."

Mostly arrived, thought Vivian as dusk settled over a still-crowded lawn. The fancy tables, now littered with remnants of fried chicken, potato salad and watermelon, stood askew as they tried to conform to the ground. Friends and neighbors clustered, drinking beer and finishing up the food as they waited for dancing music. Annabelle huddled with Vic's best friend, Hazel, and Vivian wondered what they had in common, then smiled as Hazel pulled a quilting book out of her tote bag.

"It's never looked better," Vivian repeated as she watched Shirley serve coffee and Owen's friends devour brownies while their children chased up and down along the fence keeping the geese in an uproar. John and Marsha Mathews and Joan O'Connell and her new husband, Alex, two couples from church who seemed to think they knew something about the subject, monopolized her music man. She wondered if she could rescue him.

"I know," agreed her sister, the practical one, and Vivian started, wondering if her thoughts about Harold were transparent, but Vicky went on, "There's hardly any more work to do."

Vivian shot her a sharp look.

"Well, you know what I mean . . . lots of work, like windows and paint and a new roof but it looks so good and people are so . . . so . . ."

"Happy?" Laughter rose from a group standing under the willow. "Yes, I'd say everybody's happy. Except maybe P and P." The Corgis had long since sought sanctuary in the sitting room upstairs. " Even Mary seemed to enjoy her few minutes in the sun." Quinn's mother had been gently wheeled onto the lawn at three and wheeled back to her sanctuary at three-thirty, smiling at the attention she received. Vivian's expression clouded. "I just wish Scottie were here."

"None of that." Victoria snaked an arm around her sister, shook her gently. "We'll get his letter tomorrow. This will turn out to be a blessing in disguise, just wait and see."

"I know." Vivian wiped her eyes on the back of her hand. "It's just hard, seeing the kids and all." She interrupted herself. "What's Karol doing?"

Their plump blond guest, the heels of her sandals catching in the clumpy grass, wandered without apparent direction. She picked up a paper plate from one table, a handful of plastic utensils from another and deposited them in the black garbage bag she drug behind her. As they watched, she engaged in a tug-of-war with Martha Jones, St. Paul's choir director, who apparently wasn't ready to relinquish her plate. Surrendering, Karol left Mrs. Jones to her fried chicken and continued along her meandering path.

"What *is* she doing?"

As they watched it became obvious. "She's watching her sister."

Karol's movement allowed her to keep Kristin in full view. At the moment the younger woman stood in animated conversation with Martin and three of his friends.

"That's a little weird, don't you think?"

Before Vivian could respond, music blared from the loudspeaker on the porch behind them. "Time to boogie, ladies and gents," called out the tall, skinny man who seemed to have rescued himself.

"Let's go dance," urged Victoria and she pulled her sister into the throng.

QUINN STOOD APART. ILLUMINATED ONLY BY the candles on the tables and the lights dangling haphazardly from the trees, dusk gave the scene an old movie tone. *Picnic*, she identified, the vision of Kim Novak eliciting a secret smile. *It's like the scene from* Picnic. She scanned the crowd, hard to distinguish faces in the deepening night. *So where's my William Holden?*

A sudden burst of laughter, immediately overcome by a Willie Nelson wail, drew her attention, and she saw Owen just as the crowd encircled him. Her heart bumped. A short man she recognized as John Perry thumped him on the back a few times, and then another man, taller and heavier whom she knew was Mike Sakelaris, Owen's "other best friend," draped an arm around Owen's shoulders and turned him toward a redheaded woman whose face she couldn't see. *Karle?* Two little boys wrapped themselves around his legs, and a third tugged his hand, and the quartet stood for a moment in sharp relief against the backdrop of crowd and shadow before the candles flickered Quinn back into reality.

Reluctant to show herself, unsure what reception she might get, she smoothed the silky folds of her second new dress with damp palms and tried to imagine their conversation, the talk of lifelong friends. *I don't belong here, and I don't belong with him.* Even as she doubted, her new red boots, of their own volition, began to circle the crowd.

THE MOVEMENT CAUGHT HIS ATTENTION, AND a smile took over his face as he spotted her circling, leading with her hips, a fancy flowered dress sliding smoothly over her long legs and emphasizing her tall, spare form and the deep cleavage between her breasts.

His breath quickened.

Conversation stilled as his friends followed his gaze.

With only a nod, he left them and strode toward her. At the edge of the crowded field Quinn stopped circling and waited.

"You look good enough to eat," he growled as he reached her side, wrapped an arm around her waist and kissed her full on the mouth. "Let's dance."

She tensed, so briefly he almost missed it, before she relaxed against him and let her mouth soften under his. *What,* he wondered as she returned his kiss, wrapped her arms around his middle. Then he got it. *She thought I wasn't coming.*

He reveled in the thought even as he soothed her. "Sorry I'm late. Some work came in that I needed to finish before my meeting tomorrow. How was supper?" Not really caring about her answer, he drew her onto the makeshift dance floor, nodding at Martin Edwards and a thin, blond woman as they danced past. His arm held her tight against his side as he moved into the line dance. Silent, Quinn matched her steps to his.

"Look."

"Oh, my—" Hand to her mouth, Vivian stared as her brother led Quinn into the dance. The two moved as one. 'They look like they've been . . .'

". . . dancing together forever. They do, don't they?" Not surprised, now that the evidence was before her, Victoria agreed with her sister. "Wonder what the others will think?"

Vivian looked across the field at Owen's friends. John Perry grasped the shoulder of Owen's other best friend, Mike Sakelaris, as the two watched the dancers, and then they turned away, heads together. No one else seemed to notice.

Now THEY'LL KNOW, FLASHED THROUGH HER mind as Owen led her into the dance. Acutely conscious of eyes upon them, she kept her gaze down. *I'm glad I wore these boots,* she thought as he twirled her over the uneven surface. This thought blocked *He'll be sorry,* as the red boots flashed. The new purple dress with its gaudy flowers flowed around her, and only his grasp kept her from floating away.

Dances later, when they were both panting and laughing and Quinn had forgotten their audience, Owen pulled out his handkerchief, wiped her sweaty face and then his own and murmured, "Okay, let's beard the dragons." Palm firm on her back, he steered her toward his friends.

Suddenly the night was cold and the lights glared and the friendliness of the music became the sister chorus screeching: This is bad, this is bad.

Quinn shivered and pulled away. Owen grabbed her hand and pulled her back, and she thought she heard, "You can't escape now," but she wasn't sure. The little group opened to include them.

"You've all met Quinn," he reintroduced her simply. His arm around her, plastering her to his side, made a bigger statement. "I've known these people all my life so don't believe a word they say."

"Uncle O-wen, Uncle O-wen." A little boy tugged at Owen's hand, a determined look on his four-year-old face. "Can I dance with your pretty lady?"

Quinn's hand still prisoner in his own, the honorary uncle went down on one knee, eye to eye with the child. "She sure is a pretty lady, isn't she, Johnnie Perry? You have very good taste. But I think you need to ask her yourself." He pulled Quinn down beside him, and, eyes on his scuffed boots, the boy whispered his request.

Her face shining, Quinn whispered "Yes" and held out her hand. The boy took it and as they walked toward the dancers Quinn felt the group soften. When she came back, conversation didn't abruptly halt and before Owen could reclaim her John Perry grasped her arm and started a stream of Owen

Johnson stories. The others gathered around and tossed in their own embellishments.

Owen finally protested as Mike wound up for the finish of another long-winded and well-received high school tale, "and I passed him the ball, a great pass, if I do say so myself." He paused for a well-practiced hoot from the crowd. "And this one," he punched Owen's shoulder with the hand not holding his Bud Light, "this one twisted in the air like a Houdini and caught the ball with the very tip of his fingers, the most brilliant catch of his career, and then he ran like a madman ninety yards for the touchdown . . . in the wrong direction."

Laughter erupted. Owen moaned. "Enough, enough, my credibility can't take any more."

"Last dance, everyone," Harold Anderson announced.

The rest were already packing up sleeping children as Owen drew Quinn's hand through the crook of his arm and asked, "Saved the last dance for me?"

CHAPTER 27

J ULY FIFTH, THURSDAY. THE TRAIL BOSS with his cowboys
and his string of gentle horses stood ready. In faded Levi's,
a blue plaid shirt with mother of pearl snaps secured all the
way up and a red bandana tied around his neck, Adam Singer,
scion of an old Buena Vista Valley ranching family, appeared
determined to keep the saga of the Old West alive. Tall on his
big shaggy mustang, displaying not even a hint of middle-aged
spread, the cowboy sat his mount easily.

"Howdy, ma'am, we're ready when ya'll are."

He had ridden with them before, and Quinn knew him
as a guide, a hunting scout famous for bringing back game,
and a cowboy poet. He also had a master's degree in literature
which you'd never know from talking to him. He brought new
helpers on each ride, sometimes boys from town like their
Martin, usually college students who loved the land as much
as he did. Quinn knew he treated his horses and his men well,
and she liked his matter-of-fact manner, but more importantly
she trusted that he could handle whatever today might unfold.
If Owen couldn't be here, Adam Singer was the next best thing.

He touched his hat as Quinn introduced her charges and then watched without comment as his trail hands matched the women to their mounts. The horses Adam kept were older, their behavior predictable and steady, and Quinn was almost reassured as she moved among them checking saddles, stirrup lengths and comfort levels.

She ached for Owen's presence as she performed the tasks that usually were his and for answers to her swarming questions. She wanted to know what it meant that he kissed her in public, that he introduced her to his friends.

The sister chorus was emphatic: Nothing. It means nothing. Just the polite thing to do. She hadn't been able to ask him.

"Early flight," he'd explained just before he kissed her hard and long and left her to clean up the party debris and avoid his sisters' questioning looks. "I'll be back Saturday at the latest.

Her restless yearnings had torn her bed apart. She'd waked early from a dream in which she sat at the table in her mother's kitchen, sunlight streaming around her, carefully filling sheet after sheet of binder paper with *Mrs. Owen Johnson, Mrs. Quinn Johnson, Quinn Michele Johnson* in beautiful script.

"Quinn, Quinn, look." Shirley's voice called her back. The most inexperienced of the group, Shirley, a born-again cowgirl in jeans stiff off the shelf and a white shirt piped in red, awkwardly straddled a small wide mare with a graying muzzle. A nod from Adam had posted Don, a Winnemucca boy now a UC Davis pre-vet major, at her side. She posed for Quinn's admiration.

"Looking great, Shirley," Quinn encouraged. "You're gonna love this." Quinn wished for a camera, mentally noted *photographer* on her to-do list.

Eager to be off, the horses fidgeted and filled the air with dust. Karol giggled as her mount lifted its tail and did its morning duty. The men moved among them organizing their charges.

What was I thinking? Quinn swallowed hard, wiped sweaty palms on her Levi's, worried about Kristin and the myriad things that could go wrong and tried to trust her judgment and the cowboys.

The second helper, Bartholomew "just call me Bart" Jones, an Australian also studying at Davis, positioned himself between Karol and Annabelle and, in answer to a question from Karol, launched into a tale of cowboys and kangaroos in the outback. As his heavily accented voice uttered words requiring translations longer than the story itself, no one paid much attention when Kristin, facing her horse's rump, slid her booted foot into the stirrup and swung into the saddle. Quinn watched and realized she didn't even know which leg was fake.

Adam and Quinn jostled for the lead, but she deemed his effort half-hearted as she won the contest easily. Wishing she had eyes in the back of her head, she urged George up the lane. The others fell in behind her. High-pitched squeals and Bart's stories blended with the hum of the bees and the hush of the canyon.

They rode the creek, hiked the trail and saw the eagles fly—all without mishap. On other trips the men had remained with the horses, but today they hiked along in that rolling gait peculiar to cowboys, part product of high-heeled boots and part of long hours in the saddle, exaggerated, Quinn was certain, for the women who watched. Kris' companions hovered. Quinn did not. Adam had dropped back to walk beside the thin woman, flirting outrageously, something Quinn had never seen him do before, and Kris didn't seem to mind.

Over lunch, a mobile feast produced from the back of Martin's yellow cab, they competed to surpass Bart's stories, and Annabelle's whining "But I thought all toads were horny," once again brought down the house. Kris leaned against a rock, the hefty trail boss propped on one elbow at her side, their heads close in quiet conversation. One by one the others fell silent as full bellies and the heat of the afternoon prevailed.

After stowing the remains of their lunch, Quinn announced, "Time to go, ladies," and indicated the cab's open doors.

"Ah, Quinn," drawled Kris in unconscious mimicry, "we'd rather go back the way we came up."

Quinn's protests were overturned so Martin returned scowling and alone. The others, successfully mutinous, began the hike down. Bart taught them his homeland's most famous song, and the rollicking sounds of "Waltzing Matilda" echoed off the canyon walls. By the time the group meandered the last yards to the corral, fell from their horses and staggered to their rooms, even Karol seemed content.

A knock on her door, then Quinn heard Kristin's voice, "Quinn, I know we're supposed to keep silence but could I talk with you for a minute?"

"Sure, Kris, come in." Still wearing trail grime and a wish for a long, hot shower, Quinn grimaced inwardly and opened the door to the younger woman.

Kristin stepped into the room. The denim skirt she wore was straight, tight and short. The prosthesis was no longer hidden. After a quick glance, Quinn kept her eyes on Kris' face.

"Do you want to look at it, Quinn? It's okay. I know Karol told you, even if she wasn't supposed to." She hiked the skirt up higher, displayed the leg. "Quite a contraption, isn't it?"

Quinn gawked. There didn't seem to be anything to say.

Kris explained it then, the connections, the articulations. "It took forever to learn how to use it, but I do pretty well, I think." This time Quinn was the recipient of the impish grin, and she understood why Adam Singer had ignored everyone else.

"Pretty amazing." She recognized the inadequacy of her words, but Kristin accepted them with another smile.

"What I really wanted to say," she continued, "is thank you. Today for the first time in a very long time I felt normal. Thank you."

She slipped out before Quinn could reply.

KRISTIN CAME TO DINNER IN THE same short skirt. The group had congregated on the grass flattened by dancing feet, and the flickering red, white and blue lights recreated last night's party atmosphere. Apparently it was the first time her friends had seen it also, but by the time Quinn joined them the level in the wine decanters was low, and the fussing had died down. Citronella candles fought a losing battle against the mosquito hordes.

Victoria pulled Quinn aside. "Did you know? About the leg, I mean?"

"Uh huh. Karol told me the day they arrived. It was supposed to be secret, so I just decided to see how it went, and she did just fine." Her actions clearly vindicated by the success of the day, she hated the defensive tone that crept into her voice, tried for a lighter note. "Pretty amazing."

The setting sun gleamed red, wreathed in clouds colored by fires raging miles away, the air hot, still, as if the earth held its breath.

"Does Wen know?"

"Owen? No, he hasn't been here all day." Quinn hoped her face wasn't as red as it felt. "Why?"

"I just thought you'd . . ."

Vivian called them to supper and the thought was lost.

Supper over, their satisfied and exhausted guests went off to pack, and Vivian cornered Quinn in the kitchen. "Please stay a few minutes, Quinn. We never get to talk."

They made so few real requests she could hardly refuse, so they sat on the porch and finished the last of the raspberry iced tea while Quinn nursed a very good chardonnay, a thank you gift from Karol and Kristin. The sun had set, but real darkness hadn't descended, and they could see deer nibbling at the garden. The exhilaration of the afternoon faded, leaving Quinn too tired to shoo them away.

"You look tired, Quinn," Vic observed. "Maybe you need a few days off?" Her words begged to be contradicted.

If she noticed, Quinn thought, *I must look as bad as I feel.* "No, I'm fine," she lied. Deserted without a trace by the hormones that had driven her, she sought strength in the crystal glass. The dress she wore, although she didn't expect Owen until Sunday, clung to her sticky skin.

For a time, no one spoke and the night sounds, muted and far away, filled their silence—the snuffle of the browsing deer, the water lapping against the sides of the tin trough as George guzzled, the inspirations of the women beside her, the unruly thumping of her own heart. She wondered what Owen was doing.

When she could no longer stand her thoughts, she said, "Anyway, no guests for a few days—we'll all get a little rest. We probably should space out the retreats a little better." She emptied her glass, refilled it from the bottle at her feet. "So what's up with you two?" So many twin glances had been exchanged she knew they wanted something, hoped they didn't want to talk about her and Owen. She sagged against the hard porch chair and longed for her bed.

"You know we got a letter from Scottie?"

"No." She drew the lie out. Scott's long-awaited letter had

come addressed to his uncle as though, at the last moment, the boy couldn't face them even on paper. "I guess he thought I'd run interference," Owen had muttered, angry when he told her about it Tuesday night, just before he told her about Mimi and the dead babies, before he'd pounded himself into her until she was bruised and empty, before the dance when he'd announced her to his world.

"Well, we want you to read it . . ."

". . . and tell us what your take on the matter is."

"Tonight?" Could her gritty eyes even focus?

"Please." This time it was Victoria's request.

Vivian handed it to her—two neatly typed pages, black and white and crisp as a business letter. Spots that might have been water droplets dotted the otherwise pristine surface.

Quinn held the pages and leaned back in the chair to catch the dim porch light. A mosquito darted toward her neck, hummed away as she waved the letter. She held it to the light.

"'Dear Mother and Aunt Victoria,'" she read aloud.

"He doesn't even say *Momma*. He always calls me *Momma*." Tears clotted Vivian's voice.

"And he always calls me Auntie Vic," added Victoria's peeved voice.

Quinn motioned them to be quiet. At this rate she wouldn't finish by morning, and she couldn't tolerate another sleepless night.

"You were wrong to keep me from Father," the typed words accused. "He is a wonderful man and he has suffered greatly at our separation. Now he wants to make up for all the time we have lost." Several paragraphs repeated this theme; words which Quinn suspected had not arisen in Scott's brain.

"What do you think?"

"It doesn't even sound like Scottie."

Despite interruption and fatigue, she finished the letter, re-reading the last line which seemed to say it all: "You were wrong, Mother, and now I'm going to give Father a chance to know his only son."

"What should we do?"

"I don't think there's much you can do." The hopeful expressions faded and Quinn felt panic rise. *How come I'm supposed to have all the answers?*

"Well, we want him back."

"Can't we call the police, or something?"

"That man—telling him we kept them apart." Vic's anger unfurled, and she paced in and out of the shadows that diagrammed the porch. "I'd like to strangle him." She ran her hands through her hair, paced another length. "He ran so fast we never saw him again." She threw herself into the swing beside her sister. It rocked as though buffeted by ocean waves and its legs pounded an uneven rhythm on the wooden boards. "We should have killed him when we had the chance."

She grabbed the letter and shook it under Quinn's nose. "And look at how he signed this."

Quinn retrieved the paper, smoothed it over her knee. A thin and childish scrawl proclaimed the signer: *Scott J. Harris.*

"He's using that man's name, for God's sake. That's not his name. That never was his name." Victoria shook with the ferocity of her anger.

"And not one word for nineteen years," the mother's voice, fearful for her child. "Nothing at all, and it's not as though he was looking for Scottie."

Victoria collapsed against the pillows, deflated. "Oh, Vivvy, I'm so sorry. I just can't believe this is happening."

Vivian snuggled into the comfort of her sister's hug. Quinn wanted to snuggle in, too.

"Poor Scottie," his mother sighed, "he's being charmed, just like I was."

"Like we both were, you mean."

"I'm so worried I'm beside myself," Vivian declared as they sat side by side, expectant faces toward Quinn, and Quinn stifled a grin and wished Owen were there to share the humor. *He just gets me*, she thought, forgetting for a moment her own worries.

Victoria interrupted her woolgathering. "There must be something we can do."

Quinn spaced her words as though they would be more palatable delivered in slow motion. "There really isn't. Scott's an adult. He is eighteen, isn't he?"

"Nineteen, almost twenty."

"Okay. Right, then. He is legally an adult, and the man is his father. He's offered him a job, and it sounds like he must be successful."

"Investments, his father's company," scoffed Victoria. "They probably just pay to keep him out of the way."

"Whatever. It's work, and he's safe. I know you don't want to hear this, but . . . legally he's a grownup."

They stared at her, waiting for words that wouldn't come. She wanted to shake them both, say *You didn't do anything wrong; your boy will come home*, but she did neither. Her inner walls crumbling, voice harsher than she intended, she continued, "I know it feels like you've lost your child, but he's not lost and he's not dead. Just don't push him away. Stay what you've always been, his loving parents, and he'll find his way home."

Night closed around her as she stumbled off the porch and sought her own bed. She always thought there were no tears left but there always were.

"Is she right, we just have to wait?"

"I think so, Vicky, I think so."

They looked at each other in the dim light, night shadows playing across familiar faces making them difficult to read, even to each other. Vivian sat without moving, absorbing Quinn's words, and relief warred with despair.

Her sister, accustomed to action, shook her head. "There should be something we can do."

Vivian rested against the familiar shoulder. "I think she's right, Vicky, we just have to wait and hope we did a good enough job."

"Wen's right, isn't he? She does have something deep inside, some wisdom . . ."

"Or some pain," finished Vivian. "I wish we really knew what was going on . . . with them, I mean. I feel bad for doubting her, for worrying that Wen will get hurt."

"Me, too," agreed her sister. "But I do wish she had told him about that woman and her leg. He worries about things like that."

CHAPTER 28

QUINN JERKED AWAKE, HOLLOW INSIDE, DREAMS of lost children haunting her. The guests were gone. Owen was gone. *Heavy and dark, heavy and dark.* Her heart thudded in her chest and, seeking escape, she scrambled into her clothes and stumbled to George's side. *Why now,* she wondered. *Why now?*

For the first time in months, she longed for death. Face buried in the coarse black mane, she stroked the mare's silky neck.

"Quinn, are you in there?"

Surprised, she dashed her eyes dry. She hadn't expected him so soon. Her heart beat faster, expectantly.

"In here."

He stood at the door, glowing with the light of importance which she had bestowed, stance wide, hands on his hips, hat pushed rakishly back—Robert Redford in *The Sting*. Her pulse quickened, but the smile forming on her lips retreated at the sound of his voice.

"What in the world were you thinking?"

She didn't know what he meant, each syllable an indecipherable blow. She cringed against the horse's side and held up her hand to distance him.

Eyebrows drawn together over the beak of his nose, eyes narrowed and black, Owen Johnson was hardly recognizable. "How could you do that . . . just let her go? The risk . . . they could have lost everything." His words continued as he strode toward her.

This is what happens, she noted, almost bored with the predictability of it all. *This is what happens when you let your guard down.* Like a punching bag, her body absorbed the staccato blows.

One ear laid back, tail flicking, George shifted. Her solid buttocks bumped the stall and the old building shuddered. Her soft muzzle quizzed Quinn's cheek.

"Shhh, shhh, it's okay," Quinn crooned. Her hands soothed the mare and she drew courage from the touch. *I can't let him take me down.* A strong, firm voice slipped from her lips. "Owen, stop." She didn't recognize it as her own.

He stopped, words midair.

"I have no idea what you are talking about." Each word a milestone, as though only when one was achieved could the next emerge. She released George's reassuring mane and took a step toward the man. "I repeat, I have no i-de-a what you're upset about but," another step forced him back, "but, you can not talk to me like this. Leave. Just leave. Go away. And don't come back until you can be civil."

She walked past him and got to her room before her knees let go and she crumpled to the floor.

HANDS ON HIS HIPS, HAT PUSHED back, Owen Johnson stared as Quinn stalked away, called out *Quinn, wait, I said it all wrong,* but the words were inside, and she didn't stop.

"You can-not-talk-to-me-that-way," she'd said to him, her voice firm and cold, and he'd said something but his words were wrong. He felt like she'd pushed a knife into his chest.

He'd finished his work—the lawsuit settled and his testimony no longer needed—and started home early, every minute away feeling like forever. We'll have to talk about us, he realized, a man more comfortable with numbers than words, and his laughter filled the Audi. *I couldn't help myself. She looked so hot in that dress.* He remembered how she'd pulled her hand from his and hoped she wasn't angry, but she hadn't seemed angry when he'd kissed her until he almost couldn't walk away.

Filled with excitement, the unexpected day with Quinn spinning ahead like a long-awaited treat, he called to let them know he was on his way.

Vivian answered on the second ring and before he could utter a word she poured out the story. "She has a prosthesis, Wen, a fake leg, and she hiked and she rode and . . . and . . ."

"Wait, wait, wait. She who? Who has a prosthesis?"

"A fake leg, Owen. It's the most marvelous contraption, and we couldn't even tell."

"I know what a prosthesis is, Victoria. Who has one?"

"Don't get so touchy, Owen. Kris. Our guest Kristin Amundsen, the skinny blond woman who danced with Martin and his friends at the party, has a prosthesis." Victoria's lips tripped on the word and she repeated it, "prosthesis."

On the extension Vivian joined in. "She was sick and lost her leg and this was her first trip after rehab and . . ."

Accidents, lawsuits, dangers and disasters flipped through his head so fast he couldn't follow them as he struggled to absorb his sister's words. He strained to keep his voice even. "What about Quinn? How did she handle it?"

"Oh, she knew all along. Karol, the sister, told her the day they arrived, and Quinn just waited to see what would happen."

The world dropped away, like the ledge that had failed him. *Quinn . . .* Anger replaced the anguish. *Just waited to see what would happen? Just waited?* The thought of Quinn's complacency drove his foot to the floor and the sleek silver Audi leapt to oblige. *Just waited!* Fear for his sister's well-being was not mitigated by the facts. He'd been taken in by his own lust. *She should have told me. I would never have left. I thought she cared.*

Followed by a cloud of dust, he had raced up the dirt road and screeched to a halt at the corral. *I could just strangle her.* He ignored his aching heart and strode toward the barn.

Now he stood alone, and the red dust settled.

LATE IN THE AFTERNOON QUINN SLIPPED through the kitchen door.

Eyes on the potato she was scrubbing, Victoria didn't look up. "Hi, Quinn, where've you been?"

"Wen was looking for you," added Vivian, glancing up from the carrots she was slicing. "We're having meat loaf and baked potatoes tonight. I know it's too hot but—" Her voice trailed away as Quinn, without a word, picked up the tea things and closed herself into her mother's room.

The twins finished their chores and hovered outside the sunroom door.

QUINN LEANED BACK AGAINST THE SICKROOM door, knees like rubber, hands shaking so hard the tea cups rattled. The harsh sounds of her breathing filled the room. Tears poured down her face.

When they lessened, she looked at her mother. Mary DeMello grew weaker each day. Her time awake grew shorter and her conversations more sparse. What energy remained seemed focused on her tea and her early morning visits with the twins. Now, propped on a pile of lacy pillows and covered by a thin pink blanket, she didn't stir.

"Why? What did I do?"

Mary's breathing didn't change and she didn't answer her daughter's whisper. Quinn could hardly discern the rise and fall of her mother's chest.

I'm here. I come every day. Why should today be an exception? She watched her mother breathe and thought about Mary's afternoon teas: Every day at four, Darjeeling full of sugar and cream and served with biscuits or nuts or bits of fruits and sweets—and Al DeMello had always arrived just in time, the civility of teatime bestowing, in his mind, the status his in-laws thought he lacked. Mary brightened each day at four anticipating his arrival.

Quinn sighed and pushed away from the door, waited a moment for her legs to steady. When she was sure they would support her she moved to the bedside, placed the tray on the Mayo stand and poured her mother's tea.

She knew Mary didn't notice when she poured, when she added two precise teaspoons of sugar and the large splash of organic cream that turned the dark brew a milky brown. Today as all other days Mary DeMello didn't say thank you, just grabbed the delicate cup with her skeletal hands and slurped, the little sounds audible long after the cup was empty.

Quinn sat on her usual chair, chewed her hair and watched. She imagined a conversation that began, "Quinn, why are you here?" and ended "Mommy, I have no place else to be," and in imagination her mother held her and she didn't cry alone.

Owen's voice floated into the silence, full of compassion, "She seems a little cold, your mom."

"Oh, God . . ." Her throat closed with the ache and his hateful morning words replaced compassion and folded smoothly into the corset of pain she wore whenever she lingered in this room.

A sound from the bed caught her attention and she looked at her mother. Mary's violet eyes—"Elizabeth Taylor eyes," her husband had called them—unfocussed like those of a newborn, wandered toward her. Quinn jumped up and removed the cup from Mary's slack grasp. Only the pinpoint morphine pupils seemed alive, the few seconds before they hid in sleep. There would be no holding today.

How can anyone's skin be so muddy? How can I have been so stupid?

She felt the twins' presence outside the door. *What do they want?*

Mary DeMello's snores riffled the air. It seemed too dramatic to long for death in this room so full of it, but she did. Quinn gathered the tea things and stepped out to face more Johnsons.

"Quinn, we need to talk."

The heat of the kitchen and the smell of old coffee slammed her. Sunroom door solid behind her, the twins abreast in front, Quinn balanced the tea tray on her hip and strengthened her resolve. *No weakness. Stare it down.* Tears formed. She forced them back.

"Owen asked us to explain." Vivian's sentence ended in a question mark.

She doesn't know. Quinn lowered her eyes. She knew there was more.

"He couldn't find you this morning and he had a plane to catch so he had to leave."

Defensive. She'll do anything for that shape-shifting brother. Acid burned Quinn's stomach.

"Where were you? He said he looked everywhere."

Quinn knew he had.

Hidden deep beneath her covers, she'd ignored the pounding on her door, watched through the shaded window as he went back to the barn, returned to pound on her door, and then disappeared around the guest house to check the garden. *He'll be sorry when I'm gone,* she wished, knowing he just wanted to berate her further.

Now she ignored his sister's question.

"What did he say?"

"He said to tell you he was sorry for the misunderstanding. He was concerned about the Inn's liability for the Kris woman riding and all. He worries about us too much. You know that. We explained how you knew about her and watched out for her and how successful it had been."

"And he decided that you'd probably done just the right thing . . ."

". . . and he just wanted you to know that."

"I don't know what the big deal is," added Victoria. "Everything is fine, right as rain, isn't it? But he still seemed upset, insisted that we tell you . . ."

". . . as soon as we saw you."

Gazes expectant, they awaited Quinn's explanation.

Bruised, she had none to give. She cleared her throat. "Thanks." The women stood in awkward silence. Quinn sidled around them, set the tea tray on the counter. "I think I'll go settle George."

The screen door banged behind her.

CHAPTER 29

DAYS CAME AND WENT, THE SISTER chorus in full voice dominating her thoughts: You can't ever do it right, do it right, do it right.

They reminded her of the Chantelles or maybe it was the Rondelles, no matter. Her voice—*What makes you think it will ever be different? What else do you deserve?*—joined their refrain. Exhausted, unable to eat, so wired she couldn't sleep, Quinn struggled. Memories of Owen, gentle, tender, passionate in her bed, warred with the memory of his harsh and angry words. *Of course, what did I deserve?*

The sister chorus sang her to sleep.

EACH MORNING, FOR A SLIVER OF time so thin it could be imagined, the world seemed bright—before—but then it blackened and disappeared, and she would rise, sluggish, too tired even to leave. Beyond the porch, in the poplars that lined the creek, the turkey vultures waited.

Owen was gone. Quinn thought she remembered something about a conference, or maybe it was a vacation he'd already scheduled . . . something, but he was gone nonetheless. She told herself she was glad.

Time passed, uneventful, the previously overflowing schedule now yawning empty. From dawn to dusk she harvested. Perched on the rickety ladder, she stripped fruit from tall branches, ignoring Vivian's "That's enough for one day, Quinn," and finally succumbing to Victoria's stern, "It's too dark to see them, Quinn. Get down here, or I'll come up and bring you down." She knew she was being foolish, but couldn't stop.

She picked berries until her arms ran red, their blood or her own she didn't know. Vivian winced as she poured peroxide over the wounds. Tomatoes that weighed down their vines and had to be rescued from the cutworms filled bushel baskets. The hot summer days coalesced.

THE HEAT IN THE KITCHEN HOVERED at ninety—a record for 6:00 a.m. Vivian's sundress, the yellow one with white daisies that she hadn't worn for several years, stuck like paper as she poured the last of the tomatoes into the sterile glass jars. Her sister placed the canning lids and slid the containers of succulent red fruit into the rack in the canner. "I wish Quinn would pick a little slower. If I have to skin one more tomato, I'll have to give up catsup for life."

She grimaced as she tasted her lukewarm iced tea, took a big gulp and made another face.

Victoria tossed her an ice cube. "Here."

She caught it, started to put it in the glass and instead slipped it down the front of her sundress. "Ahh. A sacrifice for the cause. Excellent." She shivered as the ice melted on her overheated skin.

Victoria chuckled, tucked a cube between her own breasts. "She is working like a madwoman."

Through the window Vivian could see the object of their conversation laboring in the garden. She knew that Quinn had already completed her yoga and her meditation, if she was still doing that, and that George, were she to investigate, would be found brushed and fed and content. "She doesn't look much better than her mother right now, does she?"

They both shot glances at the sunroom door, closed to protect their charge. Mary's bell rang a little later each morning.

Victoria set the timer and joined her sister at the window. "She does look pretty ragged, doesn't she? I wonder what's going on. A few days ago she seemed happy as a clam."

"Three weeks ago, you mean." Vivian carried the last basket of tomatoes to the sink. "And where's Wen got to? It seems like a month of Sundays since he was here."

"Right after the party, he was here and we talked about Scott's letter, remember? Do you think he's smoking pot?"

"Owen?"

"No, dummy, Scott. Do you think he's still doing that, or maybe worse?"

Vivian sorted out her sister's pronouns. "I hope not," she said, knowing she referred to Scott's father. "Surely that man outgrew his own habit."

"Maybe." Vic didn't sound so sure. Neither wanted to consider what else their boy could be doing. "I just want him to come home. Maybe we should talk to Quinn about it again."

"Did you talk about the other . . . the past stuff, I mean?"

Victoria shook her head. "No, I never got the chance. After the last retreat she stopped laughing and I didn't want to add insult to injury. Besides, maybe we were wrong, maybe there's nothing going on between her and Wen, or there was and now there's not. A tempest in a teapot."

"Maybe we should do something to lift her spirits."

"What?" Victoria watched Quinn's desultory movements and couldn't think of a thing that would raise her friend's spirits.

"I know. Let's have a birthday party for her mother, get her family here. Mary's birthday is September tenth. She told me yesterday morning, sad-like. She misses the parties and the fussing, I think. There's no retreat until the end of the month, and . . ."

"And a good thing that is, the way things are around here. Vivvy, I'm worried about Quinn, too. I don't think she's doing any of her regular stuff, the yoga and all, and when she plays that flute I just want to cry."

Vivian bobbed her head up and down. "Dirges. It all sounds like dirges." They watched as Quinn hauled another basket of tomatoes to the back step and, with a furtive glance at the house, left it there.

"I know, Vivvy, she's just not herself. She doesn't even come in to talk with us anymore."

"I feel guilty worrying about the retreat when she's so miserable, but I'm afraid we can't do it alone. Maybe it'll do her good to plan the party, to have her family around. They could even stay here if she wanted them to."

"I don't know, Viv. Quinn doesn't seem to get on with her family, at least not like we do. And that mother," they both glanced again at the door, "she's nice as pie to us, but she isn't at all nice to Quinn."

Vivian plunged the last of the tomatoes into the boiling water just as Mary DeMello's silver bell tinkled insistently. Her troubled eyes met her sister's. "Mary's dying and she's still mean to her daughter. Scott's gone. Wennie's MIA. Quinn doesn't laugh any more. Everything feels wrong, Vicky, and I don't like it one little bit."

So my mother will live to see sixty-six, and my whole family is coming to celebrate.

Quinn twisted her hair. *Nothing makes sense any more.* She was astonished when the twins, Vivian mostly, approached her with the idea of a birthday party. She'd been squatting in the garden, contemplating which tomato to kill, and they tempted her to the kitchen with the promise of a cold Corona. Her token protest, "It's not even noon yet," was shushed by Viv's, "it's noon somewhere." They didn't know about the tequila shots that jump-started her mornings.

Vivian pushed Quinn into the chair closest to the fan and overlooked the dirt that clung to her bare feet and the odor Quinn herself could smell emanating from her armpits. Neither commented that she was still wearing yesterday's shorts or that her tank top smelled more like sweat than laundry soap, so she felt obligated to listen to their arguments. Besides, she really wanted the Corona.

"Your mom misses the festivities, Quinn."

Only her hand delivering the sweating bottle to her mouth gave evidence that Quinn was present.

Vivian struggled on. "A celebration would be good for her, just a tiny one because she's not very strong."

Although not appearing as convinced about the idea, Victoria joined in the persuasion. "And your whole family would have a chance to get together."

While Mary's still with it, Quinn thought. *What else aren't they saying?*

In the end it was easier to accept the offer and promise to invite them all than to explain her family and the distances which preserved it. She knew they'd never come anyway.

"Okay. I'll invite them, but I doubt they'll come."

"Just call, Quinn, and we'll see. Use the phone in the parlor."

AS THOUGH SHE COULD BE SEEN through the phone, Quinn had to clean herself up before she called Camille. A quick shower left a pool of grit on the white tiles. She rooted through the agglomeration on her bedroom floor for a tank top that could pass the sniff test and the belt she never wore but now needed to hold up her cutoff Levi's before she felt presentable enough to—*Presentable enough to what, Quinn? To make a stupid phone call? How pathetic!*

Finally, her wet hair piled on top of her head, her skin redolent of lavender, Quinn paced the Johnson's parlor and invited her family, first Camille, and then the rest, and they all said "Yes, what a lovely idea" and "What can we do to help?" By four o'clock, what had begun as a well-intended but far-fetched notion had become a birthday party for her dying mother. It was too much to take in.

Three more Coronas and a tuna sandwich later, Quinn left the twins and made her uneven way through the late afternoon heat to the solace of the barn.

Her sisters having expressed themselves over the phone, their chorus remained silent, and she was left to the jumble of her own thoughts. George's warm neck offered more comfort than garden dirt, and Quinn brushed her and combed her yet again and then she stretched out on the mare's bare back, soaking it in. Dark, quiet, familiar—the barn lulled her, and she drifted.

"Quinn?" Owen's voice. "Vic said you were here."

Horse-whisperer.

"Will you come out and talk with me . . . please?"

A chill permeated her when she slid from George's warm back and stepped away, hoping composure would follow. George flicked her ears.

"Quinn?"

"I'm here." She walked toward the waning light.

As though no time had passed, he stood where he'd confronted her, hat pushed back, chambray shirt with the sleeves rolled up, feet planted as though he needed something to anchor him. Worry lines cut deep into his forehead and twisted the scar, and his open hands reached toward her, palms up.

"Quinn, I'm so sorry for my behavior the other day. I tried and tried to find you, to explain—"

"I know, Owen, I know. The girls told me." She hoped her voice was cold, that it didn't betray her. She struggled to smile. "I understand your concerns, really I do."

The scar returned to its original shape—she was going to be reasonable.

"Just two things though," she continued, and the scar jumped back into its question-mark pose. "No one talks to me that way . . . and," she swallowed hard, "I thought I'd earned your trust."

His face flushed. He shifted from foot to foot, eyes on his boots. "I was wrong, Quinn, and I apologize. What else can I do?"

"Not a thing, Owen, not one single thing." She turned her back on him. "Now if you'll excuse me, I've got work to do."

He watched her strut away, thinner than when he last saw her, shorts riding high, all long legs and attitude.

Sun-streaked hair streamed down her back like a river of gold and caught the rays of the sun in its ripples, but there was no light in her eyes when she looked at him. A giant hand clutched his gut and an unbearable ache filled him.

I really fucked this up big time. Think you're the only one who can handle things and just see where it gets you.

He knew he'd been unfair, that she had earned their trust and that he was the one who'd messed up, but he could explain. Hands clenched into fists so they would behave, wanting only to grab her and shake her until she'd listen, he followed her into the barn.

After one startled look, as though she thought he'd just leave when she had nothing more to say, she continued mucking out a spotless stall. She seemed surprised again when he picked up a shovel and worked beside her in silence until George's stall was cleaner than the day it was constructed.

CHAPTER 30

WHEN SHE WOKE, THE SKY STILL showed more moon than sun. The days of frantic harvest had left her physically exhausted. Requisite apology offered, Owen stayed away. *I feel lighter*, she thought, *with his absence*, no longer bearing the weight of plans, expectations, hidden desires and dashed dreams—simply carrying the day as it unfolded, moment by moment, the empty spot just left of center in her chest the only reminder of her loss.

The relentless sun turned the desert to dust. Occasional storm clouds accumulated like purple dunes. The deer came down every night to drink from a stream now dwindled into mud puddles, and the frogs sang for the rain that didn't come.

Mary DeMello continued breathing, and, in defiance of the heat, plans for her party escalated. The sisters called often, and Cecily scheduled a flight to Reno for September ninth so she could visit an extra day. "If it's okay with you, Quinn," she asked in unexpected deference. They booked her into the freshly-painted Romeo room. Even her mother seemed pleased, although most days it was hard to tell.

"Mary's excited about it, Quinn," reported Vivian, "and she wants her hair done."

In the midst of it all, the retreat scheduled to begin July thirty-first cancelled—a grandmother-granddaughter outing, the granddaughter's first place in the breast stroke had the whole family heading to Texas and the next swim meet.

"It's okay," Vivian sighed, and Victoria just smiled and emailed congratulations before she updated The Wildflower Inn Bed and Breakfast website.

Guilt prodded. Though younger, the twins always seemed older and wiser, and their easy acceptance of the cancellation confused Quinn. *They're afraid they can't do it alone. I must be really slacking.* She worked harder and tried to pay attention when they talked.

Camille faxed pictures of the cake she had ordered, a fancy two layer pink thing with mounds of whipped cream and tiny sparkles. *Gaudy,* Quinn thought. *She'll love it.*

Vivian and Victoria worried over the menu and made separate trips to town, each returning with shopping bags full of party goods and, for Vivian, a party dress in frothy pink stripes to match the cake. Victoria and Quinn watched in surprise as she modeled the pink confection and wondered, privately, where she ever planned to wear it again. Nobody mentioned that it was more than a month until the party. They agreed that no news from Scott was probably good news, and, at Quinn's instigation, began to make bets on the date of his return.

Three sets of guests, couples each, came and went with effusive praise for the food and the accommodations. Both Vic and Viv, separately, suggested to Quinn that she was working too hard.

"There's months of good weather left, Quinn," Victoria counseled. "You don't have to do everything in a day."

Vivian was more specific. "Don't pick any more tomatoes, Quinn. All we'll have is green tomato pickles. Please let some of them ripen."

I get it. I just can't stop. She couldn't explain the feeling. She didn't understand it herself: a restlessness, like ants crawling all over her insides, their tiny ant feet touching, tickling, their tiny mandibles nibbling away, a feeling that was only assuaged when she left something—a place, a job, a man—and moved on. But she couldn't leave, not now with her mother in the sunny room with the windows in the Johnson home. She went to town, and when she returned, truck laden with hay, Owen was there. Together, in silence, they wrestled the bales into the barn.

As though competing with July, August turned up the heat; the reddish-brown dust hovered, and the earth, yearning for water, held its breath. Each day promised rain. The teasing skies grew dark, but the wind that stirred Quinn's hair blew hot and dry.

Holding her sweaty glass to her flushed cheek, Vivian rocked on the porch. "Hottest August I can remember."

"Uh huh . . . even hotter than the year we graduated," Victoria added, and they exchanged their knowing glances, "and that was hot enough."

"What's the news from Scott?" Quinn asked. She showered every day now, and most days could rouse herself to a little conversation. "It must be really hot in New York." Sweat trickled off her nose and she couldn't imagine anything hotter than this porch.

"Air conditioned buildings—"

"One of those really tall ones, the twin ones," added Victoria.

The sisters had never visited New York, professed no desire to do so now. They just wanted their baby home. "I wonder what Owen's been doing. Karle called yesterday looking for him, and I had to tell her I didn't have any idea where he was. I don't think she quite believed me."

"He hasn't been around much lately, has he?" Vivian rolled her glass against her hot skin. "Good thing Martin still needs money." She glanced in Quinn's direction as though awaiting comment, but Quinn had nothing to add. She didn't know where Owen was, the ache that had settled inside familiar, comfortable, permanent.

"We've got all the fans going in the sunroom," Vivian continued when the pause had stretched long enough. "Your mother seems quite comfortable." The information was directed at Quinn, who didn't respond. "Quinn, Vic and I were thinking . . . well, maybe you should, I mean, could, visit her earlier in the day, before chores even. She really is pretty alert then."

A clap of thunder, distant, muted, interrupted Quinn's need to reply, and she wandered off the porch toward the barn. "'Scuse me, gotta reassure George."

ONCE CONJURED UP, OWEN WOULDN'T GO back into the lamp. He filled her thoughts, and her body responded. Levi cut-offs chafed her inner thighs, rubbed her crotch, and her impatient fingers fussed at them without success. The tang of manure mixed with ozone. Edgy as the weather, Quinn moved loose, disjointed, into the coolness of the barn.

The rain started then, harsh and insistent on the metal roof. Loud. She almost didn't hear his voice.

"Quinn, may I join you?"

In spite of the heat, she shivered. A genie, he blended into her fantasy, and the day was too full to hold anger. "Not my barn. Come on in."

His hat was pushed back and trickles of sweat marked his face. "I don't want you to be mad at me. I know I deserve it, but please don't."

He moved closer to her in the semi-darkness and a whiff of Jaipur and sweat caught in her throat. George fidgeted, and her tail flicked a warning. The rain drummed on the metal roof and Quinn couldn't tell if the electricity was in the air or in her skin.

"Just don't yell at me," she whispered.

He nodded. They both knew he hadn't yelled. He brushed a piece of straw off her arm, the closest to human touch she'd felt in weeks. The hollow in her center gaped.

"I've got stuff in the truck," he said. "Help me unload?"

THIRD TIME'S THE CHARM, OWEN REMINDED himself as they unloaded the truck. The routine he'd established had failed: Logic—*I apologized. I tried to explain but she wouldn't listen. There's nothing more I can do*; Work—running his hands over the armoire's polished surface reminded him of her skin, and the newly-applied stain was the honey of her hair; rational thought— *You just need to get over this.* It had been working . . . until today.

Promising rain, the navy and gray cloud-pillows gathered, and their throbbing anticipation drove him from his basement workshop. Dodging the first droplets, he'd loaded up supplies and headed his truck into the storm. His old coach's locker room advice, "What you need is a cold shower, my boy," crossed his mind, but he switched on a country western station and ignored it. Now, humming the Glen Campbell tune stuck in his head, he stood at the bottom of the ladder and stared at those legs that just wouldn't quit. His eyes swept upward to the spot where they disappeared into shorts more fray than fabric, and he set his boot on the first rung.

Third time's the charm.

SHE SENSED HIS EYES ON HER and recognized the tune he hummed under his breath. "Wichita Lineman." She knew the words—*and I need you more than want you, and I want you for all time*—and the hollowness dropped lower, resonated . . .

Betrayed by her body, she drew a shuddering breath and almost lost her footing on a ladder rung frosted with hay dust.

He steadied her, hand firmly on her back, and he sneezed.

"God bless you."

"Thank you." He sneezed again, and they both laughed, a tentative sound hinting . . . something.

Cautious now, Quinn pulled herself up the last two rungs, reached to take the tack he was carrying. Her breasts threatened to escape the sweat-drenched tank top. Good will radiated from the tiny creases around his eyes, good will and something else as he watched her nipples harden, and she backed into the loose hay, her breasts crying *touch me, touch me* so loudly she knew he could hear them. Tiny sounds, scrabbling little feet behind her. She tensed.

"We've disturbed the mice." His lips twitched, and the right eyebrow gesticulated like a Groucho Marx mustache.

She flushed.

He swung himself into the loft, dropped the tack he carried and drew off his gloves.

She scooted away.

He followed until the wall blocked her retreat, squatted in front of her and gently drew his fingers across her lips.

She followed his fingers with her tongue, savoring. The feeling settled like satisfaction deep inside and she didn't want to run any more. "Where have you been?"

"Hiding from you."

Her eyes popped open. *Hiding?* Heat rose in her cheeks.

"Your cheeks are red."

"Hot up here."

He smiled, amusement replaced by a different look. She couldn't turn away. She didn't want to.

Rain thrummed on the metal roof. Shadows filled with the bouquet of summer hay and new leather and the ragged sounds of their breathing. Nothing moved but the fingers that outlined her lips.

Eyes flashed, holding her captive. "Do you have a fantasy?"

Startled. *What a question for now.* "Do you really want to know?"

"I do." His gaze didn't leave her face, and his fingers moved along the line of her jaw.

A fine tremor coursed through and then released, and her words flooded out. "A maiden and pirate fantasy," she blurted in a voice so young it seemed to come from another. "They love each other but don't admit it until he holds her down and, very slowly, convinces her."

Her heart warred with her brain. She remembered all the loveless men who had held her down, or had she held them down, it was hard to know. "I don't mean rape," she struggled to explain, "not demeaning or violent—just . . . convincing."

"How convincing?" He responded to her words but held himself still as though alert to the vulnerability she hadn't meant to expose. The stubble on his chin brushed her cheek when he spoke. "Does he rip off her bodice, tie her wrists, touch her in places she's never been touched?"

She pulled back to see him better, surprise returning her to her original self. "You read those books?"

"Nope, just the covers." His laugh mocked, but his voice remained low—*like gentling a pony*—at odds with the new, hungry look in his black eyes. Sensation swallowed her. A piece of her hair, loose from its scarf, dangled over her eye, and he wrapped his fingers in it, pulled it and, meeting no resistance, drew her toward the vortex. "Do you want to be convinced?

His question dissipated the spell.

Owen didn't wait for an answer. He wrapped his fist in her hair and yanked her close, and his mouth came down hard, devouring her. She strained toward him, hands tugging his zipper. He slid frantic fingers up her thigh, met the resistance of fabric, tore it loose and entered her hard. He tasted her moan as she arched toward him. *Mine*, he thought, as she bucked against his hand, urging him on. *Mine*. He wanted her more than he'd ever wanted a woman and his fingers worked until she shuddered, arched and slumped against him. Mouths still welded, he tasted the soft *ohs* of her first release. Then her hands freed him from his Levi's and he plunged into her, filled her with the wanting and longing of weeks and years, and she met him stroke for stroke as he pumped. When he could delay no longer, he reared back to see her face. Open, her turquoise eyes met his with such desire he could hardly bear it. As he watched, they clouded and he felt her shudder again. He let himself go and they fell together.

CHAPTER 31

ARLY DAWN PEEKED THROUGH HER WINDOW and Quinn could court sleep no longer. Sadness, happiness, despair, euphoria. All night she had ridden these like a swing in a child's playground—Higher! Over the bar! Children's voices coaxing, then the cha-chunk as maximum height is achieved, the heart-stopping cha-chunk that signaled the drop. Love surged on the upswing, then remembrance and the downward plunge so old, so familiar the feelings permeated like dirt on summer knees.

Bruised and sated, she had lain with Owen, her head on his chest, and listened as his heart resumed the slow and solid rhythm of a good bass. In its safety she dozed and then roused to his hands and his mouth. No words passed between them; it was as though they could trust only their bodies to resume their connection. No stars shone when he half-walked, half-carried her to her bedroom door.

Now sundered, the solitary half of a Mizpah heart, she crawled from her bed. In the barn, George offered no solace, nor did the garden, although George nickered and accepted her ministrations and the dark earth offered its musty morning blessing.

He loves me; he loves me not. Her body ached.

The trees around her, green and lush, whispered in the freshening wind, the sweet smell of rain-washed foliage already surrendering to the seductive promise of another storm. On her knees, hands deep in the dirt, Quinn bent double to cushion her heart, and she heard the stirrings of her mother's morning.

All at once like a demanding child she wanted her mother. A sob wracked her. By the time she stood in the sunroom doorway tears etched her cheeks and snot ran from her nose. Just before she burst into the room, *Mommy, Mommy* on her lips, Quinn heard her mother's quivery voice and a twin's murmur in reply.

Mary DeMello must have sensed movement at her door. She hesitated, and her alert morning eyes gazed into Quinn's watery ones—a long, deliberate gaze, flat and cold—then without expression she looked away from her daughter and resumed her story. "So, you see, Quinn killed her baby."

It was the conversational tone that was so damning. In those words, in the glint of her mother's eyes, Quinn read the truth and she wondered at her own blindness—*my mother will never love me and I will never be clean.* Hollow, she drifted onto the porch, surprised when the screen banged behind her. She didn't wait for the rest of the story—for the gasps from her mother's audience—she knew it all by heart.

CHAPTER 32

n his RENO OFFICE, OWEN DRUMMED an impatient rhythm on his desktop as he waited for the client he wished he'd never scheduled. *God, I didn't want to leave her.* He felt the familiar pull in his groin. *Addicted, I'm addicted to that woman.*

It was like coming home when his mouth claimed hers and she moved against him like she belonged there, her hands as busy as his. He wanted her, wanted to be inside her so she could never leave him, and he'd pumped all his love and relief into her until they lay sweaty and panting on the dusty hay. When he looked into her eyes, he was truly lost, and taking her with him into release had been the best journey of his life.

His heart felt sundered when he left her, rumpled and sexy, but the work he'd scheduled had to be done. He forced his attention to the papers on his desk. *One more appointment and then—*

Tonight. Tonight we'll talk and I'll tell her how I feel and we'll make plans. Vivian had warned him that Quinn had issues, but then, who didn't? *She loves me. I know she loves me. She hasn't run away, has she?* His imagination placed Quinn in his kitchen, his bed. He squirmed and adjusted his crotch. *I can take care of her and she won't have to run any more. My runaway.*

A knock interrupted his reverie. Patrick Alexander, friend and office mate, stuck his head in the door. "Owen, thought you were still here. Today's your last day for a while, right?"

"Right. I'll do the rest from home."

"And take a few days for R&R?"

Owen grinned. "Do I look like I need 'em?"

With the candor of old friendship, Pat responded, "Well, now that you ask, you have been looking a little ragged lately. I didn't want to say anything but, well, is everything all right?"

"A little rocky for a while but, as my sisters would say, right as rain now. And two weeks off will take care of everything."

"How are the girls, anyway?"

Owen filled him in on the Inn's remarkable progress and Scott's defection, left out any mention of Quinn. To Patrick Alexander, old friend or not, she was just "my sisters' employee." He didn't want to talk about Quinn just then.

A raised eyebrow warned him that his ruse hadn't been completely successful. "Well, I hope things are okay." The outer door opened, interrupting anything Pat might have added. He turned to greet Owen's client. "Hello, Mr. Anderson, come on in." Stepping away from the door, he touched his forehead toward Owen in salute, "Have fun and be careful."

CHAPTER 33

EORGE WHINNIED SOFTLY AS THE WOMAN moved toward her, Quinn—an empty hull—surprised that the little mare recognized her. Her hands worked without direction, the rough blanket, her own worn saddle, Owen's saddlebags found their way to George's back. She mounted, surprised again when the saddle creaked. She felt weightless, dried like prairie grass. The mare flicked her tail and found her own way toward the hills.

Hypnotic: George's steady pace; pungent sage; expectant, waiting earth; the smell of rain. It seemed only minutes before the horse stopped and put her head down to drink, pulling the reins and bringing Quinn alert. Full from yesterday's rain, the creek bubbled underfoot and the sun directly overhead proclaimed midday. She dismounted, rinsed away sweat and tears and waited for George to drink her fill. The shell that she'd become demanded neither food nor drink.

Beside the creek, five wildflowers, survivors of the summer heat, sprang together from a granite boulder, compact, their tiny bluebell faces turned to the sun. A tight unit, a family at home in their bigger world, they swayed gently in the dusty breeze. Quinn saw and her chest tightened.

With more purpose, she swung back into the saddle and nudged George away from the stream, higher into the hills. The leather rubbed her bare thighs and the wooden stirrup worked a blister on her left ankle, but she felt nothing.

A lazy jet stream, reminder of the world that belonged to others, meandered through the pale blue sky. As woman and horse ascended, the sounds of thunder grew louder and the sky darkened, lowered. Ozone oozed. Lightning gyrated against the gray-black clouds. It was her own death Quinn sought, not George's and she urged the horse toward shelter in the rocky cliff above.

The earth paused.

George plodded upward. Darkness gobbled up the sky. Hunched, saddle horn pressed into her belly, Quinn encouraged the mare on. Like a schoolyard bully, the wind twisted her hair and threw dirt in her eyes. Lightning bolts hurled themselves at the earth; the sky roared in protest; leaves quivered at the harsh touch of the wind.

Across the ravine the tip of a tall pine exploded and the sweet, sharp smell of burning wood and boiling sap filled the air. Quinn didn't need to count the distance. Thunder boomed with the lightning strike. George trembled, her step faltered, and Quinn slid from her back and led the little mare toward shelter.

Tucked under a rocky roof, Quinn wiped George down as best she could and, from habit, began to set up camp. She ignored a stab of guilt as she removed the saddle and the blanket, exposing the mare to wind and rain, but George nibbled contentedly on a green stem growing out of the rocks so Quinn positioned blanket and saddle into a trail bed. She had no idea of time, after noon surely—she remembered the sun on her head as they stopped for water—perhaps five or six, maybe months or years later than this morning. Ignoring the fact of her demise, her stomach rumbled in protest.

Water, food—Quinn dropped to her knees and dug into the saddlebags, resisting the urge to fondle the warm old leather and soak up the last bit of Owen's touch. Her exploring hand touched metal—the gun. Her fingers closed around its handle and hunger vanished as she sank down onto the blanket and slid the revolver from its leather.

Lightning struck so close the air vibrated. George spooked, but Quinn didn't flinch. She held the gun tightly as the tidy boxes in her mind, released by her mother's words, shook themselves free of their restraints and tumbled their contents out, willy-nilly. She imagined them filling the crevices of her brain, felt them as they multiplied and spread until there was no room for thought, breath, even for her heart to beat. She felt dead but for the noise in her head.

Her hands moved into the bag and located five shells. She heard her father's voice —*Once more, Quinn, take it apart, put it together. You have to know your tools*—and sensed her eager young hands struggling to hold the heavy piece, over and over until she knew it as well as she knew her flute. She wondered what he'd think now, scrunched her eyes to see him, but there was only darkness so she loaded the gun, sliding the shells in one at a time until all five were in place. Then, cross-legged, she rocked back and forth and let memories of her daughter fill her.

She's here—Samantha, my sunny girl—here like I feel her in the morning when the day is new and all things are still possible; Samantha, Sam—my golden girl.

She cradled the gun against her breasts.

The baby's bassinet stood beside Quinn's twin bed in the basement apartment they had shared. Just a single room smelling of mold and Clorox and something dead, but sunlight streamed through the watery glass panes and created the rainbows of light in which they rocked. The teen mother dressed her daughter in tiny soft things from St. Vincent's Thrift Store on Fourth Street. She wanted everyone to know how perfect Samantha was, but no one ever came. Ten days after Samantha's birth, her teen father filed for divorce.

With memory comes emotion, charged with all the intensity of its original existence. *I remember*—in this stormy mountain theater, Samantha's life played like a motion picture and Quinn gasped as the feelings swept her.

Samantha gurgled and wrapped her dimpled baby hand around her mother's little finger and they rocked in the sunshine among the dust motes; Samantha burped and squeaked and her mouth was exotic with a sweet milky perfume as her mother wiped away the spit-up and nuzzled the folds of her neck; Samantha cried, inconsolable against her mother's full and tender breasts; Samantha lay diminished in her bassinet while strangers invaded her body and Quinn willed her to breathe and milk drenched the front of her flowered pink pajamas.

Breathe, baby, breathe—only three months to remember.

The scent of wet horse rose from the saddle blanket as Quinn rocked back and forth, pain and sorrow passing her lips like the ululations of mourning Arab mothers. *Too much . . . this is too much. I don't want to remember. I don't want to forget.* She felt the phantom pull of the baby's lips at her nipples and the ache burrowed deeper inside. She felt her uterus twitch and her breasts fill and threaten to leak so she held the gun tight against her belly and doubled over it, forcing it into the hollow left behind.

"You're young. You'll have more children," they told her, but she knew they were wrong.

My mother's right. I killed my baby.

IN RENO, THE OFFICE TELEPHONE RANG just as Owen picked up his briefcase. *Leave it, Johnson, you're late.* The client meeting had taken longer than expected. His own preoccupation made focus difficult and each detail seemed to take forever. Annoyed at his behavior, desperate to be at Quinn's side, Owen slung his jacket over his arm and took a step toward the door. *Just one more step.* The ringing persisted. *Oh, shit.* Conscience prevailing, he stepped back to his desk, snatched up the receiver and held it to his ear.

"Johnson here."

"Wennie, Wennie, come home." Vivian's voice was garbled and he could tell she was crying. His heart clutched. *Vicky? Scott? Mother?*

"Mother? Is Mother all right?"

Victoria took over. "Mother's fine. Honey, it's Quinn."

He sat down hard.

"Quinn's gone. She rode Girl George into the hills and there's a thunderstorm and—"

He let out the breath he'd been holding, not sure why this was a crisis. "She goes riding all the time, Vic. What . . ."

In a cold voice, his sister recounted the early morning scene. "And she saddled George but she didn't get any food from the kitchen and didn't say a word to either of us." Victoria drew a deep breath. "Owen, honey, you should have seen her face when her mother said those horrible words."

Stunned silent, he clutched the phone.

"Wen, are you there?" She didn't wait for a reply. "You've got to come home. We think she might be going to . . . hurt herself."

No time for questions. "Vic, call John and tell him I need Trigger. I'm leaving now." He hung up without waiting for her answer.

THE CLOUDS MERGED INTO A DARK stage curtain and the lightning retreated, taking the thunder with it. A tiny flicker of light marked the passage of a distant vehicle. Everything was hidden. Samantha was gone. The light in Quinn, the spark ignited in those morning moments, faded. Emptiness—permanent, unremitting emptiness—remained.

The gun invited her, cold metal salvation in the palm of her hand. She raised it, thumbed the hammer back, stared at it for a while and then held it to her head, the circle of steel icy against her temple. When her hand cramped from the weight she released the hammer and lowered the pistol to her lap, wiggled her fingers and rubbed out the cramp. Then, right hand resolute, raised it once again. Her index finger, flexed and active, curled around the trigger. *Just focus and squeeze.* The first shot is always noisiest, foreign to the ears, mostly felt rather than heard. There would not be a second. When her arm began to shake, she moved her finger and changed position. Elbows resting on her knees, she put the steel in her mouth, then took it out and pointed it at her empty chest.

The cold came over her then, like freezing to death must feel, peaceful and detached, and the world drifted away. Quinn and Owen's gun kept company in the dark.

JOHN HAD TRIGGER SADDLED AND READY when Owen reached the inn. A second horse stood saddled nearby. "Do you need me?"

"No, I can do this." A quick change to boots and Levi's and Owen swung onto the big horse. He settled his hat firmly and grasped the reins. "Thanks. I'll let you know if I need help."

John didn't mention the danger and futility of a nighttime search, just nodded and released his hold on Trigger's bridle.

Man and horse surged into the storm.

THE SKY WOKE, STRETCHED ITS PINK arms. Slumped sideways against a boulder, Quinn came awake slowly. Sometime in the night she had lowered the pistol to her lap, and her meditative hands clutched it still. She looked at it in wonder as the events of the night revealed themselves to her. She straightened, moving like someone very old. She forced her grip to loosen, released the hammer and set the safety. The place in her brain that had held the wish for death, the *I can't do this anymore* place, was empty. She could imagine it, see it in her mind's eye and remember it vaguely like a story long told, but she could no longer feel it. Empty, an egg from which the chick has flown. She mourned the loss.

Suffused with the smell of morning, fresh and new, dew sparkled in the green sage, and the thump of a woodpecker searching for breakfast marked distant time. The sister chorus was gone, too, leaving only Quinn. A riff of cool air and the rye grass trembled. At the horizon a ripple of white highway described humanity.

Impatient, George nudged her shoulder. Quinn searched one last time but death was gone, so she removed each bullet and returned the pistol to its holster. In moments, George was saddled and they headed home.

EYES BLOODSHOT, DARK STUBBLE ON HIS cheeks, sodden hat pulled tight on his head, Owen met them at the mouth of the canyon. *He looks worse than I feel*, Quinn thought, heart beating faster at the sight. Trigger circled once and settled in beside George. Owen's knee knocked against Quinn's own. A brief searching look took in her matted hair, streaked face, dirty hands and his saddlebags.

"Welcome back," he said, and nothing more.

As they neared the house, Quinn saw her mother's Lincoln nose-to-tail with Angelica. Her eyes questioned him.

He shrugged. "Viv must've called them."

Death would be welcome. Not only pain—now guilt and embarrassment, too. *What else do I deserve?*

He read her face. "Shall I send them away?"

Quinn wanted to say yes, to crawl into her own bed and stay forever. She shook her head. "No, I'll have to face them sooner or later."

They stopped at the guest house. Owen reached for George's bridle. "Go clean up. I'll feed George," he tipped his head toward the house, "and tell them you're okay. Come over when you're ready."

That'll be never. Quinn searched his face and saw only encouragement and fatigue so she nodded assent, slid from the saddle and disappeared into her room. Inside, the air, wet and heavy like her Grandmother's laundry on sheet-washing day, pressed her down. Resolute, she resisted, stripped away the grimy top and the wet and smelly cut-offs and stepped into the shower. *Time to scrub up and get on with it.*

They were laughing at something Owen had said when she entered the house. Yesterday's rain left wet heat behind and the big fans hummed—the only sound that remained as they all looked at her.

Camille recovered first. "Quinn, how could . . ." but Owen's "Here's our adventure girl now," cut her off. He handed Quinn a frosty glass, "Raspberry tea, your favorite," and grinned at her. Hair combed, clean-shaven and wearing a neatly pressed denim shirt—Quinn hoped she looked half as normal.

"I was just telling the ladies," his glance took in the gaggle of sisters now staring at them, "how lucky you were to find good shelter last night. It's a real challenge when you get stuck out in a thunderstorm." His arm snaked around Quinn's shoulders and he squeezed just a little. "We've created a real country girl here, I think."

He stepped away when Camille reached out to hug her sister. "Quinn, I'm sorry. I didn't realize . . ."

"I know," Quinn responded, trying not to wiggle out of her grasp, "you thought I was running away."

"Cecily said you weren't," offered Caroline, "but we didn't believe her."

"Cec is here?"

"I am, sister mine." Wiping her hands on a tea towel, Cecily emerged from the kitchen. "It's just like you to have an adventure and leave the rest of us out." She and Owen exchanged glances.

The knot in Quinn's stomach loosened.

Vivian said, "Let's eat," as though she'd planned all week for this party, and the bad moment passed. No one mentioned Mary.

SKIRTING THE PUDDLES, CECILY AND QUINN walked down the lane. Lunch was done. The other sisters were cleaning up and Owen was returning to town. Gray clouds still hovered, now interspersed with patches of pale blue sky.

"Storm's over, I think." Anything to break the silence.

"Too many sisters, I think," responded Cecily as they watched Owen's Audi disappear. "He's a nice man." She pushed up her cashmere sleeve, tucked her hand in the curve of Quinn's arm and leaned against her side. "It wasn't your fault, you know."

"Huh?" Quinn wasn't sure which *it* her sister referred to, but she knew it was her fault that Samantha had died. Who else?

"Ever wonder why none of us has kids? Besides Samantha, I mean."

In the middle of the road, Quinn gaped at her sister. No one in the family ever uttered her daughter's name.

Cecily tugged her, and they resumed their walk. "I think it's because of mother and dad—their marriage was so closed, so private."

"I know—like a house with only one room."

Cecily pondered this new idea. "That's it exactly. We weren't abused, or even abandoned. There just wasn't room for us."

"I thought it was just me."

"Oh, no. Camille and I have talked about this—it's all of us, even John Paul, though he doesn't stop drinking long enough to realize it."

Quinn felt close to her sister in that moment. "Cec, about last night—"

Cecily stepped back to see Quinn's face, reached up to place gentle fingers across her sister's lips. "Shhh, it's all right."

"No, I need to tell you. There are too many secrets."

Brown eyes met Quinn's wet blue ones. "I know you wanted to die."

"I don't anymore."

Cecily's eyes searched her sister's face and her own countenance softened. *I guess she believes what she sees,* Quinn thought, and the tension inside burst and flowed away when Cecily reached for her hand. "I know," Cecily said, "I know."

OWEN CAME TO HER AT TWILIGHT, wine bottle in hand. Only the middle of August, the days had shortened and darkness covered the hills. Lights glowed in the main house. Quinn could see his sisters cleaning up the remnants of their impromptu feast. Her sisters were gone, and, for the first time she could remember, Quinn felt sad when the Lincoln glided away. The smoky vestige of several lightning strikes hovered in the air, and through it she smelled fall. Her eyes were on the sky when she heard a door slam and she turned to watch him approach. Angelica the Auto and the old Toyota stood side by side at her gate.

He took in the small juice glasses standing ready on the porch rail. "Expecting me," he asked at the same time she curled her lip and said, "Raspberry iced tea, my favorite?"

Their answers crossed in the air. "I was," she said.

"I didn't think tequila shooters would be quite the thing at the moment," he said.

They both laughed. Awkwardness dissipated.

He poured blackberry wine, handed Quinn a glass. His fingers brushed hers and the familiar tingle coursed through her. From the porch they could see the remaining bits of sunset. He hitched his hip onto the top rail. "Do you want to tell me about it?"

"It?"

"Your daughter. And running away, too, if you want."

Silence sat gently between them. He sipped the wine and waited while she considered. Did she want to tell him, to talk about Samantha? Now that the opportunity was before her, she hesitated, as though talking might somehow diminish it.

"What did they tell you?" Her eyes burned with unshed tears, the hollow place inside scoured raw, ready to bleed forever.

He concentrated on the purple liquid in his glass. "That your mother is confused and not nice to you," he said, "and that your daughter died of SIDS, that you changed—"

"It never goes away." Her voice thickened.

He waited.

"She was my sunshine girl, and it was just the two of us." She cleared her throat, focused on the darkening sky, and regained her voice. In the distance, the owl hooted twice, twice more. "I suppose they told you I had to get married, that my pseudo-boyfriend, Parker, was a big basketball star, that he couldn't even file his own divorce papers. Did they tell you he never even saw his own daughter?"

Bitterness oozed through the tears. "And neither did my mother."

As though her legs refused to hold her, she slid down and hit the wooden planks hard, tears and mucous mingling faster than the back of her hand could wipe them away. She had forgotten that part.

Owen stepped inside, returned in a minute with a box of tissues. "Here." He squatted beside her, not quite touching, and handed her a tissue.

"I thought I'd run out of snot someday," she mumbled, "but I guess not."

He just waited, sipped his wine and handed her tissues.

"The first year I don't remember—only the dark, and that I got up each day. They tell me I started taking classes, but everything was minute by minute, and I really don't remember."

She blew her nose, a honking, untidy sound, and the laugh they shared was tentative, the thought of death perched between them. Nervy, Quinn sipped her wine, inhaled it instead and choked, coughed, hacked until she finally caught her breath and blew her nose again.

"I hate it when I do that." The tickle in her throat persisted, mingled with the tears.

He nodded, waited.

"I would wake each morning and for a split second the day would be fresh and clean and full of promise. But before I could even smile I would remember, and the permanence, the awful unremitting permanence of it, would wash over me and the lights would go out and I would get up to plod through another day because there wasn't anything else I could do."

She blinked away new tears, held out her glass for a refill. "They buried her in a little tiny box. It was yellow inside, and she wore her fuzzy yellow jammies. My mother was sick that day but the others came—Camille and Claudia and Caroline and Cecily. Even John Paul was there and he was only five."

"Your father?"

"And my father. My father held me up. He walked me when I couldn't walk myself, then took me home and put me to bed."

Owen's gaze held a question.

"Home to their house until they could ship me off to my grandparents. I never saw that apartment again. I never saw Samantha's tiny little clothes, or her brush, or . . ." Her voice stuck, cleared. "I never ever smelled her smell." A sob filled her throat and there were no more words.

OWEN TOSSED THE EMPTY TISSUE BOX in the garbage and found a new one in the Romeo room, then returned to the porch and divided the last of the blackberry wine. The curtain of night dropped over them. He didn't know what he'd expected when he came to her, maybe excuses that would release him, certainly not this. *I can't bear this,* he thought, remembering his own mother holding his stillborn child and his own father holding him as they cried together. He settled back onto the hard planks. His body aligned itself with Quinn's and he kept handing out tissues.

Finally she continued, "Sometimes just for a second, like when I'm having sex, I forget. I think she's there, in the next room, and any minute she'll chirp her morning song and I'll peek in and she'll be smiling. Then I remember . . ." The whispered words trembled in the night. "You want to escape but you don't because you have to remember. You have to make yourself remember, every day . . ."

He whispered, too. "Remember what?"

"That she's dead. That she was alive." Pain shimmered in the turquoise eyes. He sensed she'd never said these words before. "If I don't remember, then she'll truly be gone."

I know all about remembering, he thought, sitting still beside her, his arm firmly against hers, the length of his leg against her thigh. The owl hooted again, twice, and, like a ghost, disappeared into the trees. His hands were quiet in his lap as he stared into the night.

"AFTER A WHILE THE SUN REMEMBERED to shine."

Quinn thought about the day she awakened, not that she wanted to. Who could live with so much hurt and so much guilt? "It never goes away. You just get used to it so you don't notice it as much. And you think about ways to escape."

She didn't tell him about the mornings she woke stinking of alcohol or sex or about the jobs she left or the towns she abandoned or the pills she'd hoarded until that day at Cecily's. She looked directly at the man beside her and saw thoughts of the gun glinting in his eyes. He said nothing.

Later, he asked if he could stay. They undressed in silence, and he held her while she slept.

CHAPTER 34

HOT DAYS, COOLER NIGHTS. OWEN OFFERED no explanation but he parked at her gate every night. His sisters said nothing about his continued presence. *It will be very hard to leave this place,* Quinn thought as she watched the man sleep, as she resumed her morning routine, as the frantic nature of her morning chores faded and pleasure gradually returned.

No one mentioned that day. Her mother slumbered gently in the sunroom.

She often felt Owen's eyes on her when he thought she was sleeping. *What isn't he saying?* The candor of her seduction had been replaced by a wariness glimpsed just before he hooded his eyes. *What does he want?*

"What?" she would question, and then his gaze would be full on her, holding only tenderness and mischief. His mouth would silence hers and she'd be sure she was mistaken. They rode, they hiked, they danced on Saturdays at the Winnemucca Hotel and he slept at her side each night. *Maybe this is where I'm meant to be. Maybe he can—* She didn't know quite what she wanted him to do, but even as he lay beside her with his arm heavy across her breasts, and his life became more precious than her own, a part of her waited, waited for the familiar internal scurry that would signal: Time to run.

Halcyon days. She knew they couldn't last.

THE HEAT PERSISTED. LETHARGY WINNING THE war against evening chores, Vivian, Victoria and Quinn sprawled around the dinner table. Her half-eaten meal ignored, Quinn refilled glasses and added ice. In a familiar gesture, Victoria rolled her sweaty tea glass over her forehead and looked at a spot in the distance. Then, as though coming to a difficult decision, she straightened, set the glass on the table and looked at Quinn.

"Quinn."

Quinn looked up.

"Tell us about Samantha."

The room filled with the sharp intake of Vivian's breath.

Quinn blinked but didn't bolt.

Vivian reached for her sister's hand. "Please, Quinn. We'd like to know her."

Once started, Quinn couldn't stop. Samantha, Samantha—syllables as sweet as spring rain, as bold as the tree frogs' song, as soothing as the wind whispering through new leaves. For only the second time since her death, Quinn told her daughter's story.

The room was dark and silent when she finished. Victoria kept her back to the table as she stood to turn on the lights. Vivian wiped her eyes. "Do you have a picture?"

"Oh, yes," echoed Victoria, "can we see her?"

Quinn dashed from the room. In her bedroom she pushed aside the half-empty bottle of tequila and the long-ignored vibrator, grabbed the pink wallet and returned to the kitchen at a dead run.

"Here."

She pulled the picture—folded and unfolded until white creases ran through it and gave it the appearance of marble—from its hiding place between her Social Security card and her driver's license. "I took her on the bus to Penney's. We didn't have a car, you know, but there was this ad in the paper, a sale on baby pictures, a plan-ahead-for-Mother's Day kind of sale. It was the only trip we ever took."

As she explained, Quinn worked at the smudges with her shirt tail until Vivian plucked the picture from her fingers. "It's just fingerprints, Quinn. We can see her." She held the photo to the light. An anonymous baby face stared back at her, round and serious, with intense blue eyes that looked straight into the camera as though they hadn't yet learned to hide.

The three women considered the faded photo.

"What a pretty girl. She looks just like you." Vivian held the photo near Quinn's face for comparison.

"What about her father?" Victoria said.

Quinn bristled, but then she commanded her hands to loosen and her jaw to unclench. If Vivian couldn't ask about Parker, who could? She made a face.

"He was a basketball star, older than me, taller than me, and he was the first guy that ever paid me any attention. Not as pretty as your pretty boy, but I thought he was wonderful. For seventeen, I was amazingly stupid, and alcohol and sex were out of my league." *Then.*

She shrugged.

She didn't tell about Christmas Day—the day Parker brought leftovers from his parents' table and a bottle of wine with a screw-on top, then left to party with his friends; the day she sat in the dingy apartment, fat and alone, until she swallowed the little bit of pride remaining and begged Parker to return only to hear "Stupid cow" and the laughter of his friends; the day she turned to the wine bottle to blot out the pain. Sam was born two days later.

"Later on I was just pathetic."

The twins exchanged glances.

"I know, I know. It sounds pretty familiar, doesn't it?"

They shared a rueful laugh. Victoria held Samantha's picture. "Why don't you frame this, Quinn, so she's part of the family?"

"Yes, Quinn, do." Vivian turned to Quinn. "I've got a pretty silver frame that should fit perfectly."

Quinn wondered what they were thinking but didn't ask. No one mentioned her mother's words. Mary DeMello slumbered in the sunroom.

"SHE LOOKS LIKE YOU," OWEN ANNOUNCED after studying the baby face for a very long time.

"She's cuter."

He didn't argue. He knew every inch of this woman, from her soft blond hair to the deformed toenail on her right big toe, consequence of an unlucky encounter with a forbidden nail gun.

"After my toe healed," she'd told him, laughing, "my father beat me with his belt for touching his tools without permission. My mother just said I got what I deserved. It's kind of funny now, but it sure wasn't funny then."

He knew every inch of her, and he loved her, but he still didn't understand why she thought so little of herself. He listened and he wondered and he held her gently until she jumped out of bed, eyes flashing, and hissed, "I'm out of here, Owen Johnson, until you treat me like a woman and not some fucking piece-of-glass princess."

He got to her faster than she'd expected, scooped her up and carried her, arms and legs flailing, across the lane and into the barn. She scratched two deep gouges down his left side before he dumped her in the hay and threatened to tie her down with George's halter. Breathing hard, a glint in her eyes, she knelt and held out her wrists for the leather.

He took her there in the hay, quick and rough, and the intensity of their climax frightened him.

We need to talk. The old Toyota rumbled toward the Wildflower Inn Bed and Breakfast. *I need to tell her that I love her, that I want her to stay.* He rubbed at his gritty eyes. This double life was wearing him down, but Quinn's eyes still wore a haunted look and most nights she cried in her sleep. He was afraid a wrong word from him would send her scurrying away.

Earlier in the evening, over barbeque and coleslaw at the annual fundraising dinner for the Boys and Girls Club, his friends had double-teamed him.

"None of our business, man, but what are you doing? She's gorgeous and all that but—" John Perry, married forever, began the interrogation. Laughter from an adjoining table drowned out whatever else he said, but John wasn't laughing.

"Hey, guys, lighten up," Owen protested, trying to ignore the sensations that thoughts of Quinn aroused. "It's not just sex."

"Then what is it?" Mike Sakelaris interrupted. "What John means is . . . what I mean is, have you asked her to marry you? And if you haven't, why not? You know that's what you want. I mean, it's what you've always wanted, isn't it?"

Mike and John exchanged glances, both men clearly thinking about Mimi, about Karle, about their own wives even now exploring the silent auction table at the front of the auditorium.

John washed a mouthful of ribs down with a swallow of beer, swiped his foamy mouth with a shirt sleeve. "I mean, where is she right now? Mary and Patti are here spending our hard-earned money." He took another gulp of beer, punctuated his words with the mug in his hand. "Where's Quinn right now?"

Owen looked at the table. "I invited her, but there's a retreat at the Inn and . . ."

Mike interrupted again, "Ahh, Owen, she's probably a really nice woman. Hell, you wouldn't fall for her if she wasn't. It's just that . . . well, she doesn't seem quite like a Winnemucca girl."

He knew they were worried about him. They always worried about him; even sent him to a psychiatrist after Mimi left. He smiled as he remembered the businesslike woman behind the desk in the office on Ryland Street saying, "You don't need a psychiatrist, Mr. Johnson, you just need to grieve and get on with your life." *And isn't that what I'm trying to do?*

The old truck pulled up beside the little yellow Volkswagen. *Angelica the Auto, for God's sake.* He grinned. Lights still blazed in the guest house and the barn was dark. He turned the key and waited in the silence. *She's not a Winnemucca girl,* Owen Johnson admitted to himself, *but maybe I'm not just a Winnemucca boy.*

Chapter 35

M ARY DeMello's birthday approached.

Quinn sat in the parlor, a section of the sunroom door in her line of sight with the phone pressed to her ear. "Well, Camille, it looks like Mary's determined to make it to her birthday." She didn't talk with her sisters often, but now when they did talk the words came easier . The sister chorus had retired and Quinn didn't miss them. To her surprise, her real-life sisters were less critical than the chorus had been. "Should we still do something?"

"I don't think we need to, Quinn. We all saw her recently, except John Paul, and he'll have to deal with that. I'll just cancel the cake order, and that will be that. She really isn't very awake anyway, is she?"

"No. The nurse was here this morning and said we could increase the morphine a little so she's comfortable and out of it. She still visits with Viv and Vic when she first wakes up."

"Good." Quiet settled between them as they both remembered their mother's vicious words and the near-disaster that followed. In the moment of unusual closeness, Quinn thought about the tiny mound in the Mountain View Cemetery the last time she'd seen it, just before she left Reno, decorated with a tiny Christmas tree and a stuffed version of Alfie, the Wolf Pack's mascot, and braved a question. "Camille, Cec says you put flowers on Samantha's grave . . . every year. Do you?" To her own ears, her voice sounded harsh, critical.

Camille didn't hesitate. "I do, at Christmas."

When she said no more, Quinn asked, "And the toys, the stuffed animals?"

Camille's "Yes" sounded like a smile.

"Why didn't you tell me?"

Camille was quiet so long Quinn thought she wasn't going to answer. Her words, when they came, were measured. "Quinn, you know . . . well . . . well, DeMellos just don't talk about things like that."

Before Quinn could respond, Camille asked, "Have those nice sisters heard from their ungrateful son yet?"

Quinn accepted the change for the tension-reliever it was. "Got a letter yesterday. It seems he is really working in the grandfather's firm. He brags about his Twin Towers office as though he was in the center of the universe, but the praises he's been singing about his father are dwindling. He's back to signing his letters Scott Johnson, too. I predict he'll be home by Christmas."

"Good." In the pause, Quinn imagined the tiny wrinkles disappearing from her sister's forehead. Camille said, "It's good to have you back," and hung up the phone, leaving Quinn sputtering. *Have me back, indeed. You're the one who's been gone, who's been critical and mean and . . .* She laughed to herself as she replaced the receiver. It didn't matter anymore.

Side by side, the twins worked at the kitchen counter. A celebration dinner, Vivian had decreed, and they'd been chopping and stirring and mixing for two hours. Victoria wiped sweat off her forehead and wished they had a prep chef. Owen had their account books and tonight he would give them the news. They knew it would be good; they were already planning the Wildflower Inn's next season; they were ready to celebrate.

Vivian handed the berry pie to her sister, resumed the conversation that concentration on the pie's lattice work cover had interrupted. "I think we should ask her to stay."

They had been discussing Quinn. The retreat guests had just departed, leaving the remnants of a Labor Day party swollen large with friends from town and from the neighboring ranches. The sisters, Kris and Karol, had returned with two cousins, and Adam Singer had shown up uninvited but clearly welcome. From her hidden cache, Quinn had produced sparklers and filled the evening with adult children flitting like fireflies in the dusk.

Victoria accepted the pie, shoved it into the steamy oven. "Well, if we don't Wen surely will, if he hasn't already."

"And not just because she's made a difference in our business, either." Vivian stuck an exaggerated tongue in her cheek. Both women chuckled. "She's made a difference in our lives, and I, for one, want to keep her." She wiped her wet hands on a damp towel and tossed it onto the counter. "You want a beer? I think we can start our celebration without them." Without waiting for an answer, she pried off the lids and carried two bottles toward the porch.

Victoria set the timer, wiped berry juice from her fingers and followed her twin outdoors. Vivian never ceased to amaze her, one of the reasons, she was certain, that living here continued to be better than living any place else. Beer in hand, she settled comfortably on the swing and spoke her thoughts. "I want her to stay, too, Vivvy. In spite of everything, she's made us all laugh. And Wen's like a new man. I didn't realize how unhappy he'd been. I thought he'd worked something out with Karle, but seeing him with Quinn, how he looks at her . . . wow. He's clearly happier than he's been in years, since before Mimi's last miscarriage, at least."

"You're right, even before the divorce. He laughs now, too." Loving Quinn hadn't blinded her to the other woman's history, but this time Vivian kept her misgivings to herself.

"And you wouldn't be seeing Harold if Quinn hadn't lured him out here." Victoria looked at her sister through half-closed lids and grinned when she saw the tell-tale blush. "Ah hah, I knew it wasn't just choir practice running late." As color infused her sister's cheeks, she relented, "Okay, okay, I'll stop, and I'll be sure to wear something different when he comes to pick you up."

Vivian fanned her cheeks and smiled. She already knew that Harold Anderson could tell them apart. "We should finish getting supper ready, I guess." The porch was in shade, and neither woman wanted to return to the hot kitchen.

"They'll be late, Viv, they always are." The promise of air conditioning had drawn Owen and Quinn to the movies. "Will he bring the papers, do you think?"

"He said so. He's had the books for over a week. It'll be good, Vic, I know it. We had guests all summer, and the retreat guests paid so much more."

"They got their money's worth, and then some," noted Victoria, who had included their thank-you letters in the papers she had given her brother. Even he would be impressed at the effusive praise, as well as the word-of-mouth advertising their guests had provided. "And advertising didn't cost as much as we thought, and expenses weren't as high . . ."

". . . because Quinn did all the work."

"Well, not all, Viv, you and I worked our butts off, but . . . I know what you mean. And the money from taking care of *her*," she nodded toward the sunroom, "really helps, too. It's not like she's been a burden, besides the trauma to Quinn, I mean."

Vivian nodded. Caring for the dying woman had woven itself into their routine so easily that it seemed they were being paid for nothing. "Maybe it's easier 'cause it's not our own mother."

"Maybe. What did she say about Quinn?" Owen had taken Quinn to meet their mother on their last trip to town.

"She just said," Vivian mimicked her mother's cultured voice with its acquired British lilt, "'Well, she's a tall one, isn't she, Owen's gel?' and then she went back to eating her jello pudding."

"Enough chatter." Victoria rose from the swing, pulled her sister to her feet. "I want to get stuff done so I can shower before dinner. Maybe *I'll* wear your pink dress tonight."

WHEN NOT A LEAF OF THE late summer salad remained, Owen sat at the end of the long table and sipped his Merlot while the women pored over the financial report he had just delivered. He'd been surprised by the numbers, but right now his mind was on the movie they'd just seen, *Chocolat*, and how right it had felt to hold Quinn's hand in the dark theater and let worries about dissembling fathers and troublesome nephews and suddenly appearing brothers dissolve into plans for the future. *I'll talk to the twins tomorrow. And then Quinn.* He knew he didn't need their permission but they were his life, too. *Besides, they're not blind*, he thought. *They can see the way the wind's blowing.* He smiled as he folded his glasses into the pocket of his denim shirt.

Out of character in her sister's pink sundress, Victoria crowed, "We knew this would work, Owen. Didn't we tell you it would work? Look, Quinn, there's your share." Her pudgy finger pointed to a small figure at the bottom of one column.

"And, Wennie," Viv chimed in, pointing at another number, "the Inn did much better than last year." She waved her own pudgy hand over the spreadsheets on the table. "The proof of the pudding . . ."

". . . is in the eating." This time Owen completed his sister's cliché. "It truly is, girls, and I'm proud of you both." His eyes swept to include Quinn at the far end of the table. "Of all three of you. You were right, after all." He retrieved his glasses, polished them with his blue-checked napkin and slid them on. The twins folded their hands and waited. Quinn rolled her eyes, and he almost laughed out loud, remembering their first business meeting those many months ago. "But," he held up a cautionary hand, "this doesn't begin to build what you need . . . money for capital improvements, a real salary for all of you . . ." He pushed another pile of papers, several rows highlighted, in their direction.

The twins just laughed and he understood—they'd paid the mortgage; they'd had guests; they already had reservations for Christmas. They really didn't care about the drafty windows or complaining pipes. They didn't even care about the insurance money they still didn't know wasn't theirs.

He sighed and laid his glasses aside. *Enough, enough, Johnson, don't rain on their parade.* He glanced down the table for those turquoise eyes that so often reflected his thoughts, but Quinn, picking at a bit of food on her napkin, seemed miles away, and a shiver ran up his spine. *We need to talk.*

"What will you do, Quinn?" Victoria's question echoed his thoughts. "You only promised us six months."

THREE LOOK-ALIKE NOSES POINTED TOWARD HER, and she was reminded of their first meeting. But today there was no antagonism, just curiosity and concern and an odd, watchful silence, and she couldn't read his thoughts. The twins assumed her answer—of course she'd stay—they loved her and their brother loved her, what more was there to say?

He loves me, he loves me not. The knot in her stomach tied itself tighter.

Owen picked at his cuticle until he tore a piece away.

"Don't use the napkin, Owen." Vivian frowned, handed him a tissue. "The blood will stain." Ignoring her own orders, she dipped her napkin in her water glass and dabbed at his bloody thumb. "What's the matter with you, anyway?"

"She'll stay, of course," Vic interrupted the scolding and answered her sister's question. "What would we do without her? And besides," she placed her hand over Quinn's on the checkered tablecloth, "Quinn's family now."

Mary DeMello's bell tinkled.

Saved by the bell. Quinn let out the breath she'd been holding as the twins went off to attend her mother. Owen removed his glasses, polished them again, his eyes hooded. He said nothing. Quinn got up to clear the table. She felt part of this family, reminded herself that she was not. No matter, she was bound to stay while her mother remained.

CHAPTER 36

*S*EPTEMBER 10, MOTHER'S BIRTHDAY. QUINN ROLLED over, searching, but the left side of her bed was empty and Owen's reassurance had fled. After they'd settled her mother for the night, the twins had returned to the table with a new bottle of sherry and The Wildflower Inn celebration continued. Sometime after midnight, she and Owen had giggled their unsteady way across the lawn and fallen into her bed, and the question of her future went unnoticed. Days later, it remained unanswered. Like a child, Quinn scrunched her eyes closed—*If I can't see it, then it's not really there*—and buried herself in the down comforter.

Already Owen's presence at her side felt like a necessity, the fix she needed to get through each day. *You know a man isn't the answer,* her brain chided. *But maybe this one is,* her heart responded hopefully. The inner battle raged until she longed for the interruption of the sister chorus. Each morning when she woke, the sense of promise was there, quickly extinguished, but somehow the emptiness didn't seem quite as raw, and she could think about Samantha without desperation.

The big old rooster heralded the day.

What if he leaves me? Weakness filled her at the thought. *Maybe I should just leave him first.* There had been no promise nor even talk of love, just his body beside hers every night and his arms holding her when she cried. *And he laughs at my jokes,* she reminded herself, *and he gets it when I talk.* Her own voice held the answer. *He can't do this for you, Quinn.*

Her thoughts turned—*so many women in my life: my mother, my sisters, my daughter, and now Vic and Viv. How do they get through each day?* In her mind, the place that had held the wish for death, still as vivid as paint splashed on the white walls of her room, mocked her with its emptiness.

The rooster trumpeted again the cock-a-doodle-do of her childhood. *It's really hard to get up when your own mother hates you.*

Victoria's voice shattered the morning. "Quinn, wake up. Quinn, are you awake?"

I am now. Reluctant to leave her downy cave, Quinn called back. "I'm awake, Vicky, come on in."

Victoria threw open the door. Her wiry curls sprang in a million uncombed directions and she still wore her flannel nightgown. "Quinn, it's your mother—"

Quinn sat up, pulled the sheet up to cover her bare breasts. "What?"

"She passed, Quinn. Viv got up early so she went in . . . to make sure she was warm enough. You know last night was cold." Victoria took a deep breath. "Mary was lying still and it took a few minutes before Vivvy realized she wasn't breathing."

In the perfect silence, Quinn thought, *Mother died on her birthday. Well, at least we'll only have one date to remember.* She took a deep breath, let it out slowly. She could hear the music of the creek through the thick walls of her room. Tears trickled down Victoria's cheeks and Quinn kept her thoughts to herself.

OWEN JOHNSON STOOD IN THE MIDDLE of his living room, a single sheet of paper in one hand and an envelope, hastily ripped, in the other. The rest of yesterday's mail lay abandoned on the floor. He read his brother's words.

"Dear Owen," Michael began, "I apologize for the lateness of my reply, but I must admit your letter took me quite by surprise and I needed time to gather my thoughts and consider the best course of action. Better late than never, my sister would say. I hope you agree." As before, the paper was coarse and the words formed in pencil, but the grammar was impeccable, the style formal, the clichés familiar.

At least he got my letter. It wasn't all just my imagination. Struggling to decipher the pale script, Owen read on.

"Your invitation to develop a relationship, to 'be part of our family' as you so quaintly expressed it, was the last thing I expected. After our meeting and the delivery of the money to my account, I knew that you were a decent man and I was relieved that no trouble ensued. After all, my, excuse me, our existence must have surprised and troubled you more than I can ever appreciate. Whatever possessed you to think we should be 'family'?"

Owen groaned. He had feared this response, if there was any response at all. The ragged edges of the envelope caught his hair as he ran his hand over his head. *God, I'm glad I kept this to myself. Stupid, stupid, stupid. I should have left well enough alone.* Gut aching, he shuffled through the envelopes at his feet and sank into his big chair, the letter still clutched in his hand. How could he explain his need for connection? His father's chosen one—how else could he assuage the guilt?

Michael's letter continued: "Martha and I discussed your offer to visit, to get to know one another. Her grandchild, by the way, is in remission, her body and spirit mending, we hope permanently. I digress. We discussed your offer and decided that, strange though it seemed, we should accept it at face value. This letter is my poor effort to bridge the gap that lies between us."

The knot in his stomach loosened. Owen sucked in a deep breath and read the last lines.

"If you would continue with us, let us correspond for a while and develop a common ground separate from our father. I await your words." Michael's signature was an illegible scrawl.

Now I can tell the twins. No more secrets. At dinner tonight we'll make a plan together. Reprieved, Owen reached for the phone. It rang beneath his fingers.

THE NEW DAY BARELY QUICKENED THE room and Mary DeMello's nightlight angel, equal parts seashell and imagination, still glowed as Quinn reached her mother's bedside. Under the pink wool blanket, a slight bump, silent and unmoving, was all that remained. Quinn looked down on Mary's beautiful face, its pale luster already succumbing to a waxy bluish cast. With a tentative finger she touched a slender hand with its perfect pink nails and recoiled from the woody texture. Translucent lids hid the violet eyes as though Mary was just sleeping, but the air held no charge. Quinn knew her mother was gone.

She'll never look at me like that again. Quinn's shoulders slumped and she collapsed into the bedside chair. *Now I'll never know why she hated me.*

Vivian Johnson draped her brother's jacket around Quinn's shoulders and patted her gently before she adjusted the pink blanket and pulled the sheet over Mary's face. "It doesn't matter anymore, Quinn," she said as though reading the other woman's thoughts. "She's dead and you're not, and that's what matters." She patted Quinn again and left mother and daughter alone.

Arms akimbo, Quinn stood to one side as the coroner attended to his business. Her words seemed to come from far away as she answered the few questions, signed forms on the lines indicated and then watched as what remained of Mary DeMello was gently loaded onto a gurney and wheeled from the room. Twin looks alerted her to the aberration of her behavior. *I guess this isn't how it's done in Winnemucca.*

In time, flanked by Vivian and Victoria, Quinn watched the mortuary van pull away. *All that remains of the woman who bore me; the woman who hated me,* she thought, her life force trailing the vehicle as it disappeared into the early morning light. The women walked single-file and silent into the empty house.

Quinn called her sisters in the order of their birth, Camille first, then Claudia and Caroline. Vivian brought her a mug of coffee and a plate with toast cut up in squares. She couldn't swallow the coffee and the single bite of toast stuck sideways in her throat.

Cecily was the last and the hardest. Quinn's words emerged well-rehearsed and dry—as dry as her eyes, as dry as she felt. After a while she whispered good-bye and hung up the phone and there was nothing left over. Her head drooped and lank hair hid her.

Victoria said, "I'll just go take care of George so you—"

Quinn's head snapped up. "No, I can do it."

Victoria stepped back as though she'd been slapped. Vivian covered her mouth with one hand.

"Oh, Vicky," Quinn murmured, distantly aware of what she had done, "I'm sorry." She suffered the hug her apology earned. Eyes on her bare toes, she summarized the conversations. "Camille says the rosary will be Tuesday the eleventh and the funeral the next day at Walton's on Roop Street. I'll give you directions." Her throat closed up again and she couldn't tell them her mother would lie in the same little chapel where she'd said goodbye to her father.

"We'll stay at Mother's," Quinn continued, face and voice flat. "Cecily gets in tonight and I'll go home tomorrow." She didn't notice the twin look when *home* was mentioned. "The service will be at two."

Owen arrived while she was currying George, took the brush out of her hand and hugged her, but she stood like a pencil in his arms and when she shook herself free he didn't try to keep her. Without a word, she reclaimed the brush and resumed her rhythmic stroking. George seemed to sense her mood and, although she quivered with the ferocity of her grooming, the little mare didn't move away. Owen watched as though he didn't know what to say or do and Quinn wished him gone, but he pushed back his hat and picked up a second brush and worked beside her, and then she was glad he was there.

"THE SOUP'S GOOD, VIV." QUINN CAPTURED the last of the thick hand-made noodles that swam in a broth full of carrots and celery and chicken chunks. "Thank you."

It was the first she'd spoken since she'd informed them of the services and then escaped into the barn. A drop of golden liquid hovered on her lip and when she wiped it away with the heel of her hand they could see her torn and bloody fingernails. Owen had already pushed his soup away untouched and Vivian, her own spoon suspended half-way, her mouth an O of surprise, watched as Quinn leaned back in her chair, emptied her wine glass and held it out for more.

Victoria looked at Owen, but his eyes were on Quinn, so she reached across the table and filled Quinn's glass. The Merlot sparkled like Christmas in the fragile crystal.

Quinn intercepted the look. "I don't need his permission, you know." A faint slur coated her words like an almost forgotten accent. "I'm a big girl now. In fact, I'm an orphan." She giggled a little, repeated "an orphan," downed the wine in one swallow, and, like a rag doll, slouched on the hard chair.

You're drunk, Quinn. Stop it now. No, I'm not—my old friend Jose would never do that. The dusty tequila bottle, forgotten in her duffle for months, had refused her too soon and now lay in pieces on her bathroom floor. *Just one more little one and then I'll stop. And I won't say a word. They'll never know.*

A disembodied radio voice predicted another day of unusual heat. Quinn giggled again. The Johnson siblings watched.

"She hated me, you know. My mother hated me. What's wrong with a daughter that her own mother would hate her?" Quinn's words trembled into their silence. "You can't answer that can you? Your mother loves you."

She reached for the bottle, tipped the rest of the red liquid into her glass and drops like blood sprinkled onto the white tablecloth. Quinn looked at them in dismay. "Oh, Vivvy, I'm so sorry. I'll just put some salt on it and . . ." Her hand and arm seemed to work independently as she reached for the salt shaker and, puzzled, Quinn watched her wine glass materialize between her hand and its goal. She sucked in her breath. Eight eyes widened as the crystal wobbled, tipped and fell, and a waterfall of red wine engulfed the sprinkles. Quinn looked at the chaos for a minute, stated calmly, "There, I've fixed it; it's all red now," and collapsed in tears.

She climaxed before they reached the guesthouse, rubbing against him and rubbing herself as he supported her across the lawn. Owen recognized the so-familiar shiver, but he couldn't hold her drunken hands and keep her on her feet, and when he tried to carry her she slithered like spaghetti from his grasp. By the time they staggered through the screen she'd undone his belt and his zipper, and he stumbled as his slacks slid down his legs. They landed in a heap on the kitchen floor and she wriggled on top of him, freeing him from the rest of his clothes.

He knew she was drunk. He knew she was acting out of loss and desperation and habit, but the knowing didn't communicate itself to the rest of his body. He was fully ready when she impaled herself on him, her weight taking away his breath as she pushed him into the floor. He wasn't sure if she crooned "hurry, hurry, hurry" or "hurt me, hurt me, hurt me" as she rocked herself back and forth on him, hands frantic on her own body and then on his, and he was crying when he came.

SHE WOKE ALONE. THE LIGHT THAT infiltrated her room loosed tiny men with knives behind her left eyeball. Her stomach heaved and she retched, but there was nothing left. She cringed as she remembered and she was glad that Owen was gone. As she opened her right eye to check the time, the tiny men moved to attack that eye, too, and it was once again morning in the land of sex and vomit.

"Quinn, come here. Come here right now!" Victoria's scream penetrated the thick bedroom walls. Quinn leaped from her bed, men with knives forgotten as she stumbled through the door and started toward the house. The cool morning air against her naked body stopped her, and she backtracked long enough to shimmy into her shorts and pull on last night's shirt.

"Quinn, hurry." Ahead, Victoria stood on the back porch holding open the screen. Quinn took the steps in a leap and barged into the room.

"What is it? Viv?"

"Listen."

Vivian hunched over the kitchen counter, ear to the little box that usually supplied a soothing background to their nights and days. "Listen."

Tangled words spewed from the radio—"airplane, tower, watch out"—and more that Quinn couldn't quite decipher. Victoria leaned against the door frame, hand to her mouth.

"What?" Then she heard it.

His voice shocked, hollow, the newscaster announced, "and another plane just hit the second tower."

Quinn looked from twin to twin in disbelief. "Tower? What tower? Not the World Trade Center tower?"

Victoria nodded. Vivian seemed not to hear.

Quinn remembered. "Scott?"

The announcer's voice disappeared into the babble, resumed abruptly to describe the unfolding drama . . . a moment by moment recital of panic and chaos and bodies spiraling through space as the buildings smoked and burned.

Vivian looked up then, her eyes frantic. "Scottie."

HANGOVER FORGOTTEN, QUINN BREWED FRESH COFFEE and the women huddled around the radio and listened as the towers collapsed into rubble. For the first time since she'd arrived at the Wildflower Inn she wished for television. Garbled communication about another plane flying into the Pentagon and then another plane and another and a plane was down someplace in the countryside, and the United States Air Force was rising to shoot down anything that flew.

And then there was nothing new. Repetition; speculation fueled by the news that President Bush was airborne for the preservation of the government and that the vice president was somewhere else, safe; rumor that yet another plane was headed toward the White House. Quinn crept away and showered, and she gathered up her bed sheets and put them in the washer with hot, hot water and two glugs of lavender soap.

When she returned to the kitchen, the twins were dressed, too.

"Owen called, Quinn," Vic told her. "He wants us to come into town. He's got TV."

Ashamed and embarrassed, Quinn didn't ask if there was a message for her. Angelica the Auto transported them swiftly.

In Owen's tidy living room, they watched the buildings collapse again and again as health care workers stood idle, ambulances empty, no injuries to tend—just the thick gray dust, and the haunted faces of firemen who knew their friends were crushed inside. Rumor raced ahead of fact. In carnage and terror, the world stood still. *We mourn my mother,* Quinn thought, *and sit vigil for Scott, for us all.*

At three, Vivian wiped her eyes and rose from the leather hassock in front of Owen's television. A perfect imprint of her bottom remained. "Take me home, Vicky; I want to go home. He'll call me there. I know he will, so I need to be home."

Victoria, stone-faced, nodded and took her home in Owen's old truck.

"I need to go home, too," Quinn told Owen from the safety of his arms. They both understood she meant Carson City. He said nothing of the previous night. The little men still stabbed her eyeball, but with less vigor, as though, having wrecked their havoc, they were bored and ready to move on, and she wanted to forget it, too, just for now.

"Do you want me to come?"

"No, just come tomorrow for the funeral." His quizzical glance reminded her that they didn't know what tomorrow would bring. "Are you scared?"

"I just want you to be all right." He wrapped his arms around her again, tighter this time, and laid his face against her hair. "I want us all to be alright." He dropped his arms to his sides and stepped back. "Go. You need to be with your family. I'll call when we hear something."

THE HIGHWAY WAS BARREN. AN OLD green truck passed furtively and scurried into the horizon. No contrails decorated the sky. Alone, Quinn drove to bury her mother.

CHAPTER 37

HE LINCOLN TOWN CAR STOOD ALONE in the dusk. Quinn pulled into the mortuary's parking lot as far away from the vehicle as she could get before she remembered her mother would no longer ride in it. Claudia waved from the wide entry. Her lips formed words. "Quinn, hurry. It's time to start."

Quinn wiped damp hands on new black slacks and moved reluctantly to her sister's side. Claudia looked her over and nodded. "You look nice," she whispered, and Quinn was thankful for the quick stop at the town's only department store and the propriety a new black blazer bestowed. Her new black loafers felt stiff on her bare feet. The sisters entered the chapel together.

In the background, radio voices mumbled.

Open to view, their mother's coffin dominated the room. An American flag stood amidst the profusion of gladiolas and roses and baby's breath. The air shimmered with attar of roses and cleaning product. Quinn caught her breath and stumbled and Claudia's hand steadied her. She started to shrug it off, then changed her mind and leaned into Claudia's arm instead. Thus supported, she stepped forward to view her mother.

She looks like she always looks. Quinn stared at the still figure as though she could penetrate the mystery. *Why did you hate me?*

Mary DeMello wore a pale pink angora sweater and dyed-to-match wool slacks and her hands with their manicured nails, pale pink also, held her rosary, a gift from her husband on their wedding day. The silvery pink crystals glistened in the harsh florescent light. Quinn remembered: She'd been six the day she'd sneaked the tantalizing rosary out of its silver box and ran with it to the closet she shared with Claudia and Caroline. With the odor of sweaty shoes in her nose, heart pounding with fear and excitement, she knelt. Grubby fingers told the beads one at a time as she prayed for something she couldn't name.

Her mother found her just as she finished the second decade.

"There you are."

Mary DeMello snatched the sparkling chain. The silver crucifix whipped viciously leaving a thin line of red droplets across Quinn's forearm. Mary ignored the scratch, examined each pristine bead.

Quinn didn't move. Her heart pounded and she thought she might die.

Mary's voice was low, cold. "You got them dirty, you bad girl." She raised her hand. The crucifix caught the sunlight in its swing.

"I'm sorry, Mommy. Forgive me."

"No." Mary's hand slashed across her daughter's face, first one cheek and then the other. The second blow, harder than the first, drew blood from the small nose. Quinn whimpered but forced her tears inside as she waited for what would come next.

Now Quinn stared into the coffin and again forced her tears inside. *I don't understand. What did I do?*

Perfectly coiffed, lips just a little too red, Mary DeMello didn't answer.

"They made her mouth a little too smiley, don't you think?" Quinn said to whichever sister stood beside her and was surprised when no impatient voice responded *Oh, Quinn!*

"She arranged everything, Quinn. Made it easy for us." Caroline joined them.

"Didn't want us to screw things up, more likely," Quinn replied, and again was surprised when no one moaned *Oh, Quinn!* "Where's John Paul?"

Eyes shifted toward the family viewing room where a drapery obscured the view, shifted away. "In there," whispered Camille who had come up behind them. "He's not in very good shape right now."

Quinn took that to mean he was drunk and didn't ask any more questions. Poor John Paul—the price for loving their mother was high. They took their seats as Sister Benedict began the Rosary.

Prayers complete and mourners departed, the sisters ringed the coffin. Grover Brown, the old mortician stooped with years of shared grief, pushed the button and the coffin lid lowered into permanence. A metal corner jabbed Quinn's thigh—Samantha's picture deep in her jacket pocket. She had meant to slip it in beside her mother, but in Mary DeMello's final silence she had changed her mind.

One by one they left the chapel.

IN MARY'S HOME THE SISTERS RINGED the television, the vivid replays safer than talk of their mother. Quinn dozed, woke to freshly brewed coffee and low voices and the night dragged into morning—Wednesday, September 12, the day after. They showered and dressed and returned to the chapel.

In the front row, still in yesterday's clothes, Quinn stared at the polished wooden box with its shiny fittings. Closed. *Mother would hate this.* Everything about Mary DeMello, her clothes, her voice, the way she moved her hands and tipped her head, cried *look at me, look at me now,* and in Quinn's memory everyone had. *Well, no one can see you now, Mother.* The thought rose abruptly and Quinn cringed with guilt. Anxious to preserve the fragile family peace, she kept silent. She smoothed the wrinkles from her black slacks and longed for her red dancing boots and a tequila shooter.

Caroline dabbed at her eyes. Cecily seemed fascinated by the hands folded in her lap. Quinn looked around the chapel, its pinkish-beige décor absorbing sound like a sponge. Several couples had entered since the sisters had been seated, the men looking sadder than the women, and Quinn assumed some, if not all, had been suitors or potential suitors of her sensuous mother. One dapper gent, silver strands perfectly laid across his pink scalp, blew loudly into a monogrammed handkerchief. *EM*—was this the last one, the one who said *I can't stand to see you suffering* as he ran out the door? She nudged Camille to ask, but when Camille's tearful gaze failed to focus and a thick *what?* emerged from her throat, Quinn just shrugged and murmured, "Nothing."

The perfume of roses and gladiolas insinuated itself through the room, filling the spaces between the scattered mourners. In it, Quinn imagined the missing souls—her father, her grandparents, people she didn't even know who had loved her mother. Her eyes itched and teared and she blamed the flowers.

AFTER THE SERVICE GROVER BROWN SHEPHERDED the siblings into the chapel vestibule. Wedged between Camille and

Cecily, Quinn watched her brother disappear out a side door and wished she could follow. She took a deep breath, fixed a smile and willed her mind elsewhere.

A thin line of polyester suits and church-going dresses straggled by. Frail hands grasped hers for just a moment before their owners breathed a sigh of relief and escaped back to their televisions. Numb, she didn't register their names, their words. Numb, she didn't have to feel.

When Vivian and Victoria Johnson stood before her, Owen just behind, Quinn wondered who they were. Then Victoria grabbed her hand, squeezed it tight and said, "Quinn, are you all right?" and she knew them.

Vivian shoved her sister aside. "Oh, honey, tomorrow will be a better day," she said as though she really believed it, and she wrapped the taller woman in her arms.

In Vivian's embrace, Quinn wanted to believe, too. Then she looked up into Owen's questioning gaze. *What can I say?* Agonized, she turned away. She knew when she looked again his face would be impassive and his eyes guarded, but there was nothing she could give him.

Then Vivian released her and Owen stepped into her space. In his finely tailored gray suit and crisp white shirt, he looked so much like *somebody-we-should-know* that people moved aside to give him room. He grasped Quinn's hands. "Quinn, look at me."

Reluctantly, she did, hopeful that no one was watching. She had been wrong—in his unguarded face she saw hurt, longing and hopefulness, but his words were plain, "Have you eaten today?"

She smiled then. Of course she hadn't eaten.

Without releasing her hands, he nudged her out of the line. Her sisters closed ranks behind her. He drew her through an open door, pushed it closed with his foot and held her still.

She turned to him. Their eyes met. *Hold me. Make it better.* She knew he wanted to. She waited but instead of reaching for her, Owen fumbled in a breast pocket and pulled out a Chocolate and Peanut Butter Power Bar, from another a juice box sized for a child's lunch. He held them up. "Voila." He peeled away the wrapper and put the bar in Quinn's hand. "Eat." She took a bite, sure it would come back on her. It didn't. He smiled as he fit the little hinged straw into its place, handed her the juice. "Drink." She obeyed. When she had choked down half the Power Bar and drained the apple juice, he let her stop.

Almost too late, she remembered. "Any word from Scott?"

He shook his head, nodded toward the crowd that engulfed his sisters. "They've been glued to the radio and they're both convinced he'll be found. Mostly they just cry."

Quinn squeezed his hand and didn't ask what he thought. He captured both hands and pulled her close. For a minute she rested her cheek against the smooth gray wool and let the scent of Jaipur and man enclose her.

"They're ready to go home. Would you like me to stay and drive back with you?"

The moment for saving had passed. Quinn straightened and Jaipur disappeared into roses and grief. She shook her head. The slow movement of her hair reminded her that she hadn't shampooed in two days. *Mother would turn over in her grave,* she thought, *if she were in it.*

"No," she said. "I'll go in the limo with everybody else, and then get back to the Inn sometime tomorrow." She couldn't respond to the question in his eyes so she turned away. Owen let her go.

DAMN THAT MOTHER. OWEN JOHNSON POUNDED the Audi's steering wheel, cursed again out loud, "Damn woman," and imagined his hands around Mary DeMello's throat. He couldn't erase his last image of Quinn, eyes dark and lost, hair dank against the nondescript black blazer into which she had disappeared. He pressed his hand against his chest and rocked with the ache that was there.

"Don't worry, Wen, she'll be alright," Vivian's reassurance floated over her shoulder as she scurried from the car to her own kitchen radio. Victoria leaned through his open window and kissed his cheek, a gesture disconcerting in its infrequency, and followed her twin into the silent house.

I didn't tell her I love her. Christ, I didn't tell anybody anything. He pounded the wheel again. *Tomorrow, tomorrow I'll tell her, and I'll tell them all about Michael and Martha, and I'll try to believe that Scott will be found, and then things will be normal again.*

He slowed as he entered the Winnemucca city limits, pulled into an empty spot in front of Hart's jewelry store. *Tomorrow I'll make things right.*

THE AFTERNOON FILLED ITSELF WITH RANDOM scenes, *a movie before editing,* Quinn thought. Events moved in fits and starts—an old silent film: The funeral; Owen's sad eyes; the black limousine flying American flags like a presidential cavalcade as it followed the hearse. Now Quinn stood at the gravesite, her new black shoes slippery on the bright green artificial turf. The casket hovered over the earth's open mouth, and she was reminded of the eaglets, mouths gaping to receive their mother's offerings. The silence in the sky prevailed, interrupted only by an isolated birdcall, plaintive, searching.

Scenes juxtaposed and filled Quinn's mind: A neat rectangle dug deep into the soil—a tangled metal tomb; this cemetery's Wednesday serenity—searching, digging, scrabbling toward the tiniest scrap of life; the cool scent of sage mingled with roses—the rank odor of dry dust and fear and broken bodies; middle-aged siblings, properly dressed, properly subdued—hundreds of mothers and fathers and children and babies in arms surrounding the site in silent vigil.

Mary DeMello's casket descended into the ground.

CHAPTER 38

FTER, Day Two. THE GUEST HOUSE was dark, its only sign of life the kitchen radio reciting the numbers of the dead as Quinn folded her last bits of clothing. The kitchen light had just come on in the main house, and Owen's truck was not parked at her gate. The creek, its supply of snow melt exhausted, was silent, too, and only the beat of her heart filled the room.

I'm leaving with more than I brought, she thought as she forced the zipper of her duffel closed over the silky dress with its gaudy flowers squashed on top of the slinky yoga pants and the dusty vibrator. A wisp of fabric caught, a purple flag, and she left it fly. Her flute and music stand, the CD player, the yoga mat—these were already stowed in Angelica's trunk.

She'd left the cemetery before the dirt fell on her mother's coffin. A stop at Quick Cuts and a few hours at her Reno duplex completed her preparations. Minnie the Mouser deigned to twist herself around Quinn's ankles only once before she leapt to Ben the Boarder's shoulder and turned herself into a cat stole. Her purrs filled the room. Ben scratched her head absently as he accepted his landlady's newest instructions and, once again, Quinn drove off alone.

The jitters filled her and she knew she would never sleep. Three cups of coffee didn't help, and her thoughts were twisted as she drove into the night—*home*—and blinked back tears.

Now she looked around the room that had been hers for nine months. It was as she had first seen it—crisp white sheets carrying a scent of lavender, down comforter pulled up nearly to meet the lacy pillows, a wavy mirror reflecting— *Do I look the same? Am I the same?* She had no answers. On the cold hearth, her basket of offerings overflowed.

The screen squeaked and she heard his footsteps on the hardwood floor. Her left eye twitched and her packing hands stilled, but she didn't move until his knock sounded on her door.

"Quinn."

She turned then, duffel held like a shield, and met his eyes.

They blazed. "So you are leaving. They said you were, but I didn't believe it." Like desert dust, disgust coated each word.

Anger kindled. She knew he wouldn't understand, hoped he might wait for her own words before he believed. Her fingers dug into the duffel and she forced calm into her voice. "You talked to your sisters?"

"Of course I talked to my sisters." Sarcasm dripped, masking the tears and making mud of his voice. "What did you expect? But I expected more of you. I thought you were done with running away."

He stood stiff in the doorway as though he couldn't bear to be in the same room with her. *He looks awful,* she thought, averting her eyes from the tousled hair hanging over his forehead, the blurry eyes, and the wrinkled white dress shirt that she knew he'd worn the day before. *I want to lay my cheek against that shirt and smell his smell and wait until he wraps his arms around me and nestles his face down into my hair and tells me everything will be okay.* She ached with that want, looked down so he couldn't read it in her eyes. Four feet of old wooden planking lay between them, and Quinn left it there.

With an effort she kept her voice steady. "I'm sorry you talked with them first. I was coming to town as soon as I finished here. And I'm not running away."

"What then?"

"Let me finish this and I'll tell you." She waved him out of the room. "Go pour us some coffee. I'll be done in a minute."

He hesitated.

Quinn's laugh, thin and half-hearted but a laugh nonetheless, surprised her. *I didn't think I had any laughter left in me.* "Don't worry; I won't escape out the back door."

Without waiting for him to move, she slid into the bathroom. She checked the shelves and wiped an errant hair from the sparkling basin—stalling, bolstering her courage—then she straightened her shoulders and turned off the light.

He stared at the blue and white mugs set out by the coffee pot as though he'd never seen such things before and didn't know what to do with them, and the thin shell of his own anger cracked. *She's leaving. I should have told her I love her, asked . . . begged her to stay.*

Vivian's voice had pulled him from sleep, four-fifteen the bedside clock blinked as he fumbled for the receiver, and he'd thought at first, before her words penetrated, that she was calling about Scott.

"She's packing, Wen, and I thought you'd want to know."

"That can't be right. She's at her mother's. You must have misunderstood."

"Nope, the light's on in her room. She said she'd talk to us when she finished, so Vicky is making coffee and I'm calling you." He could tell from her voice that Vivian was crying.

He'd pulled on whatever clothes came to hand, and then couldn't locate his keys. It was like a bad dream, searching and searching and never quite finding until he noticed them on the kitchen counter where he always dropped them when he came into the house.

Now he was here, and Quinn was leaving. "Pour some coffee for us," she had ordered, and then she'd laughed, made a joke. As his hands reached to obey, he pulled up the shield of his anger. *How stupid am I? What else did I expect? Of course she's leaving. She always leaves. I knew that. This is just a joke to her. I'm just another bump in the road. John and Mike were right—she's not a Winnemucca girl at all.* His breath caught on the pain in his chest.

Vivian's straggly rooster announced the arrival of the sun.

"Shut up, damn you, shut up," Owen yelled. He pulled his arm back, ready to throw the mug at the bird, wanting desperately to interrupt its well-ordered existence. *I knew I should stay away. Being alone is better than this. Maybe I can talk her into staying.* Forgetting that he no longer needed to be a Winnemucca boy, he set the mugs carefully on the tray and carried them into the greatroom.

THEY SAT ON THE HORSEHAIR SOFA where no one ever sat, and its stiff hairs pricked her through the already wrinkled fabric of her new black slacks. Coffee steamed unnoticed on the table by their knees. The piano lamp cast a yellow glow and prisms of light from its crystals danced into the shadows as though ready to expose the ghosts.

"What then?" he repeated. "It looks like running away to me."

"From here to the airport. Then to Falls Church, Virginia."

"Huh?" His laugh lines deepened into questions marks, and on his forehead the purple scar wiggled like a caterpillar.

"I'm going to work. I'm a member of the Red Cross emergency response team and I'm going to work with the people at the Pentagon . . . counseling, helping prevent PTSD—that's post-traumatic stress syndrome," she added at his bewildered expression. "Helping people cope with all this." She gestured toward the radio voice in the other room.

Wrinkles smoothed, then furrowed again. "But when? I don't understand."

'They called on Tuesday. If they hadn't, I'd've called them. That's the way it works. I knew I'd be asked to go. And they were nice enough to delay my flight until after Mary's funeral."

"But the planes aren't flying." In the past two days, only military planes were allowed the sky.

"Mine is."

"I didn't know you did this."

"There's a lot we don't know about each other." She laughed again, mocking herself. "And that's not just your fault."

The rough upholstery stretched out between them like miles and miles of dirt road. Outside the sky lightened and birds conversed. The man looked at her. His hands twitched, lifted a little, then clenched in remembrance and returned to their business—running though his hair, rubbing the scar, finally refolding themselves into his lap—but his eyes never strayed from her face. Her own gaze faltered. She couldn't tell if he wanted to hold her or hit her, wished he would just hit her and get it over with.

He said nothing. A tiny muscle worked overtime along the edge of his jaw.

Say it, her mind demanded, *say it now or you never will. Say it and maybe he'll get it.* The acid of a sleepless night and too much coffee churned and threatened to overflow, and once again she longed for a tequila shooter. In awareness born of experience, she knew if she spoke her truth he would leave.

She pushed a finger against her eyelid to still the twitch and opened her mouth to begin, and he leaned toward her—just a millimeter closer. The words caught in her throat and her carefully prepared speech tottered into the room. "Owen, I've got to go." *No, that's running.* "No, no, I mean I'm ready to go." She nodded. "This," she outlined the room, the Inn, Owen himself, "has been the ultimate hiding place." She nodded again, agreeing with herself. "Hiding place, the best, but I just didn't recognize it until now."

Keeping her eyes focused downward—hangnails, flakey pink polish, ratty edges condemned her—then reached for the mug to give her hands something to do. Owen's hands lay clenched in his lap, fingertips whitening, and she took courage from his continued presence.

"Owen, it's this way—all my life I've taken a good fuck and a lot of wishful thinking and created a myth of salvation, and it doesn't work."

Her body screeched *yes it does, yes it does*, but she ignored it, and she ignored the look on Owen's face as well, but she couldn't blot out his words.

"Is that all this was to you . . . a good fuck?"

"That's not what I said." She wanted to cross the chasm between them but she sat very still, certain that he'd pull away if she tried.

"What then?"

"Two things. Number one, I used you. I used you the other night." A flush rose in her cheeks, but she forced her eyes to meet his. The heel of her new loafers chattered against the hard floor and she pressed her elbows into her thighs to stop their shaking as she remembered climbing onto him, remembered rocking them both to a furious finale, remembered his tears. "I used your body and the feelings that have grown between us." Self-loathing flavored her words. "I'm so afraid of how I feel that I use alcohol and I use sex and I used you and that's not okay."

She didn't allow herself to look away. Tears filled his eyes and his Adam's apple bounced up and down, but he said nothing. She continued, "Number two, Viv said it and she's right—I've been trying to get saved. I don't know from what but that's what it feels like—that if I just find the right man or the right job or the right place then I'll be okay. She reminded me of what Dr. Phil says when things aren't working. He always says, 'Baby, get off that train!'"

Owen looked even more confused.

"Dr. Phil . . . Oprah Show . . . psychologist—"

He shook his head. "I still don't get it. We have feelings for each other . . . don't we? I don't care about the other night. But because of this Dr. Phil you're leaving? And when does Vivian watch television anyway? And what did you do to your hair?"

In the midst of everything, he made her laugh.

"Haircut, happens to the best of us." She tossed the new do, so short it barely touched the nape of her neck, and scooted closer to him. He didn't move away. "Listen to me, Owen Johnson. I do have feelings for you and you are a great fuck and that's the problem. I can't stay here and fall in love and expect you to make my life okay."

"Why not?" She glared, and he threw up his hands. "Okay, okay—so you're leaving but it's not running away?"

"Right. For now I have to go there and help in whatever way I can, but if the world were normal I'd still have to go. I've run away from a lot of things, you know. I've got a profession that I left and a house and a cat—don't forget Minnie the Mouser—and I need to be closer to my sisters for a little while. I want to see if we can be a real family now that our mother is out of the middle." *And now that I know what a real family feels like,* she thought but didn't say.

What about me? His cry hovered in the air between them, but the words didn't escape his pursed lips.

She responded anyway. "There are emails and phones. If you want, I'll call you every day." Somehow they'd gotten to standing and she was looking right into his dark eyes. Her body flushed and she was instantly wet. She wanted him to throw her down on the couch and take her, make her his, stop the thoughts—*Omigod, my fantasy.*

The glint in Owen's eyes told Quinn he knew what she was thinking. His hands reached for her and she took a step back.

"Well, it's no secret how I'm feeling, is it?"

He stepped forward but the flat of her hand on his chest stopped him. Lightning snapped between them. "Owen, I have to do this. I wouldn't blame you if you never wanted to see me again, but I hope that doesn't happen. I want you in my life," she swallowed hard, "but I have to fix my life myself."

He gazed at her for a long time. Just as despair threatened, he opened his arms and she went into them. His hands caressed her neck, her back, her hair, and the fullness of her breasts flattened tight against his chest. Her nipples tingled. She could feel him hard against her belly, and she almost weakened.

"I like this," he said, and then groaned and held her even tighter as he nestled his face in her hair. Finally, he let her go.

"Call me," he said, "whenever you can, whenever you want. You know where I am."

The old Toyota grumbled as he drove away.

Morning sun streamed across the valley and lit the western hills with gold as Quinn said good bye to the twins. That snowy night when they'd let her in, dried her off, and introduced her to family seemed just moments ago but they were no longer Tweedledee and Tweedledum.

"Are you sure this is what you want? It doesn't sound like such a good idea to me," Victoria said. "Besides, I want you to stay. Haven't we had a good time?" Quinn winced, Victoria's words mirroring her brother's.

"She has to go, Vicky." Vivian answered for Quinn. Her belief that Scott was still alive fueled her. Defiance shone in her eyes, in the straightness of her back and the forward thrust of her chin, but the wait for confirmation had stripped away her reserves, leaving her transparent. "We don't want her to go but she has to, and, thanks to her, we'll be just fine."

The stubborn set of Victoria's jaw didn't soften. Vivian huffed. "I've explained it to you already ... her pattern of searching for love to fix things when she really needs to develop her own self-esteem and deal with Samantha and . . ."

"I get it, all right; I just don't like it."

I don't like it either, Quinn thought, *but there it is. No more knights in shining armor.*

Neither sister asked about Owen.

Victoria pulled her bandana out of her overall pocket, handed it to her sister. "Here, wipe your eyes." She turned to Quinn. "So what will you do ... after this mess is over, I mean?"

What will I do? A cool breeze from the canyon touched her. *What will I do?*

"I guess when I'm done in Virginia I'll get back to Nevada somehow. We need to sort out Mary's things, decide what to do with the house, stuff like that. I'll have to think about work, too—I can't just depend on Grandpa's money forever."

And I'll try to figure out why my mother hated me. Maybe then I can move on.

"Will we ever see you again?" The little girl voice didn't sound a bit like Victoria. Vivian and Quinn stared.

Vivian recovered first. "Of course we will, silly." She looked the same question at Quinn.

"Just try and keep me away. And if you still need me—*if you still want me*—I'll come out and help with the bigger groups."

Vivian wiped her eyes, red-rimmed and haunted. "We'll always want you, Quinn, and there's no sense crying over spilled . . ."

". . . milk," finished Victoria and Quinn together. They all laughed.

Victoria blew her nose and wiped her eyes and checked the tissue in the ritual that Quinn had come to expect. "Vivvy's right, we'll always need you and want you. And when Scottie comes home, we'll need your help with him, too."

Quinn laughed and wiped her own tears on the sleeve of her new black blazer. She hated that she was adding to their burden, to their sorrow. There was nothing more to say.

Vivian hugged her, then pushed her toward the yellow bug standing stuffed and ready. The little goats lined the fence as though to say goodbye. "Go, Quinn, you need to go. After all, this is probably a blessing . . ."

". . . in disguise." Victoria's voice was muffled in Quinn's shoulder, but Quinn hugged her tight and knew what she meant.

Then she let them go and slipped behind Angelica's wheel, started the engine and eased down the dirt lane, hurrying before one or the other could say *and tomorrow is another day.* She thought if they said those words she wouldn't be able to leave. When she looked back, they stood together, arms entwined, watching her drive away.

Epilogue

—Quinn DeMello—

MY FAITHFUL ANGELICA IS FULL. IN the rearview mirror, the Buena Vista Valley spreads wide in supplication as I pull onto the highway heading west, nine months' history fluttering behind me, reaching its tentacles to drag me back. A puffed up silver heart that hadn't been there before swings from the mirror on a fine silver chain. I catch it in my fingers, imagine the warmth of the hand that had hung it. A golden Jag with Utah plates honks, veers sharply around me as I slow, my foot inattentive on the gas, and disappears as though Angelica were standing still. It's like swimming through the mud, this leaving—each mile uphill, hard-won, bittersweet. An old Woody Guthrie song—something about times changing—jiggles out of memory, and I hum the tune. Still early, sunshine floods through the windows and torments the nape of my neck, and, forgetting its new length, I shake my hair down protectively. Seven-thirty. If I hurry I'll have time for one more cup of coffee before the plane takes off and my life changes again.

The road ahead beckons.

Acknowledgements

MANY THANKS TO ALL MY FIRST readers. You know who you are. Your love of my characters spurred me on. Thanks also for the years of support and encouragement from family and friends. My awesome critique group—Jay, Ken, Jacci, Lucy, and Kaye—deserves special recognition for helping bring *Runaway* to completion.

I am grateful to the Old Pioneer Garden Country Inn, which inspired my story. Most recently, special thanks go to Jessica Santina and her talented team at Lucky Bat Books for making Runaway beautiful. As always, I remain indebted forever to my daughter Lia and my grandchildren, Quinn and Cecily, who think everything I do is the bomb.

ABOUT THE AUTHOR

PATTI DOTY IS A NEVADA NATIVE. Although she won prizes for writing while she was a student, she chose a career in medicine as a physician assistant and marriage and family therapist. But she never abandoned her first love, and in 2013, she published her first Quinn DeMello novel, *Runaway*.

Retired now, Patti travels widely—most recently spending time in Washington, DC; Halifax, Nova Scotia; and Maui, Hawaii—always looking for new locations for her characters and their stories of love and change. When she's not circumnavigating the globe, Patti can be found at home in Northern Nevada, where she lives with her standard poodle, Izzy.